PLAYING

unravel ME

BECKA MACK

Published by Streamside Literary INC.

Visit my website at www.beckamack.com

Line art: Simply Extra Jordanary

Hockey player art: SVGForYouFromMe

Cover design: Ever After Cover Design, www.everaftercoverdesign.com

Editor: Paisley McNab, www.perfectlywrite.ca

ISBN 978-1-7781330-8-4 (special edition paperback)

To Nicole,
There's only one woman who can proudly
call herself the OG Mrs. Lockwood, and that's you.
Thank you for being here since day one.
I love you x 1,000,000.

And to Fielding,
our beautiful biggest boy who thought he was a lap dog,
not a 135lb Bernese Mountain Dog.
We still feel you around.
Rest in paradise, big buddy.

CONTENT NOTE

Unravel Me contains emotional references to the past death of parents and its surrounding grief, as well as brief discussions of foster care, depictions of child neglect (not by the main character), and the death of an animal (minimal descriptions and as it pertains to the FMC's training as a veterinarian student; not main character's pet). If you are sensitive to these subjects, please use this information to make an informed decision about whether to proceed with this story.

Playlist

UNRAVEL ME - BECKA MACK

SEARCHING FOR A FEELING - Thirdstory	♥ 3:49
IDK YOU YET - Alexander 23	♥ 3:05
SOUL - Lee Brice	♥ 2:48
FIRST DATE - blink-182	♥ 2:52
I WANNA REMEMBER - NEEDTOBREATHE, Carrie Underwood	♥ 3:34
STATE OF GRACE (TAYLOR'S VERSION) - Taylor Swift	♥ 5:22
KISS ME - Ed Sheeran	♥ 4:41
SPEAK TOO SOON - Wild Rivers	♥ 2:54
BEYOND - Leon Bridges	♥ 4:01
POWER OVER ME - Dermot Kennedy	♥ 3:20
SUPPLY & DEMAND - Wilder Woods	♥ 3:16
DANCE WITH YOU - Brett Young	♥ 3:04
FEEL LIKE THIS - Ingrid Andress	♥ 3:16
THIS IS HOW YOU FALL IN LOVE - Jeremy Zucker, Chelsea Cutler	♥ 2:55
AFTERGLOW - Taylor Swift	♥ 3:43
THE FEW THINGS - JP Saxe, Charlotte Lawrence	♥ 3:32
SKY IS THE LIMIT - Mark Ambor	♥ 2:39
I WISH YOU WOULD - Ross Ellis	♥ 3:22
I DON'T NEED ANYONE ELSE - Liam Fitzgerald	♥ 3:19
YOU MAKE MY DREAMS (COVER) - Tim Halperin	♥ 2:54
MY BOY - Elvie Shane	♥ 3:23
BEST SHOT (ACOUSTIC) - Jimmie Allen	♥ 3:13
LOOKING FOR YOU - Chris Young	♥ 3:00

ONE

THE DEVIL HAS RISEN

Adam

"I FUCKED UP."

The slurred words are buried in my pillow, where there's definitely not a warm pile of drool gathering. There's a steady beat pounding in my head, and I flip over, squeezing my eyes shut at the bright sunlight burning like laser beams through my bedroom window.

My fuckup revolves around the reason for the headache beating at my skull: the amount of alcohol I consumed last night, and Carter.

Fucking Carter. The reason behind 99 percent of my fuckups, especially of the alcohol-fueled variety.

Hence the video that's currently the hot topic in our hockey group chat, *Puck Sluts*, when I manage to find my phone.

What's the video of? Me, upside down and holding onto a keg of beer while my teammates Emmett and Garrett hold me by the legs, Jaxon videotapes, and Carter holds the spout in my mouth, shit-talking me to keep me going. And who are the Puck Sluts? Us, obviously.

GARRETT

U still sleeping, Woody?

Woody's a shortened version of my last name, Lockwood. Oh, and, uh, also 'cause the guys once caught me jerking off in my hotel room. Not my proudest moment, and one they won't let go. But hey, I was, like, fifteen hundred miles away from my girlfriend, and only nineteen. Sue a guy for trying to get some relief.

CARTER

sleeping off his hangover like a wittle baby, just like my wittle girl

Attached is a picture of his five-month-old daughter, Ireland, every ounce as sweet as her dad is annoying.

CARTER

even ollie is up n she did 3 keg stands. get it together.

Okay, well, that's not fair. His wife, Olivia, is a champ when it comes to drinking, even though she's barely the size of the pup cup I get at Starbucks for my dog. Plus, I deserve to blow off some steam. My friends are all settling down, except for Jaxon, and we aren't anywhere close to being on the same level. He goes on multiple dates a month to get laid; I go on multiple dates to come home alone, disappointed, and tired of looking for something that's probably not even out there at this point. Not for me, anyway.

EMMETT

You guys up for a rollerblade sesh this AM?

GARRETT

30 mins? Jennie's about to take me for a ride.

CARTER

fuck. u.

GARRETT

Rather fuck ur sister.

CARTER

i'm gonna fucking kill u

EMMETT

Dad??? This is where you interject.

I'm Dad, and my unofficial job is to keep Carter and Garrett safe from each other. Carter's still coming to terms with one of his best friends dating his little sister, and Garrett's turned into a bit of an antagonizing shit who loves to throw in his face that he's regularly nailing

Jennie. It's super entertaining to see someone annoy Carter as much as he annoys the rest of us, but I'm not physically capable of keeping them both alive today.

ME

I'm letting natural selection take its course today.

GARRETT

WTF? Ur just gonna let Carter come after me?

JAXON

Don't know if I can make it. Think I pulled my groin.
Also, RIP Gare-Bear.

EMMETT

Doing what?

JAXON

smirking emoji you mean doing who

Groaning, I swing my legs over the edge of the bed and sit up. All the blood rushes to my head, and I press my fingers to the throbbing ache in my temples before typing out my next message, which is more a beg than anything. I simply cannot function today without eating enough to feed a family of four.

ME

Fuck. Big Macs, please.

The boys are eager to fuck the rollerblading and go to McDonald's instead, so I crank the shower in my bathroom to wash away what I can of this hangover before drowning the rest in greasy burgers and salty fries.

My dick stands tall, bobbing against my belly button, begging me to take care of my morning woody. When I step beneath the warm water and wrap my fist around my cock, my other palm flat against the marbled wall, I drop my head and groan.

I've been fucking my hand for so long now, I don't even remember what it feels to be inside of someone. And honestly? I'm tired. It's not the sex I miss but the connection. My person used to be my whole world, above hockey, above everything.

And in a single moment, she shattered that world.

She took so many pieces of me and threw them to her feet, ground them to dust beneath her pointy-as-fuck heels.

I don't miss her. I miss the love that was once there, the body I held against mine each night, the way my heart soared every time she smiled at me. I miss the way she loved me before she…

Stopped.

She stopped, and now I don't know if I'll ever find someone who loves me for me.

Not Adam Lockwood, superstar goalie. Not the NHL's golden boy, the ticket to luxury, A-list events, vacation properties, and never having to work another day in your life.

Just…me.

I shake away the thoughts at the same moment I realize my cock has gone limp. Chuckling, I grab the soap and lather up. Nothing kills a boner faster than thinking about Courtney.

When I step out of the shower, I realize my dog, Bear, isn't in my room. He's attached to my hip, all one-hundred-and-forty pounds of him, and usually enjoys when I've been drinking because I get extra cuddly. My phone says it's after ten, so the poor guy is probably practicing his best dramatics, playing dead at his bowl in the kitchen.

I pull on a pair of boxer briefs and jog down the stairs, not pausing at the sound of dishes clanging in the kitchen. It's typical to wake up to a few teammates still around the morning after a party, but I don't expect the leggy blonde strutting down the hallway, right toward me. She finishes applying her pink lip gloss as her eyes roam over me, standing here mostly naked. "Thanks for the fun, handsome." With her hand on my torso, she presses a lingering kiss to my cheek, making it heat.

"Uh…" I run my hand through my mussed curls. "I don't know who you…what…fun?"

"All of it." She winks, steps into a pair of red heels, and takes off, leaving me super fucking confused.

We didn't…?

No, because I wouldn't ever do that. Right? And if I did, I'd definitely remember. Sex with a stranger? Not me, not in my right mind.

Unless I wasn't in my right mind.

I shake my head, sighing when I spot Bear at the edge of the kitchen. "There you are, buddy."

Chocolate eyes flick to me, heavy with disdain.

Sinking to my knees, I bury my fingers in his thick, dark fur. "I know. I'm sorry. I didn't mean to lock you out of bed, and I'm late for breakfast. I had too much to drink last night. Forgive me?"

He huffs, licks my nose, and goes right back to glaring.

Except it's not me he's glaring at.

Following his stare over my shoulder, my heart stalls at the bare legs at my stove. I track the long limbs up, to my Vipers tee that barely covers her ass. Up farther, to the vibrant red hair falling down her back as she fucking *cooks* in *my* kitchen.

"He's being super grumpy this morning," a chipper voice tells me as she adds bacon to the sizzling frying pan. "I made his breakfast an hour ago, but he hasn't touched it. Just keeps staring at me."

Rising slowly, I glare at the back of the fiery redhead, waiting for it to, oh, I donno…combust? My fists clench, blood thundering in my ears. Bear climbs to his feet at my side, a low growl rumbling in his chest.

"There he goes again with the growling. You're babying him too much, Adam. You always have."

"Get the fuck out of my house."

My ex-girlfriend spins, patronizing blue eyes pinning me with a pout I used to crumble for.

"Is that any way to talk to me, honey?" She saunters over, fingertips sliding through my patch of chest hair before her palm curves around my neck. "Once upon a time, this house was mine too."

"And then you fucked someone else in my bed." I had to get a new mattress, and Carter talked me into the outrageously expensive one I sleep on now. A win-win, really, all things considered.

She slings an arm around my neck, giving me those big blue eyes I used to love. "If you'd paid me more attention, I wouldn't have looked for it elsewhere. But I'm willing to move past it if you are." Her lower lip slides between her teeth. "You seemed willing last night when you let me in."

Let her in? Drunk or sober, there's no fucking way I'd let this she-devil into my home.

I sort through last night's memories as I pry her arm off me but come up empty. "I didn't let you in."

"Then how did I get in here, Adam? Why am I in your T-shirt, making breakfast in your kitchen?"

"Beats me. Witches have all kinds of superpowers, I've heard."

Pushing by her, I turn off the stovetop and shift the pan off the burner, jaw clenched.

This isn't the quiet girl whose hand was clammy when I reached for it on our first date. Not the woman I gave my virginity to at seventeen. Not the partner I built dreams with, shaped my life around.

Soft hands glide slowly down my back, and I close my eyes as she wraps her arms around my waist, stepping into me.

"I miss you," Courtney whispers. "Please, Adam. We can be happy again." Warm lips touch my shoulder, and for a moment, I sink into the connection.

I want *something*. I want to be needed. Appreciated. *Loved.*

No, I don't just want it. I fucking *crave* it.

And she can't give me any of that.

"I deserve more." Turning, I pull her arms away and take her chin in my hand, forcing her eyes to mine, making sure she hears my words. This will be the last time I speak them. "I deserve more than what you can give me, Courtney. I deserve better."

And I'll find it.

Her eyes widen, glossing over as she shakes her head. "No. Adam, no."

"Yes. There's nothing left. Walk away, and don't come back."

I walk forward, forcing her down the hall, until her back hits my front door.

Her expression holds all the betrayal of a master manipulator. "How can you throw away everything we had? I've given you so much time to get over this, Adam. Why can't you get over this?"

Does anybody ever really get over coming home to his girlfriend screwing another guy in their bed, the engagement ring he'd planned to give her tucked in his underwear drawer?

I open the closet, finding her purse and shoes tucked neatly inside, like she'd already decided on staying. I shove them into her hands and look at the shirt she's wearing. I don't want to know how she got her hands on that. "Give me my fucking shirt, and leave."

Her gaze darkens, and she tugs the shirt over her head, chucking it to my feet.

"Jesus Christ," I mutter as she stands before me, stark naked.

"Might as well get a good look," Courtney snaps, tearing a dress from her purse. She slips it over her head before stepping into panties. "It'll be the last time you ever see this body."

"Hopefully."

She gasps, and her palm strikes my cheek.

I whip open the front door. "Get out."

Bear barks his agreement at my side, making Courtney jump.

She steps onto the porch and opens her mouth, but before she can use it, I slam the door in her face.

Bear nudges my thigh with his wet nose. He smiles up at me, tongue hanging out his mouth, and I bark a laugh.

"I thought it was a nightmare too," I tell him, scratching his ears and heading back to the kitchen. "How else does Voldemort show up here?"

Bear woofs, prancing ahead to devour his breakfast while I survey the disaster before me. The inside of my house isn't too bad, but I cringe at the sight of my backyard. Floating unicorns litter my pool, and among them, two giant inflatable penises Carter and Emmett were sword fighting with at one point. *Thank you very much, Cara, for bringing those.* Red cups are scattered across the yard, a few haphazard bikinis, even though I don't remember a single naked girl in my pool last night. In fact, Jaxon's the only one who threatened to take off his bathing suit.

Cleaning is last on the list of things I want to do right now. I'm desperate for a Big Mac, or five, so I head upstairs to dress, forgoing the mess.

One of the bedroom doors opens, and Jaxon slips out, tugging a shirt over his head. He grins, shoving his fingers through his hair before hiding it beneath a ball cap. "Where'd you disappear to last night?"

"Huh? Disappear?"

"You dropped off the face of the earth, bud. Figured you went to bed. You don't remember? Those keg stands really fucked you, huh?"

I rub my temple. "I haven't done a keg stand since high school."

"And yet you let Carter talk you into doing three of them."

I let Carter talk me into a lot of things when I've been drinking, because he has a way of making most things sound like ingenious ideas. Last night excluded, obviously, because I'm still trying to figure out how and when Courtney got in here.

"Hey, did you happen to see a redhead here last night?" Jaxon only joined our team last year, so he never had the displeasure of meeting

Courtney. He's also the only other single guy in our group, so if anyone was around long enough last night to notice her, it'd be him.

"Redhead? Is this the devil you were referring to last night?"

"The—what?"

He shrugs. "Yeah, we were in the pool with some girls after Carter, Garrett, and Em left, and a new wave of people showed up. All of a sudden, your eyes got all huge and you said, 'Holy fuck. The devil has risen.' Then you jumped out of the pool, said, 'I was never here,' and ran away like your ass was on fire."

Shit. Okay, so she was definitely here. I shudder at the thought, but at least I'm certain I'd never touch her again, no matter what she insinuated. But what about that blonde from earlier? The one who thanked me for the, um…*fun*. Was she talking about the party, or…?

"You didn't, uh, see…I mean, I didn't, uh…did I—" I clear my throat into my fist "—sleep with anyone last night?"

Jaxon's brows dip before laughter explodes from his chest. "Dude, how would I know? I wasn't sitting outside your door. I was busy."

Right on time, pink nails land on his torso, slipping beneath his shirt. A little blonde peeks around his side, and Jaxon whispers, "Mornin', baby," before pressing his lips to hers.

"Call me." She tucks a piece of paper into his hand, smiles up at me, and kisses my cheek. "Thanks for the party, Aaron."

"Adam," I mumble as she walks by. I turn back to Jaxon, lifting my brows at his irritating grin. "You can't go a single—" My jaw drops, a brunette popping out from behind him. He calls her baby, too, when she leaves him her number. I shake my head. "No."

He grins wider. "Yes."

Unbelievably, a third girl with jet black hair steps out, another *baby*, another number. I'm 99 percent sure he's only calling them baby because he doesn't remember their names.

Still, my jaw drops a little lower. "*No.*"

"Y—"

"My parents sleep there when they visit! That's a new mattress! I just bought it!"

"It's been christened for their next visit. Deacon and Bev can thank me later."

He follows me to my room, telling me about his wild night as I tug on shorts and a T-shirt. That shit goes in one ear and right out the other, and I drop an elbow to my dresser and open my Tinder inbox. The bright red bubble telling me I have ninety-seven waiting messages spikes my blood pressure. I ignore them and navigate to the third one on the list.

ALESSIA

Can't wait to c u tonight *kiss emoji*

The kiss emoji throws me for a loop. We haven't met in person, so it feels a little forward. Carter says I'm just old fashioned, but I don't know.

ME

Me too. See you at 7. *smiling emoji*

kiss emoji *kiss emoji*

I tuck my phone away, trying not to catastrophize. I'm already regretting tonight's date, but to be fair, life's been one dumpster fire after another for the last fifteen months or so.

I look down at Bear. "Food, then hikes?"

He licks his nose and rushes from the room.

Jaxon grins. "Big Macs?"

"Fucking Big Macs."

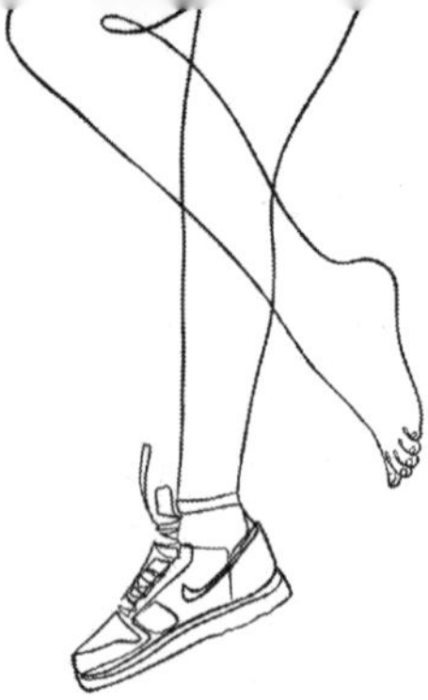

TWO

NOT THE WORST WAY TO GO

Rosie

"Do you ever take a day off?"

I look at Archie, my coworker, best friend, and roommate. He's sitting behind the reception desk, wearing blue scrubs with puppies and kittens on them. He's six feet tall, super broad, and covered in tattoos. The adorable scrubs are forever the highlight of my day.

"I'm not working today."

"Right. You're just here on your day off, and you're definitely not going to spend time with any of the animals." He cocks a brow. "Volunteering is the same thing as working, Rosie."

I roll my eyes, signing the visitor check-in. "Has anybody been in to walk Piglet today?"

Archie smiles sadly at the computer screen. "You know the answer to that."

Of course I do. Piglet is a sixty-five-pound German Shepherd with about the same amount of anxiety as me, which is, according to my entirely blunt and lackadaisical therapist, a fuckton. She needs time, patience, and love; most of those things go out the window with the other volunteers after a few short minutes of trying.

"And that's why I'm here on my day off," I tell Archie, heading toward the kennels. "Because Piglet needs someone to show up for her."

"When are you just going to bring her home?" Archie shouts after me.

"When I have more than three hundred square feet to offer her and can afford to feed her while still feeding myself," I call back.

We've currently got eight dogs here at Wildheart Animal Sanctuary, and according to the log sheet, all of them but Piglet have been walked this morning. Most barely glance up from their beds, content with the attention and exercise they've already received today, which makes me happy. But when my eyes land on that black and brown dog huddled in a tight ball in the corner of her kennel, shaking, my heart sinks.

"Hi, sweet girl," I murmur, crouching down. Her wide brown eyes land on mine, and though they brighten, she stays right where she is, watching me from a safe distance while she whimpers. Because, scared as she is, she wants to come say hello.

Four months ago, I found her tied to the bench out front early one morning. There was a note taped to the front door that said the author was tired of listening to the owner's poor treatment of the dog. We had to sedate her to get her through the doors, because she was so scared she snapped at anyone who came near. I spent the entire day outside her kennel, reading and talking to her, and have worked my ass off since to build the bond we have today.

With a lot of patience, we learned that despite her extreme fear and hesitancy, she's such a sweet, friendly girl who loves her snuggles. The kicker is her cage causes a lot of her anxiety; she's a different girl outside—more carefree, curious, and happy. She just hasn't found her forever family yet.

I hold up her leash. "Wanna go for a hike, Pig?" Her ears perk, and she cocks her head. I show her my backpack and give it a pat. "I packed lunch."

Slowly, she climbs to her feet, her legs shaking. Her tail goes between her hind legs as she ambles over, sniffing me through the cage, then the backpack. Her tongue lolls out of her mouth, she stands a little taller, and gives me a soft *woof!*

"'Atta girl." I unlock her kennel and scratch behind her ears before slipping her harness on. "Anything for food, huh?"

She licks my ankle, nudges my backpack, and looks at me with hopeful eyes.

"Damnit." I sigh, opening my bag and giving her one of the cookies she loves so much. "You know how to get me."

Piglet glues herself to my side as we make our way through the shelter, but the moment we step into the hot Vancouver sunshine, she's free. She gallops forward three steps and leaps into the air, spinning, her cute dog butt leading the way as her tongue rolls out of her mouth. When she's back on all paws, she nuzzles my hip and starts leading the way.

Wildheart is nestled into a quiet area of North Vancouver, away from the noise and crowds of downtown. The mountains and sea of green out here are the most spectacular backdrop, and I love riding the bus across the bridge each day, leaving the city behind and walking right into nature.

Like always, our walk leads us somewhere along the bottom of Mount Fromme. There's a cluster of people farther down the road where the tourists come to hike, but Piglet and I sneak between a small opening at the back of the park, rushing along the narrow dirt trail until we reach the bottom of a set of stairs.

The wooden steps are old and rickety, leading up to our favorite brand of peace and quiet. Piglet has no problem going up, leaping eagerly three steps at a time while I struggle to keep up. It's coming down later that will be an issue.

She enjoys the freedom the mountains bring, the sound of birds and running water nearby, the scent of fresh dirt and pines. You can breathe differently up here, deeper, every inhale crisp and refreshing. It wakes you up, brings you clarity you didn't know you needed.

Before Piglet, I spent so much time here by myself, wandering aimlessly through the woods, sitting with my feet in the creek, contemplating life. Sometimes I'd wish life were different, but I knew I'd never ever give up what I had now, despite the loneliness that creeps in.

Here with this girl, I don't feel so alone. It's not the life I imagined as a child, but it's what I've been given. I love it for everything it is and everything it's given me.

Even if I'll forever grieve the parts it's taken away.

Piglet and I carry on, weaving through towering pines and cedars, my eyes roaming the trunk of every pine, searching the bark for a heart and three initials I know lives somewhere in this forest. I've been looking for years, every single Saturday since I moved here, but each time I leave here with a hole in my heart that seems to, somehow, grow just a teensy bit bigger.

An hour in, my stomach starts to grumble, and Piglet slows, looking pointedly between me and my backpack.

I roll my eyes. "You give the best puppy eyes in the history of ever, you know that, Pig, don't you?" I scratch her head as she licks my knee. "We're almost to the bridge now. Five more minutes and we'll break for lunch, 'kay, girl?"

She barks and jogs ahead, stopping at the trunk of a tree to sniff. A branch snaps in the distance, followed by the rustle of leaves, and a deep voice calls a word nobody ever wants to hear when they're hiking alone.

"Bear!"

Piglet's head snaps and she stops in her tracks. I plaster myself against the rough bark of a wide trunk, trembling as footsteps thunder. Something ginormous and black bursts through the trees, stealing the breath from my lungs when it sets its sights on me.

My entire life flashes before my eyes, because I'm 99 percent sure that's a bear hurdling toward me.

"Save yourself, Pig!" I shriek, chucking her leash and shoving her behind a bush. I cover my face and brace for impact. *"I'm too young to die!"*

Something solid and fluffy collides with my body, taking me to the ground. A wet nose shoves itself in my face, sniffling rather aggressively, and before he makes me his next meal, he opens his mouth and...licks me.

Runs his big, wet tongue from my jaw right up the side of my face, before moving to the other side and repeating the action. It's rather odd, but not the worst way to go, I suppose.

I crack one lid, every ounce of fear draining from my body at the happy face panting above me.

"Oh my gosh, I *am* going to die. Yes, I am!" The burly black dog peers down at me with ginormous chocolate eyes, and I bury my hands in his soft, long fur and close my eyes, leaning into the bath he's giving me with his tongue. "You are the handsomest, sweetest doggy ever, aren't you, big boy? Yes, you are." I hug him close as his nose makes a home in the crook of my neck, tail whipping back and forth with his happy dance. "Have I died and gone to heaven? If this is heaven, I'll stay forever."

Footsteps pound through fallen leaves, cracking twigs, and a deep voice calls out that same terrifying word again.

"Bear!"

The burly dog turns around, sitting his exceptionally large butt in my lap as if he's a lapdog, not a Tibetan Mastiff nearly the same size as me. He pokes his tongue into my ear and rests his chin on my shoulder as a mountain of a man breaks through the thicket, blue eyes bouncing wildly. When he spots us, he sighs, body deflating as he grips his hips and drops his face.

"Jesus Christ," he grumbles, rubbing his eyes. He spread his arms wide, disbelieving yet amused gaze set on the dog who may or may not have claimed me as his. "You scared the shit outta me, bud!"

I giggle as the dog tucks his big head into my neck, and the man's gaze flicks to mine. His cheeks pink as he looks me over. Mine do, too, as I do the same.

"You're really tall," I blurt. "Oh my gosh, that was so rude. I just mean, like, you're…" I swallow. "Super tall."

His mouth cracks in a grin. It's so genuine and friendly, so wide, and I'm taken back by the sheer beauty of it. When a hearty chuckle tumbles out of his mouth, I nuzzle a little further into the dog at my side, hiding my blush as I study his dog dad.

He's…exceptional. His electric blue eyes are a stark contrast against the golden kiss of his skin, the dark stubble lining his jaw, and when he takes off his baseball hat and lets his dark curls spring free, long fingers running through them, I swallow.

His gray T-shirt clings to his broad body, showcasing muscular biceps, mouth-watering corded forearms, and a trim waist. My gaze follows the line of his fitted black shorts to his thick thighs, and I spy a tattoo peeking from the hem of his right leg, nearly grazing his kneecap. If you've ever wondered if thigh tattoos are hot, the answer is yes. So. Fucking. *Hot*.

Another swallow from me, and he lifts the hem of his shirt to wipe the sweat from his forehead, revealing—oh my shit, is that a fucking ten-pack? Do those exist?

My throat closes at the sight of his immaculate abs. In desperate need of water and fresh out of the kind I really require—*holy*—I reach for the backpack still attached to my back. In the process, I lose my grip on the dog, and maybe sanity, tumbling forward with a squeal, face-planting in the dirt. The dog at my side leaps to his feet with a *woof*, Piglet whimpers from the bush she's still hiding behind, and the man I've just embarrassed myself in front of rushes to my aid.

Large hands grip my waist, lifting me clear off the ground.

"I got you," he murmurs, striding across the dirt with me in his arms.

"I'm too heavy—"

"I know you're not arguing with me right now," he teases, setting me down on a boulder. Warm hands cover my knees, parting my legs as he kneels between them and peers up at me with pools of blue a girl could drown in. He brushes the dirt from my cheeks before reclaiming my knees. "I think that's the second time my dog's taken you out."

I grin, another giggle slipping free. His eyes fall to my mouth, and my heart slams against my rib cage.

"To be fair, it was your dog the first time, but this time, I just got…distracted."

"Distracted?"

"Yeah, you did that thing with your shirt, and your abs." I clear my throat into my fist. "Hot guys do it in the movies all the time."

Amusement dances in his eyes. "Ah. So we both have some apologizing to do then, huh?"

"I accept apologies in the form of ice cream or iced lattes; I'm not picky."

He chuckles as his dog licks his neck. "We'll keep that in mind when we get your apology basket together." His eyes drop, his thumb grazing a fresh scrape on my knee. "I'm really sorry he knocked you down. He never runs off like that. It's like he got a whiff of you and took off."

"Honestly, it was more my fault than anything. I saw him running toward me and I freaked out. I, um…thought he was a bear."

The man laughs and ruffles his dog's ear. "Hear that, buddy? She thought you were a big, ferocious bear. He'll be bragging about that all night." His gaze coasts over me. "You're sure you're okay? You're not hurt?"

I shake my head and wiggle my fingers in the air. "See? Totally fine."

He laughs again, and I'm struck by how much I like being the reason. "Those were some pretty half-assed jazz hands. You gotta stand and gimme the full twirl for dramatic effect. Really sell it to me if you want me to let you leave here without dragging you back to my place to check you out."

He takes my hand and stands, pulling me to my feet while I half contemplate faking a broken bone, because taking me home to check me out? *Sign me the fuck up.*

"Wanna know what's funny, though?" He gestures at his dog. "His name is Bear."

I smack my palm off my forehead as it all comes together. "Oh, duh! I thought you were warning me about an incoming bear." I give his shoulder a playful shove. "So it *is* your fault I wound up in the dirt."

He winks. "C'mon. There's a creek just up ahead we can get you cleaned up in."

I know where the creek is, of course. Piglet and I wade through it after lunch every time we're here. She loves to splash, and wading in ankle-deep water is one of the ways I've been slowly working myself back up to—one day, hopefully—swimming.

But I don't know this man, and somewhere in these bushes is a dog, hiding scared, because she doesn't know him either.

"I can't, actually, but thank you." I find the tail end of Piglet's leash, lost in all the commotion. It leads me around a rock, and I find my sweet girl cowering. "Hi, beautiful," I whisper, crouching to her level and ditching my backpack. She creeps toward me, tail between her shaking legs. I look at the man behind me, watching us curiously. Every line in his face softens as Piglet nestles into me. "Piglet's a dog from the shelter I work at."

He looks down at Bear. The compassion in both their gazes warms my heart. "Did we scare you, girl? We didn't mean to, buddy, did we?"

"I found her tied up out front early one morning a few months ago," I explain. "She was scared and anxious, and she snapped at a few of us. We don't know what happened to her, but she was severely malnourished and had a few cracked ribs." I rub the spot between her eyes, and she leans into my embrace. "She's just a sweet snuggle bug, but she's still learning to trust people. She's especially scared of men."

His frown deepens, blue eyes etched in sadness. He and Bear share a long look before sinking to the ground behind me. Bear rests his head on his paws, watching Piglet.

"I'm Adam, by the way."

My cheeks heat, no doubt turning the same color as my name. "Rosie."

"Rosie," his deep voice murmurs, dazzling eyes slowly roaming my face as his smile erupts into a breathtaking grin. "I like that."

I hide my warm face and a smile that's equal parts shy and giddy as I stroke Piglet's fur.

Adam picks a blade of grass, twirling it between his fingers before he tickles Bear's nose with it. "Do you like hiking with Rosie, Piglet? I bet you don't knock her down like big, ferocious Bear, here, do you?"

Piglet lifts her head off my lap and cocks it, blinking at Adam.

"Oh, you're a pretty girl, aren't you? Just beautiful, and I bet your heart is too."

I smile down at her as she looks from me to Adam. "You don't have to sit here with us. I know it's not very fun. She just needs a little patience."

"We don't mind." He nudges Bear. "And we can be patient, too, can't we, buddy? Except when it comes to cheeseburgers."

Bear woofs, and when I giggle, Piglet slowly inches off my lap, sliding along her belly, a little closer to the boys. Bear's ears perk, and he looks to Adam for instruction.

"Patience," Adam reminds him gently.

Bear lays his head back on his paws, waiting. Slow as molasses, Piglet moves closer, one inch at a time, her body raking across the ground, peeking back at me after each movement to check that I'm still here.

"I'm with you," I assure her, trying to keep a handle on my excitement.

Cautiously, Piglet climbs to her feet. Bear stays still as she roams his side, sniffing his ear, his neck, down his back all the way to his huge, fluffy tail, twitching with happiness. When she moves back toward his face, that tail starts a steady thump against the ground.

Piglet lies down in front of Bear, nose to nose, two pairs of chocolate brown eyes staring at each other, and I clutch my chest, right where my heart is bursting. I look to Adam and blush when I find his smiling eyes set on me.

"You're so cute right now," he whispers, chuckling at my flapping hands as I look back at the dogs.

"Me? They are!"

Right on cue, Bear opens his mouth, tongue dipping out, swiping right across Piglet's nose, and I bury my entire face in my hands so I don't accidentally squeal.

And then the most amazing thing happens. My sweet, brave Pig stands again, turning her attention to Adam. Her tail tucks low for only a moment, but as he sits still and lets her smell him, it lifts again. She sticks her nose in his face, making him chuckle, and the soft noise sends her tail wagging through the air, swiping me across the face.

"Can I pet her?" Adam asks. "I understand if it's too soon. I don't want to undo any of your progress with her."

Before I can answer, Piglet drags her tongue from Adam's chin right up to his forehead, where those curls spring free when she knocks his hat off his head.

"Pig!" I snicker, rocking forward. "At least take him to dinner first!"

My snickering takes a turn for the worst when Piglet climbs aboard Adam, straddling his lap and going to town on his face, and I accidentally snort. I clap my hands over the noise, but Adam's too busy laughing, trying to fend off the German Shepherd in his lap who seems to have claimed him as her own, and Bear decides we're missing out.

He scurries around me, nudging my shoulder, my head, before finally giving up and bulldozing me straight into Adam's lap. Piglet leaps off him as I claim the space, flopping onto her back, paws in the air as she and Bear start rolling around.

"Bear!" Adam scolds playfully, grasping my wrists as I try to right myself between his legs. "You knocked Rosie over again!"

"I'm sorry," I sputter, climbing to my knees. I grab his muscular thigh, way too close to the lump between his legs, and my eyes widen when I realize. My hand slips, and I fall forward, my chest mashing against his, sending him tumbling backward with me on top of him. "So sorry, Adam, I swear." I claw at his chest, trying to push away while he keeps laughing. When I finally sit up, flushed and sweaty, I realize I'm straddling a total stranger.

I look down. Down at his broad body, his T-shirt pushed up, exposing that exquisitely carved slab of marble, and are those—? Holy forkballs, they are. Thick, popping veins, one on each side of his torso, running below the waistband of his shorts, which I actually can't see, because I am actively sitting my crotch right on top of this man's cock.

Oops.

"*Ah!*" I shriek, throwing myself off his lap. My foot catches on his leg, and I stumble backward, still shrieking, waiting for my impending death via falling off a mountain.

Adam simply reaches up, catching a handful of my T-shirt, tugging me back to safety. I land back in his lap, hands on his chest, my breathing staggered and heavy. My heartbeat drops between my legs as those blue eyes hold mine and he whispers, "Don't go dying on me, Rosie. I'm not ready to let you go yet. We've only just met."

All the blood in my body rushes to my face, and my mouth opens and closes five hundred times before Adam takes pity on me. He gently shifts me off his lap and helps me to my feet before handing me Piglet's leash and taking Bear's for himself.

"Mind if Bear and I walk with you two?"

"Uh..." I swipe my wispy bangs off my forehead as Adam slings my backpack over his shoulder.

His brows quirk with a hint of amusement, and he cocks his head before he steps forward, making the decision for me.

"C'mon, pretty girls."

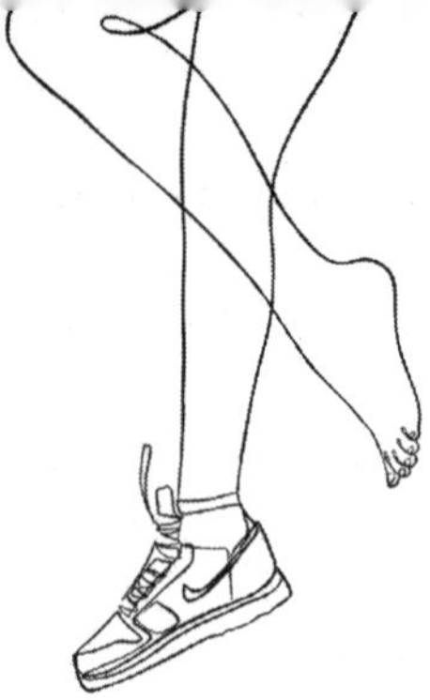

THREE

BUBBLE BUTT

Rosie

I HAVEN'T ACTUALLY MOVED YET, in case you were wondering. I know it's simple, one foot in front of the other and all that. But, you see, it's the first time Adam has graced me with his backside, and, um…

The man has a bubble butt.

Sweet mother of dragons, it's glorious. It's divine. It's—

"You comin', Rosie?"

I startle, shaking away the bubble butt fog, and let Piglet drag me over to Adam and Bear.

It's a quiet, peaceful walk, the dogs exploring ahead of us, pausing for the occasional fallen branch sniff or for a nose kiss. Adam's hand brushes against mine more than once as we weave through the uneven terrain, and when I stumble over my own two feet, he steadies me by wrapping his long fingers around mine.

There's a steady beat in my chest that thrums all the way in my ears, has me swallowing back nerves that have appeared out of nowhere. I don't know him. Not in the slightest. He's kind and friendly and here I am ready to fall all over his feet. I need to reel myself in, so the quiet is probably for the best.

We come to a fork in the path, an old wooden bridge up ahead. Piglet jogs back to us, nips playfully at my backpack hanging off Adam's shoulder, and then does her infamous jump and butt spin.

"We always stop at the bridge and have lunch," I tell Adam as Piglet leads us to her favorite spot. "It's the highlight of her day, because, food."

"Food is the highlight of our day, too, Bear, isn't it?" Adam chuckles as he hands over my bag, watching me sink to the edge of the small bridge, both dogs crawling all over me as I pull out containers of food.

I lift a sweet potato chip as Adam sits beside me. "Can Bear have a snack? They're healthy and homemade. I have dehydrated sweet potato with a bit of cinnamon, and peanut butter banana cookies. I made everything this morning, so it's extra fresh."

He nods, watching as I feed the dogs. "That sounds healthy. What are you, a vet?"

"Trying to be," I murmur, cleaning my hands after the dogs lick them clean.

"You're seriously a vet? That's so cool."

"Not yet, but next year, hopefully." I smile up at him as I unwrap my sandwich and hold half out to him. "Grilled chicken and pesto panini."

His stomach rumbles. "I can't eat half your lunch."

I snicker, stuffing it into his hands. "Your stomach says differently."

He blushes but accepts happily. "Don't judge me, but I've already had two Big Macs today."

"Oh God." I moan. "I haven't had a Big Mac in years." When you're on a budget as strict as mine, you don't stray from your carefully curated grocery list, except to accommodate whatever coupons are in the flyer that week. I look at Adam, noting that on my second bite, he's already devoured his half. I poke his hard stomach. "You look like the kinda guy who's always hungry." I blanch at my words, then quickly backtrack. "Because you're so tall, I mean. I'm not sure I've ever met someone this tall." I swallow. "And broad." *And his butt. I mean, wow.*

Adam chuckles, picking an apple pie cookie from the container I offer. "I am the tallest of my friends, and I'm hungry most of the time." He devours the cookie and swallows. "But you should see my friends, Carter and Garrett. They're human garbage disposals. I have a cupboard at home with snacks just for when they come over."

"You're joking."

"Nope. I have to refill it weekly."

Piglet stands and stretches before lying at Adam's side, her head in his lap. As she drifts to sleep while Adam gently strokes the spot between her eyes, just how she likes, I'm blown away by the instant change in her demeanor today.

"I've never, ever seen this before. She hasn't really warmed up to any man. The only person she's so relaxed with is, well…me."

"Don't worry." He nudges my shoulder with his. "I won't replace you."

I giggle. "Promise?"

"Promise." His gaze moves over me in a slow sweep that heats my insides. "'Cause you're irreplaceable, Rosie, aren't you?"

I drop my gaze to my legs, watching them swing above the sparkling creek below, unable to hold his stare. It feels intense, like he's looking for something. I don't know what, but all at once I'm both worried he won't find it and hoping he doesn't.

Whatever it is he's looking for, I'm not likely to stack up. The only thing I've ever been good at being is someone's second choice.

Fingers flutter against my cheekbone, coaxing my gaze back to Adam's. He brushes my bangs aside and smiles, twirling a lock of honey blonde and pale pink before tucking it behind my ear.

"I like your hair," he tells me quietly.

My cheeks heat as I touch one of the messy, pink buns on my head, before fluttering down to the bottom half that hangs loose, unruly waves resting an inch or so above my shoulders. "The buns? Or the color?"

"Those buns up top are cute as hell. But I really like the pink. It's kinda rosy…just like you."

My nose scrunches. "You think so?"

"Mhmm. Pretty and unique."

His kind words slow the beat of my heart. Normally the only people who gush over my hair are kids. Instead, I get judgmental looks from people in the grocery checkout line who think a person's life choices are reflected in something as trivial as their hair color. I haven't had much control of anything in my life. This is one way for me to take back control, something I do because it's my choice and mine alone.

So as Adam's fingertips skim my cheek when he pulls back, I'm sure he feels the warmth he brings there when I whisper, "Thank you."

After lunch, we wade through the shallow creek, the cool water refreshing on my bare feet. Adam goes a little farther, until the water nearly reaches his knees, and I inch back to land as my heart thuds in my chest.

He joins me a few minutes later with two happy, wet dogs, and ambles along beside me as we head back to where we came. Do I contemplate detouring several times and claiming I've gotten us lost to drag this day out a little longer? Yes. Yes, I do.

But before I know it, we're at the top of that old, rickety staircase that leads us back down to reality.

Adam starts down ahead of me with Bear, and Piglet does as she always does: digs her paws into the dirt, refusing to move.

"C'mon, girl," I coax gently. "You're safe with me; I promise."

She whimpers and lies down, and I sit on the top step, petting her head.

"Hey, Adam? Go on without us. Pig's afraid of going down the stairs. It's usually a half-hour affair. I'll just—"

"Here." Adam's at my side in an instant, taking Piglet's leash in his hand, swapping me for Bear's. "You take Bear down; I'll get Pig."

Before I can protest, he leans down, kisses her forehead, and then stands and pats his chest. Piglet rises to her hind legs, paws on Adam's torso, and he hoists her into his arms.

"'Atta girl," he chimes as my mouth gapes. "Go ahead."

I look down at Bear, and he cocks his head to the side, like he's thinking he might want a ride too. "Not a chance, big fella."

He huffs, then starts trotting back down the stairs. When we reach the ground, Piglet's looking mighty smug and content in Adam's arms.

I roll my eyes as she licks behind his ear. "You little flirt."

Adam sets Pig down and takes his hat off, running his fingers through his tousled curls before covering them up again. "Did you drive here?"

I shake my head.

"Do you, uh…need a ride? I walked here, but I don't live far. We could walk to my place, and I could drive you back."

"That's okay. The shelter isn't far from here."

Adam nods, glancing over his shoulder. He scratches his neck and points behind him. "Well, I'm going that way."

I point in the opposite direction. "And I'm going that way."

His head bobs. "Guess this is where we say good-bye."

Now I'm the one head-bobbing. It's so awkward. So I make it a hundred times more awkward by thrusting my hand out. "Nice to meet you."

He looks at my hand, then back up to me. At my hand again, then me. He grins, so wide, so amused, so damn *smug*. "A handshake, huh? So formal."

My eyes narrow, arms going across my chest. "What do you suggest?"

He shrugs, and when he takes a step toward me, my heart jumps to my throat.

"You know, Rosie. I wasn't having the best day when I ran into you. Or rather, when my dog tackled you to the ground. Maybe he knew what he was doing, though. Because my day got a hundred times better after you fell into it."

He takes another step forward, and in all the panic that ensues at the thought that this handsome, kind man might actually be...*flirting* with me, I lose control of my body, accidentally crossing one ankle over the other and promptly tripping over my own two feet, crashing into him.

Adam chuckles in my ear, low and hearty, his breath tumbling down my neck as he holds me to him. "You're trouble, aren't you?"

That t-word sparks something inside me, something lost and broken, and I cling to Adam as he squeezes me for a moment that ends too soon.

He gives Piglet's chin a scratch, and with one last look in my direction, he winks at me. "See ya around, trouble."

FOUR

I'LL TAKE THE WHOLE BOTTLE, PLEASE

Adam

I'M DYING.

Figuratively, of course. *Maybe* literally. Ask me again in two hours.

An ankle hooks around mine below the table, and I barely resist the urge to drag my hands down my face. I clear my throat, unhook my leg, and carefully tuck both of my feet below the safety of my chair. I take a sip of my red wine, set it down, and then pick it right back up and throw back the rest of the nine-year-old pinot noir when the tip of Alessia's heeled foot touches mine again.

"You really like wine, huh?" she asks, blue eyes hooded, lashes batting.

"That obvious, huh?" I don't think I've ever tossed back two glasses in less than ten minutes.

I need to quit this and quit it hard.

The dating, not the wine. The wine stays, the girl goes.

I don't know why I keep thinking this one might be different, that the more time I spend out here in the dating pool, the quicker I'll find the one. Jaxon says I'm delusional, to just enjoy the dates, take them home, and have some fun. I don't think he and I have the same idea of fun.

Look, would I like to have sex? Obviously. It's been over a year. I'm developing premature arthritis in my wrist, and I've only recently turned twenty-six. But by the time every date ends, I'd rather be subjected to a lifetime of wearing a wrist brace and giving up my career as a top-paid goalie in the NHL than spend any more time with these women.

Plus, they're not even in it for the sex. That's the problem a lot of guys on my team have: women who just want to say they've had sex with a famous hockey player.

My problem is they want more. I want more, too, but the more I want is genuine. The more they want is dollar signs.

"Oh! Hey, you!" Alessia waves down our waiter as he passes by with a tray of food. She points at the nearly empty bottle of wine. "Could we get another bottle?"

Scott lifts a brow in my direction, and when I nod, his mouth tips in a small smirk. I come here about twice a month, because Scott respects my privacy and reads my cues. He tends to my dates like royalty, and when things are looking especially grim, he tells me the chef would like to meet me. Then he shoves me out the kitchen door for a five-minute breather while he tries to speed up the rest of the dinner service.

Alessia looks around the restaurant, pouting. "We should ask him to switch our table. We're tucked all the way in the back."

"It's nice back here," I counter softly, sipping my ice water. "It's quiet."

Jesus, can her pout possibly get any bigger? How far out does that bottom lip go? "Barely anyone can see us back here."

"I like my privacy," is my simple reply. I don't feel like getting into all the reasons why she'd rather be front and center with me.

Alessia popped into my inbox on Tinder a week ago. Her profile showed pictures of her with horses and dogs, her with her arms wrapped around her grandma in her nursing home bed, and hiking through the Appalachian Trail. She was sweet and didn't say a whole lot, just that Bear was cute in my profile picture and that she loved hiking too. Three days ago, I asked her if she'd like to have dinner, and it's been downhill since. The kissing emojis, the never-ending messages throughout the day asking for constant updates on what I'm doing, who I'm with. The second I saw her out front of the restaurant tonight, she threw her arms around my neck and planted her lipstick on my cheek.

I like physical contact. I like intimacy. But I want it to feel natural. Like it did earlier today when that little honey-and-rose-colored-hair cutie tripped over her own feet and tumbled into me when I told her to shove her handshake.

My mind drifts to Rosie for the hundredth time today, the easy blaze of her cheeks, the flecks of gold that danced in those light green eyes, the way she snorted when she laughed and looked so damned relieved when she thought I didn't notice.

Everything about her was natural. Her smiles, her giggles, the timid way she kicked off her shoes and waded through the creek with me while watching the beauty around us.

"So you just re-signed your contract with the Vipers," Alessia says, breaking my thoughts. Her eyes glitter with excitement as she leans closer. "Ten-point-five million a year for the next eight years?"

"I thought you didn't keep up with hockey." Specifically, she told me she had to look me up when I told her I played professionally.

She waves my words away. "So, what are you gonna do with all that money? Buy a new house? Where do you live now? How many bedrooms? Can you see the mountains?" Her eyes widen, and she grips my hand in both of hers. "Oh my God, have you ever been to Paris? It's so beautiful, especially in the fall. We should totally go."

"I have hockey," I remind her, trying to pull my hand back. Alessia laces our fingers together, and I swallow a groan when a flash from a phone goes off from across the restaurant.

"Can you book a week off?"

"That's not how it—" I sigh. "That's not really how hockey works, not with a contract."

"Oh." She frowns, then grins. "I've heard it's beautiful at Christmas too."

"You told me you spend the day with your grandma at the nursing home."

"Grams will probably be dead by then. If she's not, I'll just skip. It's not like she'll know." She fishes her phone out of her purse and promptly shows me a series of pictures of her posing next to her sleeping grandma, giving the peace sign while she grins or purses her lips.

What in the sweet fuck have I gotten myself into?

"Um..." I pour the remainder of bottle number one into my glass, then toss it back, hoping it'll burn the memory of this conversation. "So you hiked the Appalachian Trail."

She rolls her eyes and folds over the table, clapping her hands to it. "Oh-em-gee, it was the absolute *worst*. I hate nature. I hate bugs. I hate walking. I treated myself to a five-day spa vacation after that nightmare."

Whatever was left of my heart sinks to my gut, churning.

"Your bottle," Scott murmurs, appearing at our table. He uncorks the wine, pours a sample into each glass, and smiles. "Mr. Lockwood, if you'd be so kind, our head chef would love to meet you. He's a big fan of yours."

I leap to my feet, my knees colliding with the table, shaking the dishes. I catch the wine glasses before they can topple over. "Absolutely. For sure. Yes, of course. I love meeting fans." I touch Alessia's shoulder. "I'll be right back."

Scott leads me through the restaurant and into a dark hallway.

"Next time I down half a bottle of two-hundred-dollar wine in ten minutes, I need you to pretend there's a kitchen fire and escort all the guests out. I'll cover the bills. Got it?"

Scott chuckles. "Loud and clear, Mr. Lockwood."

"So you kissed her."

"I did *not* kiss her. Have you been listening to me at all?"

Carter shrugs. "That picture on Instagram says you kissed her."

I shove Carter's shoulder, and he trips sideways in his rollerblades, stepping over the curb and shuffling onto the grass, where he catches himself against a tree.

"Motherfucker," he bites out, leaping back onto the road, tearing after me at full speed as I take off ahead of him.

Before he can catch me, Emmett wraps an arm around his head, pulling him back against him. "Don't poke the bear. Adam's gone grizzly mode."

Garrett barks out a laugh. "Adam never goes full grizzly."

Jaxon loops around me and turns, skating backward so he can smirk at me. "I went full grizzly on three girls in his parents' bedroom on Friday night."

I point at him. "You're at the top of my shitlist."

He wags his brows and spins, the five of us settling into stride together, coasting down the quiet road. "So you didn't kiss her?"

I tug on my ball cap at the uncomfy memory of last night. I walked

Alessia to her car, thanked her for the nice/awful time, but when I opened her door, she slung her arms around my neck and pressed her lips to mine. I stood there in shock before her tongue wormed its way into my mouth.

I'm not entirely proud to say that, for a whole three seconds, I considered it. I let her tongue glide against mine, and my mind wandered to a place where I wondered what it would be like to give it up for one night, to forget about what I want and get some release for once in so damn long.

But I came crashing back down to reality with the flash of her phone as she took a fucking *selfie* of us mid-kiss, and thank fuck for that.

"I stopped the kiss and said I didn't feel a connection and that it would be best if we went our separate ways." I stroke my cheek, where I can still feel the sting of her palm. "She slapped me and said, 'Thanks for wasting my time,' before she got into her car, slammed her door, and drove off."

Carter chuckles. "Never thought it'd be you getting slapped out of all of us."

Jaxon touches his cheek and smiles. "I've earned my fair share. It's fueled by some wild energy. Normally ends back in bed, or against a wall. Once, we even dropped right to the—"

"I don't need to hear it," I cut him off. "And now there's a picture of me and her floating around the internet forever."

Garrett pulls his phone out, snickering at the photo I've seen a hundred times today, the one Alessia tagged me in at the crack of dawn. "The caption is the worst part."

Emmett takes the phone, clearing his throat before reading Alessia's words out loud in the voice he reserves for his impression of his wife, Cara. "Had the best night with this man, but was so sad when I had to tell him I didn't feel a love connection. Sad emoji. Three out of five on the kiss scale. Needs some tongue work."

"Needs some tongue work, my ass," I grumble, skating up my driveway. Giggles and shrieks flow from the backyard as I flip the lock on my gate. "And *I* told *her* I didn't feel the connection!"

"Grizzly mode activated." Carter makes claws with his hand. "*Rawr*." His eyes light as they land on his daughter, but before he can get there, Garrett races by, scoops her up, and hugs her against his chest.

"Hi, angel," he coos, dotting her face with kisses while she squeals with laughter. "Uncle Gare is here."

Carter groans, balls his fists, and starts yanking his rollerblades off. "*Jennie*! Come get your boyfriend!"

Cara rolls her eyes from where she's sunbathing on her stomach. "Act your age, Carter, not your shoe size." She grins up at Emmett as he claps a hand to her ass. "Hi, baby."

My patio door slides open, and Jennie and Olivia slip out. Both their eyes light up at the sight of their men, shirtless, sweaty, and fighting over the sweetest baby. Garrett finally gives Ireland up in favor of sweeping Jennie into his arms, burying his face in her neck.

"Keep your hands above the waist, Andersen," Carter grumbles as Garrett squeezes Jennie's butt. "That's my sister." He sandwiches a babbling Ireland between him and Olivia. "My two princesses."

Jaxon steals the spotlight as he tears by everyone, screaming, "*Cannonball*!" before disappearing into my pool with a six-foot splash.

Olivia follows me into my kitchen, where I fill a glass with ice water and drain it in seconds.

"Date didn't go well, huh?" she asks, pulling a fruit tray from my fridge.

"What, that picture of us kissing didn't convince you?" I pop a piece of cantaloupe into my mouth as she snickers.

"You looked like a deer caught in headlights."

"Maybe that's why she only gave me a three out of five on the kiss scale."

Olivia snorts, but so much genuine compassion shines in her eyes. "I'm sorry it didn't work out."

I shrug. "It's cool. I'm getting used to the idea that there's no one out there for me."

She frowns. "I don't believe that, Adam. Not a single bit."

"I'm tired of looking," I admit quietly.

"Maybe that's the point. Maybe when you stop looking and just live…maybe that's when you find your magic."

I smile at the thought as I hug Olivia's tiny frame to mine before she heads outside. Magic sounds nice.

My phone rings as I pull burgers and sausages from the fridge, my mom's face staring up at me from the screen. Her deep brown eyes and wide grin as she stands next to me after my first NHL game, proud as ever and barely reaching my shoulders, bring me a level of comfort that's hard to find anywhere else.

I tuck my phone between my ear and shoulder as I set the meat on a board. "Hi, Mom."

"Hi, honey. What are you up to?"

"About to start the barbecue," I tell her as a shriek and a splash sound through the door.

"Wish Dad and I were there to join you." She hesitates, her tone somber when she speaks next. "Maybe we need to visit sooner than later."

My chest tightens. "Is everything okay?"

"Well, your dad and I are worried, because…" Another pause, and is that—

"Are you laughing?"

"No," she snickers. "It's just, we're really worried about you because —" *giggle* "—apparently you're only a—" *snort* "—three out of five on the kiss scale," she finally chokes out, nearly drowned by the boom of my dad's laughter.

"For fuck's sake. You two are brutal."

"*And she didn't feel a love connection*!" She wheezes, gasping for air, and my eyes find a permanent space in the back of my head.

"Don't forget the tongue work!" Dad shouts. "He needs some serious tongue work!"

"I hate you," I grumble.

When she finally gets a handle on her laughter—she might be crying —she says, "I'm sorry, honey. Keeping up with your love life on social media is our favorite way to spend Sunday mornings."

"Not much of a love life."

"Maybe you need to step back for a bit," she suggests.

"Yeah, Ollie was just saying the same thing."

"You've got a great bunch surrounding you, honey. If you're looking for love, take a look at the people who show up for you every day. When you find someone who makes you feel like that, an extension of your family, you'll know."

I know she's right. The laughter that surrounds me on my best and worst days brings me a contentment I couldn't live without, and as I head outside and watch my friends make my home their own, I know that if they were all I had for the rest of this life, I'd be okay.

But it still doesn't stop me from wishing for someone to call my own at nighttime when the quiet sets in.

"Hi, princess," I whisper, scooping Ireland up and kissing her tiny nose. I tug on the strap of her pink gingham sun hat, and she beams up at me, toothless, pulling in those Beckett dimples in her frilly bathing suit. "Jesus, you're cute as fuck."

"That's a Beckett trait," Carter says, swimming to the edge of the pool. "Ireland, baby, look! Look at Daddy! Watch what I can do!" He presses his feet against the pool wall and launches himself backward, flipping underwater, emerging with a gasp. "Did you see me, princess? Did you see Daddy? Ten outta ten, right, baby?"

I tickle her cheek. "Wasn't watching."

"Aw, man." Carter slaps the water and swims away.

"Your daddy is too much sometimes, isn't he?" I murmur to Ireland, setting her back down on her blanket, stretching out beside her.

Her innocent green eyes stare up at me as I drive her favorite light-up bug car around her, and I can't help letting my mind wander back to another set of green eyes. I've lost count of how many times I've done this, let my thoughts drift to Rosie. That sweet smile, those honey blonde locks with streaks of soft pink, the gold freckles splashed across her cheekbones, the way that dog looked up at her like she was her whole world.

Hours later, when I'm sitting at the edge of the pool, watching the sun sink behind the spectacular backdrop, when it's quiet and my dog's head rests on my thigh, I'm still thinking about her.

My patio door slides open, and Jaxon sits beside me, handing me a beer and dipping his legs in the water. "I'll never get tired of this view."

"Me neither." I take a long pull on my drink, licking the taste from my lips, and for the hundredth time, I wonder what Rosie's mouth tastes like. Jaxon's probably not the one to talk to about this, but he's the only other single one in our group, so he's the only one still here tonight. "I met someone yesterday."

"Yeah, dude, I know. That picture has two-hundred-and-fifty thousand likes on Instagram. Everyone knows."

I chuckle, an exhausted sound, and scrub my eyes. "Someone else. Yesterday, when Bear and I went for a hike."

His brows rise. "Oh? And? Spill the tea."

"She was...I donno." I palm the back of my neck, thinking back on

Rosie. "So cute. She's in vet school, and she was walking a dog from the animal shelter. She'd made special treats for the dog, and she shared some with Bear. Shared her lunch with me too. The dog she was with has had a rough life, she said, and she was just so patient with her." I shrug. "She was just really sweet."

"You're telling me you found someone who *actually* likes dogs and isn't just pretending? You hit the jackpot, buddy."

"Shut up, asshole."

He laughs, sips his beer. "Seriously. Sounds like something worth exploring."

"Yeah, I think so."

"And how was she about the hockey stuff?"

"Didn't come up." I remember the way I searched her eyes for any hint of excitement when I introduced myself, how her wide gaze gave nothing away. "I don't think she recognized me."

"Not a huge hockey fan, then. That's okay. Kinda what you wanted, right?"

"Would be nice to know if she likes me for me, that's for sure."

"So you gonna call her and ask her out?"

I cringe. "I would, but, uh…I didn't get her number."

"Jesus, Adam, rookie mistake."

"I wasn't thinking straight. I was all…" I run a hand through my hair, tugging. "Bamboozled."

Jaxon laughs. "So go back next weekend. Same time, same place. Bet she's there."

"That's kinda…logical. But is it too much? It feels stalker-ish. I don't wanna scare her off."

"Nah. A guy determined to track down a cutie he connected with? Girls eat that shit up. Plus, if you felt something, something that might be real…" He shrugs again. "You don't wanna lose that chance. Chase it."

I watch him quietly for a moment, casually drinking his beer as he stares out at the mountains. "You don't have a soft spot, Jaxon, do you?"

"Nah, fuck that."

"Sounds like you're a softie for love underneath that tough exterior." My grin grows as he shakes his head. "Sounds like you might know how to actually court a woman, not just sleep with her."

"All right." He yanks my beer out of my hands and strides toward the house. "You've had enough. I'm making you a coffee."

I chuckle as he heads inside, and Bear cracks his sleepy eyes, looking up at me beneath the setting sun.

"What do you think, Bear? Do we give it a shot?" I blow out a breath as the sun does its final dip and the stars begin to paint the sky. "Maybe she'll like us for exactly who we are."

~

Did I really let Jaxon talk me into this?

"What am I doing here?" I look down at Bear, where he waits patiently, then back at the small building in front of me. I throw my arms up. "Let's go. This is stupid. It's probably not even the right shelter. And she probably won't even remember us."

Bear gives me an angry *woof,* like he's disagreeing about how memorable I seem to think he is. He takes his leash in his teeth and tugs, trying to lead me toward Wildheart Animal Sanctuary.

"C'mon, buddy. Let's go. If we're meant to see her again, then—"

The sound of soft laughter steals my words when the front door opens, and a German Shepherd leaps outside, all but dragging a little thing with honey blonde and rose gold waves tumbling from the messy bun on top of her head.

I watch as Piglet trots forward three quick steps before jumping into the air, like she's never been so excited, and Rosie can't get enough of it.

Bear whimpers at the sight of them, those two girls who might have stolen a spot in our hearts a week ago, and two pairs of eyes snap to us. Piglet cowers, hiding between Rosie's legs until she recognizes us. Slowly, she steps back into the sunshine, looks up at Rosie, back to us, and starts wagging that tail of hers.

Rosie's eyes flash with recognition, surprise, and the knots in my stomach tighten as I battle between the urge to run and the desire to stay.

"Adam?"

"Hi, Rosie." It comes out super fucking croaky, and I palm the back of my clammy neck as she approaches me slowly, curiosity dancing in her soft, jade eyes. "I, uh…I wasn't sure if this was the right shelter, but it's the closest one, and I figured maybe you normally go at the same time every Saturday, and…" I clear my throat into my fist. "I thought it would be nice if the dogs could hike together again, since they seemed to really like each other. You know, for the dogs."

That grin grows, so huge, so dazzling, and Rosie bobs her head in agreement. "Oh, yes. Definitely. For the dogs."

"And maybe me too," I admit. "I, um…I liked walking with you. And talking with you. And eating you. No, fuck." I squeeze my eyes shut and shake my head. "Fuck, no, that's not what I—eating *with* you. Your sandwiches. Not your…" I gesture at her crotch. Holy fuck, *I gestured at her fucking crotch. I'm turning into Garrett.*

I need help. I need an intervention. I have a crush, and I don't know what to do with it. It's been way too long. Should I call Carter? Is he really my best bet for advice? No, I'll call Olivia. She's sensible. She can help me through this. Maybe she can gather the girls.

I point down the sidewalk. "I'll just go now."

A burst of laughter chases behind me when I turn around. Everything inside me settles at Rosie's next words, at her hand wrapping around my wrist, stopping me.

"We'd love to walk with you."

FIVE

TROUBLE WITH A CAPITAL T

Adam

SHE'S SO PRETTY. Does she know how pretty she is? Her hair looks so soft, I just want to touch it. She's got these freckles, like liquid gold, dotting the bridge of her nose and sweeping over her cheekbones. Her chin has the tiniest dimple in it, right there in the middle, and when she smiles, I—

"You're making me nervous."

I trip over my feet, jolting forward. "What?"

Rosie snickers, and when she does, her nose does this cute little scrunchy thing. "You haven't said a word in ten minutes, Adam. You're just walking in silence, staring at me." She swipes at her chin. "Do I have something on my face? I had a peanut butter and jam sandwich earlier and I tend to be an incredibly messy eater." She swings her head over her shoulder, trying to look at her butt. "Or did I sit in something? You wouldn't believe how many times I've done *that*, only to find out hours later when I take my clothes off."

I chuckle. "No, you don't have jam on your face, and you didn't sit in something. Your butt is per—" I halt. Rosie blinks at me. I blink back. "*Pur*ple." I gesture at her butt in her skintight lilac leggings. "Your pants are purple, so your butt is also…purple. Not that I was looking."

I was totally looking.

Rosie tucks a short petal-pink wave behind her ear. "Thanks…I think?"

I nod. "Yeah, they're nice leggings." I do love the leggings, almost as much as I love the ass, and not because of the color.

Because her hips are full and round as fuck, and I'm not proud to say every single time she skips ahead of me, my eyes zero in on that perfect ass in those sculpted pants. Who had any right giving her an ass like that? It lures my mind to dark, forbidden places, like what it would feel like to grab it in my hands, lift her to me and press her against a tree.

I want to feel her. Touch her. I want to brush my thumb over that tiny dimple in her chin, skim my hand over the flare of her hip, tangle my fingers with hers, and just *feel*. I want to fucking feel something, anything, and I just want it to feel *right*.

"I'm sorry," I finally say. "I'm in my own head today. Every day, really."

"That's okay. I live in mine. It's an overwhelming place to be sometimes. Oh!" She claps my shoulder and turns, walking backward in front of me. "Do you ever do that worst-case-scenario thing?"

I lift a brow. "Worst-case-scenario thing?"

She lays a hand over her chest. "I'm a worst-case-scenario expert." She flips back around and joins my side, clutching my elbow as we walk. "So I start by thinking about one seemingly insignificant thing, and then I accidentally think of something bad that could happen because of it, then another something bad, and before I know it, I've got a list of all the horrible, terrifying things that could go wrong if I wade too deep in the water, or if I go for a walk at night time, or if I grow a backbone, open my mouth, and finally tell somebody no." She watches my blank face for a moment, then cringes. "Sorry. My level of anxiety is almost always unmatched." She points at Piglet, roaming up ahead with Bear. "Except with Pig. And see, now I'm doing that worst-case-scenario thing where I'm thinking you suddenly wish you hadn't asked me to walk with you, and now you're thinking of ways to end this, and what if you're desperate enough to roll me right off the cliff?" Wide eyes stare up at me. "Please don't kill me."

A rumble of laughter escapes from deep in my chest, and I toss an arm around her shoulders. "I wouldn't dream of taking you out. How would I stare at your purple pants?"

"You mean my butt?"

"Careful, trouble."

There's that flush, the same color as her name, blotching those cheekbones.

"I get what you mean, though," I tell her. "I get lost in my thoughts, and they run away with things that could go wrong, how I might not be seeing something clearly, or how history might repeat itself. It's confusing and…"

"Daunting."

"Yeah, it is. Makes me pause about a lot of things.

"Makes me miss out on a lot of chances," she adds quietly.

"Hey." Nudging her side, I smile, because I want to see hers again. "Keep me around, and you won't miss out on anything. I'll show up at the shelter so you don't have a choice."

She cracks a wide, hopeful grin, extra parts goofy. "One might think you're stalking me."

"That's what I said! My friend said girls like that stuff, though."

Her eyes come to mine, curious and a little hesitant, another blush staining her cheeks. "You talked to your friend about me?"

There's a part of me, such a large part, that's uncertain. Worried I'm seeing something, feeling something that isn't really here. That I've gotten desperate enough to convince myself she's interested. I mean, *really* interested. And that fear steals my words.

Instead, I smile softly and take her hand, helping her over a cluster of rocks and to the bridge. She drops to her butt on the edge of the wood, feet dangling over the creek, and I sink down beside her. The dogs rush to her side when she pulls her backpack onto her lap, and I watch as Bear behaves like a perfect angel as she has him sit tall and still, showing him his cookie before she offers it to him. He takes it delicately and licks her cheek when he's done. Rosie giggles and kisses his nose before doing the same with Piglet, and after lapping some water from a collapsible bowl, the two dogs curl up together behind us.

"Piglet seems to like Bear," I observe.

"Because she's so anxious with people, she doesn't get much in the way of pup socialization at Wildheart. She's selective about who she gives her trust to, and it makes me sad to think of her spending so much time in her own head. I'm so happy that she's made a friend."

"Then we should walk together every Saturday, huh?"

Rosie smiles down at her bag. "If you'd like to."

"I would. Would you?"

This time, her blush makes its way up to the tips of her ears. "Yeah. I think I would."

"Cool. It's a date."

Rosie's eyes flick to mine, a sea of curiosity and nerves that swirl as she examines me beneath her lashes. Her bangs curtain her face, brushing her temples and not letting her hide those emotions she wears so freely. She opens her mouth but seems to second-guess, instead choosing to take her lower lip between her teeth and focus her attention on her backpack, a slight tremor to her hands.

She hands me two sandwiches and a muffin. "Here. For you."

"You made lunch for me?"

"I thought, you know, just in case we ran into you again, and you wanted to eat with us. It's a turkey bacon club with Swiss on sourdough. It's no big deal. If you don't want it—"

"It is a big deal." I lay my hand over her fumbling one, stopping the nervous way she's tearing at the edge of her sandwich. "You thought of me, and that's a big deal to me." I stroke her wrist with my thumb, and her eyes track the movement before lifting to mine. "Thank you, Rosie."

And then, to ease the thick tension in the air, I sigh happily. "I haven't eaten since second breakfast."

"Second breakfast?"

"I'd waste away if I only had the first."

There's that snicker-snort, even if she hides it behind her muffin. When she's done, she hands me a wipe to clean my hands, offers the dogs another cookie, and refills their water bowl one last time before we pack everything away.

I take her hand, helping her back over the rocks, and tilt my head toward the sparkling creek. "Walk through the water with me?"

She hesitates like she might say no, but Bear races ahead, splashing into the water, and Piglet tugs on her leash, yanking Rosie forward as she chases after Bear.

"Here," I say with a chuckle, taking Piglet's leash. I kick off my shoes and socks and follow the dogs into the water. "Go sit. Dip your toes while we play."

She nods, taking a seat on the edge of the bank, watching us as she dips her feet. The dogs plow around in front of me, wrestling and rolling, until the three of us are soaked to the bone. They stop for a rest, lying in the sunshine, and the quiet slosh of water draws my attention over my shoulder.

Rosie slowly makes her way toward us, one hand at her jaw, the other clutching the neck of her shirt. She looks up at me, an unsteady smile spreading in slow motion, and I grin, holding my hand out to her.

Her warm palm slides against mine, and I grasp it tightly, pulling her into me. I don't want to let go, but I do, and together we wade through the shallow water.

After a few peaceful minutes, Rosie's next step has the water rising suddenly to her knees, pulling a sharp gasp from her. "*Oh*. I didn't know it got so deep."

She frantically steps backward, clawing at the back of my shirt before she slips on a rock and nearly tumbles straight to her ass. I catch her around the waist, her soft curves melting beneath my palm as she fists my shirt. The tips of my fingers dig into her hips as she peers up at me, pink lips parting, each puff of breath kissing my lips as I hold her to me, staring down at her heart-shaped face.

"Careful, trouble."

Her fingers tighten around my shirt and her gaze falls to my mouth. Then she blinks, shakes her head, and pushes us both up. Piglet rushes to her side, sniffing Rosie's legs, her hands, before finally licking her wherever she can get her tongue.

Rosie pats her head. "I'm fine, Pig, but thank you anyway for the kisses." Her eyes come to mine for only a moment before darting away. "Sorry. Freaked out a bit there."

"Don't apologize. You're pretty short; we should stay where it's shallow."

She guffaws. "I am *not* short."

"That's what all short people say."

"I—" Rosie huffs, pinning her arms across her chest. "I'm not short."

I grin, tapping the corner of her pout. "What are you, five-four?"

She points a cute-as-fuck, stubborn nose to the sky. "Five-five, thank you very much. But I suppose that looks teensy tiny compared to your monstrous height."

I stifle a laugh. "Sorry I missed that last inch."

"An inch is very important."

"Oh, I completely agree. One inch might mean the difference between a disappointing night and one spent screaming for all the right reasons." The words are out of my mouth before I can overthink them, and I wait for them to settle. Rosie's mouth pops open, the heat in her cheeks returning like molten lava, and I wink.

Snapping her mouth shut, she scrunches her nose to hide her amusement and swats my shoulder. "Dirty boy. I hope for your sake, and the sake of all the girls who spend those nights with you, you've got that extra inch."

I bark a laugh. "There are no girls."

Her brows hike. "None?"

"Not a single one."

"Hmmm." She leans closer, beckoning me like she has a secret, and I dip my head, a cocktail of excitement and nerves racing down my spine as her warm breath touches my ear. "Is it because you don't have that extra inch?"

I whip away with a sharp gasp and a hand pressed to my chest. When she breaks out into a fit of giggles, I give the bun on her head a gentle tug. "You really are trouble with a capital *T*, aren't you?"

Her laughter slowly ceases, and she drops her attention to her toes.

"Not a fan of the nickname?"

"Trouble?"

"Mmm."

She stares at the bright blue sky, a far-off smile curving her lips. "Love it, actually. My dad coined it when I was two."

"Ah, so we both saw right through those wide green eyes and innocent smile."

"Hey." She narrows her eyes and pokes my stomach. "I'll have you know the most trouble I ever got in as a kid was bringing home a baby bunny I found at the park. It was all alone, so I thought it lost its mom and I was doing the right thing. Dad explained that mother rabbits leave them during the day to protect them from predators, that she would be looking for her baby when the sun went down and she came back to feed it. I was distraught with myself for taking it from its mom."

"Come on. The worst thing you ever did was save a baby bunny from what you thought might be starvation? No way, I don't buy it."

"It's true! I was a good kid. My parents and I were always so busy in our spare time, hiking, camping, exploring…" She shrugs. "I guess I never really had a chance to stray off course."

"And as a teenager?"

Something in her expression changes, the light in her eyes dimming, stealing all her excitement. "I was an even better teenager. So quiet, no one even noticed me." She turns away, wading back to shore. "I've gotta start heading back." Her reserved smile quickly spirals into laughter as the dogs claim her feet, cleaning the water off as she tries to pull her socks on. "*Stop,*" she squeals, flipping over, crawling away on her hands and knees. "My feet are ticklish!"

Seeing her on her hands and knees with her full, round ass in the air does something to me. It unlocks something dark and feral, so hungry I have to turn away, run a shaky palm over my mouth.

God, I can't remember the last time I've been this turned on, this attracted to someone. It's not just the wild fucking *curves*, the flare of her wide hips, the dip in her waist where I'm desperate to watch my fingertips dig in and disappear.

It's the way her entire body comes alive when she laughs, her nose crinkling right along with it. It's the way her eyes light with excitement and dim with disappointment, unable to hide a single emotion coursing through her, leaving her wide open, begging to be read like your favorite book. How her teeth descend on that lower lip, nibbling when she's playing shy. How she's unable to hold that smile back when it wants to break free, and the way it drags mine out like a magnet, because when she smiles, everything feels right.

It's the way she loves the dogs so wholly, shows Piglet neverending patience. It's bringing extra sandwiches on her hike, just in case, because she thought of *me*.

It's not that I feel less fractured with Rosie, but that the light streams in anyway, between all the shattered pieces left behind. I find beauty there, a sense of peace that tells me good things are waiting.

Maybe it's dense of me to be so hopeful after everything, the betrayals, the lies, the countless dates with anything but the right intentions. Maybe I've lost my mind, thinking I can find any type of solace in someone I barely know.

But I'd rather be hopeful than accept the more gutting option: that I won't find what my friends have, the type of love my parents taught me to wait for.

Rosie and I walk in silence as the dogs trot ahead of us, and after a few minutes she nudges my side. "So what about you?"

"What about me?"

"Were you a sweet kid or a terror?"

I chuckle, skimming my jaw as I admit, "I was a little shit. My parents always taught me to be kind and helpful; that was never an issue. I just found myself in a lot of places I shouldn't be. Like in a four-feet-deep hole in my Grandma's back garden when I tested whether you really *could* dig your way to China." I point a finger in Rosie's amused face. "You can't, by the way, so don't waste your energy. Then there was that time at the cottage when I collected a bucket of frogs and brought them to my mom while she was napping on the couch. She was scared of frogs, but I wanted to show her there was nothing to be scared of because they're just hoppy, gentle little guys, and a little slime won't hurt you. It, uh, really didn't go to plan." I palm the back of my neck as I remember how she cracked one lid when I whispered I had a surprise for her, how she shot up, accidentally knocking the bucket from my hand, tripped over the blanket, and face-planted on the floor as all twelve frogs leapt around the living room. "Remind me to call my mom and apologize for the hundredth time when I get home."

"Aw, come on. You were just a little kid! Your heart was in the right place. You must have been, what? Five? Six?"

I run a hand over my mouth to hide my guilty smile. "Thirteen."

"*Thirteen*? Adam! Call your mama right now and apologize!"

"I know, I know. I told you: I was a little shit. But hey, I turned out all right." I grin, extra charming, and waggle my brows. "I've even been called angelic as an adult."

She snorts, rolling her eyes. "Cocky too. And what about nicknames? Do you have any?"

"Woody, I guess, would be the only one."

"Woody? Why?"

I tell her the half truth, because I'm not telling her about the hotel incident. "Because my last name is Lockwood."

"Lockwood," she murmurs, and I hold my breath, waiting for her to put my first and last name together, for recognition to hit. Waiting for this happy, safe bubble I've found myself in to finally burst.

But it doesn't.

She smiles, holding her hand out. "Nice to meet you, Adam Lockwood. I'm Rosie Wells."

I chuckle, tugging her into my side, swinging my arm around her shoulders. "You're cute as fuck, Rosie Wells." Bear tosses me a stare over his shoulder, and I roll my eyes. "You, too, Bear." Piglet swings around, hammering Bear in the face with her butt, and bounds over to us, tongue hanging out of her mouth. "And you, too, pretty Pig."

She loops through Rosie's legs with a whimper, big brown eyes peeking at the top of the stairs as they come into view. I hand Bear's leash to Rosie and pat my chest.

"C'mon, girl."

"You're gonna throw your back out one of these days," Rosie scolds as I lift Piglet into my arms.

"Nah." I shift Piglet to one arm and flex the bicep on my other. "I'm big and strong."

"Your daddy thinks he's all that and a bag of potato chips, Bear, doesn't he?" she whispers to him as they start down the stairs, and the little shit barks his agreement. "Right, if he really wanted to impress us, he'd carry you too."

"I can hear you!"

She flashes me a brilliant smile over her shoulder. "You're doing great, Adam! Wow, you're so strong!"

"Women," I mutter, and Pig sticks her tongue in my ear.

I spend the ten-minute walk to Wildheart contemplating how to casually drop that I'm a famous professional athlete, that I think she's really pretty, and it would be super great if she wanted to maybe, like… spend some time with me. Eat a meal she doesn't make me, maybe have a glass of wine that I can taste from her lips after.

I open my mouth approximately twenty thousand times and snap it shut in favor of silence each time.

Rosie's not doing much better than me. She's standing here in front of me, twirling a pink lock and scuffing at the ground with her shoes, beat-up Nikes with a white and blue floral swoosh. Her eyes bounce between her feet and my face, her cheeks growing warmer with each pass.

"Well, I guess—"

"Do you wanna have dinner with me?" I blurt, and suddenly my cheeks are as red as hers.

"Dinner?"

"I know we agreed to hike again next Saturday, but it would be nice to see you before then."

Wide, hopeful eyes peer up at mine. "Before then?"

"Before then."

"Before Saturday?"

"Before Saturday."

She bites her lip, scrunches her nose. "Like…when?"

Tonight is on the tip of my tongue, but it's too soon. I need help. Maybe professional. I need to call a meeting.

I need a motherfucking girls' night.

"What about Wednesday? You, me, and dinner."

Something sparks in her eyes, lighting her from the inside out. Her hands curl into eager fists at her sides. "Oh, yeah, I could do that. I'm really good at eating dinner." Her jaw drops, and she claps both hands over her mouth. "Oh my gosh. *I'm really good at eating dinner*. Did I just say that out loud? I did, didn't I?"

"You did," I confirm, panic easing its grip on my throat. "But it was no worse than earlier today when I said I liked eating you and then pointed at your crotch." I take her hands in mine, my thumb moving over the chipped purple polish on her fingernails. "So…dinner? Wednesday?"

Rosie nods eagerly, then pauses. "But wait. Is it just a friend date? Or is it like…a dinner date? Like a date-date? Like two people having dinner, like a…"

"Date?"

"Yeah."

"Yeah." I grin. "It's a date."

"Okay. Cool. So cool." Her head bobs. "I like that."

"Good." I bring her body into mine for one of those hugs I've been thinking about all week. She smells summery, like coconut, melon, and fresh laundry, and I sink into the way she feels against me, soft, warm, and just right. "Because I gotta tell ya, Rosie, the thoughts I've been having would get *just a friend* into an awful lot of trouble."

By the time we've exchanged numbers and she's disappearing inside, she's still rocking a volcanic flush that paints her whole body, warm enough I can still feel it as I start back home.

Opening a new message thread, I type in Olivia, Cara, and Jennie's names.

ME

I need your help. I met a girl.

OLIVIA

OMG! Adam!!! *heart eyes emoji* *happy tears emoji* *bride emoji* *groom emoji*

JENNIE

My guy!!! *eggplant emoji* *peach emoji* *water droplets emoji*

I've got some toy recs if you two wanna get creative.

<link> This one's my fav. I threaten to replace Garrett with it at least 2x/week.

CARA

Well, well, well. Look who's come crawling to the masters for advice. You've come to the right place, young grasshopper.

Cara changed the group chat name to Journey to Pussy Palace.

Care, what the fuck???

Sorry, babe *sad emoji* I tried "Adam's Road to Hope: One Man's Journey to Pussy Palace" but it was too long.

Jesus Christ. What the hell did I just get myself into?

SIX

ADAM'S ROAD TO HOPE: ONE MAN'S JOURNEY TO PUSSY PALACE

Adam

"Welcome, everyone, to the first official meeting of 'Adam's Road to Hope: One Man's Journey to Pussy Palace.' Don't forget to pick up a gift basket and get your time cards punched on the way out. Sangria is in the fridge, snacks are on the table, and pizza will be here in thirty." Cara slings one leg over the other, clasps her hands together under her chin, and smiles. "Class is now in session."

"Cara, for fuck's sake." I bury my face behind one hand before throwing both arms out wide. "Can we stop calling it that?"

"Class? I guess, if you want to be picky."

"No, not class. Journey to Pussy Pal…ugh, forget it." I sink into the couch cushions, pinning my arms over my chest and toeing at the coffee table. "Don't even know if I want a girlfriend if she'll be anything like you," I grumble.

"Oh, sweetie." She pats my hand. "You couldn't handle me."

"And why is Hank here?" I gesture at our old friend. "No offense, Hank. I love you, but you just feel a bit out of place at this…this…"

"At Adam's Road to Hope: One Man's Journey to Pussy Palace," Cara finishes for me. "Can you believe it, Hank? Adam thinks you're too old to be here."

"I didn't say that! It's just, you know…you're eighty-six years old."

He grins, stroking both Bear and Dublin's heads from where they rest in his lap. Dublin used to be his guide dog, but when he moved into a nursing home a year ago, Dublin went to live with Carter and Olivia. Hank gets all the pup snuggles from these two when he's around.

"I've been told I'm quite the ladies' man, Mr. Lockwood, even in my old age. And something about sage wisdom, blah, blah, blah." He waves his own words off. "Why you people continue to listen to the words that come out of my mouth is beyond me, but if you need help getting women—"

"I don't need help getting—okay, I need a little help, but I really don't think it's—fine, I have no idea what I'm doing." I snatch the bowl of All Dressed chips off the table, hugging it as I toss a handful in my mouth. "Gonna die a-wone n' wif a se-wious case ub—" I swallow "—arthritis in my wrist."

Olivia pats my thigh. "That's not true, Adam."

"Yeah, Adam." Jennie snickers. "They have toys for that so you don't have to do any of the work yourself. You don't have to doom yourself to a life of arthritis."

I roll my eyes and toss a pillow at her and Cara when they high-five. I always knew Jennie had a mouth like her brother's, but it's been nice seeing her really come into herself since she and Garrett have been together.

"Okay." Cara pulls out a clipboard and a pen, then slips on a pair of glasses, which she promptly slides down her nose so she can stare at me over the rim of them. "Tell us about our leading lady."

I smash another handful of chips and frown when Olivia takes the bowl away. "Her name is Rosie."

"Rosie!" Cara scrawls it on the paper, adds my name and a plus sign, then surrounds it with a heart. "So cute. Love it. Tell us everything."

"Well, I met her last weekend when I was hiking with Bear. He knocked her over. She was walking a dog from the shelter she volunteers at. And she shared her sandwich with me. And she wants to be a vet. And I went back to the shelter this morning because Jaxon said I should go, and I accidentally insinuated that I liked eating her out, but I was talking about her sandwiches, and then it turns out she made two extra sandwiches for me just in case she saw me again. She's so kind and thoughtful, and she's really patient and sweet with the dogs. And she's got these tiny, gold freckles on her nose, and sometimes she snorts when she laughs, and she's got, like, honey-colored hair, but the ends are all pink, and it hangs above her shoulders, and she makes me smile a lot, and she's just really..." I trail off as the silence around me sinks in. Four pairs of eyes watch, waiting, smiling. I swallow. "Cute."

Olivia squeezes my hand. "She sounds so wonderful already, Adam."

"Pink hair," Cara murmurs.

"I want pink fucking hair," Jennie adds.

"Sounds like you guys had a connection," Hank pipes up. "So what do you need help with?"

"This just feels...different. I don't want to treat this date like every other date. We might actually have a chance at something here. I want to make sure I do it right."

"So where are you taking her on Wednesday?" Cara holds up her clipboard and grins. She's drawn a picture of Rosie based off my description. It's surprisingly accurate, except she has sticks for limbs. "Nailed it."

"I'm not sure yet. Somewhere private would be nice, without the pressure."

"What about a picnic dinner?" Jennie suggests. "That could be nice."

"And it'll just be the two of you, so you don't have to worry about photographers, or people asking for signatures," Olivia adds. "That can be really overwhelming at first. You hockey men attract attention everywhere you go."

I nod, but a sick feeling creeps into my stomach. "There's just, like, one super small issue." I hold up my thumb and forefinger, peeking between the tiny gap. "Teeny tiny, really. Rosie, um...she doesn't watch hockey."

Jennie shrugs. "Not a big deal. We can teach her."

"Oh, yeah, that's..." I shake my curls out. Scratch my throat. Clap a fist into my opposite hand as I jump to my feet and walk three steps to the right, then spin, shove a hand through my hair, and point at nothing. "Yeah, that's not what I meant. I mean, she, uh...she doesn't know who I am."

Jennie's brows jump. Olivia's jaw drops. Hank runs a hand over his mouth while letting out a long exhale. Cara grins, chuckles in a bit of an evil way, and starts writing on her clipboard.

"Hidden...identity..." She underlines it three times. "I love this trope."

Olivia shakes her head. "Okay, let's back up. When you say she doesn't know who you are…?"

"I told her my full name and she simply gave me hers back. She thinks I'm a regular guy."

"Well, you *are* a regular guy," Jennie argues.

Cara nods. "A regular guy who brings in over fifteen mill a year between his contract as one of the best goalies in the NHL and all his brand sponsorships. Just a totally regular, blue-collar guy." Her blue eyes stay on mine, the corner of her mouth lifted in a smirk as she adds one more painfully slow line beneath the words *hidden identity*.

I scrub my hands over my face and groan, flopping back onto the couch. "I fucked up. We haven't even had our date yet and I fucked up."

"That's not true," Olivia insists. "Has your job come up organically in conversation?"

I shake my head.

"Then you haven't done anything wrong. You can tell her on Wednesday."

I sit on her words for a few moments, contemplating everything that could go wrong rather than everything that could go right. Maybe I *am* a worst-case scenario expert, just like Rosie.

"I'm scared," I finally admit. "I know it's early, but something feels so different with her. It feels natural and easy and I've got fucking…" I throw my arm out and sigh, hating that I'm about to say this word. "Butterflies. When I'm with her, when I think of her…Everything feels new and exciting and hopeful. But what if I'm wrong about this?"

"You've spent two days with her, just being able to be yourself, without everything that comes with being a big NHL hotshot. Sure, it doesn't seem like much, but without all that pressure, neither of you has any reason to be someone you're not. Does Rosie seem like the type to be dishonest about who she is?"

"No," I answer without hesitation. "She's given me no reason to think she's being someone she's not. It's just…"

"That's what you know," Jennie says, nodding. "I get it, Adam. You're used to dating people who give you one side at first, to get your time and attention, and once they have it, they show you the real them." She shakes her head, a sad look in her eyes. "It's deceitful, and when all you're looking for is a genuine connection, a person in your corner, it's just…sad."

My heart aches for Jennie, the shit she's been through. She spent too many years being wanted for the wrong reasons too. It's where she and I are similar, and I feel a little less alone.

But I want to be where she is now, on the other side of it. Did she feel this lonely while she waited? Did she feel like she didn't even know herself? Because I feel like I'm losing pieces of myself along the way, and I hate it.

"There's no rush," Cara chimes in, gaze holding all the softness that lingers beneath the sarcasm and badassery. "Meet her where she's at, let her do the same with you, and enjoy every moment of getting to know each other along the way." She quirks a brow and tilts her head. "And if she turns out like all the others, or worse—" she gags "—*she-who-must-not-be-named,* then we get ten cartons of eggs and a Costco pack of toilet paper, and we go to her house in the middle of the night, and we—"

"No."

"But we—"

"I'm twenty-six! I'm not TP-ing someone's house, Care!"

Cara pouts, slumping in her seat. "Baby." She flips to the next page on her clipboard. "Okay, we've settled on a picnic dinner, and telling her you're rich and famous. Now let's go over the important stuff."

"That feels like the important stuff."

She rolls her eyes. "No, Adam, the important stuff is what you're going to wear, what you're going to feed her, alcohol or no alcohol, sex or no sex, chocolate cake for dessert or—"

"Sex?" Heat rushes to my ears and I shake my head. "No sex. It's a first date. I'm not even going to kiss her!" I look to Jennie and Olivia. "Right? No kiss? Yeah, you don't kiss on a first date." I sit back in my seat, relieved when Hank nods in agreement. "Yeah, that'd be moving way too fast. No kiss." I sit forward. "Or wait. Does it send the wrong message if I don't kiss her? Will she think I don't like her? And if I do kiss her, long or quick? With or without tongue? Do I let my hands wander, or do I—" I look down at my clammy hands, wiping them on my shorts before throwing them in the air, giving a little wave "—keep my hands in the air where she can see them, so she knows there won't be any funny business?"

The basement is silent for a full ten seconds.

Hank clears his throat. "I've never wished I could see more in my life than I do right now."

The girls break out in howling laughter, and even I crack a smile, forcing myself back to the couch.

"I'm just so nervous. I'm never like this before a date."

"Well, maybe that means something," Hank says. "For this Rosie to take such a solid, confident guy like you and turn him into a rambling mess…maybe meeting her was fate. And I know you've lost some of that confidence when things ended with your last girlfriend, but maybe Rosie will help you get back there. All the best people help us find ourselves when we're feeling lost."

I cock my head. "I get it now."

"Get what?"

"Why they invited you to girls' night. I don't even need them, just you."

"*Hey*!" Olivia gestures upstairs. "I brought the cute baby you love so much!"

Cara holds a tablet up. "Ollie also brought this."

I frown. "A tablet?"

"Oh, you sweet fool," she murmurs, tapping around on the screen. "*Basement Speakers* will connect me to your surround sound system, right?"

"Yes…"

"Great." She sets the tablet down as my speakers ping, letting me know a device has been connected. Her smile is extra scary, and unease slithers down my spine.

"What are we—"

"*Chapter Twelve. Isabella. My back hits the wall in the dark hallway with a thud, and I gasp at the feel of Grant's rock-hard erection pressing against my lower stomach. He's hot, heavy, and big—so damn big I whimper his name when he hikes my leg up, winding it around his waist, thrusting against me. 'I like when you whimper my name, but you're going to be screaming it by the time I'm through with you,' Grant growls.*"

"What the fuck?" I cry out, flinging my arms wide. "What is this?"

"It's an audiobook," Cara says simply, checking her nails. "You read, Adam."

"I read self-help books! Sometimes I read fantasy! I loved Harry Potter when I was a kid—sue me! I-I-I…I don't read this!"

"You're not judging Ollie and Hank's taste in books, are you, Mr. Lockwood?"

Hank waggles his brows. "This was my pick for our book club read last week."

"It was so good," Olivia adds, breathless. She fans her face. "Grant is *so* swoon-worthy."

"Can confirm." Jennie peels back the wrapper on a pack of Dunkaroos. "It was mine and Mom's initiation into the club last week, and it did *not* disappoint." She swipes a tiny cookie through some frosting, then pops it in her mouth. "Think of it as research, Adam. You're losing it over whether to kiss her, and this will help you figure it out. Those first few dates are all about reading each other's cues and body language."

"Sometimes you save that first kiss for date two or three," Olivia adds.

"And sometimes you let the arrogant hockey captain who you swore you'd never touch take you upstairs and plow you right into the next year on his California king," Cara counters, winking at Olivia.

"He told me Oprah owned the same mattress! How was I supposed to say no?"

"It's pretty easy," Jennie says. "*No*. See? Easy. Try it out with me, pip-squeak. *No, Carter, I will not have sex with you.*"

Olivia jabs a finger at me. "This is supposed to be about Adam not knowing how to date, not me being weak and horny!"

"Hey!" I push her threatening finger away. "I was happy for you two when you kissed on New Year's!" I throw my arms in the air when I realize the couple in the audiobook is naked. "Great, where did their clothes go?"

"They lost them when you all were bickering," Hank replies.

Isabella and Grant become nothing more than searing kisses, punishing touches, tortured moans that barrel out of my sound system, ensuring the memory will forever be burned into my ears, and when she takes his "thick, throbbing length" in her hand, I drop my head and groan.

"Is this necessary? It's like I'm listening to porn with my best friends' wives. You guys are like my sisters. I feel—"

Olivia presses her hand to my mouth. "Shhh. It's about to get good."

"He presses two fingers inside my soaking pussy and circles my clit slowly as his mouth moves over my neck."

"Jesus Christ. I can't." I jump to my feet and rake my fingers down my face. "I can't do it. Somebody turn it off." I point at Cara, who's typing away on her phone. "What are you doing?"

"Just texting Emmett about something I want him to try tonight."

"Cara—"

"'Is this how you like to be fucked?' he asks. 'Slow and gentle?' He thrusts his thick fingers harder, faster, and my knees buckle as I clutch his shoulders. 'Or hard and rough, like this?'"

"*Ah!*" A bloodcurdling shriek sounds from behind me. I look over my shoulder, finding my friends at the bottom of my stairs.

Carter claps his hands over Ireland's ears, from where she's clinging to Garrett. "*Cover your ears, princess!*"

"Take her, take her!" Garrett shouts, shoving Ireland into Carter's arms.

Jaxon's hands are glued to his cheeks. "What the fuck are you *doing*, Adam?" he screams.

Emmett winks at Cara. "Got your text, babe."

I stomp up the stairs as fast as my legs will take me. "I'm fucking out of here."

~

By some miracle, I make it to Wednesday.

I make it through unnecessary toy recommendations from Jennie.

I make it through snippets of *helpful scenes* from audiobooks sent by Olivia.

By the glory of God or whoever the fuck put me on this earth, I even make it through a shopping trip with Cara for a date-night outfit.

Now I just need to get through this date with my favorite five-year-old first.

"You're doing it wrong," the small voice beside me whispers.

"Shit," I mutter as the tiny pink elastic I'm trying to loop around a hook snaps, ricocheting through the air. My gaze shifts to Lily, and I cringe. "I mean, crap. Poop. Pooh? Ahhh." I rub a hand across my mouth. "Darn it."

Lily snickers, taking the tiny loom needle from my hands. She hooks another bright elastic on the loom and starts effortlessly working it with the needle. "See? It's like this."

I look down at my hands. "My hands are too big. They're ogre hands."

She shakes her head, hiding her smile as she keeps working. "I don't think so. Ogres are scary." Big brown eyes lift to mine. "You're not that scary."

Four simple words shouldn't make my heart beat a little faster, but they do. I've been volunteering at Second Chance Home for a few years now, spending time with the kids that walk through the door, in need of some extra love, the same way I was, way back when I was Lily's age.

Lily arrived at the home four months ago. She used to cry when she saw me, and as much as it broke my heart, I gave her the space she needed. Being in the off-season and one of only two single friends in our group means I've been spending a lot of time here recently. Maybe she got used to me being around, because a month ago, Lily sat down at the end of the couch I was sitting on and stared at the cover of the book she'd brought with her. I asked her if I could read it to her, and she stared at me for a whole minute before slowly sliding closer, pushing the book between us. *Wherever You Are My Love Will Find You,* by Nancy Tillman. Now we read it at every visit.

Progress is progress, no matter how slow.

I hope that's how she feels about teaching me how to make Rainbow Loom bracelets, because this shit has been a two-week affair, and it's not going well. I understand the process, I just can't get my giant fingers to work on something so tiny.

Lily hands me back the needle and tucks her chestnut hair behind her ear. "Here. Now you try again, but go slow."

"Slow. Got it."

We work on our bracelets side by side without a word. I don't mind the silence with her. Every quiet inch she's given me has always been more than enough.

I look up as a door opens and a little boy comes tearing out of it, heading for the blocks on the floor. Emily, a good friend of Garrett and Jennie's and their old neighbor, steps out of the room behind him. She shifts a pair of dark-framed glasses up her nose and smiles when she sees me.

"Is today the day Mr. Lockwood finally finishes his first Rainbow Loom?" She crouches down and nudges Lily. "About time, am I right?"

Lily giggles. "He's still learning, but he's doing great." She sets her tools down and wraps her arms around Emily's waist, squeezing. "Hi, Miss Emily. Are we gonna talk today?"

"We absolutely are, honey. I have time for you right now, but if you're busy with Adam—"

"No!" She grabs a clasp and starts hooking it into the elastic. "I'm done!"

"Aw, man," I whine. "Mine's too short still."

Lily leans over, examining the length of my bracelet. She looks down at hers and chews her lip. Then she hands me a clasp. "Do you remember how to finish it?"

"I think so." I attach the tiny clasp the same way I've seen Lily do it a hundred times, then pull my tiny bracelet off the loom and frown. "It's way too small."

Lily takes the bracelet from me and slips it on her wrist, then gently takes my hand in hers and slips her bracelet on my wrist. "I'm a little faster, so mine is longer. We can swap. Now you can think of me when you wear my bracelet, and I'll think of you too."

Something thick catches in the back of my throat, and I struggle to swallow it down. "Thanks, Lil."

"I'll go wait in your room," she tells Emily, then casts me a shy glance. "Bye, Adam."

She runs across the room and disappears before I can say good-bye, and I climb to my feet, packing up the loom.

"You're growing on her, huh?" Emily observes.

"She's the sweetest kid ever."

Emily smiles, but it's sad and a little far off. As a child psychologist who works with the kids here, she knows a lot more about them and their lives than I do. I don't want to be blind to the reason some of them are here, but I'm not sure I could stomach all of them either.

"She's a very strong little lady." She shakes the thought away and smiles. "Heard you have a date tonight. Jennie says you really like this girl."

"I do. I think. I mean, so far. Yeah. I do."

Her eyes gleam as they roam over me, as I shove my fingers through my hair and tug at my clothes. "My God, Jennie was right. You are a hot mess right now, aren't you?"

I sigh. "I'm not proud of it."

"Holy fucknuts." She grips my hand as the front door opens and my coach strolls in. "Who's that?"

"Davis."

"Davis who? I've never seen him before."

"He's my coach. He visits with the kids here and there."

"Mmm…" She traces her lower lip with her fingernail, eyes blazing. "Single?"

"Recently divorced."

"Fuck yeah. Right up my alley."

"His daughter is cute as hell too."

"Daughter?" Her arms fall with her deflating sigh. "Ugh, gross. Kids."

I arch a brow, gesturing at all the kids, the ones she works with *for free* in her *spare time.*

"I get to give these ones back, Adam. I'm not interested in keeping one full time."

The door to her office opens and Lily pokes her head out, eyes wide. "Emily? Are you still here?"

"Coming, honey!" She bumps my hip with hers. "Have fun on your date, Casanova. Don't forget to bring flowers and dessert. Chicks love that shit." She winks at me as she backs away, holding a hand up between the side of her face and the rest of the room. "They also love *being* dessert."

As if I'm taking any advice from Emily.

Okay, I'm taking *a little* advice from her.

About the dessert. Bringing one, not making Rosie mine. One day, maybe, but—*no. No, Adam. Focus.*

I tuck the freshly baked cookies and chocolate-covered strawberries into my picnic basket and set it by the front door, next to the bright bouquet of pink, orange, and yellow peonies I picked up earlier. I slip my shoes on, clip Bear's leash on, and open the front door.

Then I slam it again.

Bear looks up at me, head cocked as if to say, "What the fuck, dude?"

I run to the bathroom, flick on the light, and stare at my reflection.

My curls have been tamed, my face freshly shaved, my teeth brushed threes time just in case, and my outfit is on point, thanks to Cara. I smooth my shirt down, pat my hair, and look to Bear.

"Whadda ya think, buddy? Handsome?"

His happy tail thuds against the wall.

"Right? So handsome. Everything's gonna go great. I'm gonna tell Rosie what I do for a living, she's gonna be totally nonchalant about the whole thing, we're gonna have a great night, and maybe I'll even hold her hand, and it'll be perfect. Perfect night. Yeah."

Still, I raise my phone, flash a shaky grin, and take a picture. Then I send it to the girls.

ME

Do I look okay?

JENNIE

Handsome as ever, my dude. Go get it. *eggplant emoji* *water droplets emoji*

OLIVIA

heart eyes *happy tears emoji* You look perfect, Adam.

CARA

If my husband won't put a baby in me, will you???

I pick up the basket and flowers, then take a deep breath.

"Wish me luck, Bear. Gonna go win over the pretty girl."

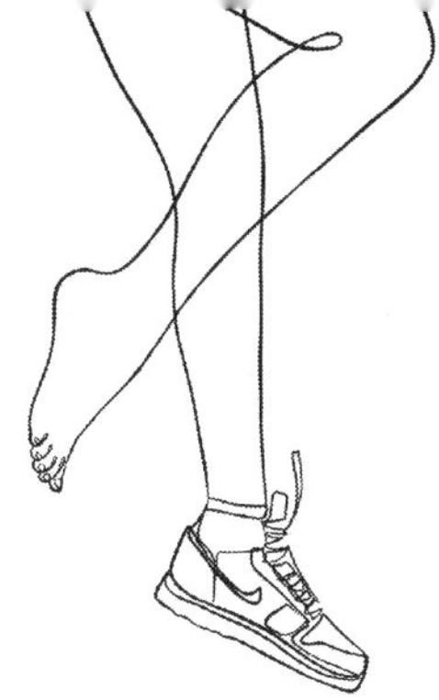

SEVEN

SPILLING SECRETS AND WINE

Rosie

"SHE WENT with the tinted balm. Nice choice."

"I didn't give her a choice."

"And the sundress? Was that you too?"

Archie hums, watching me in the mirror. "That one was Rosie, actually."

Marco slings his arms around Archie's neck from behind, chin on his shoulder. He kisses the tips of his fingers. "Chef's kiss, Ro. Easy access too."

Heat seeps into my cheeks as I check out my reflection. My hair isn't behaving today, and the flower barrettes I've used to pin my hair back aren't doing much to hide it. I run my hands down my dress. "Do I look okay? Should I change? I nicked my knee shaving. My hair's not right. What if—"

Archie shrugs off his boyfriend and pulls me into a hug. "You look beautiful, Ro."

"Very fuckable," Marco adds.

"What if he doesn't like me?" I whisper against Archie's chest.

His expression twists with disgust. "What's not to like?"

I shrug, fiddling with my fingers. "People seem to find enough reasons."

"We're never good enough for the wrong people. But you're just right for us, and we love everything about you. Don't be nervous. Just be yourself." He cradles my face, smiling. "Now what do we say?"

I take a deep breath before reciting the words these two work so hard at ingraining. "I am kind. I am strong. I am beautiful. The people who are meant to be in my life will find me."

"Damn right." Marco ushers me down the hall, swatting my butt. "Now get outta here!" When I start stepping into my sneakers, he screeches. "*No*! Not the Nikes, Rosie, *please*, for the love of God. You're ruining a perfectly good outfit!"

I look down at my shoes, the white flowers decorating the light blue swoosh. They're cute, and they match my dress. "I don't have a car," I remind him. "These are practical for walking."

His stare begs me to reconsider, so I keep going before he can argue.

"You can force the tinted lip balm on me, but it's sneakers or bare feet." I point at Archie. Besides the years we've spent as classmates and coworkers, we've also been roommates for three years. Our routine is second nature, but I have a bit of a controlling streak a mile wide about certain things. "Connor is getting dropped off at—"

"Five."

"And bath—"

"Is at six-fifteen."

"And—"

"*Yes*, Rosie, I know. I'm not new." He stuffs my wide-brim hat on my head. "Get outta here, or I'll hold you down so Marco can change your shoes." He throws a pointed look at the hallway closet, where a pair of four-inch heels wait to ruin my feet.

Any hint of humor dissipates, and I dash out the door before they can make good on their threats.

It's a beautiful, sunny evening, and I'm running early, so I get off the bus two stops early so I can entertain the thoughts that are about to send me spiraling about how horribly this date is bound to go, just like the rest of them. I waffle between being content in knowing we don't need someone in our lives who doesn't want to be here, and worrying that Adam won't want me, not all of me. It's a disappointment that already feels so heavy, one I don't want to carry with me.

I hate that I'm getting ahead of myself, living in the future instead of soaking in the now. So as the secluded park comes into view, I smooth my hands down my dress one last time and commit to giving this a fighting chance.

Adam's last message told me to call when I arrived so he could come meet me, but it's impossible to miss the huge spread laid out beneath an overgrown oak tree. My heart patters a quick, steady beat that races down to the tips of my fingers, curling anxiously into my palms. A plaid blanket lays beneath the shade of the branches, a basket in one corner, an array of meats, cheeses, crackers, bread, and fruits spread over a wooden board in the center. A stack of pillows in the corner completes the aesthetic, because Adam Lockwood is totally freaking Pinterest-worthy.

"Didn't I tell you to call me when you got here?"

My heart leaps to my throat, and when I spin around, it skids to a stop altogether. Adam is the picture of effortless perfection, someone blessed beyond belief with impeccable looks, finished with style in his crisp white short-sleeve button-up, untucked from his fitted gray shorts, dark curls swept to the side, vibrant blue eyes as playful as his immaculate, crooked grin. But the sexiest thing he wears is the confidence of a man who's certain he's going to nail this date.

"Funny thing is," he murmurs, stepping toward me, brows quirking when I take one step back. "I knew you wouldn't listen." Another step toward me, and another step back, his smile growing, like he enjoys this game of cat and mouse we're playing. "You're my favorite brand of trouble. Want to know why?"

"Why?"

His hand comes out of his pocket, catching a fistful of my dress, stopping my next backward step, closing the distance between us. His voice drops to a whisper, all gravel and husk, one that sends a hot shiver rippling down my spine when his lips pause at the shell of my ear. "Because I've never wanted to be so deep in it as I do now that I've met you."

He presses a soft kiss to my blazing cheekbone before taking my hand, pulling me toward our picnic. "C'mon, pretty girl. You look like you need a glass of wine."

A glass? I'm gonna need a whole bottle of liquid courage to keep up with *that*. What happened to the man who was so nervous to ask me to dinner, he didn't talk to me for a whole ten minutes, just kept opening his mouth and then snapping it shut?

"I had a girls' night," Adam tells me as he guides me down to a heap of pillows.

"Pardon?"

"You're wondering where the confidence came from. I had a girls' night. I was so damn nervous about getting this date right I enlisted my best friends' wives to give me advice." He holds up a bottle of sparkling water, red wine, and grape juice, pouring me a glass of the red when I point to it. "Horrible idea, by the way. My confidence comes at the expense of my dignity, which has been lost to forced listening of sexy audiobooks."

I clap a hand over my mouth as I sputter on my wine. "*Pardon*?"

"What, you've never been caught by your best friends listening to a smutty audiobook with three women and an eighty-six-year-old man?" The sun dances with the amusement in his eyes as he watches me laugh. "They thought I might need some dating help."

"I find it hard to believe you're that out of touch with the dating world."

"I'm not, I guess. I've been on plenty of dates. But this is the first one that's felt like it's meant something." He lifts a shoulder, gesturing at the spread before us. "That's probably why I was also on a four-way video call fifteen minutes ago with the same girls, freaking out about whether the pillows were too forward, if I should sit on the opposite side of the blanket, and how long into the date I have to wait before I take your hand and don't let it go for the rest of the night."

He shifts my hat back and brushes my bangs aside, fingertips skimming my cheekbone. "I can tell you're nervous, Rosie, and I want you to know that, even if I seem confident right now, I've been a mess all week over this. I'm not ashamed to admit it." When he looks at me next, beneath lashes so dark and with a gaze so heady, butterflies erupt in my stomach. "Then I saw you standing there in that hat and this sundress, and all the scary stuff melted away. The only thing I'm feeling right now is happy, and if you're still nervous, I've got enough happy for the both of us."

"The pillows are comfy, I like having you next to me because you make me feel warm and special, and if you take my hand right now, I might not ever ask for it back." The words spill out, but if I can't give him all my truths tonight, I at least want him to have these. The panic squeezing my throat eases at his kind smile. "Wow, I only had to drink half a glass of wine to say that."

"I brought two bottles in case you feel like laying it all out on the line tonight. You can tell me all your secrets."

"That's a second date kinda thing, Mr. Lockwood, and it also requires ice cream."

"Got it. Two bottles of wine, an ice cream cone, and date number two." He grins then, wide and full of mischief as his gaze drops to my legs. His hand lands on my knee, sliding along my bare skin, where he nabs the hem of my dress from where it's ridden up my thigh. Gently, he shifts it back into place, eyes rising to meet mine, a fire blazing so hot, it singes my skin. "I can't wait to unravel you."

My eyes widen at the innuendo, and I toss back the rest of my wine. It does nothing to soothe the burn in my cheeks, or the sudden beat thrumming between my legs, so I reach for the wine and refill my glass. Adam chuckles, handing me a small bottle of sparkling water too.

He reaches inside the picnic basket and produces a bouquet of flowers, holding them out to me, smiling. "For you."

My hand shoots out, fingers curling back into my palm for a moment before I hesitantly brush over the petals, hues of muted pinks and dusty lilac blues. My vision wobbles and I trap my trembling lower lip between my teeth, an expected reaction as my mom's laughter rings in my ears, memories of dirty hands and knees, peony bushes and falling leaves flashing through my mind.

"Rosie?" His voice dips, a slight tremble in his hand as he starts pulling the bouquet back. "I'm sorry. I meant to go with roses, because of your name. But then I saw these, and they were so pretty, they reminded me of you. If you don't like them—"

"They're perfect," I murmur, wrapping my hand around his, bringing the flowers to my nose. "I love them, Adam."

Sapphire eyes watch me, and Adam traps a single tear rolling down my cheek. "Then why are you crying?"

Because it doesn't feel like there's another option. "Memories."

His gaze flickers. "Good or bad?"

I smile. "The best. Sometimes I just forget that I don't get to make new ones. The realization is a little overwhelming for a moment." I set the bouquet down, and before I can second-guess it, I wrap my arms around him, sinking into his warmth. "Thank you, Adam."

He pulls my hat off and squeezes me against his solid chest. His lips touch the crown of my head. "You're so welcome, Rosie."

We linger like that, entwined together, like neither of us is ready to let go, but when my stomach growls, Adam chuckles, pulling back and brushing my bangs aside.

"Hungry?"

Another grumble, paired with a sheepish smile. "Always."

As we eat, he asks me question after question, until he's satisfied he knows everything about me, like that I grew up in Ontario and moved to Vancouver after I graduated from high school. That I'm twenty-four, but a November baby, so by the time I graduate in the spring I'll be twenty-five. That I completed my undergrad in animal sciences, and I'm on a full-ride scholarship in the Doctor of Veterinary Medicine program at Pacific Veterinarian College.

"Full ride?" His brows jump. "No shit. You're a smartie pants."

I shrug. "I had nothing better to do than study and read growing up. I didn't have a lot of friends, so I think it kind of came with the territory."

"Don't sell yourself short. You're in your last year of vet school, on a full-ride scholarship, and you're not even twenty-five. You're about to be a doctor, Rosie. Those are some incredible accomplishments. You should be proud."

My heart soars. I am proud of myself. I've worked harder than I thought possible, and having someone else acknowledge my accomplishments feels nice.

Adam refills my wine. "What do you do at the shelter?"

"Well, vet school is really demanding, so I mostly only work there during the summer, and what I can manage during the school year. Hopefully they'll hire me as a vet when I graduate, but right now, I mostly do animal socialization. A lot of the animals that come in are scared. Their whole life has been turned upside down. We work with them to start trusting humans again before they're ready to be adopted."

"It must be rewarding to see them come out of their shells."

"It really is so amazing, Adam. Especially with animals like Piglet, who have been through so much. She has so much love to give, and someone stole that light from her. I love being part of the reason she finds it again."

Adam smiles at me. "You really love her."

"So much."

"Have you ever thought about adopting her?"

"Only every day."

"What's stopping you?"

I bring my feet toward me, crossing my legs, tracing the swoop of my Nikes. "I don't have the space she deserves." Nor the money to keep up with her care. "If I did, I'd bring her home in a heartbeat. But she deserves more than what I can offer her."

"I get that. But for what it's worth, Rosie, it's not usually the space that makes a home. It's the love. And I bet you give the best kind."

The corner of my mouth quirks. "You're really refreshing, you know?"

"How so?"

"You look like someone always in control, or someone who likes to be, maybe. Maybe it's your size, or how comfortable you seem in your own skin. You're not afraid to be kind and sweet and gentle, like carrying Piglet down the stairs because she's afraid, or admitting you ask your girl friends for advice. But the way you talk sometimes, the way you…touch…as much as you like to be in control, I feel like there's a part of you dying to lose all that control, to be unrestrained. It's just refreshing to see someone so willing to be open about exactly who they are and what they need."

I clear the dryness in my throat, then drown it with wine as silence swirls around us, hoping I haven't crossed a line.

"And what about you?" Adam finally asks. "Do you like to be in control?"

"I have to be in control. At school, at work, I don't have the luxury of letting my emotions get the best of me. It's one of the hardest things I've ever done, holding it in, and I fail sometimes. Sometimes I fail often, but I'm trying. And at home, I—" I stop myself before I say too much, something I'm not ready to share. "I depend on routine. I should be more flexible, but it stresses me out to even think about changing something in my day to day sometimes. So, yes, I'm in control. But do I like to be?" I nibble my lip as I look to Adam, the way he's watching me with rapt attention, drinking in every word. "Sometimes I crave someone else to take control, just so I don't have to. Just so I can let go, even for a moment. Being in control all the time, it's…exhausting."

Adam leans back on his hands, staring at the bright blue sky slowly fading to a pretty shade of lilac as the sun dips. When his eyes find mine, something in my chest wants to break wide open, let him see inside, the fears, the insecurities, the little joys and triumphs, all the nuances that shape me. Somehow, it feels like that's what he wants too.

"What if this is your safe space to do that? What if when you're with me, you can give it up, let it go, and just…be?"

"It's a nice idea." Farfetched, but nice. The anxiety, the obsessive-compulsive tendencies that surround my routines and shape my life, they're a voice in my head that's less agreeable, less hopeful. They tell me I can't let go, because what happens when I do? Chaos, disorder. Things I'll need to fix.

"It doesn't have to be just an idea." He lays his hand on top of mine, a gentle touch that soothes the worries. "You say you're a worst-case scenario expert, and the idea of giving up any amount of control ever is probably horrifying, but maybe with time and a little trust, we learn to give and take control when we need to. For each other, and for ourselves."

I turn my palm over, watching as he traces the lines in it. "Does it make sense that the idea is as daunting as it is calming?"

"It makes perfect sense, Rosie. Nothing worth having ever comes easy, does it? We want the calm, but sometimes we have to brave the storm to get there."

His words settle around me like a cozy blanket, and a shiver runs through me when his fingers leave my palm, traveling up the inside of my forearm, making me wiggle. "So wise. What are you, a therapist?"

He chuckles softly. "Nope."

"Am I close?"

"Not even a little bit, trouble."

"Hmm…" I jerk my arm away when he tickles me again, hiding my face when my giggle starts spiraling into pig-snort territory. Taking his hand in mine, I turn it over, trading places with him as I run the tips of my fingers over his palm.

"Are you a…dog trainer?"

His eyes glitter as he shakes his head. "Nuh-uh."

"Teacher?"

"Nope."

"Realtor?"

"Cold."

"Police officer?"

"Colder."

"Heavy equipment operator? Accountant? Do you work in HVAC? Oh my God." I spin toward him, nearly crawling into his lap. "Are you a private detective?"

He laughs, snaking his arm around my waist, pulling me between his legs, back against his chest. The thunder of his heart gives way to his nerves as I wait for his answer.

"I'm a, uh…" He clears his throat. "I work with athletes."

"Athletes? Like, sports teams?"

He swallows. "Professional ones."

"Oh." My nose wrinkles. "Uh-oh."

He stiffens. "What?"

"I don't know anything about sports. I have no talking points. I'm sorry. I can barely tell a baseball glove from a hockey mitten."

He snorts a beautiful, glorious laugh. "Glove."

I lean to the side so I can look at him over my shoulder. "Huh?"

"Hockey glove, not mitten. Unless you're talking about what the goalie wears, then that's a catcher and a blocker. And actually, mitt is perfectly acceptable for baseball gloves, especially the catcher's mitt." He chuckles, poking the dimple in my chin. "But not hockey gloves."

"That's just confusing. They all go on your hands. Why so many different names?"

"Truthfully, I don't know."

"What do you do with the athletes at work?"

Blue eyes meet mine, and the worry there, the grief, it steals my breath, digs a hole in my chest and carves a home that aches. I'm not sure what he's looking for as his gaze roams my face, but if it'll take away this heaviness, I hope he finds it.

Instead, he drops his gaze. When he looks back at me, it's with a reservation that dulls the sparkle in his eyes, seems unnatural on such a kind, open man.

"A little bit of everything," he finally tells me, trailing his finger across the nick on my knee from shaving. "Training, nutrition, traveling." His mouth quirks, and he winks. "All the boring stuff."

"Do you enjoy it?"

"Very much. Wouldn't trade it for any other job."

"That's what matters, isn't it? Too many people spend their days being miserable at work. Life is far too short to not love what you do."

Adam smiles at me. "You're right. What's life if it isn't full of what you love?"

"Does it bother you I'm not into sports?"

"Not at all. It's refreshing. Gives me something else to talk about."

I cover his hand on my thigh. "Will you tell me more about you? I want to know everything."

His gentle smile slows the race of my heart, and I relax into his body as he tells me about his life in Vancouver, how he spends his summers with his dog and his friends, how he's loving being Uncle Adam to his best friend's five-month-old daughter, and that although he moved here for work and never wants to leave, he grew up in Colorado. I eat everything up, though somehow feeling unsatiated, like I'm missing big pieces of him.

We talk forever, even as he proudly displays the chocolate-covered strawberries and chocolate chip cookies he made for dessert, as he catches the strawberry juice trickling down my chin, bringing his thumb to his mouth and tasting it.

The quiet only starts to settle in when the sky dims, and I become painfully aware of everywhere we're connected. His chest pressed to my back, rising steadily. The brush of his fingers on my thighs, skimming the climbed hem of my dress. His chin on my shoulder and his lips at my ear, all of it a stark contrast to the cool breeze that starts to nip at my bare arms.

Adam runs his hand over my arms, a sizzling heat that, somehow, only elicits more goose bumps. "Here," he whispers, reaching behind the pillows, producing a sweater.

I slip the soft fleece over my head, burying myself in his warmth. A dizzying feeling rushes to my head as the smell of Adam surrounds me —an earthy, spicy scent, something clean and crisp like citrus, and the forever comforting scent of fresh laundry.

And then something magnificent happens. When the sun finally dips behind the skyline, the tree above us comes to life. Tiny lights scattered among the leaves twinkle like fireflies, making the night glow. My heart climbs up my throat and makes a home there, stealing every word I want to speak. When my gaze finds Adam's, soft and electric at the same time, I don't know if everything inside me stops working, or if something inside me restarts. It just feels *different*, and I'm thrown by the sudden imbalance, the need to reach out and grasp this man, like he's my center of gravity.

"Do you like them? They're solar powered. I was worried they wouldn't get enough sunlight hidden in the trees, so I laid them out in my backyard all day." He runs an anxious hand over the nape of his neck. "I thought we'd be able to stay longer if we had some light. Then I could keep you longer."

"You can keep me forever," accidentally slips past my lips, and I clap a hand over my filthy, traitorous mouth.

Adam grins. "Careful. I might take you up on that." He twines our fingers together, a warmth I don't want to lose. "Sounds like my type of forever."

He climbs to his feet, pulling me with him, and his smile lights my whole world on fire.

"Dance with me, Rosie."

"D-dance? But…there's no music."

"Don't need it." He winks, tugging on my hand. "Now come here."

I do, stumbling over my footing, and Adam catches me against his solid chest, his deep laugh rolling down my neck before he whispers that nickname that thrills me and pulls at so many lost memories too.

"Trouble."

"Maybe it's you who's trouble."

Broad hands coast over my hips, fingertips digging in as we sway slowly together, the leaves rustling in the summer breeze and the gentle buzz of cicadas singing a soft tune in time with the husky breath that kisses my neck when Adam dips his mouth there.

His palm skates up my spine, curving over the nape of my neck, where he squeezes ever so gently. "The only trouble I want to get into, Rosie…it's with you."

Soft lips brush my temple before he settles his chin on my head as we dance beneath the twinkling lights and the stars above us.

It's nearly eleven when we start packing everything away, and my head feels full of air and butterflies. It's a happy, carefree place to be, and because it almost never is, I hold onto it with all my might. It's a feeling I could get lost in, intoxicating and addictive, and I realize how easily Adam did exactly what he said he would: he took control, and in turn, I let go.

I let go of the expectations, the rules, the what-ifs. I let go of the questions that lead to overthinking, and I just…existed.

I watch as Adam neatly tucks everything away in his picnic basket and bag before hooking them off his shoulder, the crook of his elbow, my sun hat nabbed between the tips of his fingers.

I slip my hand into his. "Thank you."

He looks at our hands, throat bobbing. "For what?"

"For showing me it's okay to let go sometimes."

He squeezes my fingers, lifts my hand to his lips, and brushes a kiss across my knuckles before towing me through the park to a midnight blue truck where he throws everything inside.

"Did you have fun?" he asks, a spark of uncertainty in his gaze, a hopeful rasp to his tone.

So I wrap my arms around his middle and hold him tight. "I had the best time, Adam. Thank you so much for a beautiful night."

"Okay. Cool. Thank you so much for being beautiful. No. No. Fuck. Shit." He rips me off him, holding me at arm's length. "That's not what I meant. I mean, I think you're beautiful, obviously. *Obviously* I think you're beautiful." He shoves his fingers through his curls and sighs. "This is the worst. I'm the worst. Now I'm nervous again."

I snicker-snort, then clap my hand over the obnoxious sound. Just like that, Adam's nerves vanish, an arrogant smirk tipping the side of his mouth.

"Why do you keep doing that?"

I twine my hair around my finger. "Doing what?"

"Covering your laugh."

"It's not a laugh. It's some sort of strangled, dying animal sound, and it's embarrassing."

"Okay, well that'll be weird."

"What will be weird?"

"When someone asks me what my favorite sound is, and I have to describe it like that."

I blink up at him. "You're deranged."

Chuckling, he takes my hand and heads down the sidewalk. "C'mon. Where'd you park?"

"Oh, I didn't."

His gaze swings my way. "You didn't?"

"I don't have a car."

"Oh. Did someone drop you off?"

"No."

"Is…someone picking you up?"

Another snicker-snort, but I'm less embarrassed about this one. "No, Adam."

"Then how did you…how are you gonna…" He scratches his head. "Get home safely?"

"The same way I came. I'm going to take a bus."

Adam hums to himself, then pulls me around, heading back the way we came.

"The bus stop is the other way."

"And my truck is this way."

"Adam—"

"It's late. You're not walking and taking the bus by yourself."

"But I—"

"Nonnegotiable." He opens the passenger door. "Unless you want me to follow behind you the entire way in my truck. So I guess it's a little negotiable." He grins at my crossed arms and hiked brow. "You're supposed to be working on letting go, and I'm supposed to be working on being more in control, remember?"

I jab my finger into his chest. "Don't turn my own words around on me."

He laughs as I start climbing into the seat, and as my frustration grows with the difficult task, amusement rolls off him in waves.

"Something you wanna say?" I grunt as I hike a leg up in a particularly charming fashion in my sundress.

"I was about to ask you the same thing. 'Can you help me, Adam? I seem to be slightly too short to do this myself,' might be a good place to start."

My head swivels in slow motion to glare at him over my shoulder.

He waits, elbow leaning on the window frame, cheek resting in his hand, and he even pumps his damn brows. "Yes, Rosie?"

"You're insufferable." I grab the center console, but before I can pull myself up, Adam grips my waist and lifts me effortlessly into the seat. He leans over me, clicking my seat belt into place.

"There ya go. That wasn't so hard." He taps the handle above my head. "For future reference, if you grab hold of this and plant your foot on the step, you can swing yourself right up. Or I can keep lifting you in." He shrugs. "I personally prefer option two, 'cause then I get to check out your ass." Before he shuts the door, he winks, and when he climbs into the truck, he simply asks for my address like he didn't just say that.

The drive across Vancouver is peaceful. So peaceful, in fact, that when I wake with Adam's hand on my knee and his soft voice in my ear and find we're parked out front of my apartment building, I gasp.

"I fell asleep? That's so embarrassing." My face heats. "I'm almost never awake this late unless I'm studying for a test." I frown at the map display on his dash, which seems to be stuck rerouting. "Why does it say rerouting?"

"I might've gone around the block a couple times so I didn't have to wake you."

"How many times is a couple?"

He scratches his nose and looks away. "Eight."

"*Adam*."

"Okay, let's go!" He's at my door before I can count to three.

"You don't have to take me in." He *can't* come in, and the thought of me having to make excuses sends my pulse racing in my ears.

"I won't ask to come in. Just wanna walk you to your door, that's all."

With his hand on my lower back, he follows me through the lobby and into the elevator. It climbs slowly, my nerves climbing with it. By the time we reach the twelfth floor, I'm an anxious mess.

Is he going to kiss me? Do I kiss him? Do I offer him a handshake? No, I can't do that again. What if—

"Which one?"

My head snaps up. "Huh. Oh. Yeah. Here." I scramble down the hall. "I'm down here, at the end." I stick my key in the lock, pausing to listen for any sign of life, holding in a sigh of a relief at the silence. I turn back to Adam. "So I guess I'll, uh…" I shove my hand between us.

Goddammit, Rosie.

I squeeze my eyes shut and shake my head, pulling my hand back. Then I snap my fingers. "Oh! Your sweater!" I reach for the hem, but Adam stops me with his hand on mine.

"Keep it. For next time."

"Next time? Like, a…second date?"

"A second date. With wine and ice cream and all your secrets." He steps into me, and when my back hits the door, he chuckles. His face dips, and my heart leaps to my throat as he hesitates, his lips inches from mine, so close I can *taste him.*

He smiles, just there in the right-hand corner, a tiny quirk of his beautiful mouth, before he brushes his soft lips across my cheek.

"Good night, trouble."

My eyes stay locked on his as I disappear backward into my apartment. I watch through the peephole as he stands there, hands tucked in his pockets. His hand comes up, running through his curls, and with one last glance at my door and a grin that keeps growing, Adam turns and walks away.

I ditch my shoes in the hallway and drown my excitement with a glass of water before I head through the dark living room. I make it three steps before I trip over something fluffy that starts giggling.

"Elmo loves to laugh!"

"For fuck's sake, Elmo." I grab the toy off the floor and throw it toward the basket in the corner. It lands with a thud and laughs at me again, a taunting, satanic sound I hate with a passion.

I pause at my bedroom door, listening with my ear pressed against it. Nothing but white noise trickles out, so I push the door open as quietly as possible. Rustling sounds, and a tiny body rushes to standing, popping up from the crib in the corner of my room. The dim glow of the stars shining on the ceiling from Connor's favorite light illuminates the most magnificent, sleepy green eyes, and my favorite man smiles up at me as I step inside.

Connor shifts on his feet, reaching his tiny hands into the air, grabbing for me.

"Mama!"

I scoop my son into my arms and cuddle him close, my eyes fluttering closed against his fine, blond wisps.

"Hi, baby," I whisper. "Mama missed you."

EIGHT

OKAY FRIENDS; TERRIBLE ADVICE

Adam

"My junk looks huge."

I push away the photo currently being shoved in my face. "Get it outta my face."

Carter pumps his brows. "Intimidating, huh? You don't have to tell me." He flips through the photos on his phone before he leans into his wife, who sits at the end of the table with Ireland strapped to her chest. He drops his voice, but not low enough that I can't make out his words. "Don't you think the sword of thunder looks massive in my dick pics?"

"For the love of God, Carter, it's called an underwear shoot, not dick pics."

"Tomato, tomahto. I'm gonna be all over North America."

She yanks his phone out of his hands, tucking it in her bag. "Stop looking at pictures of yourself. Your friend is asking you for advice."

He waits for her to walk away, watching with a smile as she joins a small girl playing with dolls. He braces his hands out between us. "Okay, here's what you do. You wait at least five days, and hopefully she calls first. When she does, you hesitate, like you're trying to place the name."

Garrett stares at Carter. "That's the worst advice I've ever heard. Ollie would've broken your nose if you tried that on her."

"She'd have to be able to reach my nose first."

"I can *hear you*!" she calls across the room.

Emmett shakes his head, stringing a glittery pink butterfly bead onto a thread. "Listen, man, if you like her, you call her. There's no rule about how long you need to wait."

"The sooner, the better," Garrett adds from his spot on the floor, where a little boy is sitting between his legs, looking through a book about animals. "It shows you're serious."

I look at Jaxon. His eyes are closed as a girl dusts bright purple eyeshadow over his lids, then sticks two holographic flower stickers to the outside corners of his eyes.

He cracks a lid. "What are you looking at me for? I don't call girls after a date, period." Sarah, the girl currently doing his makeup, kicks his shin. "Ow, fuck! I mean, crap. Crap, what was that for?"

Sarah props a fist on her hip. "No girl is ever gonna love you with that bad attitude, Jaxon."

"My mama loves me. She's the only girl I need."

"Whatever. Tell me that again when you come crying to me for advice because the girl you like won't call you back."

"Why would I—ugh, never mind. You're eleven. You're not getting under my skin." Jaxon points at me as Sarah uses a butterfly clip to pull his hair off his forehead. "My point is this: don't ask me for advice, because I don't have any. You and I date for two very different reasons."

Sarah scrunches her nose. "Why would you date for any other reason than to fall in love and get married?"

"Because I like to f—" He stops, holding my glare. "I love friends. I love making friends. So many friends. Why pick just one, you know?"

A tiny hand touches mine, and Lily's wide chocolate eyes peer up at me.

"Your friends are weird," she whispers.

"So weird," I whisper back. "But I'm stuck with them."

She snickers into her hand. "At least you have me. I'm not weird."

"And you're my favorite of all my friends."

Her eyes spark. "Really?"

"Yup. You're always kind to me, and you teach me new things. I'm lucky to have a friend like you."

Lily flushes crimson before examining the bracelet I'm working on. "You're doing really good. Maybe you can give it to your girlfriend when you see her next." She cocks her head. "How come you and your friends are fighting over calling her?"

"Because I'm confused, and they're only making me more confused. What do you think I should do?"

"Well..." She taps her lip. "You have a crush? Like, a super big one?"

"Super-duper big."

"Easy-peasy then."

"Easy-peasy?" Nothing about this feels easy-peasy. I'm out of practice. My gut says I should call Rosie. It's been a whole thirteen hours. I don't want her thinking I didn't have the best time, or that I don't want to see her again. My heart reminds me that nothing's worked out for so long, warns me to slow down. My brain is like a fucking circus monkey; it has no idea which direction to go in, so it just keeps riding in circles.

"It's like at lunchtime when there are extra chocolate pudding cups. I love chocolate pudding, so I eat mine superfast so I can grab another one before it's all gone. That's what you're supposed to do with things you really like. Grab it before someone else does."

I drum my fingers. "I did accidentally keep her hat."

Emmett arches a brow. "Accidentally?"

I swallow. "Accidentally on purpose."

"Classic move," Carter says. "Know what I kept of Ollie's after our first time together, so she'd have no choice but to come back?" He wags his brows at his wife. "Her heart."

She rolls her eyes from across the room. "Adam, how was Rosie when you told her about hockey?"

My gaze falls to the bracelet I've barely touched.

"Adam," Olivia repeats slowly. "How was Rosie when you told her about hockey?"

"She doesn't watch sports," I say to the bracelet.

"Oh for God's sake. You didn't tell her, did you?"

"I got scared," I blurt, ignoring the surprised looks from my friends. "She asked me what I did, and I was going to tell her. The words were right there, I swear. But everything was going so perfectly, and in the moment all I could picture was everything that could go wrong." I pull at the bracelet, watching it slowly unravel, the way this little white lie is sure to at some point if I don't handle this quickly. "Hockey changes everything. I don't want to be Adam Lockwood, Vancouver Viper. Not to her. I just want to be me."

It's the perfect storm, really. I don't lie, ever. What's the point? But here I am in the off-season, nothing but free time and sunshine on the horizon. Days on end to explore things with Rosie without the time commitment hockey pulls from me. Without the media on my back, cameras in my face. I just need a few days to figure this out, to screw my head on right and explain this to her.

Olivia's brown eyes shine with compassion, but it's Lily who speaks up first.

"I don't like hockey, but I like you. Hockey isn't what makes you special." She taps her chest and smiles. "It's your heart."

She's right; I know she is. But that doesn't stop the panic that squeezes my throat at the text message that pops up on my screen two minutes later.

TROUBLE

Hi Adam. I had a great time last night, but I think we need to talk.

~

In the history of not being sure what I'm doing, this takes the cake.

Call her, they all said. And what did I do?

Said a rushed good-bye, ran out to my truck, and drove somewhere I probably shouldn't be.

And now here I am on the twelfth floor, standing outside the same door I watched her disappear behind last night with a dopey, bashful grin, and cheeks the same color as her name.

I look down at her sun hat in my hand before raising my fist to the door.

Then I pull it away, shove my fingers through my hair, and turn away.

"Hi, Rosie," I practice saying. "It's me, Adam." I squeeze my eyes shut. "No, that's stupid. She knows who you are, and she can see you." I clear my throat. "Hi, Rosie. You left your hat in my truck, and I…no, no, no. Hi, Adam, it's me, Rosie. Holy fuck." I drag my hands, and the hat, down my face. "I'm going home."

"Adam?"

I spin around, my gaze colliding with Rosie's. Besides seeming slightly amused and curious, there's an edge in her gaze, the way she says my name, too, that has me second-guessing.

This was a bad idea. I got too ahead of myself, and now we're miles apart.

Rosie shifts on her feet, glancing over her shoulder. "What are you doing here?"

"I…I…" My thoughts are a jumbled, hazy mess; I don't know where one ends and the other begins. I think that's why I open my mouth and word vomit all over her. "I had a really great time last night and I was with my friends this morning and I was telling them everything and I asked for help because I didn't know how long I should wait to call you, and some of them told me to call you right away and some of them told me I should wait, and I got really confused, and then you texted me that we needed to talk, which is normally the worst thing a guy can hear from a girl he really likes, and I was a little overwhelmed, and I kind of panicked, and I…" I trail off, rubbing the nape of my neck. "I really wanted to see you again."

A grin spreads across her face, the tiny dimple in her chin begging for a kiss. "You didn't know whether to call me, so you just showed up here instead?"

I hold up her hat. "I also kinda stole your hat so I'd have a reason to see you again."

She cocks her head. "But I still have your sweater."

I swallow. "Double whammy. You woulda *had* to see me."

She giggles, but before she can put me out of my misery, the door is pried off her leg where she keeps it propped open, and a tiny boy toddles out from behind her, holding up one shoe and one sandal.

"S-ooes," he says proudly, holding them up to her. His eyes come to mine, a vibrant shade of green. "S-ooes!"

"Well, hey there, little buddy." I crouch down in front of him. "You got some shoes?"

He nods excitedly. "S-ooes!" He shoves them into my chest, then plops down at my feet, showing me his bare toes.

"Connor," Rosie says on a sigh, kneeling beside him. "Adam doesn't want to put your shoes on." A devilish grin claims her mouth, and she starts tickling his feet. "Your feet are too stinky for him!"

The little boy squeals with laughter, wriggling his way into my lap, until I'm laughing too.

"I'm sorry." Rosie props him on her hip before wheeling a red wagon out and setting him inside. "He's usually pretty shy. He doesn't go up to strangers often." She takes the shoes from me, swapping one out so that she has a pair of matching sandals. She straps them to his tiny feet while he bounces along in his seat, like he can't wait to go wherever they're going.

"Who's this?" I finally ask.

Rosie stares at the little boy, running her purple fingernails through his wispy hair. A smile blooms on her face, one so full of love it's nearly painful, and when I watch those two sets of sage eyes peering back at each other, I'm not surprised to see the same love reflected back in the little boy's gaze. I watch them a moment longer, noting the shape of his mouth, the way it matches Rosie's, the matching honey hue in their waves, and I know before the words leave her mouth.

"This is Connor. He's my son."

NINE

LITTLE TROUBLE

Adam

SON. He's my son.

Rosie is a mama.

Her eyes close as she presses a kiss to his forehead, and when she looks at me, beyond the pride, the love, I see the hesitation, like she's worried what this might mean for us. I see the bleakest spot of grief, like she's already accepted my decision, already said good-bye.

But I don't like good-byes, and I'm certainly not willing to make her one.

I crouch next to Connor and smile. "Hi, Connor. I'm Adam."

"Dada." He pats my hand, then Rosie's thigh. "Mama."

"Oh my gosh." Rosie's face burns red. "I'm so sorry. It must be a new phase."

Connor points down the hall. "Walk?"

"Are you and Mama going for a walk? Can I come too?"

He grins, so toothy and innocent, and he's got the same splattering of tiny freckles across his teensy nose as his mom. "Walk."

"We're walking over to the park," Rosie says, setting her backpack in the wagon. "You don't have to come with us."

"I'd love to, thank you."

Her jaw drops. "I…well…but do you…" She gives up on words, choosing instead to twine her pastel waves around her finger.

"Unless you don't want me to. Is that what you were wanting to talk to me about? That you don't want to see me anymore?"

She frowns. "Of course I want to see you."

"Great." I plop her hat on her head. "The hat trick worked. Let's go." I take her hand, grab the handle of the wagon, and start pulling both green-eyed cuties toward the elevator. "So what did you want to talk to me about then?"

Rosie's eyes drop to Connor. When they come back to me, the look she gives me says she's not sure I'm all there. "That I have a son? You know, in case that wasn't something you wanted in your life."

"Why would that matter?"

She stares at her feet, tugs at her oversized T-shirt. "It matters to a lot of people."

The whispered words are carved in heartache, so I squeeze her hand and promise, "It doesn't matter to me. Now I get two for the price of one."

Her gaze rises, moving cautiously between mine. "You really mean that?"

"I know this is new, that we haven't known each other for long, but I feel something here. I'd like to explore it with you. Is that what you want too?"

"Yeah. It is."

"Then let's spend some time together. We can move at whatever speed you're comfortable with. I'm in no rush; I just want to keep getting to know you. You make me smile."

She grants me one right here and now, bright enough to rival the July sunshine. "You make me smile too."

"*Brum-brum*!" Connor shouts from behind us, pointing at a truck that whizzes down the street. "Tuck! *Brum-brum*!"

"That's his engine noise. You should see him when a bus drives by. Loses his ever-loving mind."

I park the wagon beneath the shade of a tree on the outskirts of the empty park, and we follow along as Connor tears over to the play equipment, yelling, "Pak! Pak!"

"How old is he?"

"Fifteen months. He was born in April last year." She watches me out of the corner of her eye as Connor slips his hand into hers, climbing onto the small platform, leading to the slide. "Do you like kids?"

"I love kids. I do a bit of volunteering with some vulnerable ones."

Her smile is soft, curious gaze raking over me. "That's awesome, Adam."

I shrug. "It's nothing." It's not nothing. The Family Project, my fundraising events for Second Chance Home, brings in hundreds of thousands of dollars each year, helps fund their center, and brings new families together. It's my pride and joy, my greatest accomplishment, and I like to keep it close to my heart.

"*Dada*!"

"Oh for God's—Connor, this is Adam." Rosie pats my chest. "A-dam."

Connor blinks at her. Looks at me. Back to Rosie, then me. He points at the slide. "Dada, s-ide?"

Rosie buries her face in her hand. "I'm so sorry."

"Don't be." I start climbing onto the platform. "You want some help getting to the top, buddy?"

His fingers grasp mine, and I look down at the connection. His hand is so tiny, all his fingers wrapped around my pinky, and when he tugs me along behind him, I'm struck by the warm, tight feeling in my chest.

At the top of the slide, Connor pauses. "Dada, baby, s-ide."

Rosie snickers. "Oh, baby. I'm not sure Adam can fit down the slide."

My brows skyrocket. "He wants me to…?"

"Mhmm."

"But I…" That little blue slide is narrow as fuck. I'm a fairly confident guy and I don't turn down most challenges, but this…I don't know about this. A lifetime of skating has given me what I've gracefully dubbed as a hockey butt. Hockey butts…they don't fit down kids' slides. "I'm sorry, buddy." I glance over my shoulder, down at my own ass. "I don't think…well, the thing is…"

"Adam's got a bubble butt," Rosie tells him seriously, as if he can understand the meaning behind her words. Her playful gaze rises to mine. "It's perfect, by the way, and I've caught myself staring at it way too often, but don't let it go to your head."

The corner of my mouth lifts, exploding into a slow grin. "Too late. I can feel my head getting bigger by the second." I lift my arms overhead with an exaggerated groan. "All right, buddy. Let's do this. Let's see if my perfect bubble butt gets us down this slide." I scoot around him, wedge my hips between the plastic, and Connor squeals, launching himself into my lap. Pressing his back to my chest, I wrap my arms around him. "Ready?"

I push away from the slide, starting our descent.

It's…

Entirely underwhelming. What the fuck.

I wiggle my hips as rigorously as I can, trying to gain momentum. Connor doesn't seem to mind, giggling and screeching away, and best of all? I've never heard Rosie laugh like that before.

It's beautiful and airy, so carefree and wild, letting me see how heavy it had been, the weight of wondering how I'd react to her having a son. I'd give anything to capture this moment in a photo, because right now, I see all of her, but more than that, *I've found her.*

I wonder if she'll find me too.

We make it to the end of the eight-foot slide after twenty-five grueling seconds, and the second my butt hits the wood chips, Connor's pulling me right back up. We ride it again and again, until he switches to the swing, and eventually Rosie has to pry him away for lunch.

Beneath the shade of a tree, Rosie unpacks sandwiches, fruits, and muffins from her bag. "It's simple today." She holds out a container of sandwiches. "PB banana."

"Oh, no. I can't. It's for you two."

"There's enough for us all," she assures me, placing a small plate of food in front of Connor.

"Ba-na," he says excitedly, stuffing a bite of PB and banana sandwich in his mouth. "Ba-na!"

Rosie giggles and hands me a sandwich triangle. "I never know with Connor, so I always have extra. Some days he takes two bites and says done, and some days he—"

—toddles over to my lap, plops himself in it, and takes a bite of my sandwich, apparently. All while growling like a bear and still holding onto his own sandwich, which is, to be honest, highly fucking impressive.

"—doesn't stop eating," Rosie finishes with a sigh. "There's no such thing as *mine* in our home. What's mine is his, and what's his is…well, it's his too. I get the scraps."

As if on cue, Connor offers his mom the crust of his sandwich. "Mama."

Chuckling, I tickle his side. "You're trouble, just like Mama, aren't you?" He snickers, squirming in my lap before munching another bite of my sandwich. "Little trouble, that's you, huh, buddy? That's okay. I'll share my sandwich with you any day."

Connor takes one last bite before holding the crust up to my mouth, and I eat it without thinking.

"Probably not the kind of germs you were thinking of swapping, huh?" Rosie murmurs before her eyes widen. "Not that you were thinking of swapping any germs at all. Not, like, my germs and your germs. I didn't mean that. I didn't mean, like, you were thinking of kissing me or anything ridiculous like that."

"Uh-huh," I muse, watching as she snatches up the garbage and leaps to her feet, hauling ass to the trash can.

Speaking of ass, the full curve of hers is out of this fucking world in those denim cutoffs.

"Are you looking at my bubble butt?" She slaps two hands over it, and I wanna fucking do that. Sinking back down beside me, she hides her shy smile in her muffin. "It's not like yours."

"You don't have to rub it in, Rosie. I'm sensitive about my butt. I know yours is better."

She stuffs the straw of her water bottle into her mouth, hiding her grin. "Shut up."

"You'd have to make me." I wink. "I can think of a few ways to do so if you'd like."

She manages to make spluttering water all over herself cute, and Connor thinks it's so funny he starts trying to do it too. They're a perfect pair, looking like twins as he snuggles into her lap after lunch when she pulls out his favorite book, *The Wheels on the Bus*. I smile as she sings every word as he passes out in her lap, his thumb in his mouth, Rosie's fingers running through his hair.

"I'm sorry I didn't tell you last night," Rosie says quietly, eyes dancing with vulnerability, an explanation she doesn't owe me but wants to give me anyway. "I wasn't trying to hide it, it's just…I don't date a lot. Besides it being hard to find time, it's been such a letdown. The first date I went on after Connor was born, it was someone I'd talked to a few times while waiting in line for my morning coffee. I genuinely liked him, and when he asked me out, I was so nervous to be with anyone, let alone tell them I was a mom. But he was so nice, I told him about Connor fifteen minutes into the date. He barely spoke for the next ten minutes before excusing himself to the bathroom. He came back, said he wasn't feeling well, and left. I ate by myself, trying not to cry. On my walk home, I saw him on the patio of the bar three doors down." Her nose wrinkles. "Made it home to bed before I let the tears come. I think what I felt worst about was that I'd missed out on my son's bedtime for someone who didn't care about us."

Covering her hand with mine, I give it a tender squeeze. "I'm sorry he didn't recognize what he could've had, Rosie."

"It's no big deal. I just realized we wouldn't be for everyone. I decided after that I wasn't interested in dating. But my roommate and his boyfriend always try to get me out there every once in a while." She lifts a shoulder. "I go, but with no expectations. It's my policy that I don't bring Connor into anything unless I feel a genuine connection. I've never had a second date with anyone, so…" Her lower lip slides between her teeth, and she swallows. "I've never had to deal with the rejection again."

"Does this count as our second date?"

Wide, hopeful eyes collide with mine. "Do you want it to?"

I rub the pad of my thumb over her pretty purple nails before lacing our fingers together, marveling at how perfect her small hand feels in mine.

"I'm already planning the third."

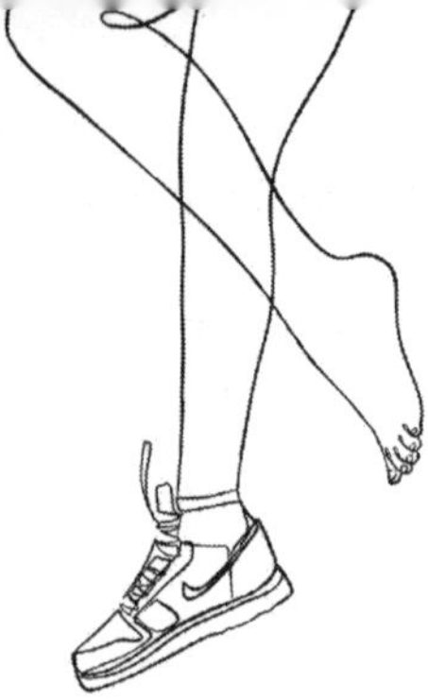

TEN

MY PEEN HERO

Rosie

"Is this date number two or three?" Marco pops his chin on his fist and cocks his head. "Or technically four?"

"Four," Archie answers. "'Cause technically their park date with Connor was two, and then their dog hike this morning was three. Right, Ro?"

"I donno," I mumble, twining my fingers through my hair, tying my French braids down, leaving the back free. It's definitely date four. This morning when I found him and Bear out front of Wildheart, waiting for me and Piglet, he took my hand and said it was date number three. He even had his own backpack, filled with fruit and cookies for dessert after lunch on the bridge.

I slip a lilac barrette onto each braid and spin around, groaning when my two-piece bathing suit is thrust in my face.

"I'm not wearing that." I shove it away, reach for the one-piece hanging on the back of the bathroom door, and then change my mind. "Actually, I don't think I'll bring a bathing suit at all."

Marco's brows rise. "Okay, Rosie's going all in. Skinny-dipping. Adam will love that. Tits and ass is always the right choice."

"I'm not going nude." I elbow past him and into my bedroom. "I'm just not gonna swim." So what if that's what he invited me over to do.

Archie squeezes my shoulder. "If you're not comfortable swimming, Ro, just tell him so. He'll understand, given what's happened."

"It's not that." It's definitely partially that. "Plus, he doesn't know what happened." I shake my head. "Okay, I'm afraid of freaking out in the pool, but mostly, he's just so *pretty*. I caught a glimpse of his abs that first day on the trail, and it wasn't even a six-pack. I swear, there were at least eight of those things. And he has that..." I gesture toward my crotch. "That stupid *V* that points right to his...his..."

"Anaconda?"

"Magic stick?"

"Dickmatizer?"

"Hospitalizer?"

I wave away their words. "Yeah. That."

Archie shrugs. "So? He's hot as fuck, what's your point?"

I look down at myself, the body hidden behind my flowy summer dress. I love my body for everything it's done and the world it's given me, but it's far from perfect. "How do I stack up to someone who looks like that?"

Archie and Marco exchange a look, and Marco nods. "She's one of those girls who doesn't realize she's gorgeous."

"I hate when she does this." Archie sighs and takes me by the shoulders. "You, Rosie Wells, are beautiful. On the outside and the inside too. Any man would trip over his own two feet to get a smile from you, and it sounds like Adam's done exactly that."

"You had a baby," Marco adds. "That doesn't make you worth any less."

"I'm not as thin as I used to be. And my scar—"

"Your scar is a badass badge of honor for having a life *you* created carved right out of you. And your stretch marks are tiger stripes, Rosie. You are strong. You are fierce. You are perfect, just the way you are." Marco sweeps my bangs aside. "Don't doubt that the right person won't see that, because he will."

"Comparing yourself to others won't get you anywhere. It's a useless way to spend your energy." Archie taps my nose and winks. "And you need to reserve that, because it sounds like Adam might be able to go all night."

I slap his hand away. "It doesn't matter, because I definitely can't. I passed out in his truck on the way home from our date on Wednesday."

Marco sighs wistfully. "There's just something about a man who drives a truck."

Archie's brows pull down. "I drive a truck."

Marco waves him off. "Please, Rosie. Wear the two-piece. The bottoms are high-waisted, they show off your curves, and Adam will be drooling."

I nibble my lip as I examine the yellow suit with little white daisies. "You really think so?"

"I know so. Now let's touch up those toenails."

A touch-up becomes a complete redo, and Marco even adds daisies to match my bikini, something I don't notice until I'm done, because I'm too engrossed with thoughts of Adam.

He was a dream with Connor on Thursday. I wasn't surprised, I guess, but I *was* surprised he was so nonchalant about the news. The man didn't even bat an eye, just got down to Connor's level and introduced himself before taking my hand and pulling us to the park. I didn't expect it to be so easy, but I'm ashamed that I'm still here, kind of… waiting for the other shoe to drop.

Fuck, I hope there's not another shoe.

My phone pings as I check my hair for the hundredth time, and I scoop it up, eager to see if it's Adam on his way over.

BRANDON

u need to come get connor. something's wrong with him.

My heart thuds a quick, anxious beat as I wait way too long for my son's father to pick up the phone he texted me from just seconds ago.

"Are you on your way?" he grumbles in greeting, and my chest tightens at the sound of Connor's cries in the background.

"What's wrong? Is he okay?"

"I donno."

"What do you mean you don't know? You said something's wrong. Is he sick?"

Brandon groans, like the conversation is exhausting him. "I don't fucking know, Rosie. He's just not right. He won't stop crying."

"Have you tried holding him?"

"He doesn't wanna be held."

"Did he eat lunch?"

"We had some Timbits."

"Timbits aren't—" I take a deep breath and let it go, reeling in my frustration. "He might be hungry still. Can you make him a sandwich? Cut up some fruit for him?"

"He's not fucking hungry, Rosie, he's just miserable. I need you to come get him; he's driving me nuts."

"Please don't say things like that in front of him."

"He's a baby. He doesn't know what I'm saying." Brandon sighs. "Look, are you coming or not?"

"I'm coming," I mumble, grabbing the folded stroller from the front closet, slipping quietly out the door before Archie and Marco can catch me and force me to put my foot down, to remind Brandon that he's supposed to have Connor until tomorrow evening, that he needs to step up and be a parent.

Instead, I type out a message I don't want to send.

ME

I'm so sorry, Adam. I have to cancel today. I hope we can reschedule.

The second I step out of the elevator, my phone rings. Adam's name lights my screen, and I steel my spine before I answer it.

"Hey, you."

"Hey, trouble. Everything okay?" There's a gentleness to his voice, one that's always there, even when his flirty side flies free.

"Yeah, totally." I squeeze my eyes shut and shake my head, before pushing through the front doors into the warm breeze. "No, not really. I don't know. Connor's having a rough day, I guess. His dad wants me to come get him."

"I'm sorry he's struggling today." He pauses a moment. "Does he like to swim?"

"You want me to…to bring him?"

"I want to spend the rest of the day with both of you. Is that okay?"

"No. I mean, yes. Yes, of course it's okay. It's just…no one's ever…I…"

"Are you going to get him now?" Adam asks, taking away the pressure to give my spiraling thoughts a voice. "Do you need a ride?"

"Brandon's only a ten-minute walk away."

"Okay, well, I can pick you and Connor up in about a half hour if you want to go home and grab his swimsuit and whatever else you need."

"No, I can't…I mean, I don't have a car seat for him. We walk or bus everywhere." I sigh, rubbing my eyes. This doesn't feel like it's going to work. "And he needs a nap, so I'd have to bring his playpen, but he might not sleep well in a different environment, and it just…I don't know, Adam. Maybe today isn't a good day."

"Hey." His quiet, patient voice stills my racing thoughts. "I've got a playpen for when my friend's daughter is over. Connor can lie down here if you're comfortable with that. I know you like routine, so if you aren't ready to change things, I understand. But I would love to see you two, so if you want to give this a try for a day, just know that I'm here."

My feet stop moving, and I ground myself in the moment. I feel the smooth, fake leather of the stroller handle in my fist, the hot sunshine on my cheeks, the warm breeze brushing through my hair. I see the way my dress sways gently, hear Adam's patient, soft breath in my ear as he waits.

"Okay," I finally say.

"Okay?"

"We'll come. We'll try it." There's a whoosh of breath on the other side of the phone, and I smile at his relief. My own relief comes at his next words, the excitement that bleeds through so vividly.

"Fuck yeah, Rosie!"

~

He's exactly where I expected him to be. Both of them are, actually.

I storm by Brandon, sitting on his couch with his feet up on his coffee table, tipping a beer back while he watches baseball, and I scoop Connor out of the playpen he's reaching for me from, crying and screaming.

"How long has he been in there for?" I ask as Connor lays his sopping cheek on my chest, grabbing a fistful of my hair as he settles himself with deep breaths.

Brandon's shoulder pops up and down, eyes never leaving the TV. "Hour or so."

"Seems like he just wanted some cuddles."

His gaze flicks to me, eyes rolling. "He needs to learn he doesn't get everything he wants by crying."

"He's a *baby*, Brandon. He can't regulate his emotions. He's crying because he wants comfort, and we're his safe place." I press my lips to

Connor's hair and rub his back, rocking him back and forth. "He just wants to be close to us. He wants interaction."

"I'm not a TV show. I don't always wanna entertain him."

"You think I want to entertain him every minute? It's hard and exhausting, but we chose to have a baby, so we do it."

"I didn't choose shit."

I stop bouncing as the color leaves my face. "What did you say?"

He sighs, setting his bottle down so he can sit up and drag both hands through his hair and down his face. "I can't do this anymore."

"Can't, or won't?"

He leaps to his feet, arms wide. "It's too much! He's too much! All he does is cry until you come back. He takes forever to get to sleep, and I lose my own sleep because of him. I just…I don't…" He tugs his hair, spinning away from me.

"Be very careful of your next words," I warn lowly. "You've walked out on him once, just to crawl back a month later. If you do it again, you won't be welcome back. He deserves to have people in his life who love him."

Brandon spins on me, pointing at me with a threatening finger. "Don't do that. I love him. He knows I do."

Then act like it, I want to scream. Instead, I walk away, pull open his door, and glance back at him. "He deserves to be surrounded by people who want to be in his life, no matter how challenging the days can be."

~

That has gotta be a nine-inch dong, at least. Maybe ten.

Do ten-inch penises exist? They must, because I'm almost certain this man is packing one.

Jesus, I wonder if his back hurts carrying that around between his legs all day.

Unless it's padding. I've heard they do that sometimes, fluff the junk up with padding to make it look extra big.

But no, I don't think so. No, the arrogant, confident look in this man's piercing green eyes says, *I've got a huge dick and I know it.*

Connor's as fixated as I am. He reaches out, laying his tiny hand over the photo of the man's package. The size difference is so alarming, it's comical.

"Connor, buddy." I take his hand and guide him back toward the bench in the bus shelter, turning my laugh into a cough. "We don't touch other people's bodies, even if it's just a picture." A gigantic picture of a gigantic dong, tucked in a tight pair of boxer briefs.

Seriously, who the hell decided a bus shelter was a good place for an underwear ad? I don't care if the man is—I squint at the words—God's gift to hockey, women, and underwear. What does that even mean? I bet the model doesn't even know. He heard his monster dick would be on display and jumped at the chance.

The rumble of an engine sounds, and Connor's head snaps up before he races toward the sidewalk. "*Brum, brum*!"

I grab the stroller and follow along, but it's not the bus.

"Tuck," Connor states proudly, pointing at the midnight blue truck as it approaches. "*Big* tuck!" He waves both hands, bouncing on his toes. "*Whoooa*! Hi, big tuck!"

The truck pulls to a stop beside us, and a man with a grin as devastatingly handsome as it is sheepish hops out.

"Well, hey there, little buddy," Adam says, crouching in front of Connor. "Remember me?"

"Dada!" Connor leaps at Adam, wrapping his tiny arms around his wide shoulders. When Adam laughs and lifts him into the air, something happens inside me.

It's the strangest thing, like something mending and unraveling all at once. I feel a pull toward a future I've always dreamt of, a stability I've craved and been deprived of for too long. And yet I'm ready to throw away nearly everything I know, all that I've worked for, for the smallest taste of this man, to feel his hands coast the valleys of my body, to make every inch of me come alive. Because, God, I feel alive with him, and all he's doing is standing there, holding my world in his arms, looking at us like we might be his.

"What are you doing here?" I take a hesitant step toward him, my hands shaking at the realization that he means so much to me in no time at all, no rhyme or reason, and I'm afraid this will end the way life has always worked for me: him, leaving, and me, walking this road alone. "I don't have a car seat."

"No, but…" He opens the door behind the passenger's seat. "I do."

I stare for so long, Adam winds up in front of me, two fingers touching my chin, closing my mouth, amusement shining in his eyes while Connor snickers and tries to do the same to Adam.

"I didn't run out and buy a car seat or anything," he quickly clarifies the longer I'm silent. "I'm not...please don't think I'm...I'm sorry if this is too much and I scared you. My friend has five cars and a seat in all of them—don't ask me why; he's just super ostentatious about all things—and he let me borrow one. He helped me install it, which, as it turns out, is super fuck—uh, *freaking* hard. There are so many rules, but he showed me how to adjust it so we can make sure it fits Connor just right." Adam smiles. It's extra wide, super gritty, and all teeth, like he's just realizing how wild this is. "I totally overstepped, didn't I? Aw, shit. I didn't mean to. I'm so out of my realm here. The thought of you two taking the bus home alone later tonight didn't sit well with me, so I...I..." He hangs his head. "I'm sorry."

Connor lays his hand on Adam's cheek and pulls his hat off, letting his curls spring free, a beautiful disaster Connor wastes no time burying his fingers in once he's tossed Adam's hat over his shoulder. "Hair," he says simply, patting the dark tresses. He points at the truck. "Big tuck. Beep-beep!"

Connor's simple words clear the fog from my head. Everything is simple to him. He's easygoing and flexible. He sees something he likes—like Adam, his hat, his hair, his truck—and he takes it. I want to be like that. I don't want to overanalyze every detail. I just want to let go and take it.

I step around Adam, peeking at the car seat. "Oh wow," I murmur. "Top of the line."

"Yeah," Adam whispers in my ear. "He's, like...super ostentatious."

"He sounds fun."

He swallows. "A little over the top."

I glance over my shoulder, and Adam's eyes drop to mine, bouncing down to my mouth, barely a breath from his with his chin dipped low, before ricocheting back up. "Connor is thirty-two inches tall and twenty-three pounds."

"So he can still rear face," Adam puffs out. "Which is what I figured when we installed it, and, by the way, is five hundred percent safer than forward-facing."

A smile tugs at my mouth. "You did your research."

"I love research." His brows pinch with his frown. "That was so lame."

A laugh bubbles from my chest, and Adam grins. The tension between us dissipates, and I tickle Connor's belly. "What do you think, buddy? Wanna ride in Adam's truck?" *Cause Mama wants to ride something else of Adam's.*

No. Fuck. No, Rosie. Think with your brain, not with your tits. Think with your brain, not with your tits. Think with your brain, not with your tits.

If I say it three times, maybe it'll come true.

Adam was right about having done his research, though he insists his friend really shoved a lot of information down his throat before he pulled out of his driveway with the car seat installed. It only takes us a minute to adjust the seat perfectly for Connor, and my little guy is happy as ever as we buckle him in.

"It's a good thing you came when you did. I don't think Connor and I could spend another minute looking at that man's peen."

Adam gives me a look, and when I gesture toward the bus shelter, he throws the truck in reverse and slowly backs up until the life-size advertisement comes into view, the arrogant, devious grin, and the extra-large —possibly padded—dong.

"Jesus Christ," Adam mutters.

"Right? Was that necessary? It's like a bad wreck. I couldn't look away no matter how hard I tried. That's gotta be ten inches, no?"

"Nine," I swear he whispers.

"What?"

"Nothing. Definitely padded." He shifts into drive, slings his arm over my seat, checks over his shoulder, and hits me with a wink before pulling into traffic. "No more bus shelter peens for you, Rosie. I'll protect you."

I cup his jaw before leaning forward, surprising us both when I press my lips to his cheek. "My peen hero."

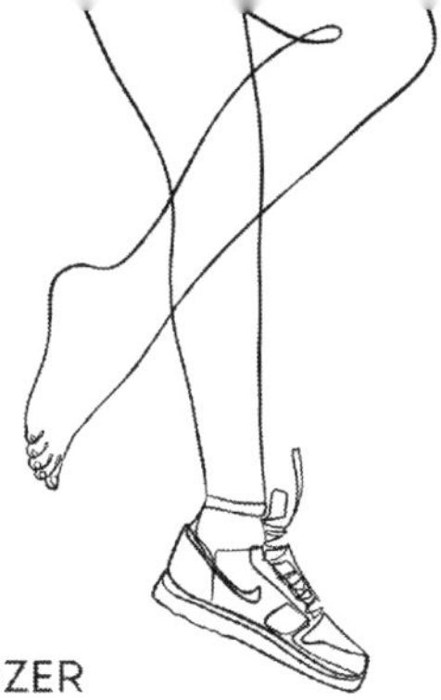

ELEVEN

CAN CONFIRM: THAT'S A HOSPITALIZER

Rosie

HAVE you ever walked into a space and been hit with the overwhelming urge to lock the door so you can live there, in that moment, forever?

That's me right now, and it's been me since Adam opened his front door and guided Connor and me inside.

Since Connor took one look at the wide staircase and started crawling up it, and then Adam spent fifteen minutes showing him how to go up and down, because we don't have stairs at home.

Since he showed us the dining room table he and his dad built together when he moved in two years ago, and then played peekaboo with Connor around it.

Since Connor found the TV remote, handed it to Adam, asked for *bus*, and the two of them watched and sang it on repeat three times.

And right now, as I run my fingers over the rustic brick backsplash, the marble countertops, along the edge of the oversized farmhouse sink, down to the cupboards. From the pristine white siding mingled with large stone, the wooden pillars, the black framed windows, this oversized farmhouse backing onto the mountains in North Vancouver is just…perfection.

But it's the olive-green cupboards that do me in.

"I've always loved the color of these cupboards, but they've become my favorite part of this house since I met you."

My gaze comes to Adam's as he strolls up beside me. "Why's that?"

He brushes my bangs aside. "Because they're the same color as your eyes."

A happy warmth pools in my cheeks, and I watch my fingers slowly skim the muted color. "My parents and I moved into our house when I was six. The cupboards were solid maple but old, and we didn't have the money to renovate." I smile at the memory of my dad dragging us through Home Depot, holding paint chips up to my eyes. "He painted them green to match mine and my mom's eyes."

"Mmm…" Adam winds an arm around my waist, pulling me back against his chest, his lips at my hair. "Your dad and I would get along well, I think."

They really would have. Lord knows he would've had my mom eating out of the palm of his hand too.

Connor squeezes between us, pulling on Adam's shorts. "'nack?"

"Snack?" Adam asks, and when Connor nods, he pulls out peanut butter, bread, and a banana. "Yeah, dude. Let me make you a—"

"*Ba-na*!" he shrieks, marching in spot, clapping his hands. He reaches for the banana. "Ba-na!"

"All right, banana it is." Adam chuckles, peeling the banana, breaking it in half, and handing it to him. "That was easy."

"Where's Bear?" I ask, suddenly realizing what's missing.

"I tucked him in my room. I wasn't sure if Connor would be nervous around him since he's so big."

"Oh no. Connor loves dogs." I ruffle his hair. "Don't you, buddy?"

"Dog," he replies, shoving the last of his banana in his mouth. "*Oof, oof*!"

Adam crouches in front of him. "Do you want to meet my dog Bear? He's my best bud."

Connor shoves the last of his banana in his mouth and grabs hold of one of Adam's fingers. The way Adam's eyes light, the corner of his mouth quirking as he looks down at the connection, makes my heart flutter.

I follow as they trot up the stairs, Connor staring up at him with wide, wonderous eyes, like he's enthralled with every word Adam speaks to him. Or maybe it's the undivided attention Adam lavishes on him. Whatever it is, I think he's in love.

Adam pushes his bedroom door open an inch, and a black nose nudges its way through, sniffing. There's a solid, steady thump of a happy tail whipping back and forth, and when Bear's tongue makes an appearance, Connor starts giggling.

"Bear, sit," Adam commands, lifting Connor into his arms as he opens the door. "Good boy. Wait." Bear's brown eyes bounce between Connor and me. He shifts from paw to paw, whimpering, and Connor starts gasping, wriggling, just as desperate to touch Bear as Bear is to touch him.

"Dog. Dog!" Wild green eyes meet mine. "Mama, *dog*!"

Adam walks into the bedroom, up to the pristine king-sized bed, and takes a seat. He pats twice and tells Bear *up* before making him lie down. Then he sets Connor on the bed.

"We're gentle with our pets," I remind Connor, and he tentatively reaches for Bear, his eyes shining with love. Bear meets him halfway, one ginormous tongue that covers Connor's whole face in a single swipe, and my little guy throws his arms around Bear's burly neck. "Hi, dog! Hi, big dog!"

Adam laughs, and my attention wanders around his incredible space, how intimate it feels to be in here with him. I walk across the chestnut brown planks, warm below my bare feet from the sunshine streaming through the double French doors. They're propped open, letting in the breeze, and I step onto the oversize balcony.

"Wow." The single syllable escapes on a breath.

A sea of evergreens peers back at me, tracking their way up the lush mountain, wrapping me in its ethereal beauty, reminding me why I moved here. Why, of all the places my family visited when I was growing up, Vancouver is the one I chose to make my home. There's a nostalgia in the green, the fresh scent of pine and earth that each gust of wind brings. A peaceful calm that settles all my racing thoughts in this moment, the uneven beat of my heart. Everything is still and quiet, and I feel…at home. With myself. With Connor.

With Adam.

Something warm brushes my back, and two strong arms cage me in, large hands clasping the stone balcony wall on either side of mine.

"Pretty, huh?"

"Pretty doesn't begin to describe it," I breathe out.

Soft lips ghost the shell of my ear. "I was thinking the same thing."

Shrieks of giggles ring behind us, and I glance behind me to find Connor and Bear rolling around on the plush rug.

Adam chuckles, a warm sound that rattles down my spine. "Think my dog's in love."

Yes. The dog. Definitely the dog. Not the…not the human. No. That's absolutely…no.

I watch Adam's hand move, so slowly, fingertips trailing my forearm before his palm splays over my belly. Instead of worrying about everything he might feel, the soft lines that speak of my love of Saturday mornings spent baking muffins and midweek batches of cookies, too many iced lattes in the summer and far too many hot chocolates in the winter, I sink into the touch. I revel in the connection, firm fingertips that seem to tingle beneath the material of my sundress, like he's touching bare skin. My heart pounds in my ears, a steady thrum that both liberates and scares me. I swallow the tightness in my throat, lick at my lips, and beg for a sudden storm to douse the heat singeing my skin.

"Your heart's going a mile a minute," Adam murmurs in my ear.

"I…" God, that's embarrassing. I curl my fingers into my palms until my nails bite the skin. "I'm sorry."

"I'm not. Frankly, Rosie, I can't tell you how good it feels to know that, for once in my life, I'm on the same page as someone."

Our gazes collide, a silent question in mine: *Are we on the same page? Really?* I'm too nervous to voice it, even though he's just said the words. But what page is he on? What chapter? How does his book end, and who does he want standing next to him in his epilogue?

I don't have a choice; my future is that little boy in there. And even if the decision were mine? He'd be my choice, day in and day out. I'll always choose him.

How nice it would be for someone else to choose us too.

Adam cups my cheek, spinning me into him. Nerves grip my throat, stealing my breath, but he simply leans forward, presses the gentlest kiss to my forehead, and soothes every worry with eight words.

"I'm glad you're here, Rosie. Both of you."

I have to start doing yoga or something if I'm going to keep up with Connor, because how am I raising a kid as flexible as the fifteen-month-old who just essentially backflipped into the playpen in Adam's spare room when I was still trying to explain to him that his nap would look different today? Maybe the breathing techniques would also help not send me into a tailspin at the idea of changing our daily routine even just once.

"Did he go down okay?" Adam whispers, making me jump as I back silently out of the room.

"Yeah, went down like a...a...a..." My eyes roll down to Adam's bare chest, the patch of dark curls that look so soft, I want to run my fingers through them. Down to the lines of thick, sinewy muscle carved so impeccably, and holy motherforking shit, I was right. It *is* an eight-pack. And, oh fuck, the swim trunks. They're tight in the worst way—because I can't look away—bright, summery stripes that wrap all the way around, hugging every single inch of him.

And, ladies, trust me when I say this: there are *a lot* of inches.

I mean, *Jesus shit.* He's bigger than the underwear guy at the bus stop; I'm sure of it. Or is it the stripes? I always avoid them because I think they make me look bigger. Does it work that way on cocks too?

Yes. Yes, it must. Because there's no way that he...that he...there's just no way, right?

This is it. I'm looking destruction right in the face. Obliteration. Total annihilation. That's the only thing that can possibly come from a dick that big. No woman is surviving a dicking from this man, not without being wheeled out afterward, and possibly in a dick-induced coma.

Oh my God. Archie and Marco were right. I've been dickmatized.

"Sorry, did you say...total annihilation?"

My eyes snap to Adam raking his fingers through those tousled curls, a faint blush on his high cheekbones. "Pardon?"

"You were talking about putting Connor down for his nap, but you trailed off and whispered, uh...*total annihilation.*" He swallows. "I think you were looking at my crotch."

I force my jaw closed, ignoring the violent cracking sound it makes. My eyes twitch, desperate to coast down, just once more, but I'm not doing it.

Okay, I'm doing it. Fuck. Damnit. My gaze bounces down, then right back up. Adam's eyes follow, and his mouth curves as molten heat rushes to the tips of my ears.

I dash by him, heading for the stairs. "I've gotta put my bathing suit on."

"I brought your bag into my room. You can change in there."

I halt, already halfway down the stairs. "Oh." Whipping around, I strut by him, keeping my eyes on my feet. "Thanks."

"Rosie?"

I pause at his door, watching his feet come closer, until all I can smell, all I can breathe, is him.

"Need help?"

I swallow. "No." *Maybe.*

"'Kay." Sizzling fingertips slide up my arm, hitching the strap of my dress back up to my shoulder. "Holler if you change your mind, trouble."

I do need help. All sorts of it. Help cooling my jets, because I haven't had sex in over a year, and looking at him, it's suddenly all I can think about. I'm flustered. So flustered. He's so sweet and kind, so patient, and then he springs these little things on me, lingering, searing touches, starved gazes, hot, teasing words drenched in intensity. I'm horny as hell, clearly, which is new and scary, but I'm not ready to jump into that, and what if that's what he's expecting?

But beyond that, I need help finding the confidence to walk out of here in this bikini.

I don't want to feel pretty for Adam. I want to feel pretty for me.

And right now, as I stand before his mirror and take myself in, I'm struggling.

I remind myself that this body gave me the love of my life. That it grew something from nothing. That it endured endless bouts of sickness, days spent hugging the toilet, aches and pains that made me feel like I'd never walk properly again, an emergency surgery that—so briefly—convinced me I was less of a woman because I couldn't push my child out. A surgery that had me unable to stand on my own for days, to take more than a couple steps with my newborn in my arms.

This body isn't perfect, but it's strong. Physically, mentally, in everything I've worked so hard to overcome.

This body isn't perfect, but for all it's done and everything it's given me, it's beautiful.

I tie the string of my sheer cover-up at my hip and take a breath before opening the door, starting down the stairs.

The photos lining the wall of the staircase catch my eye, and I pause to take them in. It's Adam in every single one of them, I'm sure of it. Even the tiny boy tucked into the side of the smiling couple is so clearly him, vibrant cobalt eyes, the most genuine grin with just a hint of mischief.

And the couple…they're everything. From the way they look at each other, full of devotion, endless love, to the way they look at Adam, like he's their whole world.

I'm so enthralled with the love flowing from the pictures, I don't notice Adam until he's at my side, towering over me though he's one step below. He's smiling at the pictures, a hint of longing in his eyes that makes me a little sad.

"Those are my parents."

I look back at the couple, their deep brown skin and warm eyes, the dark curls spilling down around the woman's shoulders.

"I was adopted."

A strange feeling grips my heart, the weight of that single word refusing to settle in my chest, questions I want to ask but can't, for fear of overstepping.

Fear of revealing parts of me I'm not ready to.

So I tell him, "You can see the love between you three."

"Mmm. I've always been able to feel it too." His mouth hitches up on one side as he stares at a photo of him on his dad's shoulders. "Even if it took my dad a little longer to figure it out."

"What do you mean?"

Adam takes my hand, pulling me down the stairs. "I was in a group foster home."

The grip on my heart instantly eases, a soaring, freeing feeling as excitement bubbles to the surface at the thought that maybe, after all, we're so much more alike than I've realized. That he'll understand all the fears, the nagging thoughts that eat at me in the darkest, quietest parts of the night, when I'm all alone, wondering if I'll always be this way.

Hope fills me so fluidly, a warm feeling that nearly spills out of me. Before the words can come, Adam goes on.

"My dad did a lot of volunteer work with the home I was in, so I met him right away. I think four-year-old me would've gone home with him that first day, I was so enamored with him. Every time he was in, I followed him around like a puppy. I wanted to be just like him." He smiles, a little far off, like he's remembering something. "I was in foster care for ten months, and my parents adopted me not long after my fifth birthday.

All that bubbling hope dies, dropping like a dead weight, sitting on my chest in an oddly suffocating way. It's a petty, dirty thing, the jealousy that nips at me, the bitterness that he spent so little time there, that he found this beautiful family that chose him, that decided they wanted to love him for the rest of their lives and his.

All I want to feel for him in this moment is happiness that he found that. Instead, I'm overcome with guilt and a stinging pile of self-hatred, because beyond the genuine happiness lies the weight of wishing there was somebody out there, *anybody*, who might understand what it's like to sit there day after day, on your best behavior, hoping, *dreaming* that someone might choose you. Might spend five minutes talking to you and go, *Hey, I think I want to take a chance on her. I think I want to keep her.*

I think I want to love her.

I bury the nasty thoughts as deep as I can, choosing to embrace the good ones as I squeeze his hand. "I'm happy you found your forever family, Adam."

"Are your parents in the city?" he asks casually as he leads me through his house, toward his backyard.

"It's just me and Connor. I came out here on my own after I graduated from high school."

"Does it ever get lonely?"

Always.

I force a smile. "I keep busy."

"Right, but…" His fingers circle my arm, stopping me. "That's not what I asked."

His eyes rake my face, searching for answers. But I'm still searching for them myself.

"How about this, Rosie." He brackets my jaw in his hand, the pad of his thumb trapping my lower lip. "How busy do you want me to keep you? Because sometimes I feel lonely, but when I'm with you, I feel full."

That fullness he swears he feels seeps into my skin, filling all the empty spaces like sand between pebbles. "I'd like you to keep me very busy."

Happiness detonates his face. "I can do that."

Adam's backyard is as immaculate as his house, exquisite and sprawling. Situated below Mount Fromme, it's a plush green oasis worthy of a magazine spread.

"Of course you have a waterfall feature," I mumble as Adam dips into the pool, long arms making circles as he pushes himself backward, waiting, watching, *grinning*.

My heartbeat threatens to pound out of my chest as I dip my toes. The water is warm, but the chill that trembles down my spine isn't.

I swim where there are lifeguards. Where the water reaches my hips and my feet touch the bottom. Where Archie and Marco are arm's length away, in case panic sets in.

My eyes flutter closed as I chant the mantra my therapist taught me.

My past is not my future. I'm allowed to be scared, and I'm allowed to choose to move slowly, so long as I move.

I move, down one step, warm water lapping at my ankles as the air in my chest rattles my rib cage.

"Rosie?" Adam murmurs, and my lids flip open. "You gonna take your cover-up off?"

"What?" I look down at myself, still covered. "Oh. Yeah. Duh." I find one of the loungers below the gazebo, and with my back to Adam, I slowly peel off my cover-up and drop it. My fingers tremble at my belly as I remind myself I'm beautiful and strong, that if Adam can't see it, it's his loss.

I drop to the first step and stop, curling my fingers into my palms three times, squeezing my eyes shut as I count each one. I hear the lapping of water, the steady *drip drip drip* as Adam climbs the steps, feel the warmth of his hands as they circle my waist, fingertips digging in.

"Rosie?" he whispers, so close, I think his lips may be nearly touching mine. I want to look, but I can't.

"Yeah?"

"Open your eyes."

"Do I have to?"

"I'd like you to, but I won't force you to do anything you don't want to."

I crack one, just a smidge. He cracks a smile, lopsided and sweet.

"What is it you're afraid of right now, me, or swimming?'

"What if I said both?"

"Well, I'd tell you that you have nothing to be afraid of when it comes to me. I'll be gentle, and I'm not going to hurt you." He sweeps his thumb over the dimple in my chin, coaxing my gaze open. Cobalt eyes lift to mine. "I wish I could tell you that you have nothing to be afraid of when it comes to swimming, too, but I don't know your reasons, and I won't undermine them. I want you to know, though, that you're safe with me. I won't let anything happen to you."

"You promise?"

"Swear it."

I take one step, then another, dropping five inches lower, then ten, and my fingernails bite into his shoulders. Strong hands squeeze my waist tighter, guiding me into him. When he sinks to the bottom, water kissing his chest, he pulls my limbs around him, letting me cling to him.

"'Atta girl," he murmurs against my temple. "You okay?"

I nod into his neck. "Don't let go, please."

"Wouldn't dream of it."

"I almost drowned when I was eleven," I blurt. "A firefighter saved me. It was a…a silly accident. In my own pool."

"Fuck, Rosie. I'm sorry." His hands still on my body. He starts wading toward the stairs. "I would've never asked you to—"

"No, please. It's okay." I drag my face from the safe spot in his neck. "It's something I've been working on for years, getting back in the water, and it's been a priority since Connor was born. I know why my fears exist, but I don't want them to control me forever. More than that, I don't want them to impact Connor's life. He loves the water, and I want him to feel confident and safe in it. We're learning together."

Adam's gaze is steady on mine, a comforting weight that tells me he's listening, taking it in. "Thank you for letting me be a part of your journey." He dips his mouth to my shoulder, pressing a kiss there that sends all the blood to my head, making me dizzy. "I won't push you to do anything you aren't ready for. You tell me where your boundaries are and I'll respect them."

"It's easier," I mumble against his neck. "With you, it feels easier."

"I feel the same with you."

I look at him, the shadow of stubble lining his rugged jawline, the sharp line of his cheekbones, the way his curls hang in effortless perfection above his eyes. "What's easier for you?"

"Being me," he whispers. "Just me."

I take his face in my hands and swallow every worry. "I like you, Adam. Just you, the way you are."

His smile is like the brightest beam of sunshine, heating the coldest, darkest parts of me. He drops his nose to mine, his lips so close I can taste the mint on his breath. "I like you, too, Rosie. Just you."

TWELVE

FUCKING HYPNOTIZING

Adam

Perfection exists, and it's right here in my arms.

It's soft green eyes that light so easily, giving way to every emotion that passes through her. It's a heart-shaped mouth, rosy lips that give way to a smile that knocks the air from my lungs. That sun-kissed nose and the way it crinkles every time she laughs.

The way she feels in my arms in this very moment, warm skin that melts into mine, the dip in her waist where I grip her, the roundness of her intoxicating hips, begging me to drag my hands lower, to explore every inch of her.

I could float through the rest of my life content in knowing I've held perfection in these arms.

Rosie lays her cheek on my shoulder with a soft sigh, tucking her face into my neck, like I'm her safe space. I think she might be mine.

"You feel really nice," perfect lips murmur against my skin. "Solid. Steady." Another sigh. "Safe."

"I'll be anything you want me to be."

"Just you, Adam. You're enough exactly as you are."

Her words tug at an invisible string, pulling everything in my chest tighter. I want to be enough for her, but I've spent the last year and a half not feeling enough for anyone. But with her, right here, right now? There's no hockey, no superstar goalie, no millionaire athlete.

There's just me, and she says I'm enough for her.

My mind races with thoughts of a life I've always dreamed of. My family in the stands, and me making them proud. Quiet Saturday nights, take-out containers, wrapped up in each other. Slow Sunday mornings, pancake breakfasts, and cartoons on TV.

Suddenly, it feels like I'm finally being gifted it.

But I know this life can't truly be mine until I give Rosie all of me, and right now, I'm struggling to find the words that give her those pieces.

So I swallow them down, bury them a bit deeper, and hope when she says I'm enough for her, she means it.

"How you doing?" I murmur against her hair, honey and rose gold tresses weaved into a braid.

"Good. I think." Her gaze lifts to mine, uncertain. "Am I doing okay?"

I chuckle. "You're doing great. Let me know if it's too much."

"It's…not. I thought it might be, but it feels okay. Though it might have something to do with the giant man I've attached myself to like a koala."

"I'm honored to be your tree branch." Questions about her past crawl up my throat, searching for answers she doesn't owe me. Instead, I tell her I'm proud of her.

"What for?"

"It's hard enough to conquer our fears, and there's a certain pressure when you're not just doing it for yourself. It's admirable that you're facing your deepest fear for both yourself and for your son."

Her lower lip slides between her teeth as she thinks. "I think my deepest fear is just…losing it all. Connor. He's my whole life. So, swimming after nearly drowning? Hard as it is, it feels like nothing more than waking up on a rainy morning in comparison to even the briefest thought of life without each other."

"Do you think about that often? Life without each other?"

"Mostly I think about having to say good-bye, how impossible that would be, but having to do it anyway. How hard it would be knowing it was the last time I'd see his face, praying that the world would be kind to him without me to protect him."

A tightness squeezes in my chest before it rolls up my throat. "That's…"

"Sad," she finishes with an anxious chuckle, shifting like she wants to pull away, hesitating because she can't. "I know. It's embarrassing. Most people don't have such morbid thoughts."

I catch one of her hands in mine, pressing a kiss to the inside of her palm before wading to the stairs with her in my arms.

"Your thoughts are painful, yes, but not morbid. I can't put myself in your shoes, but I'd stand in them if it meant one less minute where you felt that pain alone."

"Sometimes I think that's what I do," she murmurs as I set her down on a lounger in the shade, watching as she covers herself in the towel I hand her. "Put myself in my parents' shoes."

I sit beside her, rubbing my hair with my towel. "What do you mean?"

"Sometimes I wonder what it felt like for my parents." She takes a deep breath, licks her lips as her eyes roam my face, searching for the courage to go on. "When they knew it was good-bye."

Thick silence settles between us as her words settle. My mind races, remembering the look on her face the first time I called her trouble, the longing as she explained her dad's nickname for her. The way she fell apart in my arms when I gave her that bouquet of peonies, when she told me about all the wonderful memories that came with the sight of them, explained that she couldn't make more.

Because her parents aren't here anymore.

"You had to say good-bye."

"That's the thing. I didn't get to, because I didn't know. But my dad...he knew, I think." A storm brews in her eyes, angry clouds with nowhere to go. "Some days I remember everything, every single moment. Some days it's all...blurry. Distorted. But there's one image... it's like it's *burned* in my brain." The storm in her gaze dissipates, leaving behind an exhaustion I can feel in my bones, a sort of... resignation. "The way my dad tucked my hair behind my ear when he said he'd be back. The devastation in his eyes when he looked at me one last time, over his shoulder, and told me he loved me."

I wish I had the words to make this better, something to take away the grief and replace it with an everlasting happiness. But I don't, and though I haven't really lost anyone—not the way she has, at least—I know that's not how grief works.

So instead, I wind an arm around her waist, bringing her body into the groove of mine, where I can keep her safe, and I press a kiss to her temple.

She swipes at a single tear the moment it escapes. "I don't really talk about it often. It's not that I can't, but that I'm constantly trying to move forward, you know? I lost my family, but I'm building a new one with Connor. We're making the memories I can't make with my parents anymore."

"Tell me about them. The memories. You've told me about the nickname, that your dad called you trouble too. What about the peonies?"

She looks up at me, her dimpled chin on my chest, bright eyes and an even brighter smile. "Mom always wanted this huge, colorful garden, like the one she had at her house growing up. We went to this beautiful garden store at the end of September when I was eight." Her grin widens, blooming as the memory coasts through her mind. "I was enthralled. We were there forever, just walking around, taking it all in. Mom wanted something that would come back each spring. She said there was something about something as delicate as a flower that would bloom all over again after the harshest winter. I found this luscious peony bush. They were so pretty, the pink flowers. Not overwhelmingly bright, but this soft, beautiful rose hue that just captivated me."

She touches the warm pink ends of her hair. "That's why the pink. It reminds me of my mom, but my mom always said the color reminded her of me. That I was like the freshest bloom each spring, captivating." The color dotting her cheeks runs rampant, right up to the tips of her ears as she drops her gaze. "I guess I wanted to feel that way again, like I was…captivating. For someone, at least."

Captivating? But she's so much more than that. She's…fascinating. Dazzling. *Fucking hypnotizing.* Doesn't she know that?

She doesn't knock the air from my lungs when she walks into a room; she breathes the life back into me. If she's the flower blooming after the harshest winter, I'm the spring. I'm everything new and fresh, full of life and color and sunshine and hope, after it was all stolen from me the way the first bitter frost of winter steals the beauty of autumn.

Rosie gives that all to me, and she has the nerve to sit here beside me and think she's anything less than enchanting?

That just won't work.

"So you got the pink ones?" I ask, trailing my finger along the curve of her thigh, watching as she mirrors the movement on my own, tracing the black lines of my tattoo peeking out of my swim trunks.

"And the purple ones. The blue ones too." She giggles. "Then the next fall, we got the orange ones, and yellow the next. We planted a new bush each fall, and I waited by the window each spring to watch them bloom. Our front yard was a rainbow. Everybody stopped to look at it when they walked by."

"Like you, then."

She looks up at me, a noticeable swallow in her throat as she catches the intensity behind my gaze. "Like me?"

"The burst of color and life everyone stops to look at."

Her nose scrunches, a ruby flush painting her freckled cheekbones at my words. She keeps her eyes trained on her hand as it moves over my thigh, toying with the hem of my shorts. Her lips purse to the side, and she peeks up at me from beneath thick, sandy blonde lashes. "Can I?"

"Mhmm."

Something tight and thick settles in my throat at the gentle sweep of her fingers, something hot low in my belly as she drags my shorts up, exposing inch after inch of inked skin covering my thigh. The tip of her fingernail brushes over the mane of the lion painted there in black, the weathered lines of his face, the wisdom in his eyes, like he's seen it all.

"Pretty," Rosie murmurs, a slow, heated swipe of her hand that has muscles jumping that shouldn't be. "Why a lion?"

"A symbol, I guess."

"Of?"

Of everything Courtney tried to take from me, or maybe succeeded in taking from me. Of every piece of me I nearly lose with each hopeful date before it inevitably turns meaningless.

"Of strength," is what comes out of my mouth. "Wisdom from lessons learned. A reminder to do better. That I'm in charge of my destiny, not anyone else."

"I want to be in charge of my destiny," Rosie murmurs. "It feels like, no matter how much control I try to exercise, I can't control my future."

"Your future and your destiny aren't the same thing. Your future is anything that's going to happen, the things we can't pick. But your destiny…it's everything that's meant for you. The things we work hard for every day, because we *want* them. Maybe part of your destiny is a future where you aren't afraid to wade through the deeper parts of the creek in the mountain, to swim with your son without fear, to be able to say good-bye to him every morning without that fear that it might be permanent. But those things don't come easily, do they?"

The way she looks up at me, a tiny crease between her brows as she hangs on every word, mulls it over in her head, it's a heady, addictive feeling, like she's not anywhere else but right here with me.

"It's something you want, and you're putting the work in to get there, because you know it's your destiny, a life you're bound to live for however long you're going to live it, and you won't accept anything less. Your future is a life with your son. Your destiny is a life with him where your strength and courage make it the best life possible."

A beat of silence stretches between us as she watches her hand move over my thigh, her touch firmer, slower, more purposeful as it travels in a dangerous direction. A shudder of breath escapes her, and she gazes up at me with wonder. "I want that."

"Then take it," I tell her, capturing her wrist. If her hand keeps moving the way it is, something inside me is bound to snap, and I'm supposed to be in control.

There's a heat that comes over her, like it lights her from the inside out, but it doesn't touch the furthest corners of her. Not the edges of her gaze, tainted with frost, a faint uncertainty that lingers, like she's desperate to shake it. I'm not sure what it is, until I shift closer, tugging at the towel still covering her haphazardly.

She lets the plush material fall, slender fingers fluttering over the adorable daisies on her high-waisted bikini bottoms, hands coming to rest over her belly. Her gaze bounces to my thigh, the way the muscles flex as I shift closer still, then to my arms, my chest, and down farther, settling on my stomach. She swallows, fingers spreading wider, covering more of herself, and something inside me dies.

"Does it bother you that I don't look like you?"

What bothers me is the hidden meaning behind her words, so I start with humor to try to ease her tension. "That you're short? It's a little inconvenient, sure. My neck's gonna hurt once we get to all that kissing."

She rolls her eyes and swats my shoulder. "I'm not short! You're just massive!"

"Right, sorry. *Average*." I catch her flailing hand, linking our fingers, giving her a reassuring squeeze. "What's on your mind, Rosie? Let's talk it out."

Heat creeps up her neck like a vine, but she holds my gaze. "I think you're really handsome, and sometimes—especially when I'm in a bikini—I struggle being comfortable in my body. I don't have a single ab, and you've somehow got eight of them. Plus, this…" She dips her fingertip into the dip of muscles in my stomach, tracing the line of my left hip, the muscle that disappears beneath my shorts, and she sighs. "This ridiculous *V*. Who invented this? Do you know what this does to a woman?" She smiles. Soft. Honest. Vulnerable. "I guess, next to you, I'm feeling a bit average."

"If I hear that word come out of your mouth one more time, I won't be held responsible for my actions."

Mossy eyes blink up at me, wide and full of surprise. She opens her mouth like she might argue it, say that fucking word one more time. Before she can, I grip her hips, jerk her forward, until she's flat on her back, and I'm living out a vision I've been dreaming of since I met her—her, beneath me, lips parted, chest heaving, heat staining every exposed inch of skin.

"The only thing average about you, Rosie, is your height." The words are thick with gravel, a too-generous heaping of pent-up lust for a woman who's been occupying my brain for the last few weeks. My knees bracket her in, one hand doing a slow glide up her luscious side, over immaculately flushed skin, sunshine and daisies, more skin, and so, *so* much warmth. "And all the things you see as imperfections are where somebody else, like me, finds beauty." My thumb runs over the indent in her chin, the teensiest piece of perfection I've ever seen. "Like this dimple. It's so perfect, I've found myself wanting to kiss it at least five times today. And these hips…" My hands shake as my fingers rain down on her sides, grazing her waist, skimming the edge of her bathing suit bottoms where they wrap around the wide flair of her full hips. Every touch is a hunger barely restrained, a starvation I haven't felt before. "Jesus, I wanna grab them. Burn my fingertips right into them. So much, it's painful to stop myself from doing so."

The second her hands come up, a frantic touch that scrapes through the hair lining my jaw, that restraint snaps, a thread that was barely hanging on. I drop my hips to hers, and pressure explodes low in my stomach as she presses into me, a guttural, inhuman sound rumbling in my chest when she moans, like she's as starved as I am. Smooth legs come around my waist, and my hands grab onto their only lifeline, fingertips dipping below her bottoms, sinking into her plush ass as I hold her tight to me, like I'm afraid she might get away.

I won't let her.

"And these fucking legs," I breathe out, running my hands over them, a rough slide that has me pressing closer as Rosie throws her head back, exposing her long neck. My lips fall to the flushed skin there, tasting her, and *fuck*, it's not fucking enough. My mouth slides up the columns of her throat, nipping at her chin, until I finally get to kiss that dimple right there. "Not sure where you get off thinking they don't go straight to heaven. I sure as hell don't see anything but heaven when I look at you."

"Adam," she whimpers, writhing below me, fingers plowing through my hair.

"Not fucking average at all." I drag my nose along her cheekbone, settling my mouth above hers. "I never wanna hear that word again. Got it?"

She nods, a frantic jerk of her head, wide eyes ready to give up any semblance of control. "Got it."

"Good girl."

I run my hand up her throat, fingers itching to lock it in place, keep her right there. Instead, I grip her jaw, giving her a slightly less demanding version of me, gentle. As gentle as I can be right now with her below me, running that tongue across her pink lips, getting ready.

"Gotta tell ya, trouble, this isn't exactly what I had planned to earn that first kiss." I trap her lower lip beneath my thumb, my gaze tracking its drag across a mouth I can't wait to claim. "I'm gonna steal it anyway."

Our gazes collide, and through all the manic hunger, something inside me softens at the hope swimming in her eyes, the trust.

Her lips part, I dip my head, and a tiny voice calls out through the video monitor sitting five feet to my right.

"*Mamaaa*!"

THIRTEEN

2-FOR-1 SPECIAL

Adam

I CAN'T REMEMBER a time anyone has looked at me the way Rosie does.

Courtney did, once upon a time, but it's almost impossible to look back on our early years together and imagine that it was ever real, even back when we were seventeen and she looked at me like I hung the stars.

But with Rosie…I'm not the stars, lighting bits of her sky. I'm the rising sun on the clearest day, touching every inch of her world, lighting the bleakest, darkest parts where she hasn't seen light in far too long. She looks at me like I'm everything good and bright. She looks at me like she's…grateful. Grateful to be here with me. Grateful for the patience, for the understanding, for every kindness and every smile.

It's nearly painful how heavy the weight of her stare is.

Because I know, even on our best days, the way Courtney used to look at me could never compare, and it makes me feel a little…empty. It feels like wasted years and dashed dreams. Like bitter winters that outstayed their welcome, a spring that took far too long to come.

It's painful because for everything Rosie's given me, no matter how small or how hesitantly, I haven't done her the same. She gets the pieces that come easily, the ones that don't hurt, and I keep all the others in my fist, grasping them tight against my chest, afraid of what she'll do with them.

And that's the thing. When I met Courtney, I had everything I dreamed of. An incredible family who loved me endlessly, a promising career as a goalie in the NHL on the horizon. I was happy and carefree. Courtney had my bright spots, and they weren't enough. I let her steal everything good and bright and happy, one tiny handful at a time. My confidence, my trust, my faith in happy endings.

I don't think it's wrong to make someone your whole world, but I know the one time I've done it, it was my greatest mistake.

I know now that Courtney wasn't the world meant for me, but that doesn't make it easier to consider starting a new one with someone else, someone who has the power to break you all over again. I want to jump in headfirst. Fuck, I tell myself I'm already doing it, that I've never fallen so fast, started dreaming of a future with someone I barely know. But the reality is like rope tied around my ankles, letting me shuffle down the road I want to go, but each small step burns into my skin, urging me to slow down, to just…wait. Just in case.

I survived the first time, but will I survive a second?

The look in Rosie's eyes as she watches me splash around the pool with her son in my arms tells me there's nothing to survive. That she won't be the one to break me. The fissures in my chest whisper…*but what if?*

Connor wiggles in my grasp, reaching toward the steps. I know exactly where this is going; we've been doing it for the last forty minutes. I swim us to the edge and he scrambles up the steps. He rounds the patio on quick feet, stopping to take Bear's face in his little hands. "Hi, big dog," he says before pressing a kiss to his forehead. "Mama," Connor coos, patting her knee. "Mama!"

"I'm watching, baby. Are you going to jump to Adam?"

"Dada!"

I stifle a laugh at the horror painting Rosie's face, even though Connor's called me this about five hundred times today.

"I'm so sorry," she whispers. "Google says it's a phase."

I only wink, then reach toward Connor as he crouches down. "Ready to jump, little trouble?"

"Tubble," he repeats with a toothy grin. Tiny hands reach toward me, and when he launches himself off the patio and into my arms, he shrieks, "*Daaa-daaa*!"

I twirl him in the air before dunking his bottom half while he squeals with delight. He clings to my chest, little legs wrapping around me as he giggles against my neck, and Rosie can't take her eyes off us.

"Should we splash Mama?" I wade closer to Rosie, hiding my smile. "What do you think, buddy? Does Mama need to get a little wet?"

She points a finger at me. "Don't you dare. I've been wet, now I'm dry." She curls her daisy-painted toes into Bear's fur. "Bear and I like it this way."

"Mmm. Mama doesn't like being wet." The furious heat pooling in Rosie's cheeks says she doesn't miss the innuendo, but we don't have time to dwell on it as I help Connor up the steps again. "Go give Mama a *big* hug. Squeeze all your love into her."

Tiny feet tear across the patio, grabby hands reaching for his mom. She shrieks with laughter as he hurls his wet body into her lap, and I think they might be my favorite people in the world.

Water droplets cascade down my body, splattering on the concrete as I walk toward them. I grab a towel, watching Rosie's eyes move over me on a slow, heated sweep, tongue running aimlessly across her bottom lip as I shake out my hair, her throat bobbing as I rub the towel across my stomach.

"I'm gonna start the barbecue and get dinner going."

Rosie doesn't blink, gaze roaming down, then up.

I nudge her chin with two knuckles, guiding her eyes to mine. "'Kay, pretty girl?"

"Hot," she murmurs, then blinks rapidly, shaking her head. "Barbecue, I mean. It's…hot. It'll be hot. When you…start it." She nods. "Yes."

I drop my smile to her forehead, wink at Connor, and head inside. My phone's buzzing on my kitchen counter, my favorite group of Puck Sluts checking in.

CARTER

did the car seat work ok?

GARRETT

What car seat?

CARTER

im talking 2 adam, not u.

GARRETT

Fine, I'll go back to what I was doing before. Your sister.

CARTER

u motherfucker

EMMETT

Believe the correct term is sisterfucker, bud.

JAXON

crying laughing emoji Sisterfucker. Get it? Cuz he's fucking ur sister.

CARTER

I fucking hate u all. i'm only talking to adam from now on.

did the car seat work for ur girlfriend???

GARRETT

...How old is Rosie?

EMMETT

Wait wait wait...*monocle emoji*

CARTER

it's not for rosie, u turds.

GARRETT

I thought you weren't talking to us.

JAXON

thinking emoji

CARTER

...

JAXON

surprised emoji No. No no no no.

CARTER

yes.

JAXON

melting emoji Adam, buddy. Tell me she doesn't have a kid.

GARRETT

Jennie awww'd so long I stopped counting.

EMMETT

Cara says 'Stepdaddy Adam??? Man just went from a 10/10 to a solid 20.'

JAXON

ADAM. Tell me it isn't so.

ME

His name is Connor, he's fifteen months old, and he's cute as fuck.

JAXON

NOOOOO. Daddy Adam?! RIP.

EMMETT

Ayooo! That's awesome, bud. Happy for you.

CARTER

keep him away from my baby cuz no boys til she's 40.

or ever.

no girls either.

I'm not going to attempt to touch on the fact that one day Ireland will grow up and be her own person and not ever listen to her dad again, because it's a useless conversation. Carter's go-to when anyone tries to reason with him involves slapping his hands over his ears and singing *I'm not listening, I'm not listening.*

In fact, Ireland may grow up before he does.

My phone rings, and I half expect it to be Jaxon. Commitment scares him, and the thought of a toddler probably has him spiraling. If anyone's going to try to talk me out of this relationship, it'll be him.

But my mom's face smiles up at me from my screen, and I answer the video request as I shuffle out of earshot of the patio door, to the living room window, where I can see Rosie, Connor, and Bear playing in the grass with the sprinkler.

"Hey, Mom."

"Care to tell me why Garrett told me you have a girlfriend before you did?"

"I don't—what—when were you—" I scrub my eyes and sigh. "That little shit."

"Don't blame my angel." Garrett is definitely her favorite of my friends, which is why she sends him a monthly box of specialty snacks from the States that you can't get here in Canada. "He called to thank me for his snacks and asked if I was excited to meet Rosie. I said, 'Rosie who?' and he said, 'Oh, shit.' Then Jennie started cackling in the background and chanting, 'You fucked up, you fucked up.'"

"She's not my girlfriend," I mumble. "I haven't even kissed her yet."

"Well, that's understandable."

"It is?"

"Yeah, of course."

There's a snicker in the background, and then my dad's amused face pops over Mom's shoulder. "If someone publicly rated my kissing a three out of five, I'd be hesitant to kiss anyone ever again too."

They howl with laughter, and the fuckers even high-five. "Nailed it, Deac!"

I smile as Connor bounds after Bear, and Rosie after Connor, the three of them soaked to the bone as they leap through the spraying water.

"Oh my God," Mom murmurs. "He's in love."

"I am not." *I might be.* Well on the way, at the least. "Look, I gotta go. She's here right now, and I'm supposed to be starting the barb—"

"She's there? Right now? Introduce us!"

"Absolutely not."

Her dark brows pull way down. "Deacon, make your son introduce us."

Dad rips open a Fruit Roll-Up, and now I want one, so I grab one too. "Adam, listen to your mother so I don't have to, blah blah blah, happy wife, happy life."

I stifle a laugh at the look she gives him, and when Connor squeals with laughter, my mom's jaw dangles, and I pause, my rainbow treat hanging in front of my open mouth.

"Is that a…a baby?"

I stuff my Fruit Roll-Up in my mouth. "Toddler, technically. Connor is fifteen months old."

She turns to look at my dad, sniffling. "Deacon, we're gonna be grandparents."

"For fuck's sake." I knew this would happen. "I just told you I haven't even kissed her!"

"Well, what are you waiting for? And make it good, so she wants to keep you! None of that half-assed, three out of five bullshit!" She snickers at the look of pure exhaustion on my face. "Can you tell us a little bit about her? Just quick. Then we'll hang up and leave you alone. Promise."

Turning away from the window with a sigh, I pace the living room, staring at my feet, rubbing my neck. "She's…she's really beautiful. Not just on the outside but the inside too. She's in vet school, and she works at one of the animal shelters here. She's got such a kind heart, and she's the best mom." I shrug. "She makes me feel like things aren't so heavy."

Mom watches me with a quiet, wobbly smile, and Dad gives me two thumbs up behind her, another Fruit Roll-Up in his mouth. I register the soft *drip, drip, drip* of water only a moment before a tiny voice whispers, "Dada," from behind me.

I spin around, eyes locking with Rosie's wide ones from where she stands halfway inside my patio door, Connor bundled in a towel in her arms, Bear panting at her side.

"Okay, Mom, I have to go," I sorta scream.

"Did he just call you da—"

"*Bye*!" It takes me seventeen thousand tries to hit hang up. I shove one hand through my hair and gesture over my shoulder, forgetting about my phone in my hand. It soars through the air and lands with a clatter somewhere behind me. "That was my—my friend was just—I wasn't talking about—that was…" I choose to stop—it seems like the safest bet—and settle for anxious chuckling instead.

"Was that your mom?"

"Who, that?" I wave a hand through the air. "No."

"You said, 'Okay, Mom, I have to go.'"

"Hmmm. Yeah, I see how that could be construed. Definitely."

The corner of Rosie's mouth hitches. "Okay, well, we'll go get changed."

"Great. Awesome. Yeah, and I'll go start the barbecue."

She pauses at my side, smelling like coconut and lime, sunshine, hope, and everything good and right. "You make me feel like things aren't quite so heavy, too, Adam. Just in case you were wondering."

"How the hell did you get mashed potatoes in your eyebrow, bud," I mutter, scrubbing Connor's face with a warm washcloth. He turns away, sending a spray of water up around us when he splashes in the tub. "Jesus Christ, it's in your ear. Rosie! It's in his ear!"

Rosie giggles, dropping to her knees beside me as I scoop out his ear potatoes. "Connor has a knack for getting his dinner in every single crevice. Check his elbow."

I take his small hand in mine and lift his arm. Sure enough, right there in the crease of his elbow, is a clump of potatoes. I shake my head, wiping him down, and the little monkey tries to eat the potatoes out of my hand. "Big trouble and little trouble. Perfect names for you and Mama."

Rosie flicks water at me. "I think it's you who's the troublemaker."

I want to start all sorts of trouble with Rosie, but I'm trying to be on my very best behavior. It's hard, because the sun's on its way down, the air has cooled, and she's currently drowning in one of my T-shirts and a pair of my sweatpants.

Something about a pretty girl in your clothes, wrapped up in your smell…it never gets old.

Bear pushes between us, setting his chin on the edge of the tub. Connor rests his forehead against Bear's as he whispers, "Hi, big dog," and everything feels exactly right with these three beside me.

"I'm really happy you can stay," I say to Rosie as she changes Connor into his pajamas, lays him down in the playpen.

"I wasn't expecting him to do so well for his nap here. He sleeps in my room at home, and we always make it back for naps." She pushes his hair back, smiling down at his tired eyes. "I guess I don't give him enough credit."

"I don't think that's it. You have your routine, and it's not always easy to stray outside of our routines." I nudge her shoulder with mine. "It's about giving up that little bit of control, right?"

"Which I have a hard time doing," she admits.

"But you're doing great."

Her smile is soft and grateful. "Thank you for saying that, Adam."

"Mama." Connor pats around the playpen. "Cat?"

"Oh shoot. That's right." She grabs her bag off the bed and roots around before pulling out a fluffy, orange stuffed cat. "He doesn't do bedtime without Cat."

Connor shuffles to his feet, rubbing his eyes with his fists, Cat tucked under his arm. "Mama, kiss?"

Rosie takes his face in her hands, pressing a kiss to his forehead, both cheeks, and finally his lips. "Good night, baby. Mama loves you."

Connor reaches for me. "Dada, kiss?"

I plant a loud smooch on his forehead. "Good night, little trouble."

With Rosie's hand in mine, I guide her out of the room, turning off the light and quietly shutting the door. She's all nerves right now, fidgety fingers and bouncing eyes, the golden glow of the setting sun streaming through the windows, illuminating the freckles on her nose.

"I'm just gonna call my roommate for advice," she blurts, then smacks her forehead. "To tell him I'll be home later, I mean."

"Meet me out back when you're ready." I kiss her cheek. "I hope he gives good advice."

There's a weird zap of electricity running through me as I get the yard set up, Bear trailing my heels as I go. I'm nervous, but that Rosie is nervous, too, is comforting. Despite my desperate yearning for a solid foundation, a meaningful connection, and a life to share with someone, I've felt slightly off-kilter since I stumbled into Rosie those weeks ago. I know exactly where I want to take things, but in all my attempts to move forward over the last year, I haven't ever actually moved in that direction. Each step forward has ended with two backward. Each date ending in disaster, every time my face has been splashed on some social media outlet next to a woman's I barely knew, I've retreated further into the shadows, clung tighter to every piece of me.

I want to give those pieces to Rosie. I want to open my clenched fists, show her the pieces with shaky hands, and ask her to take me anyway, to like me for me.

For the first time in my life, I don't want to be Adam Lockwood, Vancouver Viper, all-star goalie. I just want to be…

I just want to fucking *be*. I want to exist exactly as I am. I want to be a loyal friend, a loving son. I want to be dependable and kind and generous because I like to be, not because I have to be. I want to be a partner, someone's best friend, the steady hand on their back when they need to be held up, the fingers laced through theirs to walk through life together.

I want to be Adam.

And like it always has, hockey will only get in the way of that.

The patio door opens, sending my heart into a tailspin, pattering against my sternum like heavy rain beating down on a tin roof. My fingers curl into my palms as I take a breath, hoping to slow the racing beat and every erratic thought in my head, and I turn around.

Rosie's a vision, a flawless beauty bathed in the dusky gold glow of twilight, scattered fragments of lavender and peach reflecting off the water, the twinkly lights illuminating the wonder in her gaze as it skates around the yard, taking it all in.

She takes a hesitant step forward, then another, one hand at her throat, the other clutching the hem of my T-shirt she wears. "Adam, this is gorgeous."

"Yeah? I, uh…" I rush to the gazebo, scooping up the flowers I'd had sitting in my dining room all day. I offer them to Rosie with a shaky hand. "I got you more peonies. I hope that's okay."

"Thank you." She takes them with a smile and looks at the inflatable mattress set on the grass, topped with pillows and blankets. "And that?"

"I thought, if you wanted to, we could, um…"

She threads her fingers through mine and squeezes, gentle pressure that settles my heartbeat. I try again.

"I'd like to watch the sunset with you while we lie together."

"I'd really like that."

My heartbeat skips. "Yeah?"

She nods, pulling me toward the mattress, holding my hand as she sinks down to it, pulling me after her. She curls onto her side, cheek resting on a pillow as she gazes at me while I pull a blanket over us.

"This has been such a perfect day, Adam. I'm so glad we didn't need to cancel."

"Connor is always welcome here. I don't want you to ever feel like you have to cancel because you're with him. I like hanging out with him."

Her smile is equal parts grateful and sad, so I give her hand a squeeze.

"Everything okay?"

"It's nice to hear, is all."

I frown. "That I like spending time with Connor?"

She nods. "Brandon, his dad…well, that's the reason I picked him up early today. Or I think so, at least. Kids weren't part of the plan. We weren't that serious, and he ran. He came back, but when Connor was a few months old he said he didn't want to do it anymore, that he wasn't built for it. Disappeared for a while again, came back again." Her eyes coast to my collarbone as I rub my thumb along hers. "It's so mentally taxing. You're either all in or you're not, you know? Connor deserves to feel loved and wanted all the time. I want to protect him from the people who can't offer him consistency."

"I think it's natural as a parent to want to protect your kids from everything that could hurt them."

"Then how come his dad is the one inflicting the hurt sometimes?" She looks away, her nose wrinkling as she worries her lower lip between her teeth. "It's just...Connor was an accident, yes, but he wasn't a mistake. He's the best thing that's ever happened to me, the greatest gift I've ever been given. It hurts that, sometimes, it feels like I'm the only one of us who thinks so."

"That's a heavy weight to carry, Rosie. I hope one day he realizes how lucky he is to have not only Connor but you, too, for bringing Connor into his life."

I stroke my hand through her hair, down her back, as she snuggles closer, nudging her leg between mine. She's given me so much today, pieces of herself she's handed over willingly while I hold back, and I want to give her something. The obvious answer screams at me from inside my head, but I shake the thought away, burying the guilt as I drag out another day without telling her what my job really is, who I am to everyone but her.

"Can I tell you something?"

She shifts back at my tone, giving me her full attention. "Of course."

"I never knew my birth mom. I only know that she was young when she had me, and she struggled with addiction. She got clean while pregnant but relapsed when I was only a few days old. She left me with my grandma and never came back." I run the tip of my finger down Rosie's arm, an anchor to reality, my steady in this unstable moment. "I don't remember my grandma, but I know she loved me very much. In every picture I have, we look so happy together. She had a stroke when I was four. My only memory is this vivid one at her funeral, where this woman with dark curls and blue eyes stared at me from the doorway, and instead of coming in, she turned around and left."

Rosie threads her fingers through mine, softly running her thumb across the back of my hand in a gentle way that lets me know she's here, she's listening.

"The thing is, I've never been mad at her. I don't think she could give me the life or love every child deserves, and she knew that. She thought there was somebody better out there for me, and in leaving, she gave that to me. A chance at something better." I wipe the single tear dripping from Rosie's eye as she cups my cheek. "When you told me about your parents earlier, how the thought of saying good-bye tears you apart, I wanted to take your hand and say you weren't alone, because I'd also lost people. But I haven't felt a loss as deep as yours. Mine is different. People chose to walk away because we weren't meant for each other. They weren't meant for me, and there's a certain peace in knowing that."

"That doesn't make your loss any less valid," Rosie says firmly. "Please don't undermine anything you've gone through because of me."

"I'm not. The truth is, I got so lucky, and I know it. There's no pain in my past, not in my memories, at least. But when you talked to me…I almost wanted there to be. I didn't want you to be alone in feeling yours."

There's a softness in Rosie's gaze, an understanding that pulls us closer, a string knotting. "I don't need you to take on my pain, Adam. I just need you to sit with me while I feel it. That's enough for me." She brushes a curl off my forehead. "Does that make sense?"

"I think so."

"Thank you for sharing that with me."

"Thank *you* for sharing your world with me."

Rosie tucks in closer, the soft inches of her pressed against me bringing me a comfort I didn't know I needed as the remaining fragments of sunlight disappear behind the trees, stars beginning to burst against the dark skyline.

"You can't see the stars with your face buried in there, pretty girl."

She props her chin on my chest, grinning up at me. "I like this view best."

I chuckle, running a thumb over the dimple in her chin. "You're the cutest ever."

Rosie flushes, averting her gaze. I nudge her chin, guiding her eyes back to mine.

"I think it's adorable when you get shy. Your whole body heats, you start nibbling on your lip, and your freckles try to hide beneath those rosy cheeks." The pad of my thumb drags across her lower lip. "You're beautiful, Rosie, and I really like being here with you."

"I really like being here with you too," she breathes. "Are you gonna kiss me now?" Her eyes snap wide and she clamps her mouth shut. "Holy fork—I didn't—no, that was supposed to be—I—"

I swallow her words with my mouth on hers, and, *fuck*, it's everything I could have ever hoped for. It's soft and gentle, the way she melts against me, the noises she makes in the back of her throat. It's everything sweet with a hint of a bite, the tang of grapefruit clinging to her lips, the frantic press of her fingertips on my shoulders, the shift of her curves against the hard lines of my body.

I sink my fingers into her hair, angling her head back. Rosie sighs, her lips parting, letting me in. Her tongue meets mine without hesitation as her hands coast over me, down my arms, my chest, clutching at my shirt as she pulls me closer, tosses her leg over my hip. My hand glides along her thigh, over her ass, gripping her waist as I hold her tight and move against her, sure that I've finally found paradise.

Rosie is bright cerulean skies and the heat of the summer sun kissing your cheeks. She's toes in the sand and crystal clear water splashing at your feet. Rainbows made of flowers and swirls of colors blending together at sunset like a flawless painting. She's escaping reality and living in pure bliss without the racing thoughts and the itch of too many bodies, too many eyes on you.

She's my version of paradise.

I cup her face in my hand, sweeping a thumb across the apple of her cheekbone as I slow us down, taking one last moment to taste her, suck on her lower lip before I press my mouth to hers once, twice more.

Rosie's erratic breath mingles with mine, color blooming in her cheeks. She presses two trembling fingers to her swollen lips. "Wow."

"Yeah."

"I…I meant to say that in my head. The kiss thing. And honestly, the *wow* too."

"I like when you think out loud."

"A lot of my thoughts are about you," she admits.

I blow out a breath of relief and pull her into my chest. "Thank fuck, because all of mine are about you."

"What's eating you?"

"Hmm?"

My eyes lift to my rearview mirror, catching sight of Connor in the back. He's passed out with his stuffie, and he didn't stir longer than a minute when I lifted him out of the playpen and tucked him into the car seat. Rosie, however, is a different story.

"You've been gnawing on your lip for the last fifteen minutes," I tell her, stopping out front of her apartment. I tug her bottom lip free from her teeth. "What's on your mind?"

"I don't want to sound…I'm nervous that I'll sound…I don't want you to think…"

"Rosie."

Her shoulders deflate and she flashes me a guilty grin under the light of the streetlamp. "I really like you, Adam."

"I really like you too."

"But…"

"Oh fuck. Not a but."

She snickers, giving me a shove. "I really like you, *but* I'm not looking for something casual. Honestly, I wasn't looking at all. But now you're here and I don't want to bring my son into something that doesn't have potential to be long term, to be real and serious and good." She takes a breath, tucking her hair behind her ears. "I know I'm only twenty-four, but I want to share a life with someone. I want us to be special to someone. I want to build a family with someone, and I have no problem parting ways with someone who doesn't want that too. Because if Connor is the only family I get in this life…he's enough for me." Dim eyes move over me, and I watch her fingers curl into her fists. "I know some people don't like to talk about commitment, and maybe it's soon. But I—"

For the second time tonight, I swallow her words, every single one of them. Her truths and her insecurities, the ones that align so perfectly with mine.

"I want that, Rosie." I rest my forehead against hers. "All of it and more."

"I'm scared," she whispers. "Nobody has ever fit into my life. I don't want to know what it feels like to lose that."

"I like being here. I have no plans of leaving." I look to the little boy in the backseat, the soft sound of his deep breathing, back to the enchanting woman in front of me. "You're a package deal, Rosie. That doesn't scare me. I'll tell you as often as I need to until you believe it."

Cautious eyes move between mine. "Promise?"

I hold my pinky out, and she grins, tucking hers around mine, pulling our hands to her chest and my mouth to hers.

"Swear it."

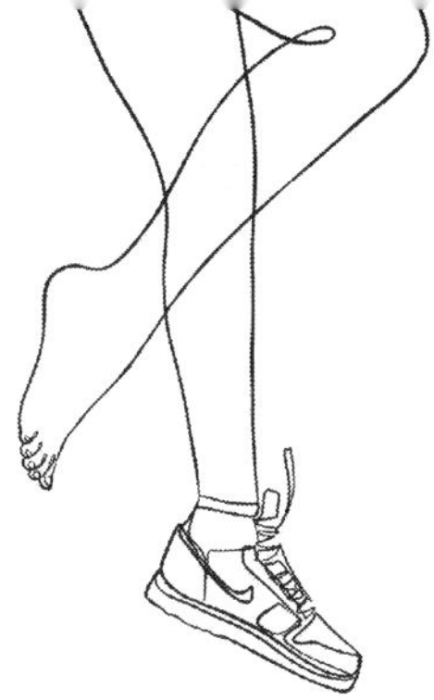

FOURTEEN

IS THAT...VIBRATING?

Rosie

"I think it's clean, Ro." Archie tears the plate I've been washing for five minutes from my hands, rinsing the suds before setting it on the drying rack. "That guy really did dickmatize you, didn't he?"

"Dickmatize is not a real word."

"It is in my vocabulary, and yours now, too, since you've been walking around with that dazed look on your face for days." Archie takes the next plate from me. "Proud of you, though. You're like a horny teenager discovering herself for the first time."

I roll my eyes, flicking suds at him. "I'm a mother; I'm hardly discovering myself for the first time."

"Practically. How many orgasms did Brandon give you while you two were doing…whatever the fuck you were doing? Two?"

"Shut up."

"One?"

My mouth scrunches as I scrub a fork with vigor.

"Rosie, tell me Brandon gave you at least one—"

"I can give myself orgasms, okay?" It comes out a little more Attitude-y Judy than I mean it to, because no, Brandon never gave me an orgasm, and quite frankly, any orgasms I manage to give myself are both fleeting and underwhelming. Better than nothing, I guess.

"I need an orgasm," I say at the exact moment Archie declares, "You need to get laid."

"I don't want to jump into anything with Adam, though." I drain the sink, washing my hands. "I want the physical stuff, but I don't want it to override everything else, you know?"

"It sounds like you guys are moving at a fine pace." He snags my lower lip and tugs it free of my teeth. "What are you really worried about?"

I nibble my thumbnail and lift a shoulder. "What if I'm boring in bed? I don't have a lot of experience, and we never really tried anything different. Is that why Brandon always wanted it to be over so quick? And we never cuddled after. He'd always roll away, or get up to play video games, or—"

"Rosie." Archie takes my face in his hands. "I know he's Connor's dad, but the guy's a total mooncalf; sorry, not sorry. He's never deserved your time, your body, or your heart, but you gave him all of it anyway."

"I just wanted someone to want me." The words are fractured and whispered, and I hate that they hurt, the way they singe the air and leave it heavy and suffocating.

"I know you did, honey. But he left you with more insecurities than you started with, and I hate him for that. You've got a beautiful heart. You're so kind, so smart, and so incredibly strong. He has a way of making you forget that. I don't know Adam, but he seems to make you remember all those things about yourself." Archie takes my hands, a gentle squeeze that always settles my racing thoughts. "Let him build you up. And in the meantime, let's get you some toys so you can work on taking care of yourself."

I slap his hands away. "I don't need a dildo."

"There are these clit suckers too."

"Archie, I'm not buying toys for myself."

He winks, throwing the dish towel over his shoulder as he starts putting the dishes away. "Okay, Rosie."

"*You're* not buying me toys either."

Another wink. "Definitely not, Rosie."

I jab a finger into his shoulder. "Stop saying my name."

A sneaky smirk. "Sure thing, Ro." His chuckle chases after me as I scoop up Connor's diaper bag. "You'd be less grumpy if you got laid."

"Mmm," I grunt out, tossing the bag by the door before I join Connor on the living room floor, where he's playing with his farm animals. "Are you ready to go to the park, baby?"

He picks up the small cow, thrusting it in my face. "Cow! *Moooo!*" The chicken is next, bouncing along my thigh. "Cluck-cluck, cluck-cluck!"

I tap on the green tractor. "And what's this?"

"Trac-*ta*! Brum-brum!"

"Hey, monkey." Archie leans in the doorway. "We goin' to the park?"

Connor leaps to his feet, tossing his animals in a basket before running toward Archie on wobbly legs. "*Pak*! *Pak*!"

I throw my arms in the air. "Doesn't care when I suggest it."

"'Cause I'm cool Uncle Arch." He scoops Connor up, setting him in the wagon and nudging my shoes toward me. "You're just Mom."

Just Mom is trying her hardest to be cool, brave Mom, which is why I'm in my bathing suit again today for my son, chasing him around the splash pad at the park a half hour later beneath the warm summer sun.

"I'm proud of you," Archie tells me when we break for a snack. "You're making big strides with the water lately."

"Connor had the best time swimming with Adam yesterday. He kept jumping in, right into Adam's arms. He was so happy. I went in too. All the way."

Archie stares at me, brows hiked, lips parted.

"Okay, I clung to Adam, and he promised he wouldn't drop me. It wasn't as hard as I thought it would be, once I was in there, but I'd guess that has more to do with him."

"Did you tell him? About—"

"That I almost drowned? Yeah."

"And your parents?"

"I told him they passed away."

"But you didn't tell him the two were related?" he guesses. "You nearly drowning and your parents passing?"

I shake my head, shame creeping up my throat.

"Hey." Archie squeezes my knee. "It's okay. There's no rush."

"It's just…what if I give him too much? Too soon? Then if it doesn't work out, I've lost it all again. That sounds silly, I know, but—"

"It's not silly, Rosie, but I do wish you weren't always expecting the worst. I get it, though. Or I try to, at least."

"Adam was in the foster system too," I tell him quietly.

"Really? What are the chances? Something for you two to connect over."

"Yeah, I thought so, too, but then..." I rub my neck, guilt making my throat tight. "I didn't tell him I was in foster care. Our experiences were different. He was four, and he was adopted in under a year."

Archie nods. "So you feel like, rather than connecting over a shared experience, they were way too different for Adam to possibly sympathize with you."

I drop my face, ashamed. "How awful am I? Nobody is in the system for happy reasons. But when he talked about finding his family, I was just...so jealous. And I feel dirty for feeling that way, Arch. I'm an adult now. I should be over this. I've got a family of my own now. I have nothing to complain about."

"Is that how that works? Your parents die, leaving you all alone in a big, scary world, you want nothing more than to find a family who'll choose to love you, and when you don't find that, you're supposed to just grow up and get over it?" Archie shakes his head. "No, your experience definitely doesn't diminish his, but neither does his diminish yours."

"I should've told him then that I was in the system too," I argue, "but I was so focused on how different our experiences were, how we couldn't possibly connect because of those differences, how jealous I was, that I couldn't share it."

"Meeting someone where they're at isn't always about finding a way to relate to what they've gone through. He shared something and you listened, which is all he could really ask for. What's going on in your head is your own business. Your feelings are valid and you need to process them, and look at you, doing it right now. You don't need to punish yourself because you immediately made assumptions about someone else."

It makes sense, all of it, and Archie's always been this person for me, the one who hears my thoughts and validates all of them before helping me through the other side. It takes me a while to get there sometimes, that's all.

"Hey." He cups my face, forcing my eyes to his. "You spent a long time convincing yourself you weren't lovable because nobody chose you. You wanted to be someone's first choice, and you weren't. But we aren't for everyone. There's always been something better waiting for you." He points to Connor. "You're that little boy's first and only choice. And you'll be someone else's first choice when it comes to love too.

Maybe it'll be Adam, maybe it won't. But what matters most, Rosie, is that you're your own first choice. Love yourself for exactly who you are and where you're at, mistakes, imperfections, and all. The people who are going to choose you will love all your pieces, not just some of them."

"Come on. Just one quick glimpse at his Instagram."

"Absolutely not."

Marco shakes his phone at me, the same way he's been doing for the last hour while trying to pry Adam's last name out of me so he and Archie can snoop his profile. "Come on. Don't you wanna see if he's got any pictures of his exes?"

"That sounds like a terrible idea." The last thing I want to do is compare myself to any woman he's dated in the past. I work hard to be happy with the way I look, and it's not always easy. Comparison is the thief of joy.

"Okay, we don't care about exes. That's good. Can't you just show your hot boyfriend off to your besties?"

"He doesn't have social media," I lie lazily, ignoring that boyfriend label that we haven't discussed.

"What kind of a loser doesn't have social media in this day and age?"

I pin my arms across my chest and scowl at Marco's ridiculous, toothy grin as Archie hides behind a couch cushion. "Me." The buzzer by the door rings and I race over to it, thinking it might be Adam. "Hello?"

"I've, uh…" The unknown voice on the other side clears his throat. "Got a couple of…packages…for Rosie Wells?"

"Oh. Okay. I'll be down in a minute." I scoop my bag up and frown at Archie. "That's weird, I don't remember ordering anything."

"Mhmm," he hums, folding his lips into his mouth. "So weird."

"I'll grab the packages and wait out front for Adam. See you later."

"Byyye," Archie calls over his shoulder.

"Nice choice on the dress," Marco adds. "Easy access."

Easy access. Psssh. *Please.* It's not like I'm hoping to feel Adam's hands on my legs during the movie tonight, below the stars at the drive-in. I'm absolutely *not* dreaming of his fingers sliding higher, dipping below the hem of my dress in the dark. And I did *not* wear my prettiest pair of pink silk panties in hopes that he might touch them, or better yet, see them.

Absolutely not.

Okay, fine, but it's not my fault. We've been spending so much time together, with Connor and without, and I've thoroughly enjoyed every single time that man has put his tongue in my mouth over the last week. I'm starting to crave…I don't know exactly, but more. A little bit more. Sue me for hoping I might get it tonight.

The elevator pops open, revealing the very man I can't stop thinking about, his head down as he examines the plethora of brightly colored packages swept up in his arms.

"Adam. Hey. I was just coming down to get those. You didn't have to…" My words trail as his face slowly lifts, mouth hanging open, cheeks pink. At the same time I note the look in his eyes—intrigued, and yet, slightly scared—I note the faint buzzing sound coming from one of the packages.

Adam takes a step toward me, and I take one back, hand at my throat in case I need to squeeze it to stop from, oh, I don't know, throwing up?

"What's that?" I whisper, but I already know.

Adam takes another careful step toward me, then another, until I'm plastered against the wall. "Uh, the delivery guy…he was…and I was coming in to get you…and so I thought…" He opens his mouth, then pauses, brows pulled down like he's lost for words. "And then I…and then this one…" He holds up the buzzing package, at least eight inches in length, hot pink with neon yellow letters that read *FOR HER PLEASURE* all over it. Adam swallows, and blood thunders in my ears. "It started…vibrating."

"I didn't buy those," I blurt out. "I-I-I…I didn't." Adam's mouth quirks, a tiny tug on one side, like he either doesn't believe me or suddenly finds this horrific situation…*endearing*. And I don't know why —I should be squeezing my throat, stopping it—but I go for it: word vomit. "Archie told me to and I said no but he-he-he never listens to me and I haven't had an orgasm in a long time and never with another person." My hands fly to my mouth, slapping over my gasp, eyes wide. "Oh my God. I can't believe I just said that."

I clear my throat, scooping the several packages out of Adam's arms and into my own. "Excuse me for a moment."

It starts a casual stroll back down the hall but turns into an angry, fast stomp.

"Figured you'd be back," Archie mumbles when I burst through the door.

"You motherfucker," I grit out, dropping the bundle on our kitchen table. Seven. There are *seven. Fucking. Packages.* "I hate you."

"Mhmm. Tell me again after you give those a whirl." He cocks his head at the buzzing sound. "You already turn one on?"

"No, Archie, I did not." I pick up the vibrating package, trying to ignore how long this thing is. "Adam picked these up for me in the lobby, and this one started *buzzing* in his hands."

He and Marco stare at each other for five silent seconds. Then they explode with laughter.

I let the pink package fly before I turn around, throwing my middle finger up over my shoulder when a satisfying *thwack* sounds as the package makes contact. "Fuck you very much."

~

My silk panties have been wasted.

Okay, not a total waste. I feel sexy wearing them, and every time Adam's hands grazed slowly up my thigh, the anticipation alone was worth it. It's not as if I *actually* expected him to get touchy during a movie, with people around, even though it was dark and we were parked all the way at the back, so if he'd *really* wanted to, he *could have.* Just saying.

Now it's midnight, we're driving along a back road in the middle of nowhere, and the last place I want to go is home.

I can't tear my gaze off Adam, one hand on the steering wheel, legs spread wide, his ebony curls ruffling in the breeze from the open window. He's so relaxed, so at home, so freaking *beautiful,* and he's here with *me.*

Adam looks over at me, the same way he's been doing every thirty seconds, cobalt blue eyes alight. A gentle smile starts in the corners of his mouth before exploding into a cheek-splitting grin when he catches me staring. He reaches over, fingers spreading over my thigh, sliding achingly slowly up, up, up, until he reaches the hem of my dress and squeezes.

"Whatcha thinking about, pretty girl?"

"I'm not ready to go home."

His eyes drop to my lips, skim down my arms, coast the length of my bare legs before coming back up to mine. "No?"

I shake my head.

"Not tired?"

"Not yet," I breathe out.

"Mmm..."

My eyes hook on his middle finger, following its path as the tip drags slowly along my thigh, around my knee, coming back up the inside. All of the air is sucked out of the car, and my heart pounds a relentless beat in my chest before dropping between my legs.

"Hmm." He steals his touch back, gripping the steering wheel with both hands. Leaning forward, he stares out the windshield, brows furrowed.

"What?"

He pulls his bottom lip between his teeth and hums. "Think we're lost."

"Lost?" I look around at the black night. In the light of the moon, all I can see are trees and never-ending fields. "Here?"

"Mhmm. Don't know how that happened." He pulls the truck over and cuts the ignition, leaving only the radio running. He fiddles with his phone before soft, slow music pours from the speakers, drenching the summer night air. "Might as well make the best of it," he says with a sneaky smirk before he hops out.

I'm not sure what he means, but I watch with rapt attention as he rounds the hood, opens my door, holds his hand out to me.

"Dance with me, trouble."

A giggle slips free, and Adam's hands swallow my waist, lifting me from the truck. Long fingers tangle with mine, pulling me before the dim headlights, beneath the dancing stars above. He wraps one arm around my waist and smiles at me before tugging me into his chest, his lithe body swaying against mine as he hums along to the music.

"Can I tell you something?" he murmurs, sinking his hand into the hair at the back of my head, holding me close. "I'm never ready to say good night. Not to you, Rosie." Soft lips touch the spot below my ear, nibble along the edge of my jaw before claiming my mouth. His tongue sweeps inside, slow, deep, purposeful, and so damn hot every inch of me singes with heat. "If I never had to close my eyes again, that'd be okay, so long as I could keep them on you. Can't seem to take them off you whenever you're around."

I curl my fingers into his curls and try my best to hold on. "You can't?"

He shakes his head. "I know what movie we saw, but I couldn't tell you a damn thing that happened." He pulls my hands from his hair, twining his fingers with mine and raising them above his head, spinning me out before pulling me right back in.

He twists a lock of hair around his pointer finger. "All I could see was the way you twined these waves around your fingers while you watched me from the corner of your eye." His finger glides across my collarbone, dragging the strap of my dress off my shoulder, touching his lips to the freckles that live there. "The way the light from the screen danced along these shoulders." With two fingers, he lifts my chin. "The way the moon shone in these eyes every damn time you smiled at me, like you were as happy to be there with me as I was with you. Fuck, I love these fucking eyes."

His name leaves my lips on a whimper, and he wastes no time swallowing it, hands on my ass as he lifts me to him, my legs winding around his waist as he carries me around the truck. There's a low *thud*, and my heartbeat trips when he drops me on his tailgate.

Adam's hands land on either side of me, bracketing me in as he leans over me. "So you're gonna need to tell me what that movie was about, because I sure as fuck don't know. All I know is you, Rosie. And I think that's all I want to know."

I lick my lips, the look in his eyes heady and starved. "I don't know," I admit.

"No?"

"No. I wasn't…I wasn't watching either."

"Mmm…" His gaze drops to my thighs, and they spread for him, inviting him in, closer. I see the pleased smile he tries to hide before he steps between them, hands gliding up my legs, fingertips dipping below my dress, grabbing my hips. "So then what were you doing?"

"I was…" Fire brews in my belly and dries my throat as he shifts my dress higher and higher. "Distracted."

"Distracted by what?"

"Your hand—you were doing—you kept—" His warm palm slides

down my thigh, thumb skimming the hem of my dress. A shuddering breath escapes my throat, and I sigh as my skin dots with goose bumps. "Yeah. That."

He chuckles lowly, warm breath skittering across my bare shoulder as he presses his lips there, trailing his mouth toward my neck, along the slope, finding its way to my ear. "I'm sorry I'm a distraction. But it's only fair, isn't it? If I'm not watching, neither are you."

"Yeah, but I wasn't..." My head drops between my shoulders as Adam pushes me back just a touch, one hand on my chest, the other wrapped around my bare hip as he opens his warm mouth against my neck. "I wasn't making you...wild...by touching you."

"Wild?"

"It was too much...and not enough. I wanted..." I gasp as he tugs the strap off my shoulder, slides his mouth along it, his teeth grazing the sensitive skin before his tongue soothes the faint bite. "More. God, I wanted more."

"Is that right?" he murmurs. "You wanted to be touched where anyone could've seen you?"

"I...I don't know." Is that what I wanted? Out in the open, under the fake security that blanketed us beneath the dark sky? Would I have let him?

I know as soon as the question skates across my mind that the answer is yes. Not just yes, but *hell yes*. I've never been bold. I'm used to blending in; disappearing, really. I've spent so many years unseen. With Adam, for the first time in so long, I feel seen. But it's more than that. I don't just feel seen; I feel like I'm the only person in his world when I'm with him.

So would I have cared about anyone else if he'd dared touch me tonight? No, I wouldn't have.

"I just wanted to be touched by you."

A rough growl rumbles from his chest, a hum of approval that vibrates so deep, I feel it in my belly and right down to my toes. His palms drag up my thighs, his touch so feral, like he's bordering on unhinged. "Like this?"

My chest rises and falls sharply. "Yes."

"And what about this?" Fingers slip beneath my panties, grabbing two handfuls of my ass, squeezing me closer.

"Yes."

"And this, Rosie? Did you want me to touch you like this?" His hands glide over my hips, bracketing the juncture of my thighs, holding them open for him as his thumbs graze along the edge of my panties, over ultra-sensitive skin, making me squirm. He hooks a finger under my chin, forcing my gaze to his as the pad of his thumb skims over my clit, making it ache more than it already is.

"Adam," I cry quietly, my head falling backward. His mouth finds my throat, and I feel his smile there, his pleasure.

"Yes, Rosie?"

"Please," I whimper. "Touch me, please."

It's that six-letter word, I think, that pushes him over the edge. He wastes no time flipping my dress up, revealing my panties, the soaked spot decorating the center of the pink silk.

"Jesus," he rumbles, a shuddering breath leaving his lips before he takes my mouth with a kiss that leaves us both breathless and hot.

With a punishing grip, he digs his fingers into my hips, hooks his thumbs into the waist of my panties, and guides them down my legs, slipping my sandals off in the process. He crushes the silk in his fist, eyes hooded and hooked on the action before he stuffs them in his pocket and comes right back, hands on mine as he nudges my nose with his and claims a kiss that belongs only to him.

"If you want me to stop—"

"God, Adam, please don't fucking stop. I'll beg you if I need to."

He grins, and I'm struck by how boyish it is. Happy and so damn proud, just the right amount of cheeky arrogance. "As much as I wouldn't mind hearing you beg, I'd rather give you anything and everything you want and need. You only have to tell me, and it's yours."

"It's been a really long time," I admit. "I want you to be gentle and patient, because I'm nervous. But mostly…" My hands slip up his corded arms, over his wide shoulders, curling into his soft curls as I brush my lips across his. "Mostly, I just want you."

"I'm yours," he tells me, right before he sinks his tongue into my mouth, lifts me to him. He grinds himself into me, and every inch of me short-circuits at the feel of him, the weight, *the need*. He needs me, wants me, as much as I do him.

"Oh God," I whimper as he tugs my head back, teeth skimming the columns of my throat.

"Is this what you wanted?" Adam whispers as his mouth moves

across my collarbone, one hand finding my breast. "To be touched in the back of my truck?"

"Yes," I cry out as he nips the delicate skin on my shoulder, his tongue lashing over it, sealing it with pleasure. The pad of his thumb scrapes over my nipple, burning right through my dress when he squeezes and rolls it, and I rake my nails down his arms. "*Adam*."

"Would you have made all these noises? Let people hear you?" Hot breath rolls down my neck, making me shiver as his teeth graze my ear. "They would've wanted to see. See the gorgeous girl come undone just for me." He grips my hips and yanks me to the edge of the truck bed before spreading my thighs wide.

"Thing is, Rosie..." His eyes drop, lock on the spot between my legs, the one that shows him how badly I crave him, and a wicked smirk tugs at his mouth. "I don't like to share." He swipes two fingers along my slit, gathering my wetness and making me gasp. Then he sinks them in his mouth, slow, savoring, and when he licks his lips, I'm sure I've died and gone to heaven. "They can't have your noises." He sinks a single, broad finger inside, and my head falls back, lips parting on a whimper. Adam tangles his fingers in my hair, pulling my gaze back to his as he works his finger in and out. "They can't have your mouth, the way it opens just for me." His thumb finds my clit, a firm pressure with a slow, torturous roll, and when my begging eyes hook on his, he grins. "And they sure as shit can't have your eyes." His mouth meets mine with another brain-melting kiss before the next words tumble out, low, promising, and so damn rough. "Because I'm not. Fucking. Sharing."

"Ohhh *God*." I shove my hands through the sleeves of his T-shirt and grip his bare shoulders below, fingernails digging in as I cling to him, and maybe sanity too.

"Just Adam is fine," he whispers, that low voice dipped in mirth, a certain smugness that's so rare from him but so beautiful too.

My hips move, lifting, rolling, chasing the friction of his hand, begging for *more*, and *harder*, and *please*, and fuck does he ever listen, giving me everything I want and more, until I'm panting, ready to combust.

"Jesus, listen to you. And you were gonna give them these noises?" He cocks his head, tsking. "No, these are all mine, trouble."

"All yours," I barely manage, sinking my fingers into the curls at the nape of his neck, tugging his forehead down to mine as I start to unravel.

"Fuck." His brows furrow, and he closes his eyes, gives his head a tiny shake. "Didn't think it was possible."

I press my lips to his, coaxing his eyes open. "What?"

The pad of his thumb scrapes across my lower lip. "For you to get any more beautiful. But here you are, looking up at me like that, your lips swollen and red, your hair a mess, and you, so…" Electric blue eyes dip, roaming over me with a wild intensity that sets fire to my skin. "So fuckin' *flushed*. Like you can't get enough. Like you're coming alive." He pushes a second finger inside, making me shake as his thumb rubs my clit, then swallows my gasp with his mouth. "Beautiful isn't enough, Rosie. You're fucking immaculate."

And here's the most incredible thing: *I believe him*.

I tell myself that's why the pit low in my stomach begins to bloom, why my spine starts to shake and my toes curl, despite never getting this far with Brandon. Because on top of the mind-blowing pleasure he's delivering, it's the confidence, the powerful sensation that comes with feeling so wanted. Treasured. *Seen*.

It's been too long since anyone has seen me.

"Was I dreaming earlier when you said you've never orgasmed with anyone?"

I whip my head side to side as my thighs begin to quiver. "Never."

"Mmm. That's a fucking crime." He watches me with a barely contained hunger as I lean back on my hands, and when my head rolls over my shoulders, he clamps his mouth over my neck, dragging it up my throat until it finds my ear. "The second you come on my fingers, this pussy is mine."

Holy mother of—yup, that'll do it. Adam knows, too, because he gets this smirk on his face, halfway to wicked.

"Ready, pretty girl?" He chuckles, a dark, gruff sound that grates against the hollow of my collarbone as he traces it with his lips. "Silly question, huh? The way you're suffocating my fingers and clawing at my shoulders tells me so."

His fingers slide into the hair at the nape of my neck, pulling my head taut as he curls the fingers inside me and whispers, "Come, Rosie," against my mouth, and I let him throw me right off the edge of the cliff.

It feels like I'm falling, drowning, and right at the last second, he pulls me up and breathes life back into me, his lips on mine as he swallows my cries.

A satisfied moan grates in his throat as I ride his fingers, rock against the waves of pleasure that beat like heavy rain inside me as Adam's mouth moves against mine, murmuring that word he promised, the only word I want to hear.

"Mine."

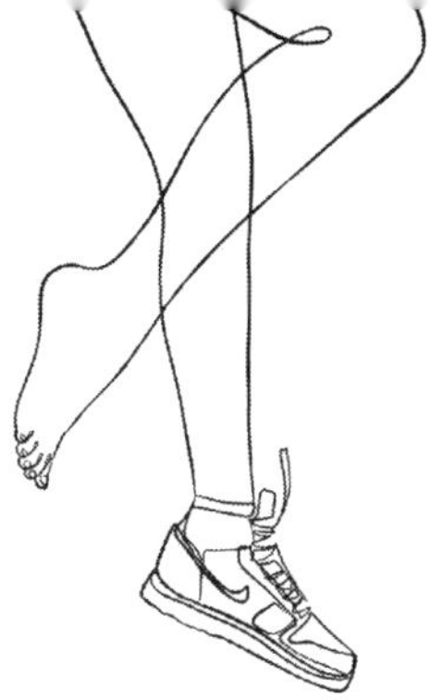

FIFTEEN

THE ONE WHERE THEY WORE FAKE MUSTACHES

Rosie

Early Monday mornings at Wildheart are near impossible to beat. It's a slow start, the quiet hum of music drifting from the radio on the front desk, the soft purr of the cats lounging in their pods while they wait for their forever homes, stretching lazily in the sunshine, bellies out and begging for scritches.

There's a certain peace that comes with being the only one here for an hour or two while the rest of the world wakes up from their weekends. It's a safe type of happiness, in a bubble of contentment, pretending for just a moment that we're not all restarting on Mondays, rushing out the door, and gearing up for a long, drawn-out week where you can barely stand by the end of it.

A wet nose nudges my pocket, and I smile down at Piglet. "You like Monday mornings, too, huh?"

What she really likes is the treats tucked in my pocket. Her nose spots those things from a mile away, and she won't stop looking up at me with those ginormous gooey-brownie eyes until I give her one. Or five.

"You're irresistible, you know that, Pig?" She takes the treat from my palm and trots happily beside me, making our way to the cat sanctuary, her favorite place to be. Turns out she's got a mothering streak a mile wide.

She's been incredible with Adam and Bear on our weekly hikes, and though she still seems so utterly depressed when I head to her kennel first thing in the morning, the moment she spots me, she leaps to her feet, tail wagging, tongue out, ready for any adventure. On quiet mornings like these, I wear her lead around my waist, let her walk around the shelter with me. She loves the newfound freedom, but, God, these cats. I don't think she'd ever seen one before, judging by the way she stared with the widest eyes at the first one through its door for five minutes straight, not moving a single muscle.

And then that cat stood, stretched, walked right over to Piglet, and touched her tiny pink nose against her big, wet black one, and all hell broke loose.

Piglet leapt into the air, spun around butt first, and promptly dropped to her back with her belly up, ready to play with the fluffball. She's been great socialization for the cats, and they for her.

Archie thinks Piglet will be ready for adoption soon. The thought makes my palms itchy and my throat thick. So badly, I want her home to be with me. I don't want to have to say good-bye to her. I want to be the person she trusts, the lap she throws herself in every morning, the face she covers with kisses.

But she deserves more than me. More time, more money, more space. I've got the love; I just don't have anything else. And Piglet deserves it all, not just the scraps.

A car door slams out front, followed by deep laughter, and I peek out the front window as two men approach the entrance. Piglet cocks her head, hesitant but curious.

I smooth the spot between her eyes as she nuzzles her head in my palm. "You want to say hi, girl? Are you up for it?"

She stays glued to my leg as she follows me to the front desk. When our guests stroll in, she scurries behind me, nearly stuffing her entire face in my butt.

"You're safe, Pig," I tell her. "I won't let anything happen to you. I promise."

"Oh shit," one of the men murmurs. "That's Piglet."

My forehead crumples. Maybe Archie's been sharing her picture on the shelter's social media page. Sometimes he does these photoshoots with ridiculous hats, and they go *viral*. I don't understand it, but people always rush in to see the animals afterward. Maybe my Pig has gone…viral.

Ugh. I don't like the sounds of that.

The men are about my age, maybe a bit older. One with golden waves and turquoise eyes, the other with brown hair and tattoos. Both ridiculously large and attractive, with happy, easy grins and a presence around them that seems oddly…warm. Friendly. They also both have mustaches, one brown and one blond, but the shape is so identical, so clean and perfect, they almost look…fake.

Yes, I'm certain these mustaches are fake as hell, but I don't know why.

Piglet doesn't seem to second-guess the mustaches, shoving her head between my legs, sending me toppling sideways into the desk, her nose going a mile a minute while she sizes them up.

"She's fucking cute, dude," the tattooed one whispers to his blond friend.

"Sorry. This is Piglet. She's one of our rescues, and she's learning to trust men. And yes, she is super cute, and she knows it."

The blond crouches down, smiling at her. "We won't bother you, pretty girl."

Pig's tail starts thwacking against the desk. She doesn't get any closer, but the tension in her lithe body dissipates as she looks between us.

"Can I help you guys?"

The blond leaps to his feet and shoves a hand through his hair, looking to his friend with wide eyes. "Uh, yeah. Yeah, we were gonna…" He slaps his friend's chest with the back of the hand. "You were gonna look at those…those…cats."

The tattooed man claps his hands together. "Yeah! Yeah, I was gonna look at those cats! For you, though. 'Cause you wanted to get Jennie a… a cat. For her birthday."

"I'm not fucking getting her a cat. It starts with one, next thing you know I'll have five cats and three dogs and I'll be sleeping by myself on the couch." He jabs his friend in the shoulder. "*You're* getting the fucking cat, douchewaffle."

"Uh…right, so…" I thumb toward the cat den. "Cats?"

"Yeah," that tattooed one says, shooting a feral look back at his friend. "But we're just browsing, if that's okay."

"Of course." That's how it always goes, mostly, and then they're back a week or two later, just to see if the cat they fell for is still here. Then a couple days after that, and another day after that, this time with adoption paperwork, a crate, and a brilliant smile to take their new friend home. We have one of the highest turnover rates in Vancouver. Our cats are rarely here more than a few weeks, unless for medical reasons. Archie says it's thanks to his cats in hats photo sessions.

Piglet and I lead the way to the cat den, and as the men's hushed whispers trail behind us, I'm fairly certain they're talking about me.

"It's definitely her…pink hair…no, dude, he didn't say it was *all* pink, he said it had pink *in* it."

My hand goes to my hair, curling around the rose ends. For a moment, I wish I blended in with the cream-colored walls.

"She heard you, dipshit. Now she's gonna think we don't like her hair."

A throat clears, and I glance back, ears heated, as the blond man offers me a kind smile. "Uh, I like your hair. It's really pretty and unique."

His friend's head bobs. "Yeah, and super cool. It suits you."

My shoulders inch away from my ears, and my hand falls from my hair. "Thank you." As I step into the room, Piglet yanks me toward a cage full of kittens. They're her favorite, rambunctious and full of love, and they're feral for her.

"Holy fuck." The blond pokes his finger through the gated door, and a tiny black fluffball attacks it. "Look at this cutie."

Tattoos rolls his eyes. "As if you're not adopting a—*oh my fucking shit.*" He stops in front of our newest arrival, a giant ball of white fluff with a few strategically placed orange blobs, like the ones on all four paws and around his right eye. "Who's this squishy marshmallow?"

"He doesn't have a name yet. He just came in a few days ago. He was left behind when his owners moved out of their apartment, so we don't have any documentation on him." The cat flops over when I open his cage, paws in the air, belly on display. The man steps forward without hesitation.

"Oh shit," he chuckles, ticking his belly. "You're a cute little fucker." Lifting one paw, he frowns. "Is it just me, or does he have too many toes?"

I nod. "He's polydactyl."

"Poly-what'll?"

"Polydactyl," I giggle, watching as he hoists the cat into his arms like a baby. "He's got an extra toe on each paw, but it doesn't impact his life." I scratch at his chin. "Just more of you to love, huh, bud?"

"It's like he's wearing mitts. Huh, buddy? That's what your name should be." He buries his face in the cat's belly, and the cat mewls, licking the man's wavy hair. "Mittens."

The blond snickers. "Mittens? Wow, big, tough Jaxon." His mouth opens on a silent scream as his friend's fist lands square against his shoulder, and he clutches the injured limb while slapping at his friend's face. "Ow, you donkey!"

The cat—Mittens?—hisses and swats at the blond. The man—Jaxon? —hides his smile in his fur. "Good boy, Mittens."

I grin at them. "You two would make such a cute couple."

Jaxon pulls his mortified face from Mittens' belly. His friend's jaw drops, and he steps back.

"No, but I—I have—Jennie's my—*I have a Jennie*!"

Jaxon gestures at him with one flail-y arm. "And I'm way hotter than him!"

"Are not!"

"Am too!"

"I'm a huge upgrade for you!"

Jaxon shoves a finger in his shoulder, and the cat hisses and swats at him again. "You're a fucking downgrade, bud! Mittens thinks so too! And Rosie. Rosie, tell him!"

I cock my head, frowning. "How do you know my name?"

Both men stop fighting, and maybe breathing. They lock eyes, fear taking hold of them, stretching across their faces. The blond's mustache dislodges from his face, hanging on to the corner of his mouth for dear life.

He comes to life then, shoving his hand in his pocket, bringing his silent phone to his ear. "Jennie? You-you need me? Okay, yeah, I'll be right there."

Jaxon tucks Mittens back into the cage. "Sorry, Mitts, gotta go!" He makes it three steps before rushing back, popping a kiss on his furry head, whispering, "Love you, chunk." He waves over his shoulder, jogging down the hall after his friend. "Bye, Rosie! Bye, Piglet!"

Through the window, we watch them hightail it into their car and speed down the road.

I meet Piglet's gaze, as lost as mine. "Men are weird, Pig. Don't tie yourself down, girl."

~

"You said you were going to drop him off to me at work." I shove the stroller through Brandon's door and blink the rain from my eyes. I'm soaked to the bone, my hair a matted mess.

Brandon doesn't look away from the TV. "Yeah, but then it started raining, and I didn't wanna go out."

"You have a car," I remind him, catching Connor as he crashes into me, scooping him into my wet chest and hugging him tight. "I'm so happy to see you, buddy."

"If you don't wanna walk, then maybe you should get your license and your own car, rather than expecting everyone else to accommodate you."

Blood rushes to my ears, thrumming angrily as Brandon tips back a beer, watching a baseball game. "I don't expect anyone to accommodate me. I do expect the father of my child might sometimes share the effort and drop him off or pick him up so that I'm not always the one doing so."

He tosses a handful of chips into his mouth. "Sounds like it's your expectations that are the issue then, Ro." Finally, he glances at me over his shoulder. "Jesus, you look like shit."

Everything inside me bubbles to a rolling boil, despite the chatter of my teeth from my soaked body and the chill of the air-conditioning. I clench my fists before strapping Connor in his stroller and tucking his stuffed kitten into my bag, ignoring Brandon.

"What's that big bag for?"

"We're going somewhere," I mutter.

"Where?"

"To my friend's."

"You don't have any friends."

I close my eyes to the outburst brewing inside me. "I'm seeing someone, and we're going to spend some time with him." It's our first sleepover, and I'm a lot less excited about it now that I feel like a drowned rat and Brandon has so lovingly pointed out that I look like shit.

Choking sounds from over my shoulder, and though I'm tempted to leave and hope nature takes its course, I glance over my shoulder as he sputters on his beer.

"You have a boyfriend?" His eyes darken, dropping down my body, a smirk tugging up his lips. "Where'd you find him? On the corner?"

"You're being a jerk."

"I just mean—and hey, no offense—but you haven't been taking very good care of yourself. You've gained some weight."

Anger clenches my jaw. I focus on Connor, his wide green eyes set on mine, so full of love and concern. "I had a baby."

"Sixteen months ago. Can't use that excuse forever, can you? Plus, you had a c-section. Isn't that the easy way out?" Brandon turns back to the TV, crunching another handful of chips. "Don't take it to heart or anything. You just gotta start hitting the gym or something." Another swig of beer. "Don't want you setting a bad example for our son."

A bad example? Like refusing to keep your son for your time because he's having a difficult day and you don't want to deal with it? Not showing him the love he needs and deserves because you'd rather hang out with your friends and get drunk? Or talking down to his mother in front of him, making her feel like shit so you can feel better about yourself?

The words are there, right on the tip of my tongue, burning like acid. But like I've done so many times before, I force myself to swallow them down, to feel the burn myself, like I somehow deserve it more than he does. Like I'd rather he forget about me like everyone else in my life has, and maybe if I'm quiet, he will.

But his words prickle at my skin, as sharp as the stinging rain slapping at my face as I stomp toward the bus stop, Connor safe under his rain shield. And when the sky opens up with a boom of thunder and a clap of lightning, something inside me opens, too, pouring down my face to remind me how weak I am, how weak I've always been, even when I've tried so hard to be strong.

The heavy, humid air becomes suffocating, and through the mixture of rain and tears, I can barely see the sidewalk in front of me. Can barely see the truck slowing down, stopping alongside me. The dark curls that pop out, rush over to me, covering me in an umbrella, the handle shoved into my fist.

But I feel the heat of his hands as they pull me into his body, an embrace that's so much more than warm. I feel his lips at the crown of his head, his fingertips as they grip my chin, feel his mouth take mine without hesitation, the way his tongue glides so effortlessly against mine before he finally pulls back, letting us both breathe.

"What are you doing here?" I whisper as he lifts Connor from the stroller, plopping a kiss on both his cheeks as my sweet boy squeals with excitement for his *dada*.

"Couldn't have my two favorite people walking in the rain," Adam says simply as he buckles Connor into the car seat in the back of his truck. He closes the door and turns to me, smile slipping off his face. "Why are you crying?"

"I-I'm not," I insist pathetically, swatting at my tears. "It's the rain. It looks like tears, because, water, but it's-it's…" I sniffle, then hiccup, and drag the back of my wrist across my nose. "I'm not crying."

He takes my face in his strong hands, thumbs swiping at the droplets rolling down my cheeks. "Then I'll kiss the rain away," he murmurs before his lips touch my cheeks, over and over, tiny kisses that make everything better and worse at the same time. And when I fall apart in his arms, he simply holds me against him, his voice in my ear, telling me he's with me.

And I know he is. I know it by the way he keeps his fingers twined through mine, one hand on the steering wheel the whole drive back to his house. As I stand at the bottom of his staircase, watching him and Connor practice going up and down for ten minutes, the way Adam scoops him into his arms, twirls him in the air, and celebrates every time they make it back down. When he pulls out the wooden stool he built just for Connor so my little man can stand with him at the kitchen counter while they make dinner together.

And when he glances over his shoulder and smiles at me and his dog snuggled on the couch with a glass of wine, I realize I'm finding a home, a family, right here with a man who walked into my life one afternoon and never looked back, chose every inch of me, not just some of me.

"Are you anxious about heading back to school in a few weeks?" he asks me as we wash the dishes side by side after dinner, Connor and Bear playing on the living room floor.

"Yes," I admit with a sigh. "My school schedule is so demanding, and this year will be even more so. Connor and I never spent so much time apart."

"What's your biggest worry with that?"

"That he'll think he isn't my priority. That he'll feel less loved, less important."

"I get that." He hesitates, like he's sorting his thoughts. "My schedule starts to pick up in September, too, and I'll be out of town a lot. I think I've been a little worried about you feeling less important to me too."

"I don't think it's about the time we have, but how we spend it when we're together." I press a kiss to his bicep before pressing up on my toes and fusing my mouth to his as his forehead comes to rest on mine. "And you always make me feel important when we're together, Adam."

"And I think you always make Connor feel important and loved when you're together. So I get where you're coming from, and I know you're feeling guilty, but if it's any consolation, I don't think there's a way in hell that kid over there feels anything other than so loved by you."

Pressing my lips together to hide my smile, I squint up at him, poke his stomach. "I see what you did there. Sneaky boy."

He chuckles, winking. "For what it's worth, I am genuinely worried. But I know I'll do my best to make you feel important, just like I know you'll do your best with Connor, because you always do. You do it effortlessly, Rosie."

"Maybe it seems that way, but it's not easy."

"No, because effortless doesn't mean easy. It's effortless because love is meant to be natural, something you feel so deeply and nothing can change it. But all love is hard sometimes."

"It's worth it though, isn't it?"

He smiles, tucking my hair behind my ear before kissing the tip of my nose. "It's always worth it."

"Dada?" Connor appears between us, tugging at Adam's shorts.

Adam ruffles his hair. "What's up, little trouble?"

"Ee-ya, ee-ya, bo?"

"Ee-ya, ee-ya, bo?" Adam's brows pull together as he repeats the sounds, trying to figure out what Connor's asking for as he drags him into the living room. "Yeah, we can ee-ya, ee-ya, bo. For sure."

Connor points at the TV. "Ee-ya, ee-ya, bo, Dada?" He puts his hands in the air and starts dancing around as Adam keeps repeating the sounds, almost silently, trying to piece them together. "*Ee-ya, ee-ya, bo!*"

Adam blinks, then throws his head back. "Oooh! E-I-E-I-O?"

Connor grins, clapping his hands as Adam finds a music video for "Old MacDonald Had a Farm." *"Ee-ya, ee-ya, bo!"*

My heart smiles so big as Adam scoops Connor into his arms, dances around the living room with him without a care in the world, the two of them singing at the top of their lungs, laughing, quacking like ducks, mooing like cows, meowing like cats. This man is so at home with a child in his arms, like it's a role he was always made to fill. That he does it so effortlessly, and with nothing but enthusiasm, only makes me fall that much harder.

"Old MacDonald" turns into "The Wheels on the Bus," about seventeen times over while I sit and watch, snap a few pictures that quickly become favorites, and as I'm about to break up their party and tell Connor it's bath time, Adam's phone vibrates on the counter next to me.

"You have a phone call," I tell him.

"Not important," he says through his laughter, Connor and Bear crawling on top of him.

"It might be. They're calling again."

"All right, c'mon, buddy." He stands, flipping Connor over his shoulder, carting him into the kitchen with one hand while he squeals with laughter. Adam takes his phone, frowning at the call before declining it. "Don't recognize the number. If it's important, they'll leave a message." He drags Connor over his shoulder, the two of them nose to nose. "It's someone's bath time, and I might have gotten some special blue bubbles, just for you."

Connor gasps, chanting one of his favorite words as we head upstairs. *"Bub-bow! Bub-bow!"*

"You didn't have to do all this," I murmur a few minutes later as Adam dips him in his bath, boats and ducks floating along in a sea of turquoise bubbles. I peek over my shoulder at the glow-in-the-dark stars stuck to the ceiling above the playpen, the tractor nightlight casting a dim glow over the room, and something thick clogs my throat.

"Sure I did. He's part of this relationship too. I want him to feel like he has a space here, and I never want you to feel like you have to deal with something on your own."

There's that *R* word, the one that stops everything inside me except the frantic race of my heart. I want to ask him about that, where we are and where we're going, especially with the end of summer looming. Me, back at school, in my busiest year, and him back at work, traveling with the athletes he works with. The worry etched on his face earlier in the kitchen seeps into my bones, but not because I think I'll be any less important to him. But because, after a summer full of him, of us, the idea of going so many days without seeing him, without being wrapped in his arms, held under the steady weight of his gaze, draped in his affection…it floods me with a startling emptiness.

It's in this moment, with Connor gazing at Adam with so much adoration as this man gives him all his attention, loves on him, acts silly with him, and just…has fun with him, I realize how full life has felt with him in it. Connor's always been the only family I needed, but I think with Adam…maybe he completes us.

Adam runs his hand up the back of my thigh, squeezing. "Connor and I can manage bedtime on our own. Why don't you go run yourself a bath to wind down? Don't wanna brag, but the one in my room is the best there is. There are eighteen jets."

"Eighteen?" I breathe out.

He winks. "Eighteen."

God, I can't remember the last time I had a bath. The idea of relaxing for a few moments, peace and quiet where my mind is all my own, it sounds…well, to be honest, it sounds made up.

I take Connor's face in my hands, pressing a kiss to both cheeks, his nose, and then his tiny pout. "Can Adam put you to bed tonight, baby?"

Connor points to Adam. "Dada."

"Adam."

He pats Adam's hand and smiles. "Dada."

"Ad—" I sigh. "Okay. Yeah. Mama loves you, buddy. If you need me, I'll be right here."

The oversized tub in the corner of Adam's bathroom is every bit as glorious as he promised. There's even a stack of fluffy towels and a brand-new bottle of bubble bath waiting for me, like Adam planned for this.

I turn the faucet until the water runs steamy and pour in a generous helping of bubble bath. Sweet vanilla mint and coffee fills the room, and I close my eyes to the smell. My bag waits for me on the bed with clean clothes to change into, but so does one of Adam's clean, oversized T-shirts, and I'd so much rather be draped in him.

Connor's stuffed kitty catches my eye, and I cart it back down the hall. He never sleeps without it.

They're still in the bathroom, the quiet lap of water, musical giggles, and soft words drawing me in. I stop short at the crack in the door, both boys covered in bubble hats and bubble beards, Adam's elbow on his knee, chin propped on his fist like he's deep in thought. It's a ridiculous sight, but one that makes me warm from the tips of my ears all the way down to my wiggling toes.

"I was thinking you could help me ask your mama to be my girlfriend," Adam murmurs to Connor, and my heart stops. "What do you think about that, little trouble? Would it be okay with you if I was Mama's boyfriend?"

Connor plops a heap of bubbles on top of Adam's already bubbly head. "Dada, bub-bow!" He pats his head. "Hair."

Adam reciprocates the gesture, coating Connor's face in another layer of bubble beard, until it hangs halfway down his chest. "You're really special to me, buddy, and so is your mama. That's why I want her to be my girlfriend. Do you think Mama would like that?" With a big sigh, Adam gently drops his forehead to the edge of the tub. "I think so. I hope so. Crap, I don't know, buddy. What if she says no?"

"I won't say no," I blurt, a pair each of excited green eyes and nervous blues coming to me as I push through the door. Dropping to my knees in front of Adam, I take his face in my hands, fingers pushing through layers of bubbles. He looks so ridiculous and adorable, it hurts.

"You are the most beautiful, kind, and thoughtful man on this planet. My heart is already yours. No isn't an option, Adam.

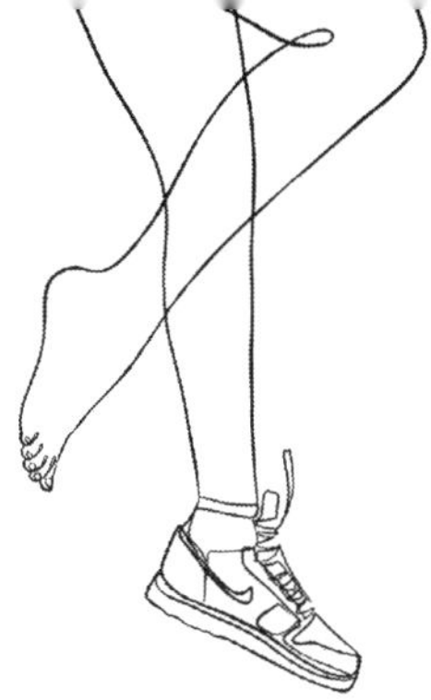

SIXTEEN

THAT'S NOT FITTING ANYWHERE

Rosie

I'VE LOST count of how many times I've wondered why loving ourselves is one of the hardest things we'll ever do.

Most of the time I find I can do it well. I remind myself of all the amazing things this body has done for me, the gifts it's given me, and I wouldn't trade it for the world. And then somebody opens their mouth without reason, and they tear your work down in seconds. You stand there in their wake, gripping the love you carry so tightly in your hands, unwilling to let it go. But sometimes the harder you grip it, the easier it is to let it sift through your fingers like sand, falling to your feet.

As I stand in front of the oversized mirror in Adam's bedroom, my eyes roam the length of my naked body, both the pieces I love every day and the ones I struggle a little extra with some days.

You haven't been taking very good care of yourself. You've gained some weight. It's been sixteen months. Hit the gym or something.

I close my eyes to words that try so hard to bring shame, hands curling into fists that shake at my stomach as I battle against the temptation to let them win. Because at the end of the day, I know that self-love isn't being happy with myself, all of me, every single moment. It's not realistic, and a recipe for failure.

Blowing out a shaky breath, I force my eyes open, force them to drink myself in right here in the mirror.

"I am not somebody else's opinion of me," I whisper. "I'm strong.

I'm resilient. My heart is big and kind. I'm always learning. I'm the only one of me." With each word, the tension in my body slowly dissipates, shoulders dropping away from my ears, fingers uncurling as my body drinks in the affirmations like it's been starved for them, waiting for me to embrace myself, because today, I need a little extra love from me.

Because, I think, self-love is as simple as giving myself grace on the hard days, loving myself extra when I need it.

The bedroom door opens, and I snap the towel off the floor, wrapping it around myself as Adam's gaze finds me. Heat pools in my cheeks at the way his eyes dim as they rake over me, the curve of his mouth as his long legs eat the distance between us.

"Hi," I whisper as he comes to stand behind me, wrapping his arms around me, his chin finding a home on my shoulder as he watches me in the mirror.

"Hi, pretty girl." He chuckles, kissing the heat dotting my cheek. "Connor's asleep."

"Thank you so much for doing that. He really loves spending time with you."

"He makes me feel like I'm doing something right in this life."

Sizzling fingertips glide up my arms, over my shoulders, before dipping down to my collarbone where I clutch the towel to me. Fire stokes low in my belly, rolling in waves in every direction, the biggest blaze of all settling between my thighs.

I swallow. "You're doing everything right."

"Everything?"

I nod, gaze hooked on his reflection as he pries my iron grip from the towel. The plush gray cloth slowly sweeps open, revealing my body inch by aching inch. For a moment, uncertainty takes control, running through me as I scramble to cover my breasts, the softness of my lower belly, the stretch marks that haven't entirely faded, a scar that never will.

"I nursed Connor for thirteen months," I blurt as Adam's fingers circle my wrists, gently opening me up to him. "So, they're…they're…"

"Perfect," he whispers, his soft touch tracing the shape of my breasts, guiding my eyes back to where his watch me so intently, holding nothing but deep appreciation, utter adoration. "They're perfect, Rosie. Please don't ever try to convince yourself any part of you isn't just right, because to me, it's everything. You. Are. *Everything*."

A single tear peels its way down my cheek. When his lips trap it, I turn into his kiss, sinking against him. "I think I really needed to hear that."

"Do you need to see it too? Feel it?" He lifts my palm to his mouth, pressing lingering kisses there as his fingertips skate across my belly. "Because I want to give you whatever you need. I want you to know exactly where you stand with me, to see yourself exactly the way I see you. The way my heart races when I'm with you, when I touch you, when I get to just fucking...*look at you*? I want you to feel that."

My gaze tracks Adam's searing one in the mirror. "How would you do that?"

"How about we start with you putting your eyes on yourself? Looking at every piece of you for exactly what it is, appreciating everything it's done for you. Seeing it for the beauty it is."

"It's not always that easy."

"No," he agrees. "It's not. Not when we're talking about ourselves." He takes my chin in his hand, runs his thumb across my lower lip. My tongue darts out, chasing its path. "Let me show you what it's like for me, looking at you. Every single thought leaves my body, except...*wow*. How fucking lucky am I? I found you, and somehow, you chose me. I get to keep you."

"Was there any other option? Choosing you? Because it didn't feel like a choice; it just felt right."

"Like it was meant to happen? Me and you? That little boy out there?"

"Like we were lost, and you pulled your truck over to the side of the road and asked if we needed a ride. We climbed in and never left."

Adam grins against my cheek. "I like that. You were made to ride in my passenger seat."

He rakes his fingers through the strands, twining a rose gold end as he grips my hip. "You paint these honey waves the softest shade of pink because you want to stand out just a little bit. I think it makes you look innocent, sweet, but what makes you stand out..." He sweeps a thumb beneath my eye. "These stunning eyes, the same color as the trees the day we met." He skims my cheekbone. "And these freckles, the way they light up your face when you smile, come out of hiding after an afternoon in the sun..." The tip of his nose rubs against mine. "This nose, the cutest fucking nose, the way it crinkles when I make you blush." Capturing my chin, he claims my mouth with the softest brush of his. "And this smile…Jesus, *this* is what makes you stand out, Rosie. This smile is what I couldn't tear my eyes from that day in the forest, not the nervous way you chewed it when you looked up at me, the way it grew when you watched that precious dog melt in my lap, the way it transformed every inch of your face when you laughed. I fell for this smile first, because there was no other choice but to fall."

There's always a choice, I almost say. *And I've never been anyone's.*

But Adam shakes his head, a glint in his eyes like he knows exactly where my mind is trying to take me. Like he's not going to let it.

He grips my neck, bringing my mouth to his, devouring me with a ferocity that steals my breath, lifts me to the tips of my toes, chasing more, everything. "No other choice," he whispers against my lips before forcing my gaze back to our reflection, where every inch of my nakedness glows red under his scrutiny.

With his eyes locked on mine, Adam steps back, reaching behind him and pulling his shirt over his head. My mouth salivates at the sight of him, miles of tanned, knotted muscles carved to a level of perfection that feels surreal. And as he steps out of his shorts, muscular thighs straining below the immaculate lines of the lion painted there, heat spreads throughout my belly.

Adam steps back into me, palm covering my torso as it glides up, up, hands skimming the sides of my breasts as he dots my shoulder in kisses.

"These," he murmurs, cupping the weight of them in his hands. "These are perfect. And they fed your son for thirteen months? I don't ever want to hear you say something negative about something so incredible. And, fuck, are they incredible. Like they were made to fit inside these hands."

"Adam," I choke out as his thumbs scrape across my nipples, pulling everything inside me tight. My back arches, pushing myself deeper into his touch, wanting more.

Fingertips dance across my flesh, dipping between my breasts, lower, across my belly, leaving a trail of goose bumps in their wake. Adam's eyes meet mine as he gently traces the faint stretch marks painted on my skin. Heat pools in my cheeks, begging me to look away, but the look in Adam's eyes begs me to stay right here with him.

"Tiger stripes," he wonders out loud. "I understand the term now more than I ever did. A beautiful reminder of the versatility of your body, the way it adapted to grow something so precious. You're unbelievably strong, Rosie. A mama who'll do anything for her son, to help him grow and learn surrounded by love, while also showing him what true strength looks like."

"What does it look like?" I ask quietly as his hands sear across my flesh like a paintbrush on a canvas.

"It's fierce. Brave. Conquering your fears so you and your son can live without the barriers you see in your mind. But it's also vulnerability. Honesty. Trust. It's seeing your faults, your fears, as setbacks and opportunities to grow and learn more about yourself, rather than a dead-end road. It's moving forward one step at a time, with someone's hand in yours, holding you tight."

"I like holding your hand. It makes all those steps a little easier."

"I feel the same way about holding your hand. But for what it's worth, Rosie, I think you'd be moving forward with or without me. I'm not your strength. You're your own strength." Fingers flutter across the line of my c-section scar, below the softness of my stomach. "If you ever question it, this right here should be all the proof you need that you're a badass with unmatched strength. Because this scar tells a story. A story of a life you grew, a life you birthed, a family you built all on your own, one anyone would be so lucky to be a part of."

He pulls me tight against him, encasing me in his warmth and something that feels a lot like love. And me? I sink into it. I embrace all of it, because I think that's what you do with love. You never know how fleeting it is, after all.

"That's how I feel, Rosie. Lucky. So damn lucky to be a part of your family, however small a part of it I may be. So grateful you let me into your lives. So grateful for these beautiful green eyes, and the kindest, widest smile that makes my heart feel so full. So grateful for this strong, incredible body that gifted me a tiny little boy I didn't know I needed, one I've fallen in love with. So, thank you, Rosie. If you can't see yourself for everything amazing you've done for you, I hope you can see everything amazing you've brought me."

My heart pounds a relentless beat as Adam takes my shaking hand in his, pulling it back.

"This, Rosie," he murmurs, pressing my palm above his pattering heart. "It's all for you."

I don't know why it feels so heavy, so deep, like being submerged in water, except it's the good kind of drowning, where it gives you life instead of stealing it away. Drowning in appreciation, in praise, in words that—for some reason—I know are genuine. The realization is staggering, pulling a shaky breath from my lungs, making my knees wobble as the feel of this man encases me. And when my knees give out, knocking me backward, I feel the heavy press of a bulge against my lower back, the sheer size and weight of it ripping a gasp from my throat.

Adam's low chuckle skates down my neck. "Yeah, that's all for you too."

Fire blooms, crawling along every inch of me as he rakes two searing palms down my sides, grasping my hips so hard it straddles that pleasure-pain line in the most perfect way, like loosening his grip might mean losing me.

"I'd kiss every fucking inch of this body, worship it all, make it my only religion if you'd only let me." He drags a single fingertip across my shoulder, my collarbone, dipping down to circle one tight nipple. "What do you say, trouble? You gonna let me?"

My back arches, pushing my aching breasts into his capable hands. "Please, Adam."

He takes the weight of them so easily, squeezing, rolling my nipples between his thumbs and forefingers, pulling every sound from my mouth. Hot, wet kisses trail my shoulder, up my neck. He traces each curve, draws a path across my belly, around the fullness of my hips. He dips lower still, and when his touch ghosts past the spot I want him most, my entire body trembles, folding forward from the teasing, the satiety I've been denied, and the handsome fucker really *chuckles* in my ear.

"I like you frustrated," he tells me, pulling my ass back into him. He dips his hand between my legs, tracing my thighs, and he hums appreciatively as he finds the physical evidence of what he does to me coating me right there.

"I'd like your hand a little higher."

"Mmm. Is that right?" Fingertips dance closer, so slowly it hurts, a desperate clenching low in my belly. "Here?" he whispers against my ear, sliding his finger through the wetness of my inner thigh.

"Higher, please."

"Here then." He traces the juncture of my thigh. "This must be the spot."

"*Adam.*" His name is a garbled cry, drowning in desperation. "Please, touch me. I'll do anything."

"Such a pretty mouth, begging so nicely. You don't have to beg though." Two fingers slip slowly through my folds, giving me exactly what I want as I fall toward the mirror with a whimper, Adam's mouth at my ear. "I'd never say no to you."

My mouth opens on a sharp gasp as he pushes two fingers inside me and shows me another side of the man I thought I knew.

Adam is soft and gentle. Every word, every action, is careful and thoughtful. The way he fucks me with his fingers right now, cobalt eyes blazing with heat, with power, is anything but. It's savage and ruthless, like he owns every inch of this body. Like he wants my body to forever remember the shape of him, the possessive grip on my hip as he holds me to the mirror, the way his hand glides down, grabbing my ass like it was made for him to hold.

"This fucking ass. Nearly forgot to tell you how much I love it."

"You don't think it's too big?" I manage.

"Too big? Is that a thing?" Fingertips dig into the soft flesh, squeezing me in his large palm. "Seems like the perfect size to me. Look how well it fits me."

"Your hands are huge."

He gives my ass a swift, gentle smack before sifting through the hair at the nape of my neck, locking our reflected gazes. "And your ass is fucking immaculate."

A shudder ripples down my spine as Adam's thumb finds my clit, moving with precision. "Why is you swearing such a turn-on?"

"Why can't I talk like a gentleman when you're naked and beneath my hands?"

I grin against his mouth when he steals a kiss. "I like you as a gentleman, but I love when you lose a little composure."

"Well, thank fuck. Because I feel like I'm losing my fucking mind right now, and you're the one stealing it." He drags me away from the mirror, into his looming body. "So come here, trouble. Because if you're stealing my mind, I get yours."

The thrust of his fingers edges closer and closer to feral as they move faster, pump deeper, hitting a spot inside me nobody's ever found. Heat climbs up my chest and wraps around my throat like a vine as my breath comes in heavy spurts.

I can't take my eyes off Adam, the way his body looks behind mine, a home I've been searching for, a shelter I've craved. The way his electric blue eyes move over me, memorizing, reverent, like he's in utter awe.

The ferocity lurking beneath his hooded lids pulls everything inside me tight. He wraps his hand around my throat, guiding my eyes to his in the mirror, his hand moving between my slick thighs.

"Fuck, Rosie. Look at you, pretty girl, dripping all over my fingers. Such a good girl, but you wanna be a little bit bad, don't you?"

"Just for you," I manage on a gasp.

"Yeah," he rasps, hot breath rolling down my neck, shaking my spine with a shiver. "Just for me." He presses his lips to my temple. "Can you do one more?"

"One more?" An edge of panic creeps into my voice, because this man's hands are *large*, his fingers *thick*. I've been with one man, and... well, he sure wasn't anything like Adam.

"One more," he repeats, gently easing another finger in, holding me close while I gasp at the intrusion, stretching around him. "That's my beautiful fucking girl, taking my fingers. Soon, it'll be my cock."

"Oh God," I cry, and my soul starts leaving my body. "*Adam*."

"I love the feel of your pussy squeezing my fingers when you're close. And you're close, Rosie, aren't you?"

I rock against his touch, clutching at his hand as I try to answer him. "So...so...*mmm*..."

"Close," he finishes for me, the single word dipped in mirth and a bit of arrogance. His fingers dive deeper, faster, his thumb strumming my aching clit, and everything inside me starts unraveling as Adam works his hot, wet mouth down the slope of my neck before whispering his command. "Come on my fingers so you can come again on my tongue."

On his tongue? But I've never—

"*Now*, Rosie." He punctuates his order with the curl of his fingers, the firm press of his thumb to my clit, and something inside me snaps. Stars explode behind my eyelids, but Adam gently squeezes my throat, and my gaze snaps to his. "Those eyes belong to me when you're coming for me. Who are you coming for?"

"You." He tilts my head over my shoulder, and when our gazes collide, I come all over his hand, giving him the words he wants before he takes my mouth too. "God, Adam, *you*."

Large hands grip my waist, flipping me around and pressing me against the mirror. He drops his forehead to mine, both of us nothing but heaving chests, staggered breaths, shaking hands. Beyond the sound of our heavy breathing, I note the quiet, slow *drip, drip, drip* beyond Adam's opened French doors, leading to his balcony. The clouds break, and the setting sun basks Adam in an amber glow, lighting him like the god I think he is.

"The rain stopped," I whisper, and my hands tremble as they slip down his abdomen to his hips, where I tuck my fingers into the waistband of his underwear, inching it down, and—

"Oh Jesus Christ." I jump backward, one hand at my throat, the other pointing at…at…"Holy motherforking…*shirtballs.*" My gaze jumps to his. "That is…I mean, that is just…" I point at his cock, shake my finger at it, then clap one fist into my opposite hand to distract from the that I'm freaking the *fuck* out. I clear my throat. "Massive. That is…massive, my friend. Wheeew." Bending over, I grip my knees and try to breathe.

"You okay?" he asks, and I hate the sparkle of humor in his eyes.

"Adam, I can't possibly…that won't…" Shaking my head, I take a step back, then another, and on the third, I trip over my feet, catching myself off the edge of Adam's mattress. He laughs, darting forward to help me up, I think, but I'll never know for sure, because I skitter up onto the bed and crawl away from him as fast as I possibly can.

"Get back here," he says on a laugh, catching my ankle. He flips me onto my back and drags me to the edge of the bed, wearing the filthiest, hottest fucking smirk I've ever seen. "Where do you think you're going?"

Literally anywhere but near that dick.

I had a c-section because Connor's head wasn't fitting through my pelvis, and this man thinks his cock is somehow going to work its way through? Sure, a cock isn't a nine-pound, twelve-ounce baby. And, yeah, it's not taking the exact same path, but, Jesus motherfuck…

I throw my hands in the air. "I think you're bigger than that underwear model on the bus stop shelter!"

"I definitely am."

"That's not fitting anywhere. Not in my mouth, and not in my vagina. You know that, right?"

He lifts a shoulder. "Things have a way of working themselves out."

"'Things have a way of working themselves out?' What the hell does that mean?"

"It means we'll make it fit."

"Make it fit," I mumble, arms out wide on the bed. I've given up. Resigned to my impending doom that is this man's cock, in and around any portion of my body tonight and in the future, whether it be my mouth or my vagina. All I know is this: there will be no survivors. "We'll make it fit. Okay, yeah, I'm sure that'll just—*whoa*!"

All the air in my body leaves me as Adam scoops me up and tosses me over his shoulder, eating the distance to the balcony. He throws open the doors and steps into the humid evening, the air fresh and earthy from an afternoon of rain, and when he sets me on my feet, the blur of rainbow smearing the pink and orange sky steals every one of my worries.

"It's gorgeous," I murmur as he steps behind me, wrapping himself around me.

"Gorgeous sunset for my gorgeous girl." His lips move over my neck. "You're gonna watch that sky while I taste you." He brushes his thumb over the sudden blaze of heat on my cheekbones. "What's this blush for?"

"You don't have to do that." I hate the softness in my voice, the shame that someone else put there because he *didn't do that.* "If you don't want to, it's okay."

"There's nothing I want more than to taste you; I promise you." He tips my chin up, eyes searching mine over my shoulder. "Have you never done this before?"

I shake my head.

"Selfishly, I'm happy to be your only. I'll make it so good, Rosie. I promise."

"No, but—" I whip my head left, then right. Adam's property is huge, an expansive oasis of lush green trees and high fences that offer nearly all the privacy you could want. But from up here on his balcony, I can see the houses nestled on either side of us, so I drop my voice as if they might somehow hear us. "Someone might see."

There's that smirk again, though he dips his head to hide it. He sits on the oversized lounger and lifts me onto his lap, wrapping my legs around him. At the thick, heavy feel of him pressed against me, right where I want him most, I dig my nails into his shoulders.

Adam threads his fingers through my hair before pulling me forward, fusing his mouth to mine. There's a slowness in this kiss, something unhurried and patient. But behind it, there's a hunger so deep I feel it in every sweep of his tongue, the way he sighs into my mouth, the slight shake to his hands. And the longer we kiss, the hotter every part of me grows, until I'm perched on my knees, pushing him down to his back, rolling my hips, wringing whimpers from the deepest parts of me, not caring who might see.

I don't know where this is going tonight. I thought I wanted more time, but with him below me, the way he claims every piece of me as his with the skim of his hands along my body, I feel ready.

"Nobody can see," he promises against my mouth. "But if you're loud enough, they'll hear. Do you wanna be loud, Rosie?"

"Yes," I groan.

"Good." He spreads out over the cushions and yanks me forward, spreading my thighs and setting my knees on either side of his face. "Tell them you're mine."

One lick. That's all he gives me. Treacherously slow, from the bottom all the way to the top, looking like a tragically beautiful masterpiece below me with his eyes locked on mine, and then all traces of my gentle Adam are gone. The man with his face between my thighs shows me how starved he is, his fingertips biting into the soft flesh of my ass as he rocks my hips back and forth, his tongue delving deep, inciting a pleasure I never knew was possible.

"*Ohhh* God." I grip his curls tight in my fists, unable to look anywhere but at him as he devours me. "So…mmm, Adam. *So good.*"

"Thinking the same thing, baby." He sucks my clit into his mouth in a way that crushes my soul. "So. Fucking. *Good.*"

I lean into the ride, one hand in his hair, the other reaching back, balancing on his thick thigh as my pelvis rolls against his mouth. It's the sight of his cock that does me in, standing so tall, so proud, when everything he's doing is all for me.

He's enjoying this. Making me feel good, it makes him feel good too. And that…that does something to me. It's not a chore; it's a choice. And by the feel of his hands on me, the way his moans vibrate against me… I'd say it's a choice he'd happily make again and again.

"Adam." Reaching behind me, I fist his cock. It pulses in my hand, and Adam's body jolts below me as he hisses, tugging at my clit. "I want to turn around."

"You don't have—"

"I want to suck your cock, please." It's part plea, part whine, and a whole lot of pout, but it sure as shit does the trick. One second our eyes are locked, and the next I'm being absolutely manhandled as Adam flips me around, my ass in the air before he jerks it back down on his face.

Adam fists my hair, holding me above him, my back bowed as I ride his face, his cock gripped tightly in my hand.

"You want it?" His mouth moves over the curve of my ass, wet kisses and teasing nips that drive me toward the brink. "Ask nicely."

"Please," I beg on a whimper as his tongue returns right where it belongs, driving me mad. "Please, Adam."

"What do you want?"

"Your cock."

"Good girl," he whispers, guiding me forward with his hand on my hip. "You can have it."

It's a distracting sight, Adam's muscular thighs flexing below me, his thick length throbbing in my small hand. He's rock hard, and I watch with wonder as a bead of cum decorates the head of his cock while I slowly stroke him. I lean forward, flicking my tongue over that glistening drop, smiling when he groans against me.

He's always so in control, but these tiny fissures, giving me a glimpse at the man below, the one craving to just let go, make me want to unravel all of him, see what's hiding beneath the calm façade.

So I grip the base of his cock and lick, from the bottom all the way to the top, slow, before swirling my tongue around the head. His thighs strain and his toes curl, and when I slowly swallow as much of him as I can, his fingertips bite into my ass.

"Fuck, Rosie." His grip on me trembles, and as his cock hits the back of my throat, his mouth falls away from me, the most beautiful throaty moan falling from his lips.

Rough palms slide up my sides before he drags them down my back, grabs my ass, and spreads me wider. Something breaks, his final tether, maybe, because every hint of gentleman disappears as he eats me like a man who's been starved for too long, lost in the desert for weeks on end. And when he thrusts his thumb inside me from behind, my whole world fades away to nothing.

"Ohhh…*fuck*. Adam. I-I-I…" My eyes roll up, up to the mountains, the sunset painting the sky as I struggle to breathe, struggle to keep my mouth on him. "God, *Adam*."

"That's my loud girl. Tell them who you belong to."

But he belongs to me, too, and I want everyone to know.

I take him into my mouth again, matching the rock of my hips, the thrust of his thumb, the lap of his tongue. We're nothing but panting breaths, biting fingernails, strangled gasps, and low moans.

Adam rips his mouth away, taking his thumb with him before replacing it with two deep fingers that have me crying out. "Christ, Rosie. So fucking good. You're a masterpiece, riding my face."

I groan around his cock as he pulls out his fingers, swiping them across my ass before he gives it a swift smack and dives right back in with his tongue. I've never felt anything like this, the soft, velvety slide of his tongue, the gentle tug of his teeth in exactly the right place, the plush press of his lips in my most intimate place. It's a taste of heaven that leaves me fiending for more, for it to never end. Everything inside me pulls taut, ready to snap, and I'm so desperate. Desperate to give all of me to this man, for him to see it, to take it, to…love it.

"Give me everything, Rosie. Come for me, baby."

And how can I not? With his hands on my hips holding me tight, and his tongue all over me, I cave. It's like walking to the edge of a mountain, looking down at all that beauty below you, closing your eyes, and just…jumping. Letting go. Free-falling into oblivion, and loving every moment of it. There's not a care in the world about who might see, or who might hear, because in the moment I know: every inch of me belongs to this man somehow, the one wringing every drop of pleasure for me as I call out his name.

He pulls away, replacing his mouth with his fingers, pulling a second orgasm from me without pause. "Rosie," he rasps, his hips jerking as he slides in and out of my mouth. "I'm gonna come." He tugs on my hips, trying to pull me off. "You gotta move, baby."

But I don't want to. I want to give him everything he gave to me.

His fingers curl inside me as he wrings another earth-shattering orgasm from my body when I thought I had nothing left to give. Digging his fingers into my hips, he holds onto me while letting go of everything else, spilling inside my mouth as he bites down on the soft flesh of my ass.

"*Fuck,*" he growls, picking me up, tossing me down to the lounger.

He crawls overtop of me, the ferocious look in his eyes telling me he's not even close to satiated. A wicked smile tugs at his lips as he grasps the nape of my neck and lifts my mouth to his, where he murmurs his next words before we dive right in for round two.

"Fucking love the way you taste when you unravel for me."

"You, on my balcony, drinking wine under the stars, wearing nothing but my T-shirt."

I tip my head back on Adam's chest, peering up at him. He's already looking at me, one hand holding the stem of his wine glass, the other trailing a path over my bare thigh. He's wearing a pair of dark-rimmed glasses because he wanted to look at every single picture of Connor I've ever taken, and it ramps up the *fuck me* factor to a whopping one hundred out of ten, but really, I've stopped counting. The man's *fuck me* score is off the charts.

His large hand brackets my jaw as he drops his mouth to mine. "My version of paradise."

"If this is paradise, could we stay here forever?"

"I'd happily stay anywhere you were." He dips his hand beneath the T-shirt I wear, trailing the tip of his finger over my stomach. "What I wouldn't give to have seen you when you were pregnant. Bet you were a goddamn masterpiece."

"I ate a lot of hot fudge sundaes, extra hot fudge. It was an addiction."

"I'd have happily fed that addiction."

"You would've contributed to the number of stretch marks, huh?"

"Tiger stripes," he murmurs against my shoulder, my neck. "And I would've spent each night kissing them too." He sets our glasses down and spins me around, wrapping my legs around him before he stands and carries me through the French doors, past Bear snoozing on a cushion in the corner of the room. Laying me down on his bed, he lifts his T-shirt off me and crawls overtop of me. "I could spend all night kissing them now."

"I think you've done that already." The words leave me a whimper as his mouth moves up my thighs, over my hips, across my stomach, covering my imperfections with tenderness.

"Just want to make sure you know how much I appreciate this body and everything it's done and continues to do."

"You make me feel very appreciated," I promise quietly. "More appreciated than I've ever felt."

The soft words bring Adam's eyes to mine, and I look away.

"Hey," he whispers, angling my face to him. "I wish you wouldn't feel like you need to hide away with me. We're partners now, Rosie. You and me. And I can't be the best partner I can if you don't feel safe with me."

"It's just…a little embarrassing."

His gaze softens, and he moves to the pillows, sitting me against his chest. He tips my chin, bringing my eyes to his. "I like you for everything you are, all the pieces you've shown me, and the ones you try to hide too. I know our insecurities exist for a reason, but there's nothing you need to hide from me."

I sink into the safety of his words and give him mine. "Brandon said I needed to lose weight. That I needed to take better care of myself, because I was setting a bad example for Connor."

"Fuck off." Adam buries his face in my hair. "I'm sorry. I didn't mean to say that out loud. I just—no, I'm not sorry. That guy needs to fuck right off. Is he for fucking real?"

Laughter bubbles and tension eases. "I love when you say *fuck*."

"Good, because I'm really fucking mad right now."

"Don't be mad for me."

"Too late. Nobody has any right to talk about someone else's body."

"He said having a c-section was the easy way out, that I couldn't use the *I had a baby* excuse anymore."

Adam grumbles a string of curses under his breath, and something that sounds a whole lot like, "Gives him the greatest gift of his life just to throw it back in her face," before he squeezes me tighter, covers my shoulder in kisses. "I'm sorry somebody said something so hurtful and careless. You're beautiful, inside and out, and you don't need to change a thing."

I sweep his curls off his forehead, feeling the rough stubble along his jaw before I press my lips to his. "Everything is easier when you're around. It's easier to love myself exactly where I'm at, because you appreciate all of me."

"You are the strongest, kindest, most beautiful person I've ever known. How could I not appreciate you?" He lies down, pulling me against him, his face in my neck. "I've been dying to do this since our first kiss. Think it's gonna be the best sleep I've ever had, and I'll never let you go again."

I don't think I want him to, because as sleep threatens to pull me under, lulling me toward a peace I haven't known in ages, there's one thing I know with certainty.

This is how you fall in love.

SEVENTEEN

BANANA-FLAVORED DICKS

Adam

It's hard to stop looking at her.

This morning, when she was snuggled beneath the mess we made well into the night. Pillowy lips that begged for kisses beneath the rising sun, honey freckles I could wake up to for the rest of my life. Bear tucked behind her knees, refusing to leave her side. The tiny boy who joined us in bed once our clothes made it back on, snuggled between us and, like me, couldn't tear his eyes off his mama while she read him his favorite book.

And now, as she strolls ahead of me and Connor, both dogs tied around her waist, her fingertips grazing the trunk of every pine tree she passes. She's at home here, in these forested mountains. I see the clarity reflected in her moss eyes after only a few minutes here, like the fresh air lifts her fog.

From his spot on my shoulders, Connor curls over my head, wrapping his arms around it. His lips press against my hat as he squeezes tight. "*Muaaah!*"

I'm not sure I've ever been so lucky, and more than that, I'm not sure I've ever felt so awake. So *alive*.

Because I've been so fucking tired. Tired of people taking only what they want, leaving the rest behind. You can't pick and choose parts of people; you have to want all of them. I've given Rosie the pieces nobody else has wanted, and she's taken all of them with eager hands.

And somehow, that makes it scarier. Before, I only had myself to lose. Now I have two green-eyed blondes who'd take everything of me with them if they left. The thought makes my palms sweaty, my hands shaky. Because at the core of my fear is the reminder that I haven't been honest with Rosie. That I've hidden a huge part of my life, all while asking her to give me everything.

I've done this whole thing backward. I always thought I'd have to convince someone to love all the regular parts of me after they fell for the hockey star. Now I have to convince her that, beneath it all, the hockey star is still me.

I need to give her all of me.

"Can I tell you a secret?" I whisper, looking up at Connor. "I just want to be good enough for you two, and I'm scared I won't be. But I promise, I'm gonna try my hardest."

He smiles at me, then rests his forehead against mine, patting my cheek. "Good Dada."

"Thanks, buddy. I needed that." My eyes find Rosie, watching us with a dazed smile. "Quit looking at me like that, trouble."

"Like what?"

I press my words below her ear. "Like you want a repeat of last night on my balcony."

She grins, teeth pressing into her pink lower lip. "You're carrying my offspring on your shoulders. I'll look at you however I wanna look at you."

"Admit it. You want round two."

"You and I both know it's round five, at least."

"Wanna see if we can hit double digits?"

"Wanna carry me everywhere the next day when my legs don't work?"

"Wanna just never leave the bed?"

She grins up at me, tucking her tiny hand into mine, and I'll never get over how perfect it feels there, the way our fingers twine together. "I wanna." She peeks at me from beneath her lashes. "Sounds like a baby-free night might be best."

My heartbeat trips. "Baby free?"

She winks, twirling out of my hold, and dances off toward the bridge, the dogs chasing after her.

"Baby free?" I repeat, Connor bouncing along on my shoulders as I dash after her. "Rosie! What does baby free mean?"

She ignores me, and when we finally catch up with her and she's dishing out lunch for everyone, she's still wearing that smug smile.

"Fuckin' trouble," I mutter, slipping Connor off my shoulders.

"What are you gonna do about it?"

My eyes flip to hers, flashing with heat so feral it makes her blush. She rolls her lips and turns to her backpack, and I nab a fistful of her shirt, pulling her lips to mine. "Guess you'll have to find out."

Connor pats our shoulders, a bubbly smile appearing between us. "Mama, Dada, kiss."

After lunch, we stroll down to the creek, Bear and Piglet flanking Connor's sides as he walks just ahead, his hands buried in their fur.

"I think Pig and Bear have adopted Connor," I say.

"I think so too," she murmurs, watching them with a smile. "I'm so happy he loves animals. And Piglet…" She shakes her head, her smile equal parts hopeful and sad. "She's just come so far, hasn't she? She's so great with you and Bear, and she loves Connor so much."

"She seems so at home out here with you."

"With all of us. So many of her strides have happened since you came along."

"I'm glad to be a positive part of her journey, but don't discount all the work you've done with her, Rosie."

"I'm not. Really, I'm not. But there was only so much I could do on my own, you know? Yes, I worked hard to gain her trust, to help her feel comfortable, but we couldn't get her near men until you. And now look at her. She's so carefree out here, so happy." Hope drains from her eyes, leaving her grieving a future she's told herself she can't have. "She's going to make some family so happy one day."

I squeeze Rosie's hand in mine. "Her forever family is going to be so lucky."

Rosie nods before focusing on the trees around us, trailing her fingertip over the bark of each tree she passes like she always does, like she's looking for something she lost. She never offers any information, and I don't press. It's her quiet time, and I'm just grateful she allows me to tag along. Plus, there's something rewarding about giving her the time and space to come to me herself when she's ready. It makes me feel worthy, and that's a feeling I've been lacking the past couple of years.

"Hey." I nudge her side. "I was thinking about you getting stuck in the rain yesterday. I've got an SUV in my garage, but I'm pretty partial to my truck. What if you used it to get around? Work, errands, picking up and dropping off Connor. It'd save you some time and save you from the rain."

"Oh, no. I can't do that."

"Sure you can. I'm happy to lend you one of my cars if it makes life a little easier for you."

"No, that's not it. It's…well…" She twirls a wave around her finger and lifts a shoulder. "I don't know how to drive."

"Really?"

"I have my learner's permit, but I never actually learned how to drive. Dad was always supposed to teach me, but…" She shrugs. "Didn't end up having anyone around to teach me." She gives me a grateful smile and a hand squeeze. "But thank you for the offer, Adam. That's so thoughtful of you. The bus is just fine, and a little rain won't hurt me."

Memories flood my head, weeks spent in the driver's seat of my dad's F-150 while I crept along quiet neighborhoods, my mom in the backseat, hanging over my shoulder and gasping every time I got a little too close to another car, or that *one time* I bumped the curb. My parents waiting for me with a poster and balloons when I finished my driver's exam, and the dinner they took me out to afterward to celebrate. Amazing memories, but ones I don't appreciate enough. Because a simple coming-of-age ritual I thought every kid had…Rosie didn't. She didn't have someone sitting next to her, worrying over how much gas she gave the pedal, every over-swing of the wheel, and whether she'd checked her blind spot. She didn't have someone watch her pull out of the driveway all on her own for the first time, someone to worry about where she was going and if she would get there safely, telling her not to be late, texting her fifteen minutes later to make sure she got there okay.

For the first time, it truly hits me how much Rosie missed out on. Can I give her back all of those experiences?

I'm so proud of her, this beautiful girl, the way she thrives despite the things she missed out on, the way she pushes herself to conquer her fears for her son. Because when Connor wants to splash in the creek, she takes his hand and splashes with him, and when he wants to wade a little farther, she takes a steadying breath and steps forward.

"I'm going to miss this," Rosie says when we start heading back.

Connor is fading fast, his small arms thrown around my neck, head resting on my shoulder, his breathing growing shallow as he bounces along on my chest.

"Summer?"

"Summer. This. Me and you. Connor. All the time we have together. I haven't had such an amazing summer since…since…" She closes her eyes, giving her head a small shake. "School starts in two weeks, and I can't wait to get back to it, to graduate, but I know I'll be so busy with all my rotations, and you'll be busy at work, too, so…I'm going to miss this. The unlimited time. The lazy days and long nights."

My stomach twists, a heavy lump that sinks to the bottom of my stomach. Two weeks. Two weeks left of summer vacation, before Rosie goes back to school and I start training camp before our preseason games.

I don't want to spend them lying to her. I want to spend them loving on her, giving her all of me, getting all of her in return. I want her at my home opener. I want her in my jersey, my name on her back. I want Connor yelling for me, calling me whatever the hell he wants to call me. And I want to make them proud to be a part of my life.

"Nothing will change between us, Rosie. It'll be hard, yes, but we'll figure it out together. We'll start a new routine, and you're going to fly through your last year of school. Before you know it, it'll be spring and you'll be a veterinarian."

"That's as scary as it is exciting."

"What's the plan after graduation?"

She grits her teeth. "I have no idea."

"Oh, come on. You, the girl who plans everything, doesn't know? I don't buy that."

She blows out a deep breath, spinning around before she sways into my side, holding my arm. "I might have a few ideas."

"Spill 'em, trouble."

"Well, the last year is for us to explore all the different aspects of vet medicine so we can decide where we want our specialty to be. So, my first chunk is at the school itself, where we do surgeries, emergencies, radiology, that kind of stuff. Afterward, we get to choose our rotations. I already know I want to go into shelter medicine, and I've arranged to do most of my elective rotations at Wildheart. I'm hoping, if I do well, they'll hire me as a vet after graduation."

"You're going to be fabulous. And they already love you there. I can't imagine them not wanting to keep you."

"Yeah, I hope so. I'd really love for Connor and me to get our own place too. I know Marco wants to move in with Archie, but our apartment is so small. There's barely enough room for Connor and me, let alone another adult. And they're so selfless, they'll never ask me to leave. If I can get a job and tuck aside the first few pays, then I should be able to afford to get Connor and I our own apartment, with his own room."

"I like your dreams. They sound perfect, and I know you'll reach them. In the meantime, we can give Connor his own room at my place."

"You don't have to do that."

"Why not? I've got four. And I plan to keep you two as much as I can, so it makes sense for him to have something a little more permanent than a playpen we stick in an open room, yeah?"

She blushes, nibbling her lip. "He really loved those glow-in-the-dark stars you hung up for him." She peers up at me. "That would be really wonderful, Adam. Are you sure?"

"I'm very sure." I roll my eyes and tip my head at the dogs ahead of us. "Now go break those two up."

"*Bear*!" Rosie dashes over to the dogs, trying to get mine to dismount hers. "You're neutered! You can't have Bear and Pig babies, as cute as they'd be!" She stares down at them, fists propped on her hips. "What are we gonna do with you two?"

I laugh quietly as Rosie has to wind back around and separate them a second time, only moments after she turns her back on them.

"We were gonna take you two for pup cups, but now I just don't know." She shrugs, as if she isn't going to climb in my front seat, give me those puppy eyes, and say, "Weren't they so good today? They deserve a pup cup, don't you think?" just like she does every single time. And just like I do every single time, I'll wind up with whipped cream all over my hands while the dogs make a mess of the pup cups I hold for them.

Connor stirs, turning to tuck his face into my neck, laying his tiny hand over my heart. I kiss his waves, tightening my hold on him, relishing the fullness I feel in this moment, right here in this forest. I look around at the dirt, all the trees, the sea of green that makes this place smell so fresh, and I can't believe here is where I found exactly what I was looking for.

A tree to my right catches my eye. It's an old, towering pine, just like the rest of them, but on its thick trunk, the bark is marked with faded carvings.

"Look," I call to Rosie, touching the bark, the old, rough heart carved into it, the three letters in the middle. *D, M, R.* Beneath it is a series of numbers that make a date from ages ago. "It's been here for thirteen years."

I hear the crunch of the earth beneath her shoes, the way they stop abruptly, the sharp intake of breath. I glance at Rosie, finding her hand at her mouth, eyes filled with tears, and I squeeze her arm.

"Hey. You okay?"

Her eyes don't leave the heart on the tree. "You found it. I-I...I've been looking. Every single hike, for seven years. I've never been able to...I couldn't remember..." Her chest rises sharply with a staggered inhale, and those tears spill down her cheeks before she throws her arms around me. "*You found it.*"

I look back at the heart, and something clicks.

D, M, R. Dad, Mom, Rosie.

"You've been here before. With your parents."

A broken sob shakes her to her core, and she buries her face against my shoulder as I run my palm over her back.

"Do you want to tell me about it?"

Rosie swipes the tears from her cheeks and nods. Taking her hand, I urge her down to the base of the tree, pulling a sleeping Connor into my lap. Rosie rests her head against my shoulder before she tells me her story.

"My parents and I loved the outdoors. We were always hiking, camping, swimming, exploring. Anything you could do outside, we did it. We spent every summer traveling, and when I was eleven, we came here. We drove across Canada, spent two weeks in Alberta, took our time driving through to British Columbia. And we finished here. Vancouver was my favorite, so we extended our stay a week, and we hiked this trail every single morning." Rosie looks up at the carving, a smile on her lips. "On our last day, my dad carved this. He promised we'd come back again, that we'd find it." She looks back at me. "You know Capilano Bridge? The suspension bridge through the mountains? It's covered in lights all winter long."

I nod. "I've been a few times. It's beautiful."

Rosie smiles wistfully. "I bet. I've only seen pictures, but it looks incredible. The snow-covered trees, all those twinkly lights…it looks like magic. I wanted to go so badly, but of course the lights weren't on in the summer. My parents said we could come back in November for my birthday to see all the lights." Her chin quivers as new tears build, sliding silently down her face. "My parents passed away in September. We never got to go."

Cupping her cheek, I swipe at the tears that come rolling down. "I'm so sorry, Rosie."

"It's why I'm here. Why I chose Vancouver, even though there's an incredible veterinarian school forty-five minutes from my hometown. Because this is the last trip we took together. Because we were so happy here. We were together, and we were happy. Because Vancouver, because here, *right here*, is where I feel my family."

Rosie climbs to her feet, holding her hand out to me, inviting me to follow suit. She traces the shape of the heart, the date, that *D* and *M*. "I don't want to lose this again. I can't. I can't forget where this tree is."

"You won't," I promise her. "I'll remember. We can put something here to mark it. Plant some flowers."

She grins. "Peonies?"

I smile, touching my thumb to the dimple in her chin. "Peonies."

Rosie stares at the heart for a long moment before she places her hand over the carving, eyes fluttering closed. When they open again, there's a clarity behind them, a newfound hope. She's not lost anymore; she's found.

She clutches to her heart. "You know what I think, Adam? I think you're the one who found it because you're my family now too. You feel like it, anyway. You didn't just find my family; I found my family in you."

I'm glad I can give her something she's been missing, something she so desperately craves and so wildly deserves.

Because I know, in her, I've found something I'd given up on.

I've found love.

"I think she's ready to have sex."

The chatter around me dies, and four sets of eyes rise to mine. Carter twists his twenty-fifth Oreo apart, slowly licking at the icing, and Garrett rips open a bag of Flamin' Hot Funyuns before sticking his hand inside, pulling a handful out at the literal pace of a turtle. Jaxon pops the cap off a bottle of beer even though he already has one, excitement gleaming in his eyes as he tips both back to his mouth at the same time, and Emmett pulls out his phone, the sound of his fingers clacking at the screen filling this awful silence.

A horrible, high-pitched, dying bird type of screech filters into the backyard from Carter's kitchen, and sweet Christ, what I wouldn't give to get that awkward silence back.

"*Rosie's ready to have sex*!" Cara shrieks from inside. "*Our sweet angel baby's getting his dick wet*!"

"Jesus fuck—" I scrub my hands over my face and look to Emmett. "Does she ever, you know…not?"

He shakes his head wistfully. "Never. Never does she not. She always does."

"When do you see her next?" Jaxon asks, reaching for Garrett's Funyuns. Garrett glares, tearing the bag out of reach.

"Tomorrow."

"And what makes you think she's ready for sex?"

"Well, she…we've been…I mean, things have progressed, naturally."

Garrett shoves a handful of his snack into his mouth. "Naturally."

Carter tosses his cookie into his mouth. "So you w-icked 'er cookie."

"I refuse to acknowledge you when you talk with cookies in your mouth and call body parts after them."

"Meh meh meh meh meh," he mimics, then tries to rip the Oreo pack out of my hand when I grab it. "No! You don't get my cookies if you're gonna make fun of me."

"Carter," Olivia warns from inside. "Share your cookies."

His brows tug so tightly together with his frown as he relinquishes the cookies. It's incredibly hard to take him seriously when he's wearing that T-shirt, *Support Your Local Girl Dads* stamped on it. He makes grabby hands at Emmett, who's holding Ireland. "Gimme my baby."

"No."

"If I can't have my Oreos, I need my princess."

Emmett tickles Ireland's belly, and she giggles around the silicone hockey skate she's gnawing on. "She's happy right here. Aren't you, angel?"

The patio door slides open, Olivia stepping outside. Her gaze sweeps the patio before landing on Emmett and Ireland. "There's my girl. I need to feed you, sweetheart, but I promise I'll bring you right back to Uncle Emmett, okay?"

"I'll be waiting." He blows Ireland a kiss and leans back in his chair, crossing one ankle over the other, looking me over. "Back to you having sex."

"You know she slept over for the first time last week. And she's been saying...she's been saying she wants this next time to be baby free. So I think...do you think..." I brace my elbows on my bouncing knees. "Does that mean...?"

The four of them leap from their chairs, high-fiving each other.

"*Ay-yo*!"

"There it is!"

"That's totally the sign!" Garrett tells me, sinking back down to his seat.

Carter nods. "Ollie always says she wants baby-free time when she wants to go all night or get super loud."

"Oh for fuck's sake." Olivia growls from inside. "*Carter*!"

Emmett clinks his beer against mine. "Looks like you're having sex tomorrow night, bud."

"Tomorrow night? But that's...so soon...and what if I..." My throat runs dry, and I lick my lips. It's been so long. Too long. I'm out of practice. And what if I'm not good? I look down at my trembling hands and blurt, "My hands are sweaty."

Jaxon watches me carefully. "So Rosie's ready...but are you?"

Am I ready? Nobody's ever asked me that before. I guess...I guess I hadn't really thought of it. I was never ready before, but then, none of those girls were Rosie. I just want to be enough for her.

I leap to my feet, knocking the Oreos to the ground, eliciting a gasp from Carter, who dives for them. I shove my fingers through my hair and blurt the first thing that comes to mind. "I-I-I...I don't have any condoms."

With his cookies safe on his lap, Carter runs a palm over his puffed chest. "I'd give you one of mine, but it'd be way too big."

Olivia's snort drifts through the patio door. "Carter, if anyone's taught him the importance of wearing a condom, it's you. Everyone here knows you don't own a single one."

Garrett exhales loudly, leaning back in his chair, kicking his legs out in front of him, resting the back of his head in his clasped hands. "I'd give you some if I had them, but Jennie lets me fuck her raw."

"*Yeah I do, baby*!"

"Take that back," Carter growls lowly.

Garrett tosses one of Carter's cookies in his mouth. "No."

Emmett puts his hands up. "Don't look at me. Me and Cara are trying to have a baby."

"What's a condom?" Cara calls.

Jaxon sighs and rises, fishing his wallet out of his back pocket. "I got you, big guy. What do you need? I got ultra ribbed, bare-skin raw, G-spot—that one's designed for her pleasure; Rosie'll like it—magnum, banana flavored, fire and ice—"

"Why do you have so many?"

"You never know what she's gonna—"

A loud crash ends his words, and we turn, watching Carter and Garrett wrestle on the grass.

"I said take it back!" Carter shouts, pinning Garrett to the ground.

Garrett rolls on top of him. "And I said no!"

"You stole my cookies!"

"Ollie said you have to share!"

"You can't have unprotected sex! You might accidentally have a baby!"

"Proof I fucked your sister! And don't call your daughter an accident!"

"Ireland, baby, Daddy loves you! You were a happy surprise!"

The patio door slides open, and Olivia, Jennie, and Cara step outside.

"Oh my," Olivia murmurs, handing Ireland back to Emmett.

"Children," Jennie mutters.

"I've got a hundred bucks on Gare-Bear," Cara says. "Who wants in?"

"Not fucking me," I grumble. Garrett's grown a whole new set of balls since he and Jennie started dating. It's a lot of fun to see him terrorize Carter. Also, I've learned not to bet on Carter. His wedding was a seven-hundred-dollar mistake I'm not making again.

"You look frustrated," Olivia says as she takes a seat beside me, Carter's lost box of Oreos now in her lap. "You know what's great for that?"

"Sex?" I guess on an exhausted sigh.

She tosses a cookie in her mouth and winks. "Sex."

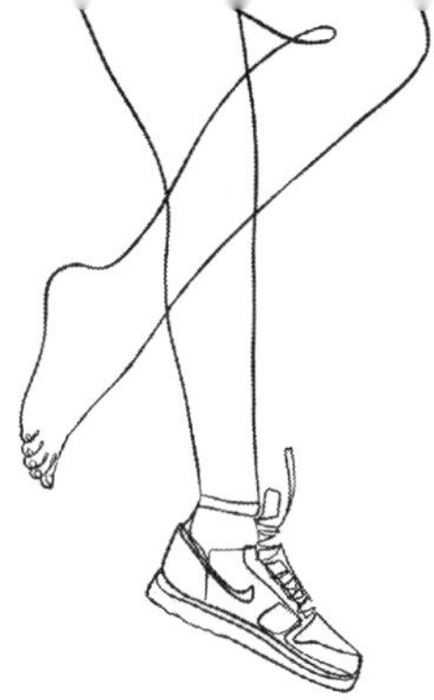

EIGHTEEN

BEFORE I FALL APART

Rosie

“Rosie’s getting laid tonight.”

“No I’m not!”

“Correction: Rosie’s getting railed six-feet deep tonight.”

I glare at Marco. “Not helpful, and not what I meant when I said no.”

He waggles his dark brows. “You’re gonna be on bedrest tomorrow. Maybe all weekend.” He props his chin on his fist and gazes at Archie. “I’ve never seen Rosie dickmatized.”

“I don’t think she’s ever really been dickmatized.”

“Hmm. Right, Brandon didn’t deliver. Pregnancy without orgasm should be illegal.”

“Okay, first of all—” I hold a finger up, one hand propped on my hip “—yes it should. Second, I’ve been dickmatized!”

Archie grins as he spoons pancake batter into a frying pan. “When?”

Crossing my arms, I point my nose to the ceiling. “Just last week, when I attempted to deepthroat his dick. That’s the only way to explain how I even *remotely* fit *part* of that thing in my mouth.” I capture my lower lip between my teeth as my thoughts wander back to Adam’s balcony, all the control I happily let go of.

“Look at you,” Marco coos. “You adorable little slut. You’re getting that dick tonight.”

“I’m not sure. Sometimes he seems content to keep things as they are.”

"A guy who likes to take it slow? Sounds like a unicorn; men like that don't really exist." Marco drops a bag of chocolate chips at Archie's elbow and pops a kiss on his cheek, a reminder that he only eats pancakes when they're loaded with chocolate. "Speaking of taking it slow, when are we gonna meet this mystery man of yours?"

"He's not a mystery. His name is Adam."

"He's a mystery to us, and I'm sick of listening to Daddy Archie late at night, worrying about his sweet Rosie because he hasn't done an ocular pat down of your boyfriend yet and cleared him to date you. Why are you keeping him from us?"

"I told you," Archie growls, "stop calling me Daddy."

"Okay, Daddy."

I snicker, kissing Archie's cheek. "I think it's sweet when you worry, Daddy."

Archie's head drops back, and he sighs. "For fuck's sake. And I'm not worried. You two have been seeing each other nearly two months now, and we haven't met him. I just want to put a face to the name." He flips a pancake and shrugs. "And make sure he's good enough for my Rosie."

"Have you met his friends?" Marco asks.

"Not yet, no."

He frowns. "Is he keeping you in his own secret bubble or something?"

My heart patters. "Secret bubble? What do you mean?"

He shrugs. "You've never even been out in public."

"You think…" My throat dries, and I scratch it. It's not as if I haven't thought about it, wondered when he'd introduce me to his friends. He's with them all the time, and they seem like family to him. I've been waiting, anxious for them to like me, but the invitation has never come. "He doesn't want to be seen with me?"

Marco grabs my hand. "No, Rosie. No way. I'm sorry, that's not what I meant. Really, it's kind of sweet. Like he just wants you all to himself."

"We really would love to meet him though," Archie adds with a soft smile. "Why don't you ask him to come for dinner Sunday? I'm sure meeting your friends will prompt him to introduce you to his too."

I force the tension in my shoulders away. "Yeah, okay. You're right. I'll invite him for dinner."

"Maaamaaa!"

I smile, starting toward my bedroom. "And there's my cue."

Connor grins as soon as he sees me, reaching his arms up high. "Hi, Mama," he murmurs as I scoop him into my arms. "Dada?"

"You'll see Dada later today, honey."

"Bear? Dada, Bear?"

My heart does something funny, a flutter that drops to my belly, erupting like butterflies.

He's asking for Adam, not Brandon.

Connor's grown to love Adam so much, and I can't blame him. He gives Connor everything he needs, at the forefront of those needs being unconditional love, patience, connection, the things his own father struggles to give him. I don't want it to be a competition; I want my child to get the love he deserves from all the important people in his life.

"Uncle Arch made pancakes," I tell Connor as I get him dressed for the day. "Chocolate chip."

"Pa-cakes?" he whispers with wide eyes. "*Wow*."

"*Rosie*!" Archie calls. "Your phone! Why is the dean calling you?"

"What? The dean?"

He appears in the doorway, phone in his hand. "How'd you already get yourself in trouble? The school year hasn't even started yet."

I tear my phone away. "I never get in trouble."

"Aw-chee! Pa-cakes?"

Archie swings Connor up into his arms. "Come on, little man. I made yours heart shaped."

I wait for them to leave before answering the call. "Professor McKee? Hi."

"How many times do I have to tell you to call me Eva, Rosie? You know I don't like last names and titles."

"I'm sorry. I panicked."

Eva laughs, and I sigh, the panic melting. Kinda. Sorta. Not really. Eva's the kind of professor you hope to have. Approachable, kind. She makes it her mission to make everyone feel comfortable in her presence. But still, it's August, she's the dean, and she's calling me. If that isn't reason to panic, I don't know what is.

"Any chance you can pop by my office today?"

"Oh." *I might vomit.* "Yeah. Totally. I have my son today. He doesn't go to his dad's until later. Is that okay?"

Eva pauses, and the panic in my stomach knots, pulling taut. "It would be for the best if it were just you and I."

Definitely going to vomit. "Am I…am I in trouble?"

"Of course you're not in trouble, Rosie. What kind of trouble have you ever gotten yourself into?"

None, but that doesn't mean bad things haven't happened to me.

"We need to talk, that's all. It would be best if you were able to give the conversation your full attention, and I know how challenging that can be when you've got a little one to keep your eye on."

My eyes burn, and I swallow the urge to cry as I start mentally cataloging all the worst-case scenarios. "I'll drop Connor at his dad's and come by."

"Great. I'm here until three. And Rosie, try not to worry."

The thing about anxiety is that you have no control over it at all. Your brain senses a threat, and every alarm in your head starts sounding. The nerves in your body jump, and you're left trying to fight the urge to get up and run while every worst-case scenario plays out in your head. Sometimes, what's hardest to wrap my head around about anxiety is that it's so damn *easy* for people without it to just let the thoughts roll off their back, all while I look like I'm losing my damn mind over something so pointless. Because it is pointless, isn't it, to worry about something out of your control? I just wish my brain got the memo.

My nails bite into my palms to stop the slight tremor in my hands before I call Brandon. It goes to voice mail, and when I call a second time, he answers with a groan.

"I'm trying to sleep."

"Sorry to wake you. Something's come up. Can I drop Connor off a bit earlier today?"

"What? When?"

"One, maybe?"

Another groan. "He's not supposed to come over 'til four thirty. The guys are coming over to watch the baseball game."

I try to rub the headache from my eyes. "I wouldn't ask if it weren't important."

"Why don't you ask your boyfriend to watch him?" His tone is sour, and I have no patience for it.

"Because you're his fucking dad, Brandon, and frankly, I'm sick of you acting like you have better things to do than spend time with your son. Now can I drop him off early, or do I need to find someone else who cares about him?"

"Jesus, Ro, who shit in your coffee this morning?" He sighs, long and low, like he has to think about it. "Yeah, whatever. Drop him off, I guess. I'm not canceling my plans though."

"Thank you, Brandon."

"You owe me. You're dropping him off three-and-a-half hours early, so you owe me those hours back."

I hang up without a word, because I'm incredibly close to reaching my limit. I think I'm a pretty patient person, but Brandon has a way of testing every last one of my nerves when it comes to our son.

Connor wasn't planned, I get it, but it's been seventeen months and Brandon still acts like it's a chore to father his child. It's just another stressor today, and when I'm knocking on his condo door several hours later, I can't help but want to wrap Connor in my arms and take him with me so I know he's getting all the love he deserves.

Brandon opens the door, a beer in one hand, nacho chips in the other. "Hey," he tosses out, his back already to us as he heads back to his living room where his friends are spread out on the furniture.

"No," Connor whispers, staring up at me with wide eyes as I start taking his shoes off. "Mama, no."

"You're gonna hang out with Dada." My smile is so fake it hurts. "Mama will see you tomorrow."

"No." He shakes his head, yanking at the hem of my dress. "*No. Nooo!*"

"Fuck," Brandon mutters, scrubbing a hand over his mouth. "Here we go. Starting already."

My chest tightens, and when Connor stares up at me with tear-filled eyes, my eyes fill too. I take his sweet face in my hands, swiping at the silent tears as they fall. "I wish I could stay with you every single day, honey. That would make my mama heart so, *so* happy. You're going to stay with Dada tonight, and Mama will be thinking about you. When I pick you up tomorrow, I'm going to give you the biggest hug *ever* so you can feel how much I missed you."

Brandon leans against the wall, watching me with disinterest. "You think you're gonna stop smothering him anytime soon? He doesn't need you to explain every single thing to him like he's a baby; he needs you to leave. He'll forget about you as soon as you walk out the door."

I have this thing about fighting with Brandon in front of Connor. Call it being a mature adult who wants to model respectful relationships, but I don't think airing our grievances in front of our son is a particularly healthy display of communication. Needless to say, Brandon and I are not on the same page.

I'm also about two minutes from snapping and punching my son's father square in his tiny, useless dick.

So I close my eyes and breathe, rubbing Connor's arms. I take his hands in mine and smile, giving him a tender squeeze. "Mama loves you, and I can't wait to see you tomorrow. I'm going to miss you, but I hope you have so much fun with Dada and his friends."

"Dada," Connor whispers, beautiful eyes searching mine as he points at the door. "Bear."

I press my lips to his tiny pout and pull him into my arms, hugging him tight. "We can see them tomorrow," I murmur against his ear, savoring the way his little warm body melts into mine. I manage one more squeeze before Brandon pulls him away, leading him into the living room.

"Hi," Connor says to the three men lounging on the couch. He points to the Batman logo on his T-shirt. "Ba-man?"

Three gazes flick to his before moving back to the baseball game on TV, and my heart sinks.

Connor roots through a small basket of toys, pulling out a plastic cow. He displays it proudly, grinning widely. "Cow. *Moo-moo*!"

"They don't wanna play," Brandon tells him flatly.

Connor places his hand on his dad's knee, holding his cow out to him. "Ee-ya, ee-ya, bo?"

"I don't know what you're saying."

"E-I-E-I-O," I clarify gently, remembering the patience Adam showed him, the way he worked so hard to figure out what Connor wanted, how he sang and danced with him all through his living room. "He wants you to sing 'Old MacDonald' with him."

"No thanks."

Connor's face falls at the same rate my heart hits the floor.

Brandon picks him up and sets him down in the playpen in the corner of the room, emptying the basket of toys in there. "Here. Play in here."

"Okay, well..." I swallow, wringing my hands. "Call me if you need me. Bye, baby. Bye, guys."

While I'm waiting for the elevator in the hall, I root through my bag for my phone so I can tell Adam I'm heading to school. My hand brushes something furry, and I groan when I pull out Connor's stuffed kitty. He'll nap without his kitty, but he will not—*no matter what*—go to bed for the night without it.

I head back to Brandon's, pushing the door open.

"She's so fuckin' weird," someone says, and my feet stop.

"You're telling me," I hear Brandon mutter.

"A little overbearing, no?"

"Controlling as hell is what she is. Drives me up the fucking wall."

Quiet laughter rings out as my chest heaves, my head dipping down. My hand trembles on the doorknob, the other one gripping the stuffed toy so tight.

"Can't believe you had a kid with her."

The words hurt, but not nearly as much as Brandon's response.

"You think I chose this? Chose *her*? She wasn't supposed to be anything more than a casual fuck for a few weeks of summer fun. You know her parents died when she was a kid and nobody ever adopted her. Sometimes I think she poked a hole in the condom or something, just to get the family she wanted. Now I'm stuck with her forever. You think that's what I want?"

My fingers dig into the stuffed animal, and I try to ground myself in the moment. Feel the softness of its fur, listen to the whir of the air conditioner, inhale the scent of the food spread out on the counters.

But it doesn't work.

Instead, I hear the words in my head, again and again, like they're etching themselves there for me to replay at my darkest moments.

You think I chose this? Chose her?

Nobody adopted her.

Now I'm stuck with her.

The words are sharp and vicious, a knife plunged deep and twisted so forcefully. The stuffie falls to the ground as my hand moves to catch the quiver of my chin, to stifle the wounded whimper dripping from my lips. I take a step back, and then another, watching the door slam in my face when I let it go.

I make it to the elevator before I start to crumble.

"Are you feeling okay, Rosie? You look like you're going to be sick."

"I'm okay," I lie, wringing my hands in my lap. They're wet with sweat, shaking with the urge to fall apart. It took everything in me not to on the way here, not to give in to the gnawing compulsion to cry over a man whose words shouldn't hold any weight at all.

Except in a few simple sentences, he touched on every one of my insecurities. He brought to life every fear I've spent years in therapy combating the legitimacies of, and validated all of them in one fell swoop.

"I didn't sleep well last night. And I've got a bit of a headache." I wave a flappy hand through the air. "This weather, I think."

The look in Eva's eyes says she's not buying it. "How's your summer been?"

"It's, uh, it's been great. Connor and I—" Squeezing my eyes shut, I shake my head. "Actually, could we not do this? I'm sorry. I don't mean to be rude, but I'm incredibly anxious about why you brought me in here. I'd rather get this over with so I can stop catastrophizing in my head."

"I can certainly appreciate that. I didn't mean to cause you anxiety over this, Rosie, but…well, look. To be honest with you, it's not the best news, so in the spirit of getting this over with, I'll just come right out and say it." She rests her elbows on her desk, twisting a pen between her fingers as she watches me. She drops her gaze for only a moment, blowing out a sigh. "You've lost your scholarship."

The half-assed grip I had on my bag fails, and it falls from my lap, the contents spilling out on the floor. "*What*?" Eva rushes around the desk to help me. I hold my hand up, stopping her. "No. Stop."

"Rosie," she urges gently, watching me scramble to pick my things up, stuffing them in my bag. "Let me help you."

"I've got it," I snap, emotion bubbling in my throat. "What do you mean I lost my scholarship?"

"The donor felt you weren't serious about your studies, and they wanted to go in a different direction."

"*Not serious*? But I-I…I've worked so hard for this!" I scramble to my feet, clutching my bag to my heaving chest. "I ace everything. I study so hard. I-I…I don't have a life outside of school. I barely have any friends. I don't go out, don't party. School is my *life*."

"You're an excellent student, Rosie, and you have been since the moment you stepped foot inside this school."

"Then help me understand," I plead, my eyes burning with tears that want so desperately to fall. "What did I do wrong?"

Eva steps forward, taking my hand. "You've done nothing wrong, sweetheart. The donor's values…it's become clear they don't align with yours."

"What does that mean?"

She pulls her bottom lip between her teeth, like she's debating whether to tell me. Sighing, she guides me back to the chair. "They were disappointed to learn that you took an academic break."

"An academic break? But I was on maternity leave. I was raising my son."

"They felt that in choosing to take a maternity leave at such an important time in your academic life, you decided where your priorities lied."

"We live in Canada." I press my fingers against the headache forming in my temples. I can't be hearing this right. "I'm entitled to a full year maternity leave."

"You absolutely are."

"I'm being penalized for making my son, *my family*, my priority?"

"Rosie, you're not being penal—"

"I'm losing my scholarship!" Blood thunders in my ears as I jump to my feet. The room spins, the edges of my vision blurring. "How am I supposed to pay for school? Oh my God." I spin away from her, trembling hand pressed to my mouth as my world starts collapsing around me, the weight of the realization hitting me right in the chest. "How am I supposed to pay for school?" I whisper. "I used the last of my inheritance to supplement my maternity leave for the last year. I've only been back to work for four months. And only part time. And I have daycare expenses. I-I…I don't have enough saved up. Not even close." A choked sob escapes my throat, and I slap my hand over my mouth as my stomach threatens to empty itself. "Oh God."

A hand lands on my back, and though the touch is meant to be soothing, I feel no comfort.

"What are my options?"

Eva pauses. "I've looked into some additional funding, some bursaries, but, Rosie, this close to the school year starting…everything's already been spoken for."

I hug my bag to my chest, staring at the ground. "I deserve this," I whisper. "I've earned it."

"I'm not arguing that, but ultimately, it's up to the donor." She squeezes my shoulder. "You can take a year off. Work at the clinic and save up. The team is prepared to save your spot for next year. What's another year?"

What's another year? Another year means me working as much as I can, long days and nights so that I can cover my rent, pay for daycare, and somehow save enough money to cover the cost of vet school. It's two more years at Archie's and being the reason he and Marco can't move in together, because I can't afford to move out. It's less time with my son, a mental battle I have to face for letting both of us down, putting our future on hold for another year.

Slipping my backpack onto my shoulder, I head for the door. "Thank you for taking the time to meet with me," I tell her quietly.

"Rosie—"

"It's fine," I lie. "I'm fine. Enjoy the rest of your summer."

She watches me closely, and I see the anguish in her eyes. She hates that she has to do this, and I know it's not her fault. But in this moment, I need to get away from her.

She finally nods, smiling faintly. "We'll be in touch. Take care, Rosie."

I rush through the hallways, bypassing the professors and few students roaming around. My throat burns, a tightness that squeezes like a vice. Everything feels blurry, confusing, a muddled mess I can't see through. I burst through the front doors, stepping into the warm sunshine and fresh breeze, but it doesn't help. It brings no clarity, and I hurry aimlessly across campus, unsure where I'm going, what I'm looking for.

I won't find it here anyway, right? I don't belong here. Not right now, at least.

I…I'm not sure I belong anywhere. And the realization is gutting, buckling my knees, threatening to wipe me off my feet, pull me to the ground.

But I make it to a bench before I fall apart.

NINETEEN

DIPSHITS

Adam

"I SWEAR TO FUCK, Adam, if we lose one more time because of you, I'm gonna lose my shit."

"He's distracted as fuck today."

"Leave him alone. He's getting laid tonight for the first time in forever. That takes a lot of mental prep."

"I'm not—no, I'm—that's redic…" I sigh, my TV screen splattering with the blood of my character as I die yet again, disappointing my teammates on the other end of my headset for the umpteenth time today. "Yeah, I'm definitely kinda-sorta thinking about it."

I mean, fucking sue me. As Emmett said, it's been forever. And also, Rosie is Rosie. Have you met her? She's got the kindest, most patient heart I've ever known, and being with her makes me feel alive. Of course I can't fucking think straight right now.

"He's doing it again," Jaxon mutters. "Buddy, you better hop in the shower and rub one out before your girl comes over. Otherwise Rosie's gonna need to finish herself off tonight when you bust your nut five seconds after you get your dick wet."

"Fuck you." *Definitely squeezing in a shower.*

"What time is she coming over?" Garrett asks.

"I'm waiting for her to text that she's ready to be picked up. She had to go into school to meet with one of her teachers." My Apple Watch vibrates, and I chuck my Xbox controller in all my eagerness. "This is probably her." I frown at the number, swiping the call away. "Never mind. Not her."

"Who else would it be? Do you have other friends you're not telling us about?" Carter accuses.

"With your larger-than-life personality? I don't have room for any more friends."

"You're damn right you don't."

The same number jumps at me from my watch face, and my brows tug together. I don't know it, but I recognize it as being the same one that called last week when Rosie and Connor were over. I decline the call again and sit forward on the couch, rubbing my eyes.

"I'm gonna get going."

"He's gonna go jack off in the shower," Jaxon clarifies.

"Hey, Jaxon?"

"Yeah, dude?"

"Shut the fuck up."

"Oh shit." He chuckles. "Watch out, Rosie. Daddy Adam's feeling fiery tonight."

I toss my controller and headset to my coffee table, patting Bear's head before I stand, stretching my arms overhead.

"Where's Rosie, huh, Bear?" I scoop my phone off the kitchen island. Her last text message came in two hours ago, right before she dropped Connor off at Brandon's.

TROUBLE

Do you think I'm getting kicked out for being a bad girl?

ME

You're a good girl, but if you wanna be bad later, I can make sure you're punished accordingly.

We should call you Trouble, not me. I'm an angel, and you're a bad influence.

You can call me whatever you want as long as your eyes are rolling back into your head while you do it.

The most trouble, and the baddest boy.

Am I catastrophizing?

Maybe. But the best of us do sometimes. I'm sure it's nothing.

I hope so. Can I still be a bad girl later?

You can always be a bad girl, just as long as you're mine.

smile emoji Thanks for making me feel better and taking my mind off this. I'll call you when I'm done. Can't wait to see you.

I smile down at the messages, rubbing my hand over my chest, the way it puffs with pride, with happiness, with fullness. Because Rosie makes me feel all those things, and it's been so long since I've felt anything but disappointment.

I shoot off a quick text, asking her if the meeting went okay, and jump in a quick shower. It's not quick because I don't jerk off—because I absolutely do. It's quick because Jaxon was fucking right—it's been too long, and I'm way too worked up over this girl to last longer than a few minutes thinking about her body below mine.

There's no response from Rosie when I step out of the shower, and when I call her, it goes right to voice mail. Standing at my kitchen island, I tap my truck keys against the marble, trying to ignore the prickle of unease that makes the back of my neck clammy.

"Fuck it." I toss my phone in my pocket and my hat on my head before I head out the door and climb into my truck.

Something feels off, and the closer I get to the school, the more I worry. Rosie's phone is still off, which isn't like her. She always keeps it on and close by when she doesn't have Connor.

Driving slowly down the road, my gaze roams the grounds, looking for Rosie. I don't know what my plan is if I can't find her. I don't have a clue where she might be in this building, and I can't very well just stroll through it and hope no one recognizes me.

I'm about to try her one last time when I catch a flash of wispy blonde and rose gold waves beneath the shade of a towering oak. Rosie sits by herself on a bench, and I know. I know something's wrong by the defeated slump of her shoulders, the hang of her head, the way she clutches her bag to her stomach.

I throw the truck into park, cut the ignition, and rush across the lawn without so much as a care about who might recognize me, only that Rosie's alone right now, and I need to fix that.

"Rosie," I murmur when I reach her. "Baby, what's wrong?"

She doesn't flinch, not a bit, like she knew I'd find her.

I almost expect her to say nothing. To sit here silently, unable to find the words she needs.

But she doesn't. She has the words, and she gives them to me. Quietly, and so easily, like they're the only truth she knows.

"My parents died in a house fire when I was eleven. My house was destroyed. My entire life was lost. I was the only one who survived, because my dad chose to save me first. He chose me." Slowly, Rosie's gaze lifts to mine, and the never-ending grief that shines in her eyes like shattered glass, far too fractured to be repaired, rocks me to my core. "That was the last time I was anyone's first choice."

The murmured, broken words snap the last of my resolve. I sink to my knees, right there before her, and as the dam breaks and those tears pour down her face like rain, I sweep her into my arms, clinging to her just as much as she's clinging to me.

~

I can't take my eyes off her, the way she's snuggled up beneath the quickly fading sun and a warm blanket, my dog curled up at her side, refusing to leave her. I don't blame him. She's different tonight, and she has been since I loaded her into my truck, ditched our dinner plans to pick up her favorite takeout instead. She's quiet and distant, and the silence is ear-splitting and painful in an earth-shattering way.

My world isn't right without her laughter.

Stepping through the patio door, I make my way to her, replacing her wine glass with a mug of her favorite blueberry tea. She takes it with a small smile, red-rimmed eyes peering up at me, and when I sit beside her, she wastes no time folding herself into my side.

Squeezing her to me, I kiss her head. "I think you belong right here."

"With you?" she asks, chin on my chest.

"Where else?"

She lays her cheek over my heart, her words soft. "I've wanted to belong to someone for a long time. So long, I'm not sure my brain will let me believe it now."

"I'm a patient man. I don't mind needing to prove it to you every day."

Rosie smiles, and for the next few minutes, we sit in the peace of the evening, the quiet breeze rustling through the trees, the buzz of the cicadas, the fading song of the birds settling in for the night.

And then Rosie tells me her story.

"I woke up in the middle of the night to my mom screaming my name. My bedroom door was closed, but it felt so warm in there. I remember the glow coming from beneath the crack in my door." A tear slides down her cheek. "I just thought the hallway lights were on."

I pull her tighter against me, rub her back while I listen.

"My mom kept screaming, telling my dad to get me. It made me scared, and I started crying, calling for my parents. Then my dad came into my room. He knelt next to my bed, told me to wrap my arms around his neck and my legs around his waist. And he told me to close my eyes." Rosie's eyes find mine, shining with tears beneath the light of the moon. "I listened. I always listened to my dad."

"Such a good girl," I murmur, swiping the tears from her eyes before they can fall.

"Even with my eyes closed, I knew. I could hear it. Feel it. My dad held me so tight, he left bruises. It was so cool when he ran outside. It was September, and the weather had started turning. It felt like such a relief to be outside, but I could feel the heat at my back as my dad kept me turned away from the house."

Rosie looks up to the sky, pulling in a shaky breath. When she releases it, her tears spill down her cheeks. "'Stay right here,' Dad told me. 'Don't move. Wait for help.' He told me he had to go, that he had to get my mom. I asked him if he was coming back, and he looked at me for a minute before he promised he would. 'Right back,' he said. 'I promise, I'll never leave you.'" Her eyes flutter closed, and she sits in the moment, the memory, while I kiss her forehead, smooth back her hair from her wet cheeks. "I knew he was lying. He wasn't coming back, and he knew it too. He kissed me, hugged me so…*so* tight. Tucked my hair behind my ear and told me he was proud of me. And right before he disappeared inside the house, he looked at me one last time over his shoulder and told me he loved me for the last time."

My chest pulls tight, I feel like it's breaking wide open as Rosie buries her face in my neck and cries for the parents she lost, the good-bye she should have never had to say, not at eleven years old. I press my lips to her shoulder, over and over, any words that might make this better completely lost to me. Is there a better? I really don't know, but I don't want her to feel alone.

"He was only inside for a minute when it happened. I could hear the fire trucks close by. But suddenly there was a loud crash, and every window shattered. The front door blew open, and flames spilled out. I screamed, ran through the gate to the backyard just as the trucks pulled up. Right in time for the back door to explode," she adds on a whisper. "It scared me, and I tripped. Over my own two feet. Fell backward, right into our pool. The sun cover was on, and I got tangled in it. I started sinking, and I couldn't get free. I couldn't find my way out. I thought that was it, Adam. I thought I was dying, and I just wanted to be with my parents." Rosie swipes at her eyes with the back of her wrists, sniffling. "The next thing I remember, I was lying on our back deck, and a firefighter was giving me CPR. It was already too late for my parents."

"Ah fuck, Rosie." I pull her onto my lap, wrapping her around me, feeling her against me. She's here and she's solid, but the race of my heart reminds me how close I came to losing her, to never knowing her, and the thought is staggering.

"Hey," she whispers, cupping my face, bringing my gaze to hers. "I'm right here. I'm okay."

"I'm sorry," I try, but it's hoarse, broken. The two words aren't enough, but they're all I have. Closing my eyes, I rest my forehead against hers while I get my bearings. I tuck her hair behind her ears, staring into the sweetest green eyes that hold so much love, compassion, strength, unending grief. "I don't think he was lying, Rosie. Your dad. I know it feels that way. But he told you he'd never leave you because he never will. You can't see him, I know, but he's there. Your mom too."

"I know that; really, I do. But I was alone. So many times I wished I'd gone with them, because I was left with no one. I was all on my own, and I was only eleven."

"What do you mean you were all alone? You had other family, right? Someone who took you in?"

She looks at me for a long moment, letting my mind work, and I know before she tells me. "I went into the foster system, Adam. Group foster. Just like you."

There's a tiny part of me, this small little boy who wants to jump for joy at a connection we share, but I know. I know by the lonely look that lives in the corner of her eyes, the longing that's always there. "Our experiences were very different, weren't they?"

She nods, a sad smile on her face. "I aged out. I sat there alone, year after year, wanting nothing more than to be chosen. I wanted my family back. I wanted any family. I just wanted to belong, to feel safe, to feel wanted. And I—" She sniffles, catching a tear the moment it drips from her eye. "I didn't understand why nobody wanted me. I was such a good kid. I was always kind and respectful. I loved school and was an A-plus student. Nobody wanted me, Adam. And still..."

"What do you mean, 'still?'" I grip her chin when she turns away, forcing her gaze back to mine. "What do you mean, 'still,' Rosie?"

She sniffs, nibbling her lower lip. "I overheard Brandon today when I dropped Connor off. His friends were over, and he said...he said he would've never chosen to have a child with me. That I was just supposed to be temporary fun, but he was stuck with me now."

"What a fucking dipshit," I accidentally blurt.

"It's my own fault for expecting more from people who've never given me reason to. He's not even listed on Connor's birth certificate, for God's sake. I gave birth alone, because he couldn't step up and support me in my most vulnerable moments."

"Fuck that guy," I bite out, blood thundering in my ears. "Rosie, *fuck him,* and fuck his worthless opinion. He doesn't know what he has, how fucking *lucky* he is to have you as the mother of his child. You gave him the most beautiful gift in the world, and he's done nothing but take it for granted. So fuck him."

"That's not all of it," she whispers. "I lost my scholarship today."

"What?"

"My teacher, she told me he—the donor—felt like taking a break for my maternity leave was my way of stating where my priorities lied. That I should've chosen school over staying home with Connor for the year."

A dark, bitter chuckle leaves my throat. "You've gotta be fucking kidding me. That's the most misogynistic bullshit I've ever heard. He pulled your scholarship because you chose your son when he needed you?"

"It's just...For years, nobody chose me. I had no one, and I so desperately wanted a family of my own again. Someone to love, someone to love me. And then Connor came, and by some miracle, I had it. I had the family I'd been dreaming of. I told myself I'd always choose him, so I did. I chose him, and honestly, I chose myself. Because nobody else ever did it, and I wasn't going to begin my son's life by not putting him first, not when I have this opportunity to take this time with him. But now, in doing so, I've lost the only thing I've been chosen for in years." She shakes her head, a furrow between her brows. "I worked so hard for this, Adam. I poured my heart and soul into my education, and I've earned this scholarship year after year. And now…now even they don't want me."

"They don't deserve you, Rosie. Nobody who treats you like this does." I brush my thumb over her lower lip. "I'm so sorry that somebody overlooked you when you were growing up, that they didn't take the time to know you, to see how beautiful your heart is. I'm sorry Brandon is a useless twat-waffle."

Rosie snorts a laugh, music to my damn ears after a day without it. "What's a twat-waffle?"

"I'm honestly not sure, but my friend calls her boyfriend and brother one every time they're being dipshits, so it felt fitting." She laughs again, and I smile, tasting it from her mouth. "I'm sorry you lost your scholarship. I know how hard you've worked for it, and it's not right. We're going to figure it out, okay? Together."

"There's no figuring it out, Adam. I don't have the money to pay for it, bottom line. I'm going to have to take the year off again and work to save up for it."

I shake my head. "Nope. What's option two?"

She laughs again, quietly this time, a tired, resigned sound that I hate. "I don't have another option. I had some money after my parents passed, but I used the last of it to support Connor and me on maternity leave. There's no other way."

"Then I'll help."

"You absolutely will not," she says firmly. When I open my mouth, she raises her brows, and I snap it shut again. "You will not, Adam Lockwood, do you hear me?"

"I don't want you to put your dreams on hold, Rosie."

"What's one more year?" she murmurs, and the words sound like they hurt to say just as much as they hurt to hear. She shifts off my lap to the seat beside me, pulling her knees into her chest. She looks so small, so vulnerable, I want to wrap her in Bubble Wrap so nothing can ever hurt her again. "Today's been a stark reminder that I've never belonged to anyone or anything. That I've never been enough, never been just right to be anyone's first choice." She rests her chin on her knee, staring off at nothing. "Maybe it's less about being someone's first choice, and more about being loved, being loved enough to *be* someone's first choice." She shrugs. "No one has ever loved me enough to make me their first choice."

"Hey." I take her hands in mine, pulling her back to me. "We'll never be right for everyone, but we'll be perfect for the right person. And when that person comes along, there is no choice. It just…is. We exist exactly the way we are, with exactly the right people, because there is no other way to be."

I press my lips to hers, and she opens without hesitation, her fingers sliding tenderly through my hair as she sighs against my mouth.

"I want you, Rosie. I want all of you. And there is no other choice."

TWENTY

SPLITTING HER IN HALF, BUT POLITELY

Adam

I SWEAR this body was made for me. Warm and soft, curled around me tighter than it's ever been, gentle fingers that drift along my arms, a tender gaze that doesn't sway.

This body is perfect, every sweet inch of it, and I don't want to let it go.

We sit for so long beneath the stars, tangled limbs huddled together under a cozy blanket, Bear sprawled out at our feet. Rosie's different now than she was before. Freer, like she doesn't need to hide anymore. She's dropped her last wall, put it all out there, and now she can just…be.

She never needed to hide, but I understand the hesitancy to let someone all the way in. I'm just thankful I'm the lucky fool who gets all her pieces.

She tells me about the house she grew up in, big and beautiful, an old Victorian with stained glass windows framing the front door, and a sprawling wraparound porch with a swing. Her favorite places were the bay window in the living room where she curled up to read, and the garden of peonies she and her mom planted out front. She loved all the charm the house came with, and tells me that, despite the old wiring that led to the short-circuiting that caused the fire, she only looks back on her memories there with so much fondness.

"Adam?" Rosie rubs the spot between Bear's eyes, smiling down at his head in her lap. She looks up at me, her eyes moving between mine. "I want to apologize for not telling you sooner that I was in the foster system too. I know the ideal time to tell you would've been when you shared the same with me, but when you told me about your time in the system, I felt a bit jealous. You found this beautiful family, and I found nothing. Your experience sounded so wonderful, and mine was so lonely. The jealousy didn't last, but then I felt dirty and guilty for ever feeling that way, and I didn't know how to talk to you about it. My biggest insecurities were formed during my time there, and I've spent the years since trying to combat them, to hype myself up, love myself enough so that I didn't have to rely on someone else to give it to me. But some days are harder than others when it comes to remembering all the strides I've made. So, I'm sorry, Adam."

"You don't need to apologize for being human. Those feelings are real and valid, and you deserved time to sort through them." I press a kiss to her palm. "Thank you for being honest with me about this."

We stay snuggled together for another half hour, no words spoken as we hold each other. She's had a long day, so when she buries her third yawn against my arm, I shift her off my lap.

Standing, I hold my hand out to her. "C'mon, sweetheart. Let's go to bed."

Bear doesn't make it past the living room before choosing to pass out on the couch. I keep Rosie's hand in mine as we move silently through the dark house, and when she disappears into my bathroom to get ready for bed, she does so with a kiss on my lips first.

I strip down to my boxer briefs and plug my phone into the charger. I've got nineteen missed notifications. Two are more calls from that unknown number; the other seventeen are my *Puck Sluts* group chat. Garrett's sent four eggplant emojis, four peach emojis, and eight question marks. Emmett says Cara wants to have another girls' night so they can analyze our first time. Jaxon wants to know how many of his condoms I used. Carter wants to know if we had post-sex snacks in bed. Apparently, that's his and Ollie's favorite bonding time.

I'm too exhausted to deal with any of them, so when the bathroom door opens, I turn my phone right off.

"Ready for be—ahhh. You're naked." *She's fucking naked*. I shove my hand through my hair, then gesture at Rosie's beautiful, full, naked body. "You are…really fucking naked. Fucking spectacular, too, in case you were wondering. Also, naked."

My favorite brand of trouble giggles, that adorable nose crinkling when she does, her hands wringing at her stomach. She steps forward, and my eyes bounce from her immaculate tits to the swing of those round hips. Christ, she's flawless. Have I already said that?

"Can confirm, I am, indeed, naked. In case you were wondering." There's a hint of mischief in her eyes that shines so bright, hiding nearly all the nerves. "Would you like to get naked too?"

"Well, I…I…" I rub the nape of my neck, then point at the bed. "To do naked stuff?"

Rosie nods. "To do naked stuff. If you want to."

"I don't want to take advantage of you feeling vulnerable."

"I am feeling vulnerable, but not in a bad way. I feel safe, Adam, and it's freeing. Tonight made me feel closer to you. Maybe I dropped my last wall." Her shoulder pops up and down. "I don't know, but I feel good, and being with you makes me feel even better."

I swallow the lump in my throat when she stops in front of me. "Being with you makes me feel better than I've ever felt."

She takes my face in her hands, her smooth, warm touch gliding along my stubbled jaw. "Can I kiss you?"

My heart thunders, and I give her the most articulated whispered response I can manage. "Duh."

She beams, the most incredible, breathtaking sight, and guides my face down to hers. This kiss is everything Rosie. Patient and slow, soft but confident, the gentle way her lips move on mine, her tongue sweeping my mouth with certainty, fingers gliding into my hair, sifting through the curls. It settles my heart and sends every nerve ending racing at the same time.

"You're shaking," Rosie murmurs, head cocked as she watches me. "You're nervous."

"No," I lie. "No way. I'm totally prepared and super excited and not at all nervous. Look!" Dashing to my bedside table, I yank open the drawer with my super-steady hands. "I even got all these." I hold up the massive wad of rubbers Jaxon shoved at my chest yesterday, waving them in Rosie's face. "Condoms!" I start sorting through them. "Ultra ribbed, bare-skin raw, banana flavored, mag—"

"Adam." Rosie laughs, placing her hand over mine and my gigantic collection of condoms. "Why the hell do you have so many?"

My face burns, and I can feel my heartbeat in my throat. "My friend gave them to me."

"He really likes his variety, doesn't he?" Rosie picks through the assortment, setting one aside, tucking the rest away. With a smile so sure, so certain, she steps up to me, and my brain short-circuits as I stare down at everything I've wanted, craved for so long. She's finally here, this incredible woman in front of me, and part of me is terrified to reach out and take it. It feels like there's no turning back after this, but what if she wants to? What if she decides I'm not enough?

"I keep trying…" I swallow, shaken by the nerves rolling off me while Rosie stands there so sure of this. She takes my hands in hers, steadying the tremor in my hands when she squeezes. "I don't mean to rush you. I'm trying to take things slow with us."

"Do you want slow?"

My eyes move between hers, hoping she sees it all. The commitment, the awe, all my best intentions. "I want…you. I just want you, Rosie."

"You have me, Adam. I don't feel like we've rushed anything or moved too slowly. Everything feels right." She brushes my curls from his forehead before pressing her lips to mine. "Very right."

And maybe that's exactly what I needed to hear, that I'm just *right* for her. Because the tension stacked in my shoulders dissolves, and as I stand taller, my chest swells with pride.

"Ah," Rosie muses. "There's that smirk. One part playful, two parts cocky." She slings her arms around my neck as I yank her into me. "Just the way I love it."

"You know what else you're gonna love?" My mouth moves over her shoulder, up her neck, pausing at the shell of her ear. "The way I fuck you."

Rosie's fingernails bite into my shoulders as I walk her backward. The back of her thighs hit the bed, and with my hand on her collarbone, I force her down to the mattress. Her wide eyes follow the path of my hands, down to the waistband of my boxer briefs, and when I lose them on the floor, she licks her lips.

"God, I keep forgetting how big your cock is. I'm almost certain this is going to hurt."

"I'll be gentle," I promise. "I'll try to be, at least." Trailing my finger up her thigh, I watch her skin pebble with goose bumps before her legs fall open to me, letting me step between them. "We can stay in bed all day tomorrow and eat hot fudge sundaes while you recover."

"Careful. Serve a girl hot fudge sundaes in bed, and she just might fall in love with you."

"Note to self," I murmur, reaching down to grip the back of Rosie's neck, hoisting her mouth to mine. "Serve Rosie hot fudge sundaes in bed."

Stepping back, I fist the base of my hard cock, taking a moment to appreciate the scarlet flush creeping over Rosie's body, the way it makes me hot from the inside out.

"Feet flat on the bed. Let me see how wet that pussy is, gorgeous girl. Show me you're ready for me."

She doesn't hesitate, propping herself up on her elbows, spreading her legs wide for me. The sight is glorious, her delicate skin a dusty rose color, glistening and needy, begging to be touched, tasted. I stalk toward her, and her pupils dilate as she scurries backward, up to the pillows. I grin, grabbing hold of her ankles, dragging her beneath me as my knees hit the bed.

"Get back here," I murmur, fingers sliding into the hair at the nape of her neck, gripping it, tilting her chin. "Can't taste ya way up there."

I claim her mouth first, because I love the way she lets go against me, releases that breath that seems to hold every last bit of tension, like she melts just for me. When I glide along her jaw, trail wet kisses down her throat, her breath hitches. I palm her hip, squeezing the soft flesh in my hand as I take one rosy nipple between my teeth, dragging my tongue across it while she writhes.

"Adam," she whimpers as my mouth moves lower, across her stomach, swirling my tongue around her belly button, nibbling on her hip bone.

"Yeah, baby?"

"I…I…" She covers her face with her hands, hips lifting off the bed when I trace the juncture of her thighs with my tongue. "Oh fuck."

I settle between her legs, hooking my arms around her hips. "You trying to say something?"

"I…I…" Bright green eyes bounce between mine. "I just…" She swallows, the simple action audible. "I really like you."

"I really like you too. Want me to show you how much?"

"Please."

"'Kay." With my eyes locked on hers, I lick a slow path up the center of her, watching as she tosses her head back with a rough moan. Her fingers plow through my hair, and when I pull her swollen clit into my mouth, she bucks against me, crying out my name.

"More," she pleads. "God, give me more, please."

"I told you before. Just Adam is fine."

Her head rolls backward. "You're infuriating sometimes."

"If it's you I'm infuriating, I'll gladly do it for the rest of my life."

Rosie comes alive when I push two fingers inside her, and *shit*, if that isn't a stunning sight.

She keeps one hand in my hair as she grinds against my face, rides my fingers, a brilliant flush staining her immaculate skin, crawling up her throat like a vine, pooling in her cheeks. Her soft pink waves graze her slender neck, full red lips parted as she struggles to breathe, each one a strangled cry as she chases her high.

I curl my fingers inside her, pulling a gasp from her throat, and suck her clit until she comes undone, spilling all over me while my name rings in my ears.

Rosie sits up, scrambling to the head of the bed as I head to the bedside table, grabbing the condom she picked for me. *Magnum.*

I fucking love her.

I hold her wide gaze as I tear the wrapper with my teeth and sheath my throbbing cock in one fluid movement. My knees hit the mattress, and I crawl over her, cupping her cheek as she lies down.

"You're sure?" I ask quietly.

"So sure."

"Good. Because I'm so sure about you."

She smiles at me then, free and gentle, and I know I'm going to remember the way I feel right now for the rest of my life.

Rosie wraps her fist around my cock, guiding it between her thighs. Despite all her confidence in this bedroom tonight, I feel the slight quiver in her touch. I take her hand off me, instead holding it in mine.

"Hey," I murmur, smoothing her hair off her face. "It's okay to be nervous. I am too."

"It's been a long time," she admits on a whisper.

"For me too. But I'm glad for that. It means I waited for something special. You're my something special, Rosie."

She tips her chin, running the tip of her nose against mine before kissing me. "I'm ready."

I grip my cock, pressing it against her. My chest tightens and my heartbeat leaps to my throat as Rosie holds my gaze, and slowly, *so slowly*, I sink inside her. Her mouth opens on a gasp, fingernails scoring my shoulders as she tenses below me.

"I'm sorry," I whisper against her neck, holding myself still. My body trembles with the desire to plunge forward, to feel every inch of her squeezed so tight around me.

"I don't want this to go to your head, but it feels like I'm being politely split in half."

I chuckle. "As long as I'm doing it politely."

She lifts her hips, urging me deeper. I squeeze my eyes shut to the overwhelming euphoria as she takes me to the hilt, pausing there to adjust.

"Christ, Rosie." I drop my forehead to her shoulder, struggling to hold onto my sanity. "You're so fucking tight." Slowly, I rock my hips against hers. "Is that okay?"

"Yes," she moans, matching each rock with one of her own. "Please, more."

I give her more, pulling out before I sink back inside, inch by aching inch, careful not to push her. She takes it all, opening her legs wider, lifting her hips higher, and I grip her chin as I drive a little deeper, a little faster.

"Such a beautiful girl, taking all of me. You're doing so good."

Hazy eyes roll down to mine, pink tongue swiping across her swollen lips. She tosses one arm around my neck, pulling me closer, the other strewn haphazardly above her head as she meets every one of my thrusts. "So good," she mumbles. "So perfect. Don't stop, Adam. Please."

I don't think I could stop if I wanted to, but if she asked me to, I'd find a way. I'd give her anything, whatever she wants, because as she stares up at me like I'm the sun in her sky, I realize she's mine. She's everything bright and good in my world, and in this moment, I'm so fucking thankful. Thankful for an ex that treated me wrong, because she showed me what I deserved. Thankful for dates that went to shit, because they showed me what I wanted. Thankful for every single thing that hasn't worked out the way I wished it did at the time, because all of it—all the bullshit, the broken trust, the hurt—led me right here, to this incredible woman below me, the only one I want at my side.

And the knowledge makes me feral.

Something comes over me. Something dark and hungry that wants to claim this woman so everyone knows she's mine. My hand goes to her throat, closing around it, dragging her drugged gaze to mine as I growl out my next words.

"You wanna belong to someone, Rosie? You belong to me. These eyes are for me. This smile is for me. This heart? All mine." I drag my hand down her side, over her hip, digging my fingers into her ass as I bring her closer, drive myself deeper and deeper, until there's nowhere left to go. "These hips. This ass. This fucking pussy? *Mine.* All of you belongs to me, Rosie."

"Oh *fuck,*" she cries, squeezing me tighter. "Adam, I'm gonna come."

"Not yet, you're not. Not until you tell everyone who you belong to." I hike her leg up, tossing it over my shoulder. She cries out as I plunge deeper, and thank fucking *fuck* I took that shower, because I'm about thirty seconds from blowing my load. "Who do you belong to, Rosie? Better make it count, 'cause I'm only gonna ask once."

Her eyes widen, legs trembling, and when her head falls back, I grab her hair and bring her gaze right back to mine. Her walls shake, and the faster I thrust, the more she tears at my shoulders. My thumb finds her clit, and she explodes around me with a cry, screaming my name.

"*You,*" she cries as I bury my face in her neck, combusting inside her. "I belong to you."

Crushing my mouth to hers, I haul her slick body against mine and reach for another condom, because I'm not fucking done. Not with her, and I'm gonna make sure she knows it.

"You're not my first choice, Rosie. You're the only goddamn option."

TWENTY-ONE

WE USED SEVEN CONDOMS

Adam

I'VE THOUGHT about fate a lot in my life.

Recognized that if my first mother hadn't made the decision to not raise me, if my grandma didn't die, I would have never found my parents and the incredible family who chose to love a kid they had zero obligation to love. Without my family, I likely wouldn't have been able to follow my dream to be a professional hockey player. Hell, I don't know if I even would have had the dream at all.

If I hadn't been drafted to Vancouver and relocated to Canada from Colorado, I would have never found my best friends.

If I didn't travel for hockey, I might not have come home from a twelve-day road trip to find my girlfriend fucking another man in our bed.

If I hadn't caught Courtney cheating on me, I would have never forced myself to leave.

If I hadn't forced myself to leave, I wouldn't have been on that trail through Mount Fromme nearly two months ago.

If I hadn't been on that trail, I wouldn't have found the very best and brightest thing in my world.

I think about fate a lot. I think about all the shit things I've had to overcome to get to where I am now, the happiest I can remember ever being, with a sweet little beauty tucked into my side, her flushed cheek resting on my shoulder, soft hand splayed over my stomach. I wouldn't have these freckles, delicious flecks of honey sprinkled over sun-kissed skin. Not this nose that crinkles in the sweetest way when she's trying not to smile, these wide, plush hips that demand my eyes follow them everywhere they go, this brilliant smile that manages to turn my whole day around and give me hope for a future I'd given up on.

I've learned not to ask why, but I find myself always wondering how. How the hell did I find myself here? How did I get so damn lucky? How did I find her, and how do I make sure I get to keep her?

Thick lashes flutter, and sleepy moss eyes blink up at me. A shy smile tugs up one side of her mouth first before giving way to a brilliant explosion that this perfect girl tries to hide by burying her face in my chest.

"Why are you staring at me?" Rosie mumbles against me.

"Why are you hiding from me?"

"I asked you first."

"I asked you second."

She lifts her face, hair a wonderful mess, playful gaze narrowed. "You're annoying."

Chuckling, I roll her onto her back and sprawl out on top of her, holding her wrists above her head. "I don't know how I found you, but I don't want to waste my time wondering. I can't believe I just stumbled on you on a normal day, that you walked into my life and didn't turn around and walk right back out. I don't want to know how or why I got so lucky; I just want to accept that I did and never question it.

"I don't want to waste my time asking pointless questions, imagining a life where you're anywhere other than right next to me. I want to spend my days giving you the love you've always deserved, the kind you've dreamed of, and I want to show you how thankful I am for giving it back to me. You're mine, Rosie, and I'm yours. That's all I need to know. *That's* why I'm staring at you."

"Oh." She tilts her chin, sweeping a breathless kiss across my lips. "Guess that's okay then."

"Mmm, you guess? Well, I can't have you guessing. Need to have you certain."

"And how do you plan on doing that?"

I trail my nose down the slope of her neck, then lower, until I can cup her full breast in my hand, twirl my tongue over that taut, dusky bud. My fingertips glide over the dip in her waist, push their way between her luscious thighs, plunging into a pool of heat, wringing a cry from her throat. "By fucking it into you."

"We only have one condom left."

Sitting back on my heels, I grab the last sealed wrapper from the pile of torn ones on the table. I lift a brow and sheath my cock as Rosie watches, captivated. "Better make it count then, huh, trouble?"

The name does something to her, makes her come alive with confidence, maybe. Because she gets this wicked gleam in her eyes, trying and failing to bite back her smirk. She climbs to her knees, her palm hitting my chest as she pushes me down to my back and straddles my hips, trapping my cock between her wet pussy and my stomach.

"Look at you," I murmur. "So sexy when you're taking control. Are you gonna sit on my cock?"

"I don't know. Teasing you might be fun."

"Teasing me?"

"Mhmm…" One hand disappears in her hair, the other braced on my abs as she slowly—*so fucking slowly*—slides along the length of my cock, right up to the head, and then back, soaking me. "Teasing you."

"Rosie," I warn, gripping her hips when she does it again, grinding her to a halt at the tip of my cock. "I'm not always patient."

"But you're always kind."

I push up on my elbow, bringing her mouth to mine with a fistful of her hair. "Don't mistake my kindness for weakness. I'll put you on your hands and knees, bury myself inside you and fuck you from behind until the only word you remember is my name, and you can feel me even when we're not together." I nip her lower lip. "I'm weak for you —*so fucking weak*—but the bedroom is the last place you'll see it."

Rosie grins, smug and proud, before she takes my cock in one hand, pushing me back down with the other. She sinks down my length, a magnificent sight as her head lolls backward, lips parting on a low, long gasp while everything inside me lights up like a pinball machine, begging me to take control.

"Oh God. This is…" She shifts, rocking forward, and falls forward with a whimper, nails biting into my chest. "Yep, this is it. My favorite of your collection. Tell your friend thanks."

I pick up the crumpled wrapper, chuckling when I read it. *G-Spot, For Her Pleasure.* I open my mouth to tell her I'm not going to tell Jaxon shit —it'll go right to his head—but she picks herself up and sinks down a second time, deeper this time, seating herself all the way on my cock, and I toss my head back with a low growl, fingers digging into her hips with a punishing grip.

Rosie leans over, waves falling around our faces. "I like you weak for me," she whispers. "I'm weak for you, too, except, somehow, I feel so much stronger with you." Her soft hand grazes my cheek, and she presses her mouth to mine, coaxing it open. "Thank you for building me up, for making me feel safe enough to be myself, for being the type of man I'm so proud to have my son look up to. Thank you for being you, Adam, exactly as you are."

Fate has taken so much only to grant me so many invaluable things in this life. And as much as I've tried not to question it, to simply take what it gives me, I'd be lying if I said I didn't sometimes question the process of getting there.

Because if Courtney had loved me exactly as I was and it still didn't work out, I wouldn't have lied to Rosie about who I am.

But Courtney didn't love me for who I was.

And I did lie.

And Rosie has no idea who she's really dating.

But this isn't fate's fault. It's mine.

~

"Did you use them all?"

"I'm not telling you how many times we had sex." If I were bragging, though, I'd definitely be telling my friends that it's a miracle my dick is still attached to my body, and that I'm no longer at risk of developing premature arthritis. I don't feel like bragging though. I'm nervous, and my stomach hurts.

Jaxon wags his brows. "So you *did* have sex."

"What? No, I—ugh." I cross my arms over my chest and look away. If I don't make eye contact, there's a better chance of me not spilling the *juicy deets* everyone keeps asking for. "Shut up."

"I'm not asking how many times you had sex. I'm asking if you used all the condoms."

"Telling you how many condoms we used tells you how many times we had sex."

Carter winks. "Unless you went in bare after you ran out."

"I did not."

"You fucker," Jaxon muses. "You *did* use all the condoms. Jesus, that's, like, six times."

"Seven," I mumble, ignoring Carter's hand when he holds it up for a high five. He resorts to high-fiving Garrett. "But the last one was this morning." I point at the two of them, shoving their hands into a box of Oreos. "If you two don't stop eating, you're gonna be covered in cookie crumbs for your interviews."

Garrett frowns at his hands before wiping them on his pants. Carter, on the other hand, crunches another cookie between his teeth while looking me dead in the eye.

I roll my eyes. "I don't give a fuck what you look like in your interview, but I know for a fact Ollie dressed you in that outfit this morning, and if it's covered in crumbs, it's gonna be your ass."

"I can handle Ollie," he says, licking his fingers, and I snort a laugh.

"Okay, bud. Let's pretend your five-foot wife doesn't have your balls in a vice."

He jabs me in the shoulder. "Five—" *jab* "—foot—" *jab* "—*one*. She's just got such a powerful personality. You know she's got those teacher eyes." He points two fingers aggressively at his eyes. "Sees everything. And don't get me started on that teacher voice. Turns me on and scares the fuck outta me at the same time." He sets his cookies down, dusts his hands off, adjusts his junk, and frowns. "Guess I'll put these away for now."

Emmett hops off the stool he's been sitting on for the last ten minutes, shaking hands with the sports journalist who's been interviewing him. His eyes widen with his grin as he jogs over to us.

"Did I hear you say you went through *seven* condoms last night? Cara's gonna lose her shit. She says you've been ignoring her messages. She's upset with you."

Groaning, I pull my phone out of my pocket. I've got twenty-three notifications, and all of them are from my group chat with the girls.

OLIVIA

Why is he ignoring us?

CARA

We know where you live, Lockwood. Nobody ignores Cara Brodie and lives to talk about it.

JENNIE

Our man def journeyed to Pussy Palace last night. Might've gotten lost there too.

OLIVIA

I just wanna know if she treated you right.

Oh! Did you try that move from the audiobook? You know the scene, where she's on her hands and knees???

JENNIE

I feel like Adam's a freak between the sheets. It's always the quiet ones, you know?

CARA

If we don't hear from you in the next ten seconds, I cannot be held responsible for my actions. Do you hear me, Lockwood? I. CANNOT. BE. HELD. RESPONSIBLE. FOR. MY. ACTIONS.

This motherfucker is going down.

JENNIE

**Rosie-fucker

I tuck my phone away like I've been doing all day, because I can't deal with these three right now. My head hurts when I think about Rosie. It means acknowledging the mistakes I've made, the ways I've failed her, and I'm not sure I'm ready to face a version of me who's been anything other than honest.

Scrubbing a hand over my mouth, I spin away from my friends, tossing an excuse over my shoulder about needing some air. I'm not surprised when I hear the door open behind me a few seconds after it closes, but I am a little surprised to see Jaxon take a seat beside me on the bench out front.

He hands me a bottle of water. "You okay?"

"Yeah. Fine."

He huffs a laugh, looking down at his feet. "You know, I suck at relationships, but when a woman says she's fine, she's almost always lying."

"I'm not a woman."

"But you're not fine, either, are you?"

I glance at my friend, the easy way he sits there, like he doesn't have a care in the world. "Do you really want to know?"

"Sure. I'm here, aren't I? Plus, you look like you're gonna puke, so you should probably do it before you get behind that camera."

Bracing my elbows on my thighs, I focus on the water bottle in my hands, picking mindlessly at the paper label. "I'm in love with Rosie."

"Yeah, I figured that much. You talk about her all the time, and you're constantly grinning at your phone like a high school girl texting her crush. Or Carter texting Olivia. Garrett and Jennie too." He sighs. "And Emmett and Cara. You guys all suck, to be honest."

I laugh but finish with a sigh, dragging my hands through my hair. "I really fucked up, man."

"With Rosie? I thought last night went well."

"It did. It was great. Perfect. She's…she's fucking perfect. It's just… something changed last night. She opened up about some serious stuff, some vulnerable shit that's just…awful. Not fair. She hasn't had an easy life, and she sat there and told me all about it."

"Are you feeling bad about having sex after that? Because she was vulnerable?"

My knee bounces, and I squeeze the water bottle. The words are on the tip of my tongue, but I keep trying to swallow them down. I've never been so careless, so selfish, and I can't accept that the one time I was, it was to somebody who means so much to me, somebody I've never wanted to hurt. "I'm feeling bad because she's given me everything, and I lied to her."

Jaxon hesitates, then hangs his head. "You still haven't told her."

"No."

"*Dude.*"

"I know. Fuck." I drop my exhausted face to my hands. "*Fuck,* I'm such an asshole. I feel sick about it. It's gone on so long now, way longer than I ever planned."

"Why, man? Why'd you let it get this far? Fuck, Adam, you could've been outed by anyone at any time. Training camp starts soon, and then preseason games. What were you gonna tell her when you were out of the country?"

My stomach churns. "I was just…scared. Fucking terrified. Being Adam Lockwood, NHL goalie, has brought me nothing but trouble. I just wanted to be me. And that's all I was to Rosie. I've never had to worry about her wanting me for anything other than me. Never had to worry about her lying to make me like her. It was easy. Fuck, it was just…*nice*."

"I get it, Adam, I do. But you realize that everything you were worried about her doing to you, you turned around and did to her, don't you? You lied to her because you wanted her to like you."

What I've been doing has never been lost to me, and maybe that makes it worse. All this time I've been terrified about being deceived. Turns out I'm the only one doing the deceiving.

My throat burns, and a headache knocks at my temples. "What if she doesn't forgive me?"

"Aw, man." Jaxon squeezes my shoulder. "She will, buddy. I know she will. You're still the same guy you've always been to her. Just richer, and famous." He sighs, spinning the hat on his head. "Look, man, you just gotta come clean. Be honest with her, and don't hold back. Chicks love that shit, when you're vulnerable with them. Tell her why you were scared, apologize, ask her to forgive you, and then move forward."

"It's that easy, huh?"

"The solution? Yeah, it is. I think honesty pretty much always works. But stepping up and being honest when you haven't been? Not so easy."

"Fucking tell me about it. I kept telling myself I'd tell her everything, but the longer it went on, the harder it got. I liked the life we created, like we were in our own little bubble. I wanted to hold onto it just a little longer. Now the thought of telling her—after everything she's given me, especially after last night—feels impossible."

The sound of the doors opening has both our heads swiveling. One of the assistants pops her head out. "You're up, Adam."

Jaxon stands, squeezing my shoulder. "Talk to Rosie. Be honest with her. It'll work out."

I don't normally put much stock in Jaxon's relationship advice, but this time I'm determined for him to be right. It'll work out, because there's no other choice. Rosie belongs in my life, and I'm going to make sure she stays there. I know this means getting vulnerable, opening up about insecurities I've been fighting against. But Rosie has given me so much, trusted me with her secrets, her fears, her heart, and most precious of all, her son. She's trusted me with all of it, even when it wasn't easy for her to do so.

She's been so much stronger than I have. This time, I'm going to be strong.

That's what I'm telling myself as I walk back inside. It's all that's on my mind as I sit down in front of the cameras, turn on the Adam Lockwood charm everyone loves.

We do these preseason interviews every year, at the end of summer when everyone's gathering back in Vancouver to get ready for training camp. It's the same questions every time: *What did you get up to this summer, how are you preparing for the upcoming season, what are your hopes for the season and for the team?* Each interview ends with the reporter trying to dig up what people really care about—something about our personal lives. For most of the guys, it's a chance to brag on their families. Carter brought a stack of pictures of his daughter to show off, and even though he's the last interview, everybody's already seen every picture at least twice today. Garrett nearly brought the engagement ring he's planning on giving to Jennie, until he realized she'd be watching the interview when it airs in a couple weeks. Instead, I watched him beam from ear to ear while he told the journalist all about the house he and Jennie just moved into, the dance studio she's been working so hard at getting ready to open.

My friends are happy, and I love watching them brag on the people that make them that way. But I'm happy, too, and I'm tired of not being able to brag on the two people who make me this way, the ones that matter most to me.

"How do your parents feel about you re-signing with Vancouver for another eight years?" Chuck, the sports journalist, asks. "Word on the street is your dad was hoping you'd take Colorado up on their offer."

Laughing, I skim my hand along my jaw. "Yeah, my parents would have loved to have me back home. My mom said something about me moving back in with them. But my heart is here in Vancouver, and my parents know that. I'm working on convincing them to relocate, but then Garrett wouldn't have someone to send him over snack packages from the States."

Chuck laughs. "Yeah, he mentioned something about Dunkaroos and special edition Pop-Tarts. But let's circle back to what you said just now."

"That I'm trying to convince my parents to move here?"

"Aw, c'mon now, Lockwood. You know that's not what everyone wants to know."

I smile at my lap, rubbing the nape of my neck. I know where this is going, because nearly every interview not game related goes down this road at some point.

"You said your heart is here in Vancouver." Chuck holds up his hands in surrender the second my mouth opens. "Now I know, I know. It's only meant to explain that you belong here. But I'll have a lot of angry women on my hands later on if I don't ask the question everyone wants the answer to, especially since the NHL's resident serial dater seems to have completely disappeared off the dating scene in recent months."

Chuck taps his pen off the papers in front of him, grinning. "So, Mr. Lockwood, everyone wants to know...is there someone special in your life?"

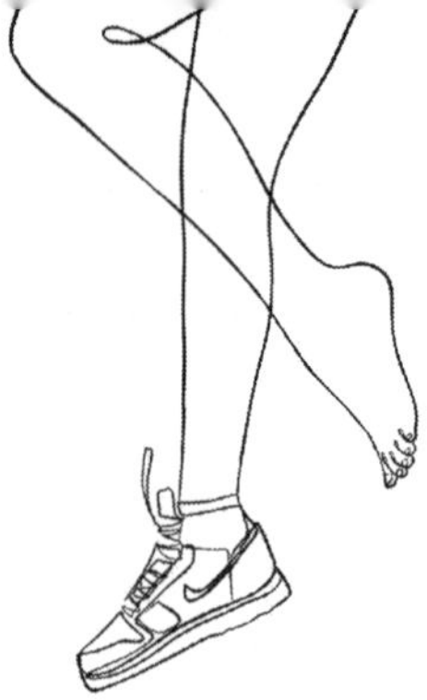

TWENTY-TWO

THE OTHER SHOE

Rosie

"WHY DOES he have so many toes? Is that normal? Cats are little freaks, aren't they?"

"Mittens is polydactyl," I tell Marco, scratching my fluffy friend's chin. "He's got extra toes. And cats are not little freaks. Little demons who terrorize you in the middle of the night, yes. But little freaks, never."

"How many times have you asked Archie if you could bring a cat home?"

I frown, scooping Mittens against me. He purrs, nuzzling my cheek. "Too many to count. He won't let me. Says he doesn't want cat hair all over the furniture. Funny thing to say for someone who gets so excited when his new hats come in the mail for his cat photoshoots."

Marco rolls his eyes, spinning around me so he can lean on the cat condos with one hip. He's been following me around for the last fifteen minutes, waiting for Archie to finish work. "I'm ninety-nine percent sure he's gonna be a crazy cat dad when we get our own place and I'm gonna be subjected to a lifetime of cat hair on furniture. There's just not enough room right now for all the cats he plans to bring home."

My smile starts to fall before I paste it back on. "Connor and I will be out as soon as we can; I promise. I know it's not ideal, and—"

"Rosie, no. That's not what I meant. You can stay as long as you need to."

"I know you're waiting for us to move out so you can move in. There's not enough room for all of us; I get it." I tuck Mittens back in his home, and he gives me those huge, sad eyes of his, paired with the tiniest *meow*, because he hates being alone in here. He's a people person, although he seems to be very particular about *who* his people are. His favorite so far has been that tattooed man that came in here with his friend, and I really thought he'd be back to adopt him. I think Mittens and I are both upset that he hasn't. "I was planning on moving out after grad next spring, but now, with losing the scholarship—"

"Rosie." Marco grabs my hands, stopping my spiraling thoughts. "I know you think so, but you aren't holding us back. There's nowhere else Archie would rather be than with you and Connor right now. And I stay there most nights anyway. But we're happy, okay? Really, we are. Plus, my mom isn't ready to let me move out yet anyway."

"You hate living with your mom."

"Because she drives me up the fucking wall. But I'm her favorite child—naturally—so I persist."

I drop my stare to my runners. "If I ever become a burden—"

"You are family, not a burden. I love you, Ro. You're like my annoying little sister. I can't get rid of you, but no part of me actually wants to."

I give his dark hair a tug before turning back to the cat dens, checking on a litter of kittens and the stray mama who were brought in last week. "You're way more annoying than me."

"Watch your filthy mouth."

"Can't. I just let it run." I press a kiss to a tiny, gray-striped kitten before tucking it back in its bed. "Archie should be out of surgery soon. Are you guys going out for dinner?"

"Nah. We're gonna grab Connor and pick up some takeout."

My head snaps up. "What?"

"Archie told me what Brandon said about you yesterday. We're gonna pick up Connor on our way home so you don't have to."

"You're going to say something to him." If it's not Marco, it'll be Archie. Hell, it might be both of them.

Marco smirks. "What would we possibly say?"

"Marco."

"I *might* drop that you got dicked so hard last night you're limping today."

"I am *not* limping!" *I'm definitely fucking limping.* My legs might've worked well enough today if we hadn't used that last condom this morning. But instead Adam drew a total of four orgasms out of me while he was inside me—on my back, my legs over his shoulders, on my knees, and up against the wall—before he *finally* came. When I stood up to follow him to the shower five minutes later, my legs shook so hard my ass was a split second from hitting the floor when Adam caught my waist and scooped me against him.

I got dicked so hard I feel it in my brain.

"Rosie, you got dicked so hard you're staring off into space while *grinning*."

I snap my mouth shut. "I am not."

"Hello," Marco breathes out, shoving me aside. He puts his sunglasses on just so he can shift them down his nose as he stares out the window. "Hottie alert. And he's got flowers."

I follow his stare, and when I spy the dark blue truck, the impossibly large man stepping down from it with a bouquet of peonies, my heart free-falls to my stomach. "Oh my God."

I press myself to the window, watching as Adam pulls off his sunglasses and folds them into the collar of his T-shirt, spinning his keyring on his finger.

"Oh my God," I murmur again, fogging the window up. I turn to Marco, folding my hands at my stomach. "How do I look? No, wait. Don't answer that. It's too late to change anything. Adam likes me the way I am." I shove him aside, rushing past him. The door opens just as Marco crashes into me from behind, and I smile up at Adam as he halts, staring at the two of us staring up at him, breathless. "Adam. You're here." I raise my palms and gesture around me, in case he doesn't know where *here* is. "In my work."

He's always waiting for me outside, the sight of his truck pulling up fifteen minutes before my shift ends making my heart flip-flop, or every Saturday morning when he and Bear join Piglet and me out front for our hike. Something about him being here, inside, it feels so personal.

I take a step toward him before stopping myself, unsure how to act. He's just watching me, his eyes moving between me and Marco, who may or may not be hyperventilating beside me.

And then suddenly, Adam grins, crooking his finger at me. "Get over here, trouble, and gimme your mouth."

I dash across the lobby to Adam, and he hooks one arm beneath my butt, hoisting me to him before he drops his mouth to mine.

"Couldn't wait to see you tonight. Wanted to pop by and say hi."

"Hiii." Marco approaches slowly, a goofy smile on his face. He arcs his hand through the air. "I'm Marco, Rosie's amazing, beautiful friend who she loves *so* much."

Adam chuckles, setting me on my feet. "Yeah, that tracks with everything she's told me about you." He offers him his hand. "Hi, Marco. I'm Adam."

"Mhmm." His eyes move down Adam, then back up. "That you are, that you are. I've heard a lot about you, too, Adam, but not quite enough."

"Maybe we could have dinner soon," I suggest excitedly, looking to Adam. The sight of him, so imposing, so flawless, makes me nervous, and I find myself backtracking, twirling my hair around my finger. "Or whatever."

His blue eyes move over me, and the corner of his mouth lifts as he pulls my finger free from my hair. "I'd love if we all had dinner, or whatever." He holds out the bouquet of peonies to me, bright pinks, dusky yellows, and deep oranges, my favorite sunset. "These are for you."

I lift the flowers to my nose to smell them but gasp when I see what's waiting inside.

Tucked in the middle of the bouquet is a hot fudge sundae from Dairy Queen.

"Extra hot fudge," Adam whispers against my temple with his arm around my waist.

It's the silliest thing, something so small and sweet, and yet it's bringing three little words to the tip of my tongue, ready to roll right off it. I want to say it. I never have, because I've never felt it. I thought I wouldn't be sure I was in love, that I'd have to wonder, but I know now there is no wondering.

Love is, without a doubt, the most certain emotion I've ever felt. It's steady and sure, constant, like the gentle ripple of the creek winding through the mountains, the quiet song from the birds in the treetops. I opened my eyes one morning and there it was, carved into the deepest parts of me, like it was always there.

Like Adam had always been a piece of me.

There's a happiness radiating throughout me, a slight quiver in my hands as I stare at him, like my body is begging me to reach out, to take him into my arms, and God, I want to.

He sweeps his thumb across my lower lip. "Quit looking at me like that. It's dangerous."

"How am I looking at you?"

"Like you'd marry me right now if I promised to bring you flowers and ice cream sundaes every day for the rest of our lives."

I completely fail at biting back my smile when I tell him, "I'd settle for weekly."

His brows quirk, a playful challenge. "Don't tempt me, trouble. I didn't come prepared with a ring."

"Wow. You two are adorable." Marco gestures at us with circles of hands. "I almost feel like I'm interrupting a beautiful moment."

Adam casts him an amused glance. "Almost, huh?"

"Oh, don't mind me. Get your freak on. Ro's already wrecked. Been limping around here all—"

"*Marco*!"

Adam laughs, winding an arm around my waist and tugging me into his chest when I try to decapitate my friend. "I gotta go. Don't kill Marco before we can have dinner. But for the record, Rosie…" His lips dip to the shell of my ear, sending a shiver down my spine. "I like you a little bit wrecked." With my chin between his fingers, he presses a lingering kiss to my lips. "See ya later, gorgeous."

I stay rooted in place, watching Adam head to his truck, hitting me with a wink before he climbs in and drives away.

"If you're not gonna eat that sundae—"

"Back off." I tear my ice cream bouquet away from Marco, setting it on the reception desk while I dig out my sundae. There's an obscene amount of hot fudge on this thing, layered on the bottom, top, and halfway. I don't think I've ever been happier.

"You have some explaining to do, Miss Rosie."

My gaze lifts to Marco, my spoon pausing just before my mouth. "What?"

His smile is particularly huge as he watches me with his chin propped in his hands, elbows on the desk. "Don't 'what' me. You know exactly what."

"I do not."

"Mhmm." He drops his forearms to the desk, tapping his fingers. "So all this time you've just conveniently *forgotten* to mention that you're dating Adam Lockwood?"

"What do you mean? I told you we were dating."

"You told me you were dating a man named Adam. You did not tell me you were dating Adam. Motherfucking. *Lockwood.*"

"I don't get it," I say slowly, lowering my spoon. "Do you know him?"

Marco frowns. "Do you not know what Adam does for a living?"

"He works…he works with professional athletes." I don't know why it's a murmur, or why it sounds more like a question. I don't know why my stomach knots either.

"Rosie, Adam Lockwood *is* a professional athlete. He's the starter goalie for the Vancouver Vipers."

"H…hockey?"

"One of the best and highest paid in the league."

My head shakes, and the tremor in my hands returns. Adam wouldn't lie to me about something so important. He just wouldn't.

"He just re-signed with the Vipers for ten-point-five million a year. And that doesn't include any sponsorship deals." Marco pulls out his phone, typing. "Google says at the end of the last season, your man had a net worth of thirty-four million."

"Thirty-four million?" I place my hand over my stomach. It's lurching like my lunch might make a reappearance.

"I swear, Ro. Do you even know him? Here, look." He flashes me a picture. "Here he is in one of his game-day suits. Look how well he wears a three-piece. Imagine him in that at your wedding?"

I can't; all I can focus on is the pictures. So many of them, all Adam. I click on one, and the screen fills with a photo of Adam on the ice, looking utterly massive in a pair of skates and huge, clunky equipment, a mask that matches his green and blue jersey.

My stomach turns itself over as I pull up another photo. Adam with his lips pressed to the temple of the gorgeous redhead tucked into his side. There's a caption included, one that makes me stop breathing.

Are they really done? Hockey's golden boy Adam Lockwood and longtime girlfriend, Courtney McLean, end their seven-year relationship amid cheating rumors.

I swallow down the bile climbing my throat and, against my better judgment, pick a new photo. In this one, Adam doesn't even appear to know his picture is being taken. He's sitting in a restaurant, drinking wine with a pretty brunette. This caption?

Adam Lockwood, hockey's most eligible bachelor and serial dater, not settling down any time soon!

My racing heart slows to a crawl before I swear it stops beating altogether, and my ice cream sundae slips from my grip, splattering at my feet.

I can't be sure, but I think that's where my heart winds up, too, after it shatters.

TWENTY-THREE

I'LL SEE YOU

Adam

I've circled Wildheart five times. *Five goddamn times.*

I've repeated my speech over and over, the same one I recited to Bear eight hundred times before I left the house, after making sure my hair looked nice and I was wearing my lucky T-shirt. My hands won't stop shaking, and I tell myself my sweaty palms sliding against the steering wheel are the reason I miss the entrance to Wildheart a sixth time.

"Fuck." I grip the steering wheel, softly banging my forehead against it. I should've done it a long time ago; maybe it would've knocked some sense into me.

But I can't fuck around about this anymore, so when the light in front of me turns green, I turn into the parking lot at Wildheart Sanctuary and park myself in the same spot I always do, where I have a front row seat to Rosie puttering around in there, finishing the last of her paperwork, doing her final rounds in the cat den, showering them with love one last time before she says good-bye.

Unbuckling my seat belt, I stare down at my trembling hands before wiping them on my jeans, scrubbing one over my mouth, running the other through my hair before fixing my hat back on my head and, finally, getting out of the truck.

The two girls standing behind the desk lift their heads when I walk in, and a cat ambles up to me, dropping itself at my feet and showing me its belly. Silence falls over the room, and my shoulders pull taut as I stoop down, rubbing the cat's belly.

"Is Rosie around? Can you tell her Adam's here?"

The girls exchange a look, eyes bulging and heads tipping in my direction. The blonde clears her throat, turning to me. "Uh, Rosie's not here."

"She's not?"

"She wasn't feeling well. She went home early."

Standing, I slip my fingers up the back of my hat, scratching my head. "Oh. Okay. Was she okay?"

"Ummm…" They look at each other again.

"Never mind. Thank you." I give the cat one last pat before heading for the door, and when I'm halfway through it, their hushed words send my heart into overdrive.

"Oh my God. It really *is* him. Rosie's dating Adam Lockwood."

~

I'm not sure there's a word to describe what I'm feeling now, bypassing the elevator and racing up all twelve flights to Rosie's apartment. There are no nerves left, just sheer, unadulterated panic, and it spills out of me with the frantic rap of my knuckles against her door, the way I knock my hat clear off my head and yank at my curls while I wait for her to answer, to tell me I can make this right.

But it's not Rosie who opens the door, and the narrowed gaze and crossed arms of the tattooed man waiting for me tell me I might be too late.

"Archie—"

"Oh, that's interesting," he bites out. "You know who I am, even though we've never met, yet you've been fucking around with my best friend for the last two months, and she had *no idea* who you were."

"No, it's not—it's not like that."

"Really? You didn't lie to her about your job?"

"No, I—" *Fuck*. "I did. But I had a—"

"Good reason?" His brows rise. "Can't wait to hear it."

The door pulls away from him, and my sweet girl steps into view, pink waves piled on her head and grazing her neck, gaze trained on the hands she wrings at her stomach. When her name leaves my lips, it's a desperate plea, drowning in the grief I feel rolling off her.

"Rosie."

She looks at me then, stares up at me with those green eyes, impossibly wide and so wrecked, begging for it to make sense. Everything I want to say to her, everything I practiced when I was in control of this situation, it all dies somewhere in my throat.

I need to hug her. I need to feel her, need her to feel me. To feel how sorry I am, how deeply I care about her. How I'm not fucking going anywhere, because she's been the one since she walked into my life. If I can just hug her, she'll know. I'll squeeze all of it into her, all the love I have.

But she crosses one arm over her stomach, grabbing onto her opposite elbow, and more than I see it, I can feel the wall she's just erected between us.

"Here if you need me." Archie presses a kiss to her temple before shooting me a castrating glare and disappearing.

Tears of betrayal swim in her guarded eyes, but the hopelessness might be worst of all. Eyes that shone with so much faith, so much warmth, are now shattered and muted. There's a certain resignation to them, almost like she was waiting for something bad to happen, for the floor to fall through.

"You lied to me," she whispers, swiping at the tears that start dripping down her cheeks.

I step toward her, but she steps back. "I'm so sorry, Rosie."

"Sorry for lying, or sorry you got caught?"

"I was going to tell you. I swear, Rosie. I was going to tell you tonight."

A huff of laughter escapes her. She tugs the sleeves of her sweater —*my sweater*—over her hands, wiping at her eyes. "Convenient timing, huh?"

"Dada?" A tiny voice floats down the hallway, stopping my heart. Connor toddles into view, eyes locking with mine and filling with so much excitement before he starts racing toward me. I crouch down, ready to catch him, because I think the only thing in the world that might make me feel better right now is holding this little boy in my arms. *"Dada!"*

"Connor, no." Rosie catches him before he can crash into me. For a moment, I stay stooped there on the ground, trying to shove away the startling feeling clawing at my chest. It matches my arms: fucking *empty*.

Connor points at me, looking at Rosie. "Dada, hug?"

She squeezes his hands in hers, her words hoarse. "Not right now, baby."

His sweet face crumples, and I'm ready to fall to my knees, beg her for forgiveness, scoop them into my arms and tell them how much I love them.

But then Marco appears, taking Connor's hand. "Hey, bud. Let's go play trains."

"Say bye to Adam, baby," Rosie tells him, and the simple words bring those tears right down her cheeks again, faster this time, and she turns away to rid her face of the evidence.

"Bye, Dada," Connor whispers, waving at me. "Lub you."

I close my eyes to the two words I've never heard before, not from him, ones I want to hear all over again but might never get the chance to. "Love you, too, little trouble."

He points at Rosie. "Big tubble? Lub?"

"Marco," Rosie chokes out. "Please."

He scoops Connor into his arms, casting an apologetic glance at me. "Come on, buddy. Uncle Arch is setting up your tracks."

"Rosie, I—" My phone rings in my pocket, cutting me off. I pull it out, silencing it without looking at it, but before I can tuck it away, it rings again. "Sorry," I mumble, frowning at the number, the same damn one that's been lighting it up for over a week now. "I'll turn it off."

"You can get it, Adam," Rosie says, scrubbing her eyes.

"No, I don't—" It rings again, and Rosie sighs.

"Adam, please. Just answer it."

Bringing my phone to my ear, I keep my eyes on Rosie. "Hello?"

"Adam? Oh thank God. I've been trying you for days!"

I frown, dropping my gaze as I try to place the voice on the other end. When it hits, the frantic plea behind my name, something drops from my chest, sinking low in my stomach. "Courtney?"

Rosie's face falls, and I know immediately that she knows who Courtney is.

And I refuse to let this woman mess up any relationship other than the one she already lit on fire a year and a half ago.

"I blocked your number for a reason," I bite out in a low voice as Rosie looks down, giving me space I don't want.

"I know, but I had to talk to you. It's about—"

"There's nothing to talk about. Don't call me again." Before I throw my phone in my pocket, I block her number. "Sorry about that. Nobody important."

Rosie nods, scuffing the floor with her bare toes before she finally meets my gaze. "You're on Tinder."

My brows pull down. "Tinder? No."

She pulls out her phone, showing me my profile on that fucking dating app. "This isn't you?"

"No, it's—I mean, yes, it is. But I'm not—I mean, I *was*—my profile is still—ugh." I scrub my hands down my face, because nothing is coming out right. I'm all fucked up, panicked, and my words aren't wording, so I take a breath and try again. "I haven't used it at all since I met you, Rosie. I promise."

She looks down, and I hate how quiet her voice is when she speaks next. "Why didn't you delete your profile? Were you not sure about me?"

I step forward, saying a big *fuck you* to the distance between us, the part of my brain that warns me to give her space. I take her hands in mine, clutching them between us. "You are the only thing I've *ever* been sure of." I sweep my thumbs over her knuckles. "It's a shit excuse, but I just didn't think about it. I wasn't logging on, so it wasn't on my mind."

Her eyes move between mine as she tugs at her lower lip with her teeth. "The websites are calling you 'hockey's most eligible bachelor,' and 'the NHL's serial dater.' You've dated a lot of women in public, but not me. You dated me in private, Adam. Why didn't you want people to know about me?"

I shake my head, and when she tries to pull away, I yank her closer. "No. No, that's not it. That's *never* been it. This isn't about you, Rosie. This is about me, and I won't have you thinking I was trying to hide you, that I was embarrassed in any way, because that's simply not fucking true."

"But it feels that way, you get that, don't you? Everything I've read about you this afternoon tells me I'm different."

"You *are* different. You are absolutely everything they weren't for me, in the best and most surprising way. I'll apologize for a lot of things, because I know I've fucked up. God, I've fucked up. But I won't apologize for wanting to keep you to myself, for wanting to wrap you up and keep you tucked away from this world."

"From *your* world, Adam. This is *your* world. And I don't know it, not at all. And finding that out now makes me feel like I don't know *you*." She steps back, looking up at the ceiling, fighting so damn hard to keep more tears from falling. "God, how dense am I? I'm dating one of the most famous goalies in the NHL, and I have no clue. I feel like such a fool."

"Fuck, Rosie. I'm a goddamn mess, and I'm so disappointed in myself. I didn't mean to hurt you, I swear. And I hate more than anything that I've made you feel like a fool. I fucking panicked. I told you my name the day we met, and you didn't react. When you asked me what I did, I realized you had no idea who I was, and I just…I couldn't. For some reason, the words wouldn't come."

I know what I've done. Fuck, I know *exactly* what I've done. In lying to her, I've perpetuated her deepest fears. She's spent her whole life wanting someone to choose her, and she's been let down time and time again. And now, I'm no different.

"I know it feels like you weren't important enough for me to be truthful with you. I know you're feeling like I didn't choose you."

"It feels a whole lot like you chose us, just only for the summer. You got to play house for a couple months and now you get to go back to being a famous hockey player. You didn't just hide your job from me, Adam. You put us in a bubble and hid us away from the rest of your life."

"I did. I saw an opportunity and I ran with it. You didn't know about the hockey, and I liked it. I didn't have to wonder which version of me you liked."

Something in her eyes softens, but then, they've always been soft. Kind and gentle, even right now, when I've broken her heart.

"I need you to understand that this isn't about the hockey, Adam. I get that somewhere along the way, as a professional athlete, you've been made to feel like that's all you are. And I can tell you with absolute certainty that's not true. You are a beautiful human being with so much more to offer. But in letting those worries consume you the way you did, you didn't just lie to me. You kept whole pieces of yourself from me because you didn't want to trust me with them. And all I've done is trust you. I've given you everything. My heaviest, earth-shattering truths." Her voice drops, and her eyes move to Connor over her shoulder, watching us from his spot on the floor where he plays with Archie and Marco. "And my entire heart. I trusted you with my son, Adam, and you lied to us. You've made me feel convenient, temporary, when I thought this might be..." Every one of her insecurities shines in her devastated eyes. "I thought this might be permanent. You promised you wouldn't hurt me, but this? This hurts."

Her shoulders slump, and she seems to shrink before my eyes. "I don't know how to trust you right now. And if I can't trust you, I don't know how we can be together."

Panic bubbles, and the world around me slows to a crawl. "You're breaking up with me?"

Tear-filled eyes lift to mine. "I...I don't know. Honestly, Adam, I don't. When you came into my life, you grounded me. You pulled me to my center, and for the first time since my parents died, I felt like I was finally on level ground. I felt safe, and I felt loved. Now I feel like I've lost my footing all over again. I don't know which way is up, and I hate it. I fucking hate it."

I swallow down the lump in my throat. "You're my family, Rosie. You and Connor."

"Families are built on honesty. Hard truths and scary vulnerabilities. You don't hide who you are."

"I don't want to go back to before. To without you. I don't want to forget what it feels like, being a family with you." Something breaks inside me, if anything was still whole. It crawls up my throat, clawing its way out, shattering my next plea as a tear drips from my eye. "Please, Rosie. I can't let you go. I won't."

Rosie steps forward, cupping my cheeks. Her thumbs brush beneath my eyes, coming away wet, stealing my heartbreak and making it hers too. She takes my hands in hers, slender fingers lacing through mine. They're so small, so warm, so fucking perfect, and I'm terrified it'll be the last time I hold them.

"I need a minute, Adam. I need some space to breathe, to wrap my head around this and figure out what it means for us, if we can get past it. Can you give me that? Some time? Some patience?"

I look down at our twined hands, the way they fit together. "I'd give you anything you want." *Even if it's the last thing I want to do right now.*

"All I've ever wanted is you, Adam. Even the parts you're scared to share." She takes my face in her hands, her touch tender and compassionate, just like the way she looks at me. "We have to get comfy with the uncomfy parts of ourselves before we can really know who we are and love that person, before we can let someone else know and love us. I want to know you, but I want you to know you more. Then you can share that person with me. Okay?"

Hope sparks in my chest, a frantic pounding that hurts the way hope can sometimes. "It's not good-bye? Not forever?"

Her mouth quirks with a sad smile. "I don't like good-byes."

I bury my trembling fingers in her hair and bring her forehead to rest against mine. "Promise me. Promise me, Rosie."

Her eyes flutter closed, lashes lying against her rosy skin as tears cascade down her cheeks. "I don't think my forever exists without you somewhere inside it."

In this moment, those words are enough. Enough to breathe life back into me, even if for only a short moment, while we stand here holding each other, her chest rising and falling in time with mine, so close, I can't tell if that's her heart or mine beating so fast.

It's when she finally releases me and backs away that I realize it's my heart. Because in this moment, it stops beating altogether, a silence so loud, so ear-splitting, I hear every tiny fissure that splinters all the parts of me Rosie and Connor made whole again.

Rosie backs into her apartment, and right before she disappears, she whispers the three words I'll cling to until she comes back to me.

"I'll see you."

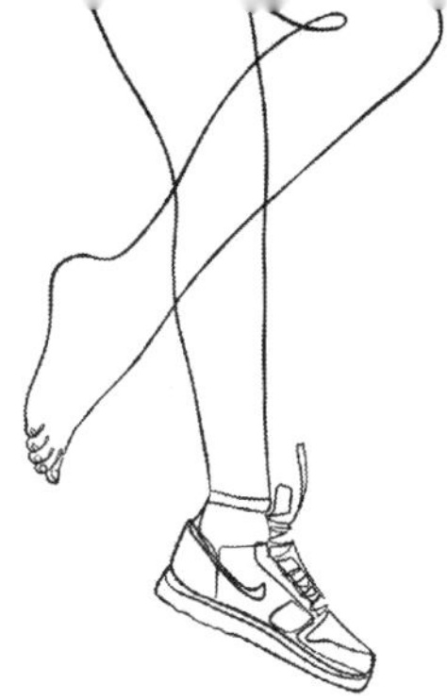

TWENTY-FOUR

STARDUST LANE

Rosie

I'm certain these hands have never felt something so soft as these waves, fine blond wisps scattered across Connor's forehead. They're perfect in every way, this sign of innocence I hope never fades away.

I run my fingers through the wisps, brushing them off his temple, sweeping my thumb over the apple of his cheek, where it's just as soft as his hair.

And yet, I can't help but remember the roughness of Adam's calloused palms as they grip mine, the way they scrape down my sides, grab my hips, and pull me against him. They're soft in a different way, drifting down the curve of my spine while I lie wrapped up in him, twining through my hair, the pad of his thumb running over the dimple in my chin before he presses his lips to mine.

And I miss him. Miss the way he makes me feel so savagely needed while so utterly treasured with the simple sweep of his gaze over my body, the touch of his hands. So passionately *loved* with the quiet, sure words he presses against my ear.

He's everything soft and gentle, greedy in only the warmest way. A man who's happy with everything he has, yet insatiable, a feral need to keep his happiness tight within his grasp, unwilling to let it stray.

I saw it last week in his gaze, the reluctance to give me what I needed. Time to think, space to breathe. He didn't want to give it to me, but like he said then, he'd give me anything I asked for.

But all I've ever asked for is him.

I've spent this past week searching for clarity, but I'm not sure my brain has gotten any less foggy.

One part of the *why* is clear. It's written in every headline that mentions Adam's superstar status as a goalie in the NHL, how much money he's worth. Every headline that violates his right to privacy when it posts a picture of him and his ex-girlfriend, speculates the reason of their breakup, the unwanted pictures of him on date after date, wondering which girl will be the lucky one to finally nail down *the NHL's most desirable and available heartthrob.* It's clear Adam had a difficult time knowing which relationships were genuine and which were self-serving, and I can't imagine how challenging that would be to navigate with the severe lack of privacy this man has.

But the other part of the *why,* the part that lied to me, it wonders why, after all the time spent together, learning each other, loving on each other, he still didn't feel safe enough with me to trust me. To choose me to share all of himself with.

All the horrible insecurities I've spent years fighting try to claw through my mind, and at the forefront is that I've never been anyone's first choice. That not a single person has looked at me and seen the possibility of forever, a certain permanence that comes with a chosen family, an unconditional love I've spent my life chasing.

Deceit doesn't speak of permanence. Beyond the intentional pain inflicted by the twist of the knife lodged in your back, is the emotional turmoil of being only a fleeting moment in someone's life. Because lies are never forever, and I can't understand the point of them with someone you intend to keep in your life.

Despite the fears that have sunk their teeth into my bones over the years, I pride myself on never having given up hope on finding my people. It's not always benefited me, like the time I spent trying to force something to work with Brandon just to be a family. And I'd be lying if I said I wasn't worried about putting myself in a position where I'm repeating history. There's not an inch of me that has ever been worried about that with Adam.

Until last week, when the life he'd been hiding from me was thrust in my face.

"Rosie?"

My gaze snaps to Eva, waiting in the doorway to her office. Her smile is easy; I wish I could appreciate it more.

"Thanks so much for coming in again last minute." She waves me inside, pouting at Connor as I carry him past her. "Sleeping?"

"We spent the morning at the park, and one of the day camps was going on a trip, so Connor wanted to watch all the buses drive off." I don't tell her that he asked for *Dada* and *Bear* twenty times over after he found Adam's hat in my bag. I don't tell her that he put the baseball cap on his head and toddled around saying *Dada hat.* And I don't tell her that when Connor took his first bite of his peanut butter and banana sandwich, then held it up and asked for Dada again, wanting to share his sandwich with him like he always does, the first tear broke free.

"Sounds like a fun day so far."

Thrilling.

At least there's no mascara left on my lashes for when I cry again at the reminder Eva's about to give me about my future being delayed another year. Hell, maybe she'll tell me they can't hold my spot anymore, not two years in a row. To figure it out and get the money together in four days so I can start next week, or give up my spot in the program altogether.

I'm going through a bit of a pessimistic period right now, if you can believe it, so when Eva called this morning and asked me to come in for another chat, I was pretty much resigned to being kicked out.

"You don't already have all your textbooks and materials for this year, do you?" she asks, sitting on the edge of her desk, gesturing to the chair across from her.

Connor stirs when I sit, tucking his face into my neck and stuffing his thumb in his mouth.

"I've been buying the materials one at a time to make it more affordable." I press my lips to Connor's hair, my knee bouncing. "I could probably sell them, though. I'm sure there's a student who hasn't purchased yet. It's no big deal."

"Rosie, what are you talking about?"

"I can't afford to pay my tuition this year without my scholarship. Isn't that why I'm here? You're going to tell me they won't save my spot for me anymore? That I have to pay and attend this year or leave forever?"

She stares at me for a long moment, and when she finally laughs, I don't know whether to laugh, too, or cry. I have no idea what's going on in my life anymore, but it feels like it's unraveling before my eyes.

"Rosie, you're our top student. We recognize how damn hard you've been working over the years, and the veterinarian world would be taking a huge hit losing you before you've even gotten the chance to get started. We are so proud of everything you've accomplished. You're an incredible student, an eager learner, and a dedicated mama. We're so lucky to have you."

"Oh. Uh…" Heat crawls up my neck, prickling my cheeks. "Thank you. It's really nice to hear that. To be recognized."

"You must realize how much you bring to the table, no?"

"It's hard to see what you bring to the table when no one sits down at it with you."

"Here's the thing, Rosie. You don't need anyone to sit at the table with you. You need to be happy sitting there with yourself. That's the only way you'll ever understand and treasure your own worth."

I catch the tear as soon as it sneaks out of my eye. My gaze falls to the little boy in my arms, the only person who thinks the world of me. But maybe he's the only one that matters.

"Well…" Eva walks around her desk, sinking down to the chair behind it. "I'm glad to hear you have all your materials together. I'd hate to have you scrambling just four days before classes start."

"Pardon?"

"And I do hope you'll find your worth this year. I'm sure you will, at the very least here in the classroom."

My pulse thunders in my ears. "I'm confused and emotional because, quite frankly, this has been a shit week. So I'm going to need you to put me out of my misery and tell me what you're speaking in code about."

She chuckles softly. "A gentleman stopped by my office yesterday, wanting to set up a new annual scholarship fund for our veterinarian students. Outlined all the qualities he'd like to see in the recipients, not just as students but as real people. Someone dedicated to their family, someone who prioritizes the things that really matter, someone caring and compassionate who's committed to helping animals. Someone who sounds a lot like you, Rosie."

"Who?" I ask, the single word breathless as my chest heaves, my eyes prickling with tears. "Who's the donor?"

"He wishes to remain anonymous."

"Eva, I can't—"

"You can, Rosie. You can accept this for exactly what it is: someone who wants to see you succeed in all your dreams, because you deserve it."

My chin quivers. "What are you saying?"

"I'm saying go home and get some rest this weekend, Rosie, because you've got a wild year ahead of you. You're the first recipient of the Stardust Lane Scholarship."

It's hard enough to wrap my head around being gifted a scholarship at the last minute, allowing me to finish my schooling when I'd just about given up hope. But hearing the name of the scholarship is what brings the tears streaming down my face.

Because Stardust Lane? That's the name of the street I grew up on.

The last time I was home with my parents.

~

"Gastric what?"

"Gastric dilatation and volvulus," I repeat to the woman standing before me, one hand clutching her purse strap, the other laid protectively over her dog's stomach. "It's when a dog's stomach fills with gas and bloats, or what we call gastric dilatation. It progresses into a volvulus when the bloated stomach twists, blocking the entrance and exit of the stomach."

"And Pepper…she needs surgery? There's no other way?"

"GDV requires surgery to correct."

"And it will? The surgery will work, and Pepper will be okay?"

I look down at the beautiful, docile St. Bernard on the examination table, the pink bow she wears on her collar. Big brown eyes stare back at me, and I wish I could lie. "Surgery is not a guarantee."

"What's the mortality rate?"

"The survival rate—"

"I asked for the mortality rate, not the survival rate. I want to know what the chances are that my dog dies if I let you put her on that table."

I clench my fists in an attempt to still the violent tremor in my hands. "In uncomplicated cases, the mortality rate is about fifteen to twenty percent. Depending on how long the stomach has been twisted and whether other issues are present during surgery, the mortality rate can jump as high as thirty-eight percent."

She nods, staring at her dog. "I need some time to decide. Maybe I'll bring Pepper home, and we'll see how she does over the weekend."

"Mrs. Greene, with all due respect, GDV is a life-threatening emergency and requires *immediate* intervention. It's crucial we relieve the pressure on Pepper's internal organs as soon as possible."

Her eyes pool with tears, and she looks to Dr. Holmes at my side, like my professor might tell her I'm wrong.

"Rosie is correct," she says simply. "And the longer a dog goes without treatment, the higher the mortality rates are. Untreated, a dog with GDV *will* die. Is surgery a guarantee? No. But we can guarantee we will do everything in our power to help your girl. Your other option is euthan—"

"No. I won't consider that." Tears slide down her cheeks, and I fight to keep myself in check, biting my tongue to draw the pain out of my chest as Mrs. Greene stares down at her best friend. "I don't understand how this happened."

"There isn't any rhyme or reason," I tell her gently. "It does tend to favor bigger dogs, like Pepper, but it can happen to any dog."

She wipes at her tears. "Can I have a few minutes alone with her?"

"Of course. We'll start prepping for surgery."

Dr. Holmes follows me into the operating room, watching as I organize the required instruments. "Is this how you imagined finishing off your first week of fourth year?"

"Prepping for surgery? I'd hoped so, honestly. I've been so eager to be on this side of the glass. But for GDV?" I think about Pepper, unconscious in her mom's SUV when she rolled up here, how Mrs. Greene said she was sick all morning. "No, this isn't how I imagined finishing this week."

But truthfully, it's on par with how it's been going. There was no easing into the year. We jumped right into the emergency setting at the campus clinic, and there hasn't been a quiet moment since. I'm exhausted, barely keeping my emotions in check, and last night I passed out on my bed with my shoes still on and my dinner—an apple—half-eaten in my hand. I'm beyond grateful to be here, but I can't wait for a break.

Dr. Holmes hands me Pepper's chart as she's rolled into the room. "Can you tell us about Pepper before we get started?"

I smile down at the sweet, gorgeous girl as she stares up at me. "Hi, sweetheart," I murmur, stroking the brown spot between her eyes. "Pepper is a three-year-old, one-hundred-and-twenty-seven-pound St. Bernard. Her mom reported that she didn't seem well earlier this morning. She didn't eat breakfast, was quiet and lethargic, and was favoring her bed, all of which are unusual for Pepper. Mom brought her in when she collapsed trying to walk to her water dish." I smooth my hand over her ears, giving her a scritch. "And she's got the most gorgeous brown eyes."

"She certainly does, doesn't she?" Dr. Holmes fixes her mask over her mouth and pulls on her gloves. "All right, let's make sure we keep Pepper comfortable, and let's get started."

I don't release Pepper's paw from my hand. Not when we put her under anesthesia, and not when I hand Dr. Holmes the scalpel so she can make the first cut into her abdomen. I don't let go when her stomach suddenly ruptures before surgery can even really begin, and I don't let go when the energy in the room becomes frantic as Dr. Holmes works as fast as she can, does everything in her power to save her.

I don't let go, even as I watch her pulse drop lower and lower, until she flatlines right there on the table in front of me, her paw still warm in my grasp.

I don't let go when Dr. Holmes touches my shoulder, tells me this is the toughest part of the job and she's sorry I had to see it so quickly.

I don't let go until the room empties, until it's time for the moment I dread, something I've spent these years hoping I'd somehow never have to do.

"Does it ever get easier?" I ask on a whisper, peeking at Pepper's mom through the small window in the door.

Dr. Holmes hesitates. "Never."

"I was afraid of that."

"Rosie." She catches my arm, stopping me before I can open the door. "You did great today. You were thorough and quick with your assessment of Pepper earlier, allowing us to get her onto that table as quick as we did, even if we were still too late. Give yourself some grace. We need to keep our emotions in check here, yes, but I don't need you to be a robot. If you need to cry after this, scream, swear…give yourself the grace to feel what you need to feel. I find we can't move on until we do."

I nod, and before I lose my nerve, I push through the door.

Mrs. Greene jumps to her feet, wringing her hands. "That was fast. You said it would be longer." She smiles, but it's shaky. "Is that a good thing?"

I don't want to do this. I don't want to be responsible for breaking her heart, for telling her that her best friend isn't going home tonight, that she won't be curled up at her feet, or resting her head in her lap.

I clear my throat and step toward her. "Mrs. Greene—"

Her breath hitches, and she presses her hand to her throat, stepping back. "No."

Everything pulls taut, so tight I feel like something has to snap. There's a lump in my throat making it harder and harder to breathe. "Pepper's GDV was extensive and advanced. Her stomach ruptured from the pressure shortly after we began, and we were not able to save her."

My eyes burn as I watch hers fill with tears, spilling relentlessly down her face. I blink my own away, press my lips together to stop the sob that wants to escape.

"She was not in pain when she went. We made sure she was comfortable and loved. She was not alone." My voice breaks on the last word, and I feel a gentle touch on my shoulder.

"Rosie held Pepper's hand all the way through," Dr. Holmes tells Mrs. Greene. "We know this is a lot to process. Would you like a moment alone, or would you like a shoulder?"

"I…" She sinks down to her seat. "I don't…but Pepper…she was fine last night. Just last night she was fine." Her gaze is lost, fixated on the floor, but I'd bet she's not seeing a damn thing. Her eyes start roaming, bouncing around the room, like they're making sense of the news.

Like she's realizing she just lost her best friend.

I do fine. I *swear* I'm doing fine, even as her chest starts heaving. But when her face crumples, when a sob breaks free and she collapses into herself, burying her shaking hands in her hair and crying out for her dog, something inside me shatters. I clutch at my chest, trying to claw the pain right out of there, and Dr. Holmes whispers a simple, "Go," in my ear before she takes a seat next to Mrs. Greene.

And I go. I throw my clipboard down at the doctor's station and burst through the double doors leading to the reception area. I rush past the stares and out the front door, into the warm September afternoon, and I run.

I run across campus, until I wind up at the same bench I fell apart at two weeks ago, when Adam found me here after I lost my scholarship.

And I do the same thing I did then.

I don't want to, but I give in to the pain, burying my face in my shaking hands and letting it go.

Like I did right here on this bench in the safety of the arms of someone I loved and trusted, I fall apart.

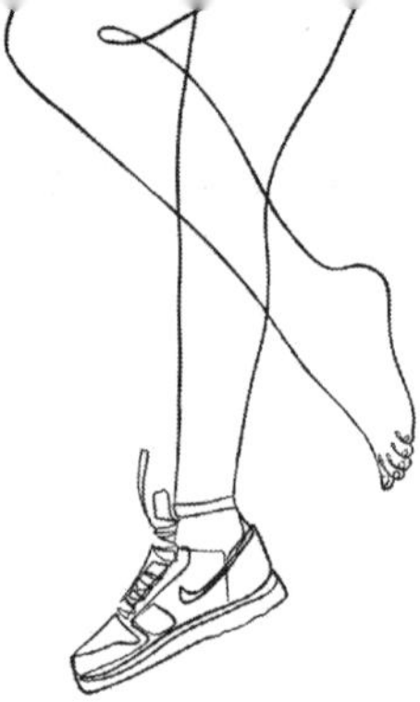

TWENTY-FIVE

FOREVER FAMILIES

Rosie

Adopted.

There's this silly part of me, this small child buried so deep down, who sees that seven-letter word scrawled across the animal cage and, every single time, without fail, actually feels…jealousy. Grief for a family I lost, and a second one I was never given a chance with.

It doesn't change a thing about how excited I am for the animals going home to be with their forever families. There's nothing I want more than for them to live out the rest of their lives in luxury.

Luxury is being surrounded by all the love you need to walk through life. It's having someone to laugh with on the good days, and arms to hold you up on the bad ones. Luxury…it's the people who make it all worth it. Every single day.

I've lived with luxury, and I've lived without it. I know which one I'd choose.

I pull Mittens from his den, snuggling him against my chest. "I'm glad you're getting your family, Mitts."

He crawls up my shoulder, clinging tightly to me as I walk through the shelter.

"It'll be okay, buddy." I smooth my palm down his back as I reach the room where his new dad is supposed to be waiting. "You're going to love your new family."

He makes a low, growly sound, like he doesn't believe me.

I push through the door, stopping when I see the large, tattooed man inside.

Jaxon Riley, who I now know to be the Vancouver Vipers superstar defenseman, one of the NHL's most notorious fighters, a gigantic playboy, and one of Adam's best friends, smiles. "Hi, Rosie."

Mittens' head whips around, and with a *meow* that echoes across the galaxy, he launches himself off my chest. Jaxon chuckles, crouching to catch him in his arms. My heart warms at the sight, Mittens tucking his fluffy white and orange head into the crook of Jaxon's neck, the perfect fit.

"Hey, Mitts," Jaxon whispers against his fur. "You're coming home, marshmallow."

I disguise my laugh as a cough when Mittens scurries up Jaxon's shirt and drapes himself over his broad shoulders. "Does your shirt say *Cat Daddy*?"

Jaxon doesn't even bat an eye. "Fuck yeah, it does. I wanted it to say *Slutty Cat Daddy*, but Adam wouldn't let me. He's no fun sometimes."

Clearing my throat, I start flipping through the adoption paperwork. "Almost didn't recognize you without your mustache."

His smirk is proud as he rubs the spot where that fake monstrosity was when I first met him. Now, there's only stubble. "Thinking of growing a real one. I can rock it, right? Garrett looked ridiculous with his, though. Right? I looked better?"

"Is who wore the fake mustache better when you came to spy on me really a competition?"

"Everything's a competition between me and Garrett. And we weren't spying on you." He chuckles at the sassy eye roll I hit him with. "Okay, we were spying on you, but only 'cause Adam wouldn't shut up about you, and we were tired of waiting for him to bring you around."

My heart sinks at his harmless words, and I clutch the clipboard in my hands. "Um, so, you brought a carrier to take Mittens home, that's great."

"Rosie."

"I don't think you'll have any issue, given how much he loves you—"

"Rosie."

"—but there may be an adjustment period where he hides away and—"

"*Rosie.*" Jaxon's chest appears in my field of vision, and Mittens reaches across, laying one paw on my shoulder. "That came out wrong. Adam wasn't hiding you away from us or anything."

"Wasn't he?"

"Nah. That's not his style." He laughs suddenly, scratching his stubbled jaw. "Actually, he would, but only because he'd be afraid we'd scare you off. We're kind of an overbearing group. Like a big, dysfunctional family. A big, dysfunctional, *very loving* family," he adds with a pointed look.

"I believe you," I say quietly, moving past him to inspect his carrier.

"You do?"

"Of course I do. The media loves your relationship."

Not a lot of what I found online made me smile, but one thing that did was this little family Adam seems to have formed with some of his teammates and their partners. Every time they're photographed on a night out on the town, they're together. The media loves referencing their social media accounts, too, especially Carter Beckett's, the underwear model with the huge dick from the bus shelter and, apparently, the team captain. His Instagram account is bogged down with pictures of his family: his daughter, his wife, and his best friends, always together.

"The media doesn't know everything," Jaxon reminds me. "They spin stories to make them seem more interesting than they are."

"So Adam isn't really the NHL's most eligible bachelor?"

He hides his smile behind his hand. "Nah, he really is. Or was, until he met you. But look me in the eyes and tell me all those articles about him being a serial dater didn't make him sound like the biggest fuckboy." Amused eyes move between mine. "You can't, can you? *I'm* the fuckboy, not Adam. I was just trying to get laid; he was just trying to find his happy place. And he failed, every time, until he took you on a picnic date and stole your hat just so he'd have a reason to see you again."

My heart flutters, and happiness crawls up my face, tugging at the corner of my mouth. "He told you about that?"

"I told you, he never shuts up about you. Connor too."

I take Mittens from Jaxon, snuggling him for the last time. "Did he tell you he started a new scholarship at my school just so I could graduate on time?"

"I thought he was staying anonymous?" Jaxon's face falls at my smile. "Ah *fuck*." He shakes his finger at me. "You sneaky little shit. Adam's gonna kill me."

It hurts to think about Adam, all the ways he's been so selfless, so supportive. I've wanted to be angry with him for being selfish in his decision to hide himself from me, but in all my research, in everything I've read between the lines on the internet, I understand. I don't like it, but I do get it. He's been hurt, time after time, and I can't fault him for being afraid to get hurt again.

Aren't we all afraid of heartbreak? It comes in too many forms, from the people you least expect, and it never hurts any less.

Thing is, though, in trying to guard his heart, he broke both of ours in the end. And Connor's, who asks for *Dada* every single day, breaking my heart all over again.

Hugging a purring Mittens against my chest, I close my eyes. "I'm gonna miss you, buddy, but I'm so happy for you." He nudges his soft head against mine, and I press a kiss to it before securing him in the carrier.

"You can come visit him sometime, maybe," Jaxon says, taking the carrier and following me out to reception. "He's gonna live like a king."

"I have no doubt."

He pauses at the desk, looking me over. "You okay?"

"Fine."

"You'd be surprised, but years of fuckboy behavior have taught me that when a woman says she's fine, she's never fucking fine."

I manage a tired laugh, scrubbing my exhausted eyes.

"Seriously, what's up? You look like you're ready to crumble."

"It's just been a tough couple of weeks. It's nothing." I sniffle. "I'm fine."

I wait for him to nod, to walk out the door with his new best friend, but he doesn't move. Just stares at me. Waits.

"I lost a dog yesterday," I blurt. "At school. Her name was Pepper and she was still just a baby. I held her paw while she took her last breath, and then I had to tell her mom..." Tears blur my vision, and the memory squeezes my throat. "I had to tell her mom she wasn't going home. And all I wanted was to go to Adam, because he just listens, he doesn't try to fix things that can't be fixed. He lets me feel what I need to feel, and he makes me feel safe while I do it. But I'm still *so* hurt. He was my safe place, but I wasn't his." I swipe at my cheeks. Of course I'm crying again. Feels like all I've done these past two weeks. "I want to be someone he's proud to be with, but instead, it feels sort of like I was his dirty secret rather than his first choice."

The carrier hits the desktop on my last word, and Jaxon's arms come around me, bringing me into his chest. He holds me like that until my body stops shaking, until my tears stop coming, and when he finally releases me, I can't look at him.

I watch out of the corner of my eye as he rounds the desk, shakes the mouse to wake up the computer, types on the keyboard. Then he pulls me back into him. I feel his chin on top of my head, and for a moment, I sink into the compassion.

"I know it doesn't feel like it right now, but I promise you everything will be okay." He releases me, picks up Mittens, and walks to the door before pausing once more. "You were never his dirty secret, Rosie. You're his world, and I'm pretty sure it's stopped spinning since you've been gone."

Thoughts of Adam run rampant in my mind as I watch Jaxon drive away. Footsteps approach, and Archie's familiar whistle sounds behind me before it comes to a sudden halt.

"Rosie? What is this?"

Archie's leaning over the desk, staring at the computer. He gestures me over with the tip of his head, and my heart tries to claw out of my chest at the video waiting for me on the screen, the caption up top.

Adam Lockwood breaks hearts everywhere: he's taken!

The video is cued up, paused at a spot halfway through. Adam is sitting on a stool, wearing the same outfit he had on the last time I saw him.

Archie reaches for the mouse, but I grab it away.

"Jesus," he mutters as I press Play. "I was gonna do that, bossy girl."

"Not fast enough."

Everything in my body rolls to a slow stop when the video starts, Adam's heartbreaking smile on display, his blue eyes electric, the deep timbre of his voice as he talks about his life in Vancouver. My stomach squeezes like a fist at the reminder from the reporter that I wouldn't have ever found Adam if he hadn't re-signed to Vancouver shortly before we met.

I might've lived through a whole life before him, but now it hurts to imagine one without him. Because when Adam tells the camera his heart is in Vancouver, I know mine is too.

"I'll have a lot of angry women on my hands later on if I don't ask the question everyone wants the answer to, especially since the NHL's resident serial dater seems to have completely disappeared off the dating scene in recent months," the reporter says. "So, Mr. Lockwood, everyone wants to know…is there someone special in your life?"

I'm hyperaware of Archie's stare, ricocheting between me and the video, the way everything around me falls away and slows, until all I can hear is the patter of my heart, the drum of blood in my ears. My hands tremble, and I'm nearly about to shut off the computer when Adam's eyes come alive, a familiar spark that holds so much love, the grin that comes over his face, splitting his cheeks.

"Yeah, there is someone special. Two someone specials, actually."

The reporter's brows jump. "*Two*?"

Adam chuckles. "It's not how it sounds. She's got a little boy."

"*Stepdaddy Adam*!" someone shouts from off camera, followed by a slew of hoots and whistles. His cheeks blaze before he ducks his head to hide his smile.

"You look pretty smitten," the reporter muses. "It's nice to see you so happy."

"I wasn't sure I'd be this happy again." Adam rubs the back of his neck and shrugs. "They make me want to be the very best version of myself."

"So, it's serious then? This woman and her son?"

"The only thing I take as seriously is hockey."

"Are you planning on following in your captain's footsteps?"

"I normally strive to do the exact opposite of Carter," he says with a chuckle. "But I assume you're referencing him settling down, getting married, starting a family…"

"Exactly."

Adam's fingers tap against his knee for a quiet moment, and then he smiles. "I've always loved the idea of being married. It's always been an important part of my life plan, because my parents have been an incredible example of two people who love each other working through the toughest parts of life. They're proof that you don't have to do it alone, and I don't want to. I want to do all the hard stuff with the right person by my side.

"So, do I see myself settling down with her? Yeah, I really do. And starting a family?" Adam looks directly into the camera, and for a moment, it feels like he's looking right at me. "We already have one, but I can't wait to keep building it."

~

This is the first time I've been here on my own in over two months.

I've had Adam at my side since I stumbled into him in July. Without him, I haven't been able to bring myself to come back here.

But this is my space. Before Adam, this was where I felt safe. There's something so innately comforting in the feel of earth beneath your feet, where everything is so green, so fresh, a sign of life, renewed energy. Where each breath of mountain air makes you feel alive with clarity.

Clarity. It's been missing for two weeks, and right now, it's all I need.

"Quit looking at me like that, sassy girl," I tell Piglet as we trudge through the forest, because it's about the hundredth time she's thrown that grumpy look at me over her shoulder. "I get it: everything is way less fun without Adam and Bear. I'm not exciting enough."

She cocks her head, those beautiful brown eyes blinking at me. Then she trots back to my side, nudging my hand before carrying on beside me. She has a funny way of slowing my racing thoughts, reminding me to go easy on myself. Maybe that's why we get along so well. We give each other the patience and love we both need.

"I know it's here somewhere," I murmur, creeping through the trees. I'd long since given up on finding those thirteen-year-old initials my dad carved into that tree when I was eleven. I must've looked a hundred times over my years in Vancouver. It's silly, but when Adam found them, I thought maybe it was my parents' way of letting me know they were with us, that they approved of Adam.

And I think that's part of the reason I haven't been back here since. Because I know if I don't find it now, when I really need it, I'll wonder. My mind will wander to that dangerous *what-if* territory that I hate, where I second-guess everything. And I'm so damn tired of second-guessing. I just want to be sure. I want to move forward with certainty that I'm making the right decision for me. No matter which way this goes in the end, I want to know that I believed in myself, that I gave myself a true chance at love, at a happy ever after with someone who only lifts me up.

And if I can't find this tree, if my brain tries to convince my heart it's a sign...what if I'm not strong enough to battle that voice? What if the voices overwhelm me, and I give in to the pressure to give up?

I tell myself I'm not really looking, that if I find it, I find it. But five minutes turns into ten, and when I've been wandering in circles for forty-five minutes, everything in my chest pulls taut.

"It's here," I tell Piglet. "I know it's here. It has to be."

But the longer I come up empty-handed, the more I doubt myself. And the more I doubt myself, the more I just want to crawl into the arms of my parents, remember how it feels to be surrounded, protected by that kind of unconditional love.

So when my heart grows heavy and those voices try to win, I give myself grace. I pick a tree, just any old one, and I sink to my butt at the base of it. Piglet drapes her head over my lap and licks my fingers as I fix my sight on the blue sky filtering through the trees, focus on pulling in breath after breath of fresh air, clearing my mind.

"I am stronger than the voices in my head that tell me I'm weak," I remind myself. "I prioritize myself and my family, and I make decisions with my well-being at the core." I take a deep breath and sink into the moment, the earth beneath my hands. If I listen carefully, I can almost hear it. My laughter ringing through the trees, Mom telling me to stay close, Dad suggesting a splash in the creek. I can hear the slosh of the water as we dance through it, feel its chill kiss my feet, and in this moment, I feel them. Placing my hand over my beating heart, I say with certainty, "Even though I can't see them, my parents are always with me."

Piglet and I stay there for a half hour, and when I finally pick myself up again, my head is clear. There are no voices telling me what I can or can't do. Everything feels steady. Sure. Like I know exactly where I'm going, and the relief that brings, the sense of freedom, it's staggering.

For the past two weeks, I've been battling the overwhelming ache inside me that's felt so damn hollow. I've never been empty, though, and I had to remind myself of that. I have Connor, and our little family is enough. It will *always* be enough. He's sunshine seeping through the cracks of shattered glass that's been glued back together: he fills every empty space with light.

The thing is, when some of those broken pieces came loose and I tried to stuff them back into place, Adam helped me realize it was okay to leave them where they lie, out in the open. He held them in his hands and showed me how much more light shone through when you learned to let go and let things be.

I guess what I'm saying is that even though I have everything I need with the family Connor and I have created with each other, the family I think we both want...well, I think that family includes Adam.

Because even when he's not here, he's everywhere.

Maybe that's why I'm not surprised when my eyes settle on that heart carved into the towering pine before me, nestled in the thick of the forest. My gaze traces the lines of those initials, the numbers that mark the time I spent here with my parents. And finally, my eyes coast down. Down the trunk, where the tree meets the earth.

Where stems of bright pink peonies lie scattered around it, making this tree impossible to miss.

Because even when he's not here, he's everywhere.

And I don't think I want him anywhere else.

TWENTY-SIX

THEY CALLED MY MOM

Adam

I FORGOT how physically exhausting heartbreak is.

It's staring at your phone until late into the night, rereading old messages, smiling at pictures. Typing out a hundred new messages, only to second-guess and delete every single one. Heartbreak is forgetting to eat, not sleeping at all, or sleeping way too much. It's brain fog and stomach aches, skipping your morning workout, and forgetting you made plans.

Heartbreak is a thousand times worse when Rosie is the one your heart is missing.

I wish it were as easy as getting on my knees and begging for forgiveness, but as I sink down to one of the couches in the main living space of Second Change Home, I know it's not. I lied to Rosie, someone who trusted me with everything precious in her life. And instead of being furious with me, instead of yelling, telling me she'd never forgive me, she comforted me. She took my pain in her hands and gave me grace. For space, for patience. And, like I told her then, I'd give her anything she'd ever ask for.

A quiet shuffle brings my gaze up, finding little Lily standing at the opposite end of the couch, hands clasped, head down.

"Hey, Lily."

"Hi, Adam." She scuffs at the floor, big brown eyes bouncing to mine, then back down. "Could I sit with you?"

I pat the cushion next to me. "You can always sit with me, sweetheart."

She shuffles over, leaving a gap between us. "Did I do something bad?"

"Something bad?"

She nods, eyes fixed on her hands in her lap. "Sometimes at home Daddy would say he didn't want to see me. He said it was because I was being bad, but I never knew what I did. He would lock me in my room for a while."

A muscle tics in my jaw. "A while?"

"Yeah. I wasn't allowed to go outside or go downstairs to watch TV or play with my toys. Mama would bring me sandwiches and stuff and come play with me while Daddy was sleeping." She tugs at the hem of her dress, over and over, her knuckles turning white. "I thought maybe I was bad and you didn't want to see me anymore."

Anger moves through me, and I force my fists to unclench. I don't know Lily's story, but I know I don't want to be anything like her dad. That I've inadvertently made her feel unwanted while I was in my own head these past two weeks makes me sick.

I reach across the gap, hooking my pinky around her tiny one. "I'm sorry, Lily-bug. I was having a couple of tough days, but I shouldn't disappear like that. I'm sorry I scared you, and I'm so sorry I made you feel like it had anything to do with you. You're special to me, and I'd never do anything to intentionally hurt your feelings like that."

Slowly, she slides her small hand into mine. "How come you called me Lily-bug?"

"I'm not sure. But it sounds kinda happy, doesn't it? And I feel happy when I'm with you. Feels a little like my heart is smiling."

Her ears burn red, and she scrunches her nose and mouth, trying to hide her smile. "Mama used to call me Lily-bug. Before Daddy sent her to heaven."

Fuck. "If you want, I won't call you it again. You can keep it your special name that you shared only with your mama."

Lily stays quiet, scooching close and turning our clasped hands over in her lap, running one tiny fingertip over my knuckles. "Why are you sad today?"

"Not doing a good job of hiding it, huh?"

Her nose crinkles. "Maybe you're better at hockey?"

"I hope so," I chuckle, then sigh. "I hurt someone's feelings. Someone special to me. I lied to her about something silly, and it really hurt her."

"How come you did that?"

"I was scared of getting hurt, and I didn't want to lose her. I thought maybe she might like me better if she didn't know I played hockey."

Lily cocks her head. "But why? I like you even though you play hockey."

"Yeah?" I squeeze her hand. "Why do you like me?"

"Because you're nice to me, you make me laugh, you make bracelets with me, and on days when I'm really sad, I forget why I'm sad when you play with me."

Something warm moves through me, and I fight the urge to wrap this little girl up in my arms. "That makes me feel really special, Lily. Thank you."

"You are special, Adam." The compassion shining in her gaze rocks me to my core. In this moment, I realize how much she reminds me of Rosie. "I could give you a hug, if you want. Mama said I have magic hugs. They always made her feel happy when she was sad. So if you want…" She shrugs. "I could give you a hug."

"I'd love a magic hug."

Cautiously, she wraps her tiny arms around me. I wind my arm around her back, holding her gently, and as she snuggles into me, everything feels like it'll be okay. I guess that's the magic.

"Adam? I think you could call me Lily-bug. Like my mama did."

"That would make me feel really special to share something with you that you only shared with your mama."

"I think she'd like it if I shared it with you." She lays her head against me, sighing softly. "You feel safe, just like my mama."

~

They called my fucking mom.

My dad, too, but he simply clapped my back and slid out into the backyard with the rest of the guys, murmuring a quick, "Good luck," before leaving me alone with this pack of vicious hyenas.

"Quite frankly," my mom starts, "it's about time I was invited to girls' night, since *somebody* has been ignoring my phone calls."

I scuff at my floor. "I've been busy."

"Busy wallowing in self-pity," Cara clarifies with an eye roll.

"Busy missing Rosie," Olivia corrects with a sharp look at Cara.

"Busy taking care of his premature arthritis 'cause he's back to jacking off now," Jennie mumbles, checking out her nails.

I drag my hands down my face. "*How*?"

"How what?" Cara asks.

"How are you guys my best option?"

"Hey!" Olivia props her fists on her hips. "I take great offense to that! I'm mostly normal *and* mature!"

With my elbows on my knees and my head in my hands, I run my fingers through my hair. "Maybe we call it a night." I ruffle Bear's ears, and he cracks one sleepy lid, staring up at me from my lap. "What do you think, bud? Am I a lost cause?"

"Adam." Olivia squeezes in beside me. "You're not a lost cause."

"I know how easy it is to give up on yourself," Jennie offers gently. "But we aren't going to let you do that."

"I just really miss her." I rub my chest, trying to soothe the ache beating there. "It's not getting any easier, giving her space. I only get angrier with myself each day that goes by without her."

"I hate Courtney," my mom mutters.

"I'm with Bev," Cara says, slinging one leg over the other. "And it's not too late to circle back to my original idea of running her down with my car."

"We're not running anyone over," Olivia says. "But if she were to be accidentally pushed—" She holds up a hand, stopping herself and shaking her head. "Of all the terrible things Courtney has done, the worst by far is breaking you down to the point of believing you—exactly as you are—are unworthy of someone's love."

I hang my head. "I don't even know who I am anymore."

"We know who you are, Adam," Jennie insists quietly. "You're eternally hopeful. Somebody who always tries to see the best in others."

"You root for everyone, and you always stand by your friends' sides," Olivia adds.

"You cheer for the little people who can't cheer for themselves," Cara tells me. "Some of those kids didn't have a reason to smile until you came into their lives."

"You've got the biggest heart out of anyone I know," Garrett says from behind me, and I turn, finding my friends and my dad in my patio doorway.

"When I feel like a failure, I find you," Emmett tells me. "You lift me up and remind me how far I've come."

"You make me want to be a better person," Jaxon mumbles, gaze bouncing from me to the floor. "I think I kinda already am, and it's because I follow you."

Carter leans against the doorway, his daughter in his arms. "You believe in me when no one else does."

I huff a tired laugh. "That's proven to be an expensive trait of mine."

"And you give the best snuggles," he coos in a baby voice, waving Ireland's arms around as she giggles. "And you're definitely the most handsome and strong of all my uncles, almost as handsome and strong as my daddy, but not quite."

Laughter rings throughout the room, and Carter sets his smiling daughter down in my arms. "Seriously, man, you don't see yourself clearly. And we get it. How could you after everything you've been through? But if you look around this room, you'll see a bunch of people who love you." He shrugs. "But you need to love you too. Especially if you want Rosie to love you."

"Why do you feel like you don't deserve her?" my dad asks.

"I never said that."

"Not with your words, maybe. But that's what your actions said, isn't it? You hid who you were because you felt like that person might be less deserving of her love."

Rosie is everything good and bright in this world. She's got the purest heart, made of the warmest sunshine. She's the embodiment of compassion and grace, the kindest person I've ever known, someone who strives to give people the understanding she didn't receive when she needed it most. She's continuously working on herself, taking difficult steps to give her son the life he deserves. She's always trying to be the best version of herself, but I don't think she needs to change a thing; her drive and her heart ensure she's someone who only puts her best foot forward every time she moves.

"What if I can't give her everything she's spent her life searching for?" I whisper. "I can't be a partner who's at her side every day when I'm traveling seventy-five percent of the year. I'll miss birthdays and anniversaries, and I won't be holding her hand through some of her toughest moments. How can I be the partner she deserves? The family she and Connor need?" I shake my head as the truth grips my throat. "I can't be."

"Ah," my mom murmurs. "So that's why you only chose her with half of your heart."

The girls are all nodding, but I'm sitting here, so lost I can't figure out left from right.

"Here you have this beautiful woman who's lived her life not being chosen. Who has wanted nothing more than for someone to see her and love her enough to choose her and her son. And you chose her, Adam, you really did. But you didn't choose yourself. You took all of her, and you only gave her half of you in return. All those broken pieces don't make a whole unless you give all of them to her."

All this time, I wanted someone to like the parts of me that weren't defined by hockey. I wanted someone to see me outside the sport and everything it's brought me, and want those parts too. Because for so long, that's all I've been. But the truth is...hockey is a part of me. It's made me everything I am today, both the good and the bad. I'm loyal and supportive because I know how to be part of a team. I'm empathetic because I know what it feels like to lose, to put so much pressure on myself to succeed, and I know what it's like to have people support me every step of the way when I don't think I deserve it. I love as hard as I do because people have loved me just as hard back.

And because people have broken me, and I never, ever want to be like them.

I found Rosie. *Finally, I fucking found her*. Someone who makes me feel like a *person*. I forget when I'm with her. Forget that I've been broken. I forget to put on an act. I forget how much money I'm worth and yet still, with her by my side, I feel fucking *priceless*. Irreplaceable. When I'm with Rosie, I feel like there's no one alive who can love her the way I do, the way I want to promise to love her for as long as she'll let me.

But when I'm alone, I remember.

I remember that I've been replaced by someone I loved. That I've been nothing but dollar signs, a fancy house, and a handsome face. I forget all the things Rosie loves about me, the things I love about myself, and I fixate on everything else. Everything that pulls me deeper into the lie I've spun, where I can't face the possibility of giving Rosie everything, because everything has never been enough.

"What if I give her all of me and she decides she doesn't want it?" The words are hoarse, halfway to broken, barely hanging onto a thread of hope. "I don't have anything else to give her."

Olivia lays her hand over mine. "You give what you can, Adam, and if she doesn't want it, that's her loss, and it's a big one. But for what it's worth, I can't imagine her not loving all of you. What you've given her is who you are; the hockey is just an extension of yourself. It doesn't change a single thing about your heart. She needs to give you a chance to show her that—and she will, because she's always been so patient, so good at making you feel seen. And you need to be willing to let her have all those pieces, to trust her with them."

"It's okay to be scared, Adam," Jennie murmurs. "Because when you have trouble loving your own broken pieces, nothing seems scarier than giving them to someone else." Her eyes flit to Garrett, and something soft moves across her gaze. "But sometimes those people show you exactly how to love the broken bits of yourself. To them, you're not broken at all."

My mom smiles softly from across the room. "Go show Rosie how well you can love her, simply because you're you and she's her. Show her that she and Connor are the family you choose because you're each other's perfect fit. Show her that the man she's fallen for and the hockey player she's only just met are one and the same. Show her you love her, Adam, because we know you do. And deep down, I think she knows too."

Cara wipes a single tear from her eye, sniffling. "I knew calling your mom was my best work yet. I can't wait to see how I eventually top it."

My dad comes to stand behind me, nudging my shoulder. "Maybe two weeks is long enough to wait idly on the sidelines. You've been patient, and that's great. Now maybe what Rosie needs is for you to step up and remind her that you're still here, and you're not going anywhere. That when she's ready, you'll be right here, ready to move forward with her." He winks. "Women love men who chase them just a little. Just ask your mom."

"And Ollie," Carter adds with the pump of his brows. "She wanted me from the beginning, but she pretended she didn't—"

"Carter."

"Fine," he grumbles, crossing his arms. "But it was relevant."

Mom hugs me from behind, kissing my temple. "I'm proud of you, honey. I want you to be proud of you too." She brushes one of Ireland's curls from her forehead. "Jesus, Carter, I can't believe you had a hand in making anything so beautiful and pure. Thank God for your incredible wife." She straightens, patting my shoulder. "Garrett, I've got a box of snacks for you out in the—"

"Say less," he says, breathless as he dashes down the hallway.

It's amazing how, just like that, my worries begin to fade. I guess that's what family is for, though: to lift you up when you've fallen so hard you can't see your way out. Even the hardest things feel more manageable with my family surrounding me.

So as we spend the rest of the evening soaking up the last of summer on the patio, drinking beer and eating barbecue, I feel content. For the first time in two weeks, I fall asleep peacefully, and when I wake in the morning with sunshine streaming across my face, I'm optimistic.

The time on my phone tells me it's after nine, which is probably why Bear isn't in bed. If I haven't fed him by seven, I can find him waiting at his bowl in the kitchen, acting like I've starved him for days.

I wander downstairs, the smell of my mom's French toast wafting from the kitchen, making my stomach rumble. I drop a kiss to her cheek, stealing a piece of bacon from the platter.

"Morning, honey. I tried to feed Bear, but he wasn't interested." She gestures at the yard. "He's lounging out back in the sun. Seems like he's moving a bit slow today."

"Thanks, Mom." I head out back with his bowl, whistling for him. His head pops up from where he's curled up beneath the shade of an oak, but he doesn't move except for the excited whip of his tail as I approach. "What's up, bud?" I set his bowl down in front of him, ruffling his floppy ears and kissing the spot between his eyes. He lays his head back down, and I frown, running my palm over his belly. It's hard to tell beneath all the fur, but it feels swollen, bloated almost. "You got a belly ache, big guy?"

Huge brown eyes stare up at me as his tail slows to a happy, steady thump on the grass, but he makes no move to eat his breakfast.

"Grandma's making bacon," I try, and that steady thump turns frantic before he climbs to his feet. "'Atta boy. C'mon, big guy. It's the good stuff, double smoked and maple flavored."

He jogs ahead of me, a happy skip to his step before he stops suddenly. His eyes come to mine over his shoulder, and for a moment I think he's waiting for me to catch up.

Until all one-hundred-and-forty pounds of him collapses on the patio.

TWENTY-SEVEN

HOW MANY FUCKING SHOES ARE THERE?

Rosie

Clarity has a funny way of making you feel like you've been tied to a bundle of helium balloons, floating above the skies with the sharpest view of your world, where all the answers lie before you like an open book. The type of clarity that comes with pausing, taking the time to reflect on your priorities so you can choose your future with certainty.

Connor is my everything. He's my past, my present, and my future. But Adam, he's *our* future. That's the type of knowledge clarity has brought me, had me Googling *Vancouver Vipers training camp dates*, and *Vancouver Vipers preseason game schedule* last night. Google told me he leaves tomorrow for his first preseason game in Edmonton, so if I want to talk to him—and I do—it has to be today.

That has to be why I've been floating through my morning emergency rotation with a smile on my face, not an ounce of tension in my shoulders.

All right, I have to credit the extra shot of espresso I added to my iced vanilla latte this morning. And okay, it also helps that the emergencies have been nonexistent so far. We've spent the morning looking at old X-rays and their corresponding clinical notes and telling Dr. Holmes what we think was going on with the animals. I've nailed all of them so far, so I float a little higher as I head to reception to file the records away.

"It's hard to believe after days like Friday," Dr. Holmes says, "but we do have good days around here. Enjoy them when they come."

My mind wanders back to a warm summer night when I crept out the front door, determined to triple-check on the baby bunny we'd returned to its empty nest in the park, to make sure its mom really did come back. My dad caught me at the end of the driveway, and we walked over together. That was the first time I told him I wanted to be a vet like him, and he told me the same thing Dr. Holmes did: that despite all the hard days, where all I'd do was cry and want to quit, there would be so many good days too.

The good days weren't always the easy days, he'd said. And he was right. Sometimes, they were the days you felt like you were hanging by a thread, where you wondered why you chose something that could be so painful, only to watch a furry friend open its eyes when you weren't sure they'd open again, when the arms of their human came around you without warning, hugging you so tight as they thanked you.

The days where you can look back and know you made a difference, he'd said. *Those are the days that make it all worth it.*

I know the days will be hard. I want to be someone who takes the pain of somebody's hardest day and makes it a little easier to carry.

An engine roars close by, followed by the squeal of tires in the parking lot. Murmured chatter erupts around me as my colleagues gather by the front windows to watch our first emergency unfold.

"Sorry to cut our easy day short, everyone," Dr. Holmes says. Her eyes come to mine. "Ready?"

I nod, pulling my stethoscope from my pocket, hanging it around my neck. My legs carry me quickly toward the doors, and I nearly trip over my feet when a dark blue pickup truck skids to a stop out front. When the passenger door opens, my heart stops.

"Is that Adam Lockwood?" someone wonders out loud, and when Adam jumps down from the passenger seat, his one-hundred-and-forty-pound dog limp in his arms, I'm already pushing through the door, running toward him.

"Rosie!" Adam screams as professionals and students alike surround him, reaching for Bear. "I need Rosie!" He clutches Bear to his heaving chest, his eyes tearing through the parking lot, sliding right over me. "No! You can't take him. Only Rosie can touch him!"

I shove my way through, grabbing Adam's face and pulling his tortured gaze to mine. "Breathe, Adam. Breathe, baby. I'm right here."

Sapphire eyes settle on mine, red-rimmed and panicked. "They can't take him," he whispers. "I don't trust them. I-I-I…I trust you."

I cover Adam's trembling hand, his fingers tangled in Bear's fur. "I'm going to look at Bear, okay? But you can trust everyone here, I promise you. They want to help."

"You're gonna look at him?" Hopeful eyes bounce between mine. "You? Because he knows you. He-he…he loves you."

"And I love him too. Very much."

A handsome, broad man with deep brown skin climbs out of the driver's seat of Adam's truck, coming to stand behind him, squeezing his shoulder. I know this man from the happy photos lining Adam's staircase, but what I didn't know about him until Google told me is that Deacon Lockwood, Adam's father, is a retired NFL player. A quarterback, to be specific, and I guess that's kind of a big deal.

Among the worry, his gaze shines with kindness. "Hi, Rosie."

"Hi, Mr. Lockwood." We share a soft smile before I run my fingers through Adam's mussed curls, cupping his cheek. "We need to take Bear inside so we can look at him right away, okay?"

His chin quivers, tears clinging to his dark lashes. When he blinks, they run down his cheeks. "I can't lose him, Rosie. I-I-I can't. He's my best friend."

"We're going to do everything we can for him. I promise."

"Mr. Lockwood, I'm Dr. Holmes, Rosie's professor and the head of emergency surgery here." She guides Adam and his dad inside. "Let's walk and talk so we can get caught up on Bear and get him stabilized right away. Can you tell us what happened?"

"I don't know." Adam sets Bear down on the exam table. "He was fine last night. He was playing with his friend in the backyard, and he took up the whole bed at nighttime like he likes to, Rosie, you know? And then this morning, he wouldn't eat breakfast, and you know how much he likes his food. Then he just…fell. He was walking, and he just collapsed."

I smile down at the heavily panting dog, lifting his burly front paw as I press my stethoscope to his chest. "Did he vomit at all?"

Adam squeezes his eyes shut, his forehead creasing. "I can't…I can't remember." He looks to his dad. "Dad?"

"Yes," Deacon answers for him. "Bear vomited three times in the backyard."

"Hi, Bear," I murmur, brushing my thumb along Bear's snout. "I missed you. What are you doing not eating your breakfast, huh? You never pass up food." My big, burly guy whimpers, nuzzling my hand. The weak throb of his pulse in my ears squeezes at my throat. "I'm going to help you breathe a little easier, okay, big guy?" I tell him, fitting him with an oxygen mask. My palms slide along his rib cage, moving gently over his belly. Dread claws its way up my chest when I feel the swelling there, and the look I share with Dr. Holmes says she knows exactly what I've found.

This can't be happening, not again, not this soon, and not to our Bear.

I wipe my forehead on my wrist before curling my fingers into my palms, nails biting in to still my panic. "I'd like to start Bear on an IV right away. He's in shock, and this will help to stabilize him. I'd also like to do an X-ray."

"What for? Do you think he broke something?"

"The X-ray will give us more information. His stomach is bloated, and there's a chance it might have twisted."

"What does that mean? How do you untwist it?"

I squeeze his forearm, and his shoulders drift away from his ears as he leans into my touch. "Let's take a look inside and see what's going on first. You and your dad can stay with him during the X-ray, and then Dr. Holmes and I will discuss what we see, and we'll come back to talk to you about a plan of action. Does that sound okay?"

Adam agrees, and once Bear has an IV in and is stabilized, an X-ray tech comes to wheel him to another room.

Adam's hand comes down over Bear's belly, panicked eyes shooting to mine. "Rosie? I want you to do it."

Warmth rushes through me when I cover his hand with mine, like my body has missed this, comes alive just for him. "This is Maribel's job, and she's really amazing at it. She has a Tibetan Mastiff at home, too, did you know that?"

Maribel smiles. "Even bigger than Bear, if you can believe it."

He looks down at Bear, and I squeeze his hand, bringing his eyes back to mine. "I can't wait for you to see how gentle Maribel is with him. He's going to love her. Maybe even more than he loves me."

His gaze flickers with something like disbelief. "That's not possible," he murmurs before giving Maribel a weak smile. "Okay. We're ready."

I tell myself I'm not jumping to any conclusions. I tell Dr. Holmes that I'm hopeful, that the X-rays will show the stomach still in proper position, so we'll be able to remove any gas quickly and easily.

I tell myself everything is fine, but when those X-ray pictures land in my hands fifteen minutes later, showing me the damning evidence, they fall right to the ground, Dr. Holmes's eyes following.

"Bear's stomach is twisted. He has GDV."

"I don't understand." Adam's quiet, lost voice punctures my chest as he stares down at Bear, his head resting against his torso. "Is it something I did? Is it my fault?"

"GDV doesn't have much of a rhyme or reason," I repeat the same information I gave to Mrs. Greene just three days ago, only this time, I can't swallow the heartache. "Bigger breeds with a deep chest, like Bear, are at a higher risk, though it can happen to any dog, and even cats. GDV happens when the stomach expands with gas and then rotates, or twists, blocking the entrance and the exit."

"So the gas has nowhere to go," he murmurs, a protective palm sliding over Bear's belly. "How common is it?"

"The chance a dog Bear's size contracts GDV is about twenty-one to twenty-four percent."

"Fuck. Have you ever treated a dog with GDV?"

I look to Dr. Holmes, and she nods, gesturing for me to continue. "This past Friday we diagnosed a St. Bernard with GDV."

"What happened?"

The words are lost to Adam's brilliant eyes, holding onto that spark of hope but dimming fast.

"Rosie," he whispers. "What happened?"

"Pepper—" Her name catches in my throat, breaking, burning. "Pepper passed during surgery. Her stomach couldn't handle the pressure any longer and ruptured before we could release it." A single tear leaks from the corner of my eye, and I sniff, swiping it away. "I understand why that might make you hesitant to proceed, but surgery is the only option. We would release the gas and set Bear's stomach back in the normal position, then perform a gastropexy, which is where we attach his stomach to his abdominal wall to prevent future twisting." I hesitate. "If Bear doesn't have surgery, Adam, he will die. There isn't another outcome."

His chest rises sharply, and he strokes a hand down Bear's side. "Okay."

"Okay?"

"I trust you, Rosie. If you say he needs surgery, let's do it."

Trust. It's a double-edged sword sometimes, isn't it? I want it. I'm honored to have it. And yet I'm terrified to be the one to break it, even unintentionally.

So I only nod, praying I don't have to do that today, and then excuse myself to have the operating room prepped.

Dr. Holmes catches me in the hallway. "Are you okay to do this? There's no shame in stepping back. It's always difficult, but when you have a personal tie to an animal—"

"I want to stay with Bear. Please don't take me out of this."

"If you feel your control slipping at any time, you let me know, and someone else can step in."

"Thank you, but I won't lose control." It's only a half lie; I'll keep it together until the surgery ends.

When the OR is ready, I make my way back to the exam room where Adam waits with Bear and his dad. Deacon smiles at me, getting to his feet.

"Your mom is on the way over. I'm going to meet her out front." He claps Adam on the back, kisses his head, and then takes Bear's face in his hands. "You, big boy. I know I'm gonna see you later. I can feel it all the way down to my feet you love to sit on so much." He presses a kiss to his nose, and Bear reciprocates the sentiment with a languid flick of his tongue over Deacon's face. "You're such a good boy, Bear."

Deacon pauses at my side on the way by. "Thank you for taking care of my boys, Rosie. I know how much they love you."

The words hang heavy in the air as he walks away, leaving Adam to stare at the deep flush the sentiment leaves on my cheeks.

"We're ready for Bear," I tell him. "Dr. Holmes will perform the surgery, and—"

"But you—"

"I can't do the surgery, Adam. My job is to assist her with instruments and monitor Bear while I watch and learn."

He nibbles his lower lip. "You won't leave his side?"

"Never. I promise."

"He's going to be okay, Rosie. Right?" His words are drenched in desperation, just like the heartbreaking look dimming his cobalt eyes, begging me for a promise he knows I can't make.

"He's going to be surrounded by love, Adam. I can promise you that."

"Yeah," he murmurs, watching our hands dance alongside each other down Bear's side, nearly touching. "I know. You give the best kind of love." He sniffs, his gaze coming to mine, and the trust that lives there grips my heart. "Thank you, Rosie."

Adam crouches, taking Bear's face in his hands. Beautiful eyes pool with tears before he rests his forehead on Bear's, and I turn away, swatting away the single, fat teardrop that escapes and steals its way down my cheek.

"I love you, Bear," Adam whispers to him. "You're the best dog in the world, and my best friend." He presses one last kiss to Bear's head, and on the way out the door, his fingers find mine, tangling together, squeezing tenderly.

As he disappears into the reception area, I can't help the fear that claws its way up my throat. And minutes later, when big brown eyes stare up at me before they close, the sedation doing its work, those claws sink deeper, unwilling to let go.

Because if Bear doesn't make it through the other side of this, what if Adam never forgives me? What if, today, I lose them both?

Adam

I didn't think it could get worse. I thought all the shoes had dropped, and yet here I am, faced with the possibility of losing not only Rosie and Connor but now my Bear too.

How many fucking shoes are there?

My only solace is that I'm surrounded by my family. My dad paces the reception area, and Carter is crouched by a small enclosure, quietly showing Ireland a litter of kittens while Jaxon takes turns snuggling them. Jennie sits next to Garrett, her head resting on his shoulder, and

Olivia and my mom flank my sides, whispering reassuring words to me as I wait with my head in my hands.

I made the mistake of looking up GDV the minute I sat down. Article after article that left me suddenly sure I'd never see my dog again because he displayed some of the most advanced symptoms. I didn't stop until the clinic doors opened behind me and my friends walked in, Carter tugging my phone away and reminding me why he's our team captain, a born leader, with a handful of words.

We're not gonna do that. We're not gonna focus on all the bad numbers. We're gonna sit here together, because that's the way we're strongest, and we're gonna find peace in knowing that Bear is in the most capable hands right now, and we're gonna hope. That's what we're gonna do, got it?

So instead, I've been sitting here for the last hour thinking about everything good Bear has brought me. The loyalty, the friendship. The warm body snuggled next to mine in bed after having my heart shattered, the tip-tap of his paws as he follows me through the house, keeping me company. The goofy laughs, the belly rubs, and the gentlest heart.

And Rosie.

Bear brought me Rosie, and Rosie brought me Connor.

I wouldn't have one without the other, and it doesn't feel like my family is complete without all three of them.

Silence falls over the room, and Olivia gives my hand a small squeeze. My gaze lifts to her, and I drag my head out of my hands, following her stare.

Rosie stands in the doorway, weary green eyes sweeping the room, settling on me. Her hands curl into little fists at her sides, and she steps toward me as I rise from my seat. She meets me in the middle of the room, all five foot four of her staring up at me, that dimpled chin trembling.

"It's okay," I tell her quietly. "If he didn't..." The thought of a life without him far sooner than I should ever have to think of it seizes my lungs, and I swallow against it. "You can tell me."

Tears glisten in her eyes, and the corner of her mouth hooks. "Bear did great."

"He...what?"

"The surgery was successful. Dr. Holmes released the trapped gas and attached his stomach to his abdomen wall. There were no complications."

My heart kickstarts, thrashing against my rib cage. "He's going to be okay?"

Rosie takes my hands in hers, clutching them tightly. "He's going to be okay."

The room dissolves into cheers, and my family comes around me, a tangled web of arms hugging me tight as relief slides through me. The feeling is so strong, so palpable it knocks the air from my stomach, makes my limbs weak. I sink into the love, the family I'm so lucky to have found.

My eyes open in time to see Rosie slipping silently out the clinic doors, hurrying into the parking lot.

"Be right back," I murmur, detangling myself and chasing after the woman who just ran out of here with my heart in her hands.

"Rosie! Wait."

She glances over her shoulder, waving me off. "I'm fine, Adam. Don't worry about me."

I catch her wrist, pulling her back to me. "Hey. Stop."

Green eyes wobble, each breath sharp and staggered. "I'm fine," she repeats, and the lie is so weak I nearly laugh. "You should be with your family. Bear will be awake soon. I just need to do something."

"I am with my family, and I'll be with Bear as soon as he wakes up. So tell me what you need to do and I'll help you."

She shakes her head, trying to pull free from my grasp. "I just need to…I just need to do something," she cries, chest heaving as her face starts to crumble. "Please."

"Rosie." I run my palms up her arms, squeezing her shoulders. "Let go, sweetheart. Let it go."

That lower lip trembles, and all I want to do is trap it beneath my thumb, take it between my lips. I want her pain, her worries, her trust. I want her to give up control, give it all to me. I'll take care of her.

"I was so afraid," she finally whispers, the words fractured and meek. "I was so afraid we were going to lose Bear. And I was *terrified* that you'd never forgive me for it. I thought I might lose both of you forever, and I—" A sob escapes her throat, racking her body. "I've survived a lot of things, but I don't know how I'd survive that loss."

Her agony wraps around my throat like a fist, threatening to cut off oxygen. When a fresh wave of tears cascades down her cheeks and she curls into herself, covering her face with her hands as she cries, I yank her into me. This time, I refuse to let her go.

"You will never lose me, Rosie. As long as you want me here, there's nowhere else for me to be." I press my lips tenderly to her temple as she clings to my shirt. "I promise."

TWENTY-EIGHT

LONG TIME COMING

Adam

"What are you doing?"

I shift my reading glasses up my nose and flip the page. "Reading."

"I know that," Garrett grumbles. "But reading what?"

"A book."

He pins his arms over his chest and slumps in his plane seat. "You're so annoying sometimes, you fuckin' turkey."

I smile to myself, sticking a blue tab to a passage in my book. Riling up Garrett is fun. He starts spewing all kinds of weird, colorful insults, most of them picked up from Jennie, who also likes to rile him up. For different reasons than me, though. Something about hand necklaces and other shit I'd rather not know.

"What's that you're doing there?" Jaxon gestures at the tabs I'm sticking in my book. "With the tabs?"

"It's called annotating," Carter answers for me, pulling a box of Oreos from his bag. "Oooh, fudge dipped. Fuck yeah, Ollie." He rips open the package and tosses one in his mouth. "Aw-wie does it wif her spicy books." He swallows the cookie so he can talk like an adult again. "She marks out all the sexy stuff she likes, and then we try it. Like this blindfold—"

"No." I hold up a hand. "Stop. I hate how much I know about your sex life."

Jaxon frowns. "So, you're marking sexy shit to try with Rosie?"

"No, I'm—"

"Cara bookmarks porn she likes," Emmett says. "That's kinda like annotating, but with a movie, not a book."

"What? No, that's not the same—"

He smiles, a far-off look in his eyes. "Last week, she came out of the bathroom wearing this leather—"

"For fuck's sake, I don't want to know about any of your sex lives!"

"Whoa," Garrett murmurs, eyes wide. "Someone's testy."

Carter licks at the icing on a new cookie. "'Cause he's not gettin' any right now."

"He smashed through all of my condoms in one night and now he hasn't had sex in three weeks," Jaxon adds unnecessarily.

Emmett pats my shoulder. "It'd make the best of us grumpy."

"Holy fuck." I tuck my book away; clearly reading's not happening anymore. With my MacBook and AirPods, I stand and point to an empty seat down the row. "I'm gonna watch a movie."

"Have fun looking at pictures of Rosie," Garrett calls as I walk away.

We've been on the road for three days for our first two preseason games in Edmonton and Calgary, and Garrett's been my unlucky roommate.

No, wait. *I'm* the unlucky roommate. He came back to the room one night and found me looking at all the pictures Rosie's been sending me of her and Bear while he's been recovering from surgery at the school clinic, and I came back to the room one night to him furiously scrubbing a *mess* off the carpet while Jennie was cackling at him over FaceTime. He screamed at the both of us that he'd scored a goal and deserved to let loose, even though it was only an exhibition game. Which scene would you rather come home to?

Popping my headphones in, I open my laptop and pull up my message thread with Rosie. Our preseason started the day after Bear's surgery, but knowing Rosie would be there every day to give him lots of love made it easier to get on the plane. The pictures and videos she's been diligently sending don't hurt either.

I pull up my favorite one, sent this morning.

Rosie smiles at the camera, bright and happy. "Let's go see if Bear is up."

She pushes through a set of swinging doors, and his head pops up from his bed. Slowly, he gets to his feet, tail whipping back and forth, thudding against the wall of the oversized kennel.

"Look at you, big boy," Rosie coos, propping her phone up as she gets down on her knees, burying her fingers in his fur. Bear wastes no time covering her face in kisses, and she giggles, hugging him close. "Do you wanna tell Daddy how much you miss him?" She points at the camera as Bear gives a little woof. "Say, 'I love you, Daddy.'" He barks again. "That's my handsome boy."

A text cuts across my screen, and I sigh at the interruption from my publicist.

ANGIE

She's called me three times today, Adam.

There's no name, because Angie knows we don't say it when we can avoid it.

You'd think blocking her number not once, but twice, and telling her to never call me again would do the trick, but after Courtney called me that night at Rosie's, in the middle of all the chaos, she resorted to calling Angie.

The woman hasn't been in my life since I tossed her—and the guy she was fucking—out of my bed over a year ago, and suddenly she wants to chat. I don't have the time of day for her, and I certainly can't be bothered to see her again. I still cringe at the thought of her in my kitchen that morning in July, wearing nothing but my T-shirt, acting like she belonged there, claiming she'd been at my party the night before.

Drunk Adam doesn't always make the brightest decisions, but Drunk Adam has never made an oopsie that size.

ME

I don't want to talk to her.

And I've told her that. Approximately 25,000x. Honestly, Adam, how you were ever with this woman is beyond me. No offense.

I could swear up and down that Courtney was nothing like this at seventeen, but the more reflecting I do, the more signs I see that I didn't before. Still, on my bad days, I sometimes wonder if I'm responsible, if I didn't love her the way she needed to be loved, if the hockey made me too absent. All the same fears that led to my downfall, to the lies I never should've told Rosie.

I think you should meet with her. Hear me out.

Abso-fucking-lutely not.

I know, I know. But she says she's got something you'd want to hear.

That's bullshit. What could she possibly have to say that I'd want to hear?

I agree, but I also know you like to stay out of the media when it's not hockey or fundraising related, and I wouldn't put it past her to drag you into something if she wants your attention that badly. So I say we meet her somewhere public, I do the talking, and we give her five minutes, nothing more.

Courtney has embarrassed me enough in the media, but nothing is worse than the hurt it causes, knowing that after all we've been through, all the years I gave her, she cares so little for me that she would go to such great lengths to tear me down in whatever way she can. Like all she wants to do is wreck everything I've worked so hard for, take away this life I've earned.

So I agree to five minutes, not a single second more, this Saturday. I just want this over with.

Tension stacks in my shoulders, so tight it curls me forward. I roll my neck, but the stiffness has already dug its claws in. My fingers move on their own accord, hitting that Video Call button, and my knee bounces as I pray for it to connect.

Rosie's face fills my computer screen, and I melt into the seat.

"Hey," she greets me quietly, a spark of hesitance in her eyes. Through all the messages since Bear came out of surgery, we haven't spoken face to face.

"Sorry for calling so late."

"It's okay. I just climbed into bed two minutes ago." She looks like an angel, lit only by the glow of her phone, pink waves scattered around her face, the sleeve of her oversized sleep tee hanging off one delectable shoulder. "Congrats on your…oh God, this is going to be so embarrassing. I know this is wrong, but I know it's close. Shut-up?"

I bark a laugh, and she blushes my favorite blush. "Shut*out*."

"I told you it was gonna be embarrassing. But it still made sense in my head. You didn't let in any goals, so it kinda shuts up the other team, you know?"

"I like it. Petition to change it from shutout to shut-up."

"I know you're just placating me, Adam Lockwood."

"And I know I'm in trouble when you or my mom use my full name." I smile at the way she giggles. "Did you watch?"

She nods, brushing her bangs back. "Both games. Carter Beckett is really fast. And Jaxon likes to fight a lot, which I wasn't expecting, given that he fell head over heels for a cat at first sight, called him Mittens, and then adopted him."

"He hides his soft side behind tattoos and punches."

"And you, you were so…" She blows out a breath, eyes widening. "*Big*. I didn't think you could get any bigger, but you really did. And, um…flexible. I mean, I knew you were flexible, of course." Her eyes widen. "Oh God. That's…that's…" She swipes a hand through the air. "Just never mind me."

Christ, she's so damn cute, I'd give anything to pull her into my arms right now. "I, uh, called because I…wanted…to…" *Tell you I love you and I've hated every single minute apart from you?* "Thank you. For taking care of Bear."

"You don't have to thank me for that, Adam. He makes school better, getting a hug and kiss whenever I want."

"That's why he looks so smug in all the pictures you send me, huh?"

"You know I can't say no to him. Plus, he's thriving on all the attention. He's got the girls here wrapped around his paw." A rustle draws her gaze away from me, and then she dives under the covers with her phone. "Oh shoot. I'm waking Connor. I better get going."

"I'll see you in the morning? When I pick up Bear?"

"I'll be there, Adam. We're so excited to see you."

We're. The single word sends my stupid heart into a tailspin, and I fixate on it for the rest of the flight, and two hours later when I'm lying awake in bed. When I'm walking into the clinic after breakfast the next morning, spinning my keys around my finger and whistling, the six-word sentence is still playing on repeat in my head.

"Mr. Lockwood," the receptionist greets me. "It's a beautiful day to bring home a happy, healthy pup."

"It definitely is." I slide a box of donuts onto the desk. "These are for everyone."

"We love donuts. I'll let them know you're here."

A woman walks out from the back a minute later, and she most definitely doesn't have pink hair. "Come on back with me. I'll walk you through what to expect from Bear's recovery at home."

"Is Rosie here? I brought her breakfast, in case she didn't eat this morning. She forgets sometimes."

"Rosie's working on an emergency that came in about twenty minutes ago. She'll be sad she missed you, but I can take those for you." She reaches for the iced latte, the bag with a piping hot bacon, gouda, and egg breakfast sandwich on a croissant, with a warm and gooey ginger molasses cookie.

And what do I do? I pull the items into my chest, because apparently, I'm a child.

"I'll make sure she gets them, Mr. Lockwood," the woman assures me. "I promise I won't eat her breakfast."

"Oh." I look down at the food in my hand before slowly handing it over. "Okay. Thank you."

A gloomy feeling settles low in my stomach. With Bear coming home, Rosie has no reason to check in. As I follow the doctor through the clinic, my brain is already working in overdrive, conjuring up a hundred ways to *accidentally* bump into her. If I can get my hands on her hat again, she'll *have* to see me.

"Rosie came in early this morning to get Bear ready," the doctor tells me. "She took him for a short walk around campus and said he was very happy to get out in the sun." She gestures me inside a small examination room, where Bear greets me by hopping up on his hind legs, front paws on my stomach.

"Oh, buddy." I drop to my knees, letting him lick my face, my hands in his thick, silky fur. Relief expands in my chest, clogging my throat as I hug my dog to my chest. "I love you, Bear," I murmur against his floppy ear. My hands slide over soft cotton, and I pull back to look at the bandana tied around his neck. "What's this?"

"Rosie wanted to surprise you. And as you can see, Bear looks very dapper in his new bandana."

The Vipers logo and my jersey number, forty, cover the blue bandana. But right in the center? A drawing of me and my best, furry bud, the words *Daddy's biggest fan* scrawled beneath it.

I should've known. If ever there was going to be somebody who would see past it all, the goalie mask, the fears, and the insecurities, I should've known it would be Rosie.

It's always been Rosie.

Rosie

Think with your brain, not with your tits. Think with your brain, not with your tits.

No matter how many times I repeat the words, all I can see is muscles. Miles of muscles. Intricately carved, golden like honey, moving lithely under a soft, Saturday morning sun in September, ebony curls falling over bright blue eyes. For the best, really, because I know what will happen when I see them.

I'll drown. I'll lose myself in those eyes, all the love, the kindness, the patience that swims in them. I came here to talk to him, to figure out where to go from here, but when I look at him, the only words that come to mind are *I love you*.

I only make it another three steps down the winding driveway before my heart free-falls to my stomach, my feet halting. The bright garden Adam has been working at since I appeared at the end of his driveway comes into focus, lush petals splashing a rainbow of colors across his front porch, lulling me forward, closer to a feeling that screams of home.

"What are you doing?"

Adam's eyes flip up, and he jumps to his feet, all six foot five of sweaty, barely-covered muscles. "Rosie."

Bear leaps up from the dog bed on the porch, whining as he jogs toward me, pressing himself into my side.

Adam swipes at the sweat beading on his forehead, leaving a smudge of dirt above his eyebrow. "You're here."

I zero in on a droplet running a river down the center of his broad chest, through the flawlessly etched abs flexing as he yanks off his gloves.

"What are you doing?" I repeat, eyes flicking to the bushes that weren't here before.

He wrings the gloves, gaze ricocheting between me and the bushes.

"Adam…" I skim the soft pink petals, fighting the sting of emotion behind my eyes. "These are peonies. You're planting a peony garden in your front yard."

He nods.

"Why?" I whisper, heart pounding in my ears.

The haze in his eyes clears, leaving them vulnerable. "Because I wanted you to feel like you were home if you decided to come back to me."

There's too much space between us. Too fucking *much*, the only logical decision is to eliminate it by throwing myself at his chest, wrapping every inch of me around him until there's nothing left.

Adam chuckles softly, his hand running down my back.

"I forgot how good you feel," I cry softly into his neck, and then he sighs, his body relaxing as he hugs me tighter.

"I missed you so much, Rosie."

I slide down his body, wiping the traitorous tears from my cheeks. "I came to check on Bear, and then I was gonna segue into asking if we could talk about things. I wasn't planning on jumping on you."

He laughs again, and I'm not sure there's a more beautiful sound.

"For future reference, jumping on me is always acceptable." He gestures at my bag, discarded somewhere along the way on the driveway, and the dog jumping at my feet. "Do you want to check on Bear and then segue into asking me if we can talk here, or should we do it inside?" He cringes, checking his watch. "Shit, I forgot I have to meet someone in a half hour. It's kind of important. My publicist said I have to be there."

"Oh. That's okay." Disappointment slumps my shoulders, and Adam palms the back of his neck.

"I could push it? Yeah, I'll just push it. Then we can have as much time as we need to talk."

"It's okay. I shouldn't have shown up unannounced. I dropped Connor off at Brandon's and instead of going home I wound up here instead."

"I won't be long. If you want, you could wait here with Bear, and I'll come right home."

"That works." I scrub Bear's ears, smiling down at the happy boy. "Let's go inside and get you comfy on the couch so I can check you out, 'kay, handsome?"

Inside, Adam sets his gardening tools down in the hallway and heads upstairs to shower as I unpack my bag.

"Oh shoot," I mutter, pulling Connor's stuffed kitty out. Being with Adam this past summer helped me realize my son is a lot more flexible than I gave him credit for, but the one constant in his life is this kitty in his bed every single night, no matter where he sleeps. I've had to walk it over to Brandon's house while Connor screamed on the other end of the phone far too many times.

Once Bear has been thoroughly checked and I'm confident in his healing, I snuggle beside him, his head in my lap as I call Brandon. It takes three tries before he answers.

"What?"

"I forgot to leave you Connor's kitty."

"Fuck, Rosie." He blows out a deep breath, one I barely hear over all the noise in the background. "That was stupid of you."

My chest pulls taut at the six-letter word he wields so easily. "I can bring it over later."

"Yeah, you better," he mumbles distractedly. "Aw, bullshit! He was on the bag! He's safe!" Another sigh. "I'll be home in a couple hours. Bring it over sometime after four."

"Did you guys go out? That's fun." I bite my tongue to stop from asking him if he has our son at a bar while he watches a baseball game.

"Nah, Connor's at home."

"Oh. Who's watching him? I could've kept him longer if you wanted to go out."

He barks a laugh. "Sure, and then you'd bitch at me for not spending more time with him. He's fine anyway. I set the alarm before I left."

"You set the…what?"

"The alarm."

I rub the headache forming in my temples while I process the meaning behind his words, the sound of Adam's footsteps as he comes down the stairs thumping along with the beat of my agitated heart. "Who's watching Connor?" I ask again.

"I set the alarm," he repeats.

"Who the hell is watching Connor, Brandon?"

"Relax," he says on a muffled whisper. "I put him in his playpen for his nap, and I set the alarm on my way out. I'm just at the bar downstairs."

"You left our *toddler* at home alone while you went to get drunk and watch a fucking *baseball* game?" My last restraint snaps, and I leap to my feet as the words rush out of me, an angry, violent wave that pulses through me. "How can you be so damn careless with your son's life?"

I don't stick around to hear his bullshit excuse. Instead, I stuff my phone in my bag and march down the hallway, angry tears flooding my vision as I struggle to put my running shoes on.

"I'm sorry," I say as Adam forces me to sit on the stairs, slips my shoes on for me. "I have to go. I don't know how...does he not love him at all? He's his father, for fuck's sake." My fists ball, fingernails biting into flesh, and I mumble a distracted thank you as he helps me back to my feet, opens the door for me, and follows me outside.

"Rosie," he calls as I start my trek down his driveway.

"I'll call you later, Adam."

"*Rosie*."

I stop, glancing over my shoulder. He stands at his truck, holding the passenger door open. There's a tic in his sharp jawline, veins popping in his forearm as he clenches his keys in his fist, anger radiating off him.

"Get in the truck."

"You have to meet someone. You said it was important. Your publicist—"

"Canceled. Get in the truck."

"But—"

"Connor is a million times more important. There is *nobody* as important to me as you and that little boy, so for the love of God, Rosie, get in this truck before I throw you in it."

My heart thrums, and he doesn't take his eyes off me as I walk toward him, as he helps me into the seat and shuts me in. He doesn't say a word the entire drive, silently following my quiet, panicked directions. The truck is barely in park before he's hopping from his seat, towing me from mine, pulling me through the lobby to the elevator.

As soon as the doors open, Connor's wails pierce my ears, floating down the hallway of the condo.

"Fuck," Adam mutters, hot on my heels as I race to the apartment door.

"It's locked," I cry, jiggling the handle.

"Maaamaaa," Connor screams, sending hot tears cascading down my cheeks as Adam gently sets me aside, playing with the lock.

"It's okay, baby!" I fight to mask the anxiety clawing its way up my throat. "Mama's here!"

"We're coming in to get you, okay, buddy?" Adam tells him. "Just hang tight."

"What do we do? Should I go find Brandon? Get his keys?"

"I've got it," Adam mumbles.

"How are you going to—" I gasp as Adam shoves his shoulder against the door. "Adam, it's a reinforced door. There's no way you can—"

His shoulder connects with it a second time, and the door pops off the top hinge. With a grunt, he shoves his body into it once, twice more, and he catches himself against the frame right as the door swings open and the elevator opens behind us.

"What the fuck?" Brandon yells. "My fucking door!"

"Imagine you cared about your family as much as you cared about your door?" Adam bars his arm across the entrance, stopping Brandon from following me as I race through the apartment. "Don't fucking follow her."

Connor's tear-streaked face appears from where he's trapped between the floor and his tipped-over playpen. Little hands reach for me, fear-stricken eyes colliding with mine, and I rip the playpen off him, scooping him into my arms, pressing my lips to the small gash on his forehead.

"I'm here, baby," I weep softly into his hair as he buries his face in my neck. "It's going to be okay. Mama's got you." I scoop his bag off the floor, and Adam takes it from me, his hand on my back as he guides me toward the door, past a confused and half-drunk Brandon. "He was trapped under his playpen."

"He...he..." Brandon's eyes ricochet from the mess in his living room to the blood trickling from Connor's forehead. "He must've tried to climb out and it tipped over. It was an accident. Right? It was just an accident, buddy. You're okay."

He reaches for Connor, and I yank him away.

"Don't touch him," I seethe. "Never again. You've had a million chances. *Too many chances,* and like a fool, I kept giving you more because all I've ever wanted is for Connor to have a family. But you're not his family, are you? You don't care about anyone but yourself."

"That's not true," he tries weakly, eyes flicking to Adam. "I…I love him."

"You don't have a clue what love is."

He rolls his eyes, giving up the act. "And you do?"

"I know it feels nothing like this. This toxic, selfish bullshit you call love does nothing but harm people. And I won't let you hurt him anymore."

"So what? You guys are done with me then?"

"You're not even on the birth certificate."

He snorts a laugh, shaking his head as I turn to leave. "Whatever. Big fucking loss. Sick of being a goddamn babysitter."

I spin around, the words on the tip of my tongue, but Adam beats me to it.

"And that's your fucking problem, isn't it?" He looms over Brandon, watching as he shrinks away. "You're not a babysitter, you're his goddamn father, and the last thing you've ever done is act like it."

"Who the fuck do you think you are?" Brandon looks at me, a bitter chuckle rising in his throat. "This is who you're dating? Adam fucking Lockwood? You must be mental if you think this guy cares about anything other than getting pussy." He looks to Adam. "She must be holding out on you still, otherwise you'd know it's not worth it."

"Leave," Adam says, so quietly, the single word scatters a shiver down my spine. "Rosie, leave. Now."

"I—"

"What is she, your newest charity case? She's a worthless piece of ass, Lockwood. You must know that, though, right? That's why I've never seen her in any pictures with you. You're embarrassed."

"Leave," Adam repeats, eyes locked on Brandon as he points at me. "Take Connor and get in the truck."

"She poked a hole in the condom just to get a baby out of me," Brandon spits his lie when I try to walk away, knowing full and well that fucking latex ripped right down the middle. "Because she was so desperate for a family. For someone to fucking *want* her. Someone as rich and famous as you? What do you think she's gonna do to trap you?"

The door slams in my face, a force so heavy and brutal it knocks me back a step. But that's not what brings the gasp ripping up my throat.

It's the sound of Adam's fist connecting with flesh and bone.

Once.

Twice.

Three times.

His whispered threats are barely audible, and I'm rooted in place as they float through the door, touching my ears.

"You shut your goddamn mouth and quit acting like those two walking out this door and never looking back won't be the worst thing that'll ever happen to you. Because I promise you, it fucking is. You're only gifted something like this once in a lifetime, and somebody else is going to appreciate and love the beautiful family you were given, the same one you took for granted."

"Who?" Brandon struggles to ask. "You?"

"Yeah. Me."

The door swings open, and I stumble backward before Adam's fingers wrap around my arm, catching me. He takes my crying son into his arms without hesitation, hugging him tight as Connor buries his *Dada*s in Adam's neck. His hand slips down my arm, fingers linking with mine, and my gaze settles on his swollen, bloodied knuckles.

Adam pulls me into the elevator, his heated gaze coming to mine as his chest heaves with each ragged breath. "I think we need some hot fudge sundaes."

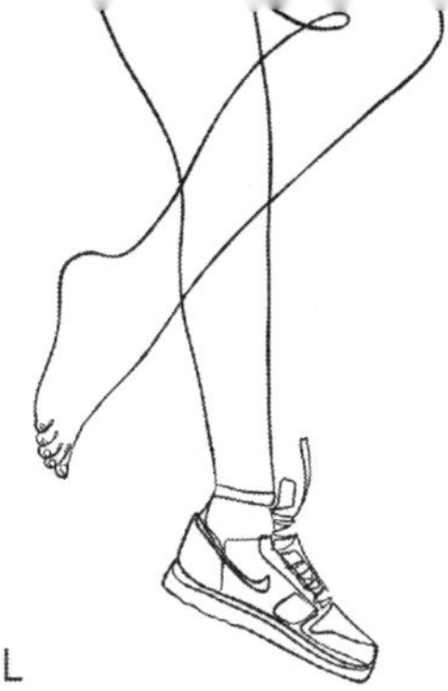

TWENTY-NINE

BATMAN ALWAYS GETS THE GIRL

Rosie

"You're really good at that."

God, he's so cute, sitting here beside me, trying to make conversation. Why else would he be surprised that I, a fourth-year vet student and mom, am good at tending to injuries? It's been a slew of remarks since we got here ten minutes ago, less compliments and more general observations. *You've got a braid in your hair today. I like your purple hair clip. You smell like oranges. Is it just me, or is this grass* really *green?*

My favorite? When he looked at me, swallowed, and whispered, *There are thirty-six trees in this park. I counted.*

I finish cleaning Adam's busted knuckles, smearing ointment over them. "Do you want a Batman Band-Aid to match Connor's?"

Connor taps the bandage on his forehead. "Ba-man." He pats Adam's hand. "Dada, ba-man."

"Do you think he's calling me Batman?" Adam whispers as I stick a bandage over his knuckles.

"I think you very well might be his personal Batman."

His chest puffs with pride, and I swallow my snicker. This man is nothing short of a superhero. I thought it when he stormed out of Brandon's apartment, and it was the only thing on my mind when he walked out of Dairy Queen with my son on his shoulders, bloodied knuckles wrapped around Connor's foot, a tray of sundaes in his other hand. The sight did something feral to me, and I was back to chanting my brain/tits mantra in my head.

"Thank you," I whisper as we watch Connor and Bear in the grass. "For sticking up for me and Connor."

"I'm always going to have your back, Rosie." He lays his hand over mine. "How are you feeling?"

"A little scared, to be honest. I know it's the right decision, removing Brandon from Connor's life for now. He's been halfway out the door since before he was born, and putting Connor's safety at risk is unacceptable. But doing it all on my own now sounds kinda scary."

"You're not alone. You have Archie and Marco. You have me."

I focus on the napkin I tear apart between my fingers. "We're not anyone's responsibility."

"No, you're not. You're our family." Tentatively, he tips my chin up, brushing my bangs back. "I'm sorry my actions made you feel like you and Connor weren't a priority. Of all the things I've regretted in my life, lying to you about who I am takes the cake. The thing is, Rosie, when I lied to you, it was myself I wasn't choosing. My heart has chosen you every step of the way."

"Will you tell me what happened?"

He rests his arms on his knees, his eyes on Connor and Bear.

"It's always been about hockey, you know? It was about hockey when we got Bear because Courtney said she was bored being at home by herself, and it was about hockey when he was three months old and I had to start leaving him with Carter's mom when I wasn't home because Courtney was tired of being responsible for him." He pulls a blade of grass, fiddling with it between his fingers. "It was about hockey when I came home from a trip and found Courtney in bed with another man, and it's been about hockey for every single woman I've been on a date with since."

His gaze comes to mine, quiet, reserved. "Ironic, isn't it? Courtney said she cheated because I wasn't home enough to give her the attention she needed, but she wouldn't leave, either, because hockey supported her lifestyle. Every date has been questions about contracts and salaries, vacation properties, and how many cars sit in my garage. It's *always* been about hockey, Rosie, and it was so damn exhausting not being enough for anyone without it."

He looks down, shrugging. "I got to this point where all I wanted to do was give up. And then I met you, and you had no idea who I was. And you liked me anyway, all the pieces nobody else bothered to look at. I saw a chance, and I ran with it. I'm not proud, but I also won't lie to you: this summer with you, forgetting about all the shit that came with being the famous version of me…it was the best summer I've ever had. It was about me and you, about Connor, about the time we spent together and everything we were building. I know I hurt you, and it's no excuse, but fuck, Rosie, having you choose *me*…it fixed something inside me. For the first time in a long time, I felt worthy."

It's heartbreaking seeing him like this, curled in on himself, so unsure of how incredible he is and everything he has to offer, at the hands of people who never deserved any part of him. I hate that careless people broke such a kindhearted man, wore him down to a place where he felt he needed to hide something so important just so someone would give him a chance.

I cover his hand with mine, stopping his fidgeting. "You did the same for me, you know? You fixed something inside me. Something that had been broken for so long, I thought it couldn't possibly be made whole again. I'm not sure I really saw my worth before you. Not as a mom, a friend, or my potential as a partner. Now I'm certain in it."

Proud blue eyes move between mine. "I did that?"

"You did that. I'm sorry people didn't take the time to see what a wonderful man you are beyond hockey, Adam. But it's their loss." I watch as Connor crawls across our picnic blanket and into Adam's lap, settling against his chest as Bear follows suit, draping his head across both their legs. "And our gain."

"What if you don't like the hockey side of me?"

Thing is, I already know I love it. I've spent the last two weeks watching him. Highlight reels, postgame interviews, preseason games. The one thing I saw with clarity was that he's the same type of person on ice as he is off it. Full of life. Dominating. He celebrates all the victories and lifts his teammates up when they're struggling. Someone who tries to stack everything on his own shoulders, even though his friends don't let him. He's fiercely protective of his team, the same way he is his family.

How do I explain to him that I see him?

"What was the first thing you noticed about me that day on the trail?" I ask him.

Adam grins, electric, like he can see the memory play out right before his eyes. "Your smile. It was so big, so genuine, while my dog sat his hundred-and-forty-pound ass in your lap. And then you laughed, and it was just as beautiful, just as happy and addictive as your smile, and I knew right away your heart would match." The smile in his eyes traces the shape of my mouth, his thumb running along the dimple in my chin. "Those were the first things I noticed about you."

"Do you remember when I said I dye my hair pink because of my mom?"

"You reminded her of the pink peonies you planted. Fresh and captivating." He cocks his head, smiling. "One of my favorite descriptions of you."

My heartbeat trips, buzzing at the confirmation that this man has always heard me, always seen so much more. "That's half the reason. The other half is because I wanted to be noticed. So badly, I wanted someone's attention. I hadn't been able to capture anyone's all those years in foster care. I thought if someone noticed me for my hair, if they were curious enough and spent any amount of time talking to me… maybe they'd notice other things. Maybe, if they'd just give me a chance, they'd find other things to like. And it worked often enough, though not really the way I hoped. It was always the first thing people noticed about me, but not you. You saw so much more, right from the beginning. You made me feel seen for all the right reasons."

I reach across the blanket, lacing my fingers through his. He's so warm, the way he always is, this firm touch that makes every mountain seem small. With his hand in mine, I've never been more confident.

"I've always seen you, Adam. And I've loved everything I've seen. I know you've hidden this part of you for a reason, but I'm certain I'm going to love it too."

He stares down at my sleeping son in his lap, sifting his fingers through his blond waves. "I just want to be perfect for you two."

"I don't need perfect. I need the mess, the chaos, all your fears and your insecurities. I've given you mine, and you've walked me through all of them. Let me walk with you through your chaos."

"What if it's too much? All the time apart, the games, the media. What if it's too hard?"

"That's life, isn't it? Figuring it out when it gets hard? It's how we grow. And I've spent so many years growing by myself. Now I want to grow with somebody else."

Hope sparks in his eyes, and I swear his body comes alive. "With me?"

"With you, Adam."

He grins down at our hands, watching his thumb move along my skin. When he looks up at me, there's a patience there, a reminder that this man has always understood even the deepest parts of me. "I think you need me to take it slow."

"I think so too," I admit, gauging his reaction. But he just smiles.

"I think that might be what I need too. I'm so certain that you belong in my world, but I want to do this right, Rosie. I want to give you all of me, give you the time to get used to all this at whatever speed you need." He lifts my hand to his mouth, sweeping a featherlight kiss across my knuckles. "So take your time, okay? Because when you're ready, I'm not gonna let you go again."

~

I've always been a fan of silence. The good kind, where everything is comfortable. The kind of silence that comes with peace, with laying it all out there, working through your problems together and, finally, finding the path where you can walk together, side by side. It's the kind of silence I'd be happy to stay in, and I do just that as we ride the elevator up to my apartment.

The door opens as soon as we stop in front of it, almost as if someone had been watching through the peephole. Archie stands there, his gaze moving cautiously between us, and Adam sticks his hand out.

"We haven't formally met. I'm Adam."

Marco's face appears over Archie's shoulder. "Oh my God. He's here. For research purposes, Adam, could you lift your shirt up? Rosie says you have an eight-pack, but Archie thinks she's exaggerating. We have a bit of a bet going, and—" he lays his hand over his chest "—I bet on you, *obviously*—so if you—"

Archie silences him with a hand over his face. "Please keep your shirt on. Marco's working on boundaries, but it's nice to formally meet you." He crouches down, scratching Bear's ears. "Hey, big boy. You are every bit as handsome as Rosie promised." His eyes come to mine, searching. When I smile, he smiles too. "Connor, wanna play trains while Mama says goodnight to Adam?"

Connor races through the door with a scream, then skids to a stop. He runs back to us, tossing his arms around Bear's burly neck. "Bye, big dog. Lub you." He collides with Adam's legs next, wrapping his arms around them. "Bye, Dada. Lub you."

Adam scoops him against his chest. "Bye, buddy. Love you too."

The door closes behind Connor, leaving us alone in the hall.

"I missed that," he says quietly. "Dada. I know it doesn't mean..." He shakes his head, tucking his hands in his pockets. "It makes me feel special to him, that's all."

"You are special to him, Adam. You're special to both of us." I study this man before me as he nods, eyes on the ground, the strangest, most endearing mix of confident and bashful, the purest heart underneath it all. "How did you know?"

"Know what?"

"Stardust Lane," I murmur the name of the street I spent my childhood on. The name of the scholarship that conveniently appeared after mine was lost.

Adam flushes, chuckling nervously. "You knew that was me, huh? I, uh, Googled you."

I snort a laugh. "I guess this whole mess would've been avoided if *I'd* Googled *you*."

Adam looks down at his dog, sitting exactly halfway between us, like he refuses to choose just one of us. "I think Bear brought me you, you know. I would've never had you and Connor if he hadn't knocked you on your ass that day in the mountains. And while he was in surgery, I realized that."

He takes a step closer to me, and my heart jumps to my throat. "But I also realized I had your parents to thank. That you wouldn't have wound up in Vancouver if they hadn't brought you here and made you fall in love. That you might not have ever wanted to be a vet if it weren't for your dad, or for the way your parents raised you, gave you this incredible, empathetic heart. I couldn't sit back and watch you put your dream on hold for another year, not after all the work you've put into this. I know you didn't want me to pay for it, Rosie, but giving you this...it's one of the best things I've ever spent my money on. And as for Stardust Lane? I wanted to find a way to honor your parents' role in your life and your future. Because I know they've been with you every step of the way, proud as hell of their daughter."

Sneaky tears sting my eyes, and I sniffle, fanning at my face. "Why do you always have to make me emotional?"

He chuckles softly, brushing a stray tear away. "I love your heart, Rosie. It's what's going to make you such an amazing vet. It's what makes you *you*."

"Thank you for believing in me, Adam."

"Thank you for giving me a second chance. I won't need a third, though. I promise."

The promise feels as good as the warmth of his hand cupping my cheek, and I sink into both of them. "No more secrets, though, okay?"

"Okay." He pulls his hand back. His eye tics, and he flexes his fingers, curling them into fists before he blurts, "I love Fruit Roll-Ups. I know it seems like I mostly only eat healthy food, but I love Fruit Roll-Ups so much, I've got eight boxes in my pantry right now. I've tried to stop, but I can't." He exhales, so long and so loud, a hand on his torso as he deflates. "Wow, I feel so much better."

That that's the worst of his secrets is so damn telling about the type of person he is, and when I laugh, he grins.

His fingers find mine, twining them slowly. "I spent most of the last two weeks in my kitchen, staring at my green cupboards, because I didn't want to forget what color your eyes were." His eyes roam over me, and my heart kicks into high gear at the heavy look there. "I wouldn't have given up, just so you know. And now, I'll do everything you need me to do until you're ready. I'll take it as slow as you need me to. I'll be patient."

"Ready to spend your days waiting on a woman, huh?"

"If that woman is you? Absolutely." He drops a kiss to my cheek, soft lips finding my ear, lingering there with his whispered words. "I'm gonna marry you someday, after all. Batman always gets the girl."

He backs away, a proud smirk on his face, before he heads to the elevator. Playful eyes come to mine before the doors slide closed, and he winks. "Night, trouble."

THIRTY

SHIRTLESS DADDIES DO IT BEST

Adam

"WOULD you just fucking text her? I'm sick of watching you open your messages, stare at them, and then close them again!"

"Geez," I mutter, glowering at Jaxon. "Someone's testy this morning."

"Mittens thought my goddamn wiener was a dangly toy when I got out of bed, and he whacked it with his sharp fucking talons before I could shield myself." He grips his junk with one hand, the other arm flailing wide. "Of course I'm fucking testy!"

"Maybe you should guard your *testes,* and then you wouldn't be so *testy,*" Carter says. He wags his brows, holding his hand up for a high five. "Eh? Get it? Because I said—"

"No, we got it," I assure him.

"Oh." He frowns at his hand. "'Cause no one high-fived me." He chugs his post-rollerblade smoothie, then twists an Oreo apart. Balance, I guess. "How come you're not texting Rosie?"

"It's barely after seven a.m."

"She has a kid and school," Emmett says, as he and Garrett slather mashed avocado on several pieces of toast. "She's definitely awake."

"Dey takin' tings swow," Garrett mumbles around his bite.

Jaxon blinks at him. "What?"

"They're taking things slow," Garrett repeats. "So he can't text her first thing in the morning, 'cause that's not slow."

Carter chuckles, stretching his arms overhead. "Yeah, I know that game. Ollie and I were never good at slow. Her more than me. We were supposed to be taking things slow, then she climbed on top of me in the limo after Cara and Em's engagement party. Had to fight her off."

Olivia walks by with a steaming mug of tea, flicking him in his head. "That's absolutely not how that went." She smiles at me. "I think it's sweet you guys are slowing things down for a minute. It can't hurt. And yes, you can text her. Women love to know they're your first thought in the morning."

"So I should—"

"Yup."

"*Yes.*" I pull out my phone and immediately start typing out a message, not a fuck to give about the way my friends are laughing at me.

Good morning. Did you have a good sleep?

No. Lame. *Backspace.*

Hello, Rosie. Are you well today?

How did it get worse? *Backspace.*

Good morning, beautiful. I thought of you in bed last night.

Oh my God, Adam, what's *wrong* with you? *Back-fucking-space.*

Olivia peeks around my shoulder. "A simple *have a good day* would do wonders, Casanova. Don't overthink it."

ME

Morning, trouble. Hope you have a good day.

TROUBLE

Thanks, Adam. Not off to a great start.

A photo follows, a tearful Connor wrapped around her.

Connor has a stomach bug.

Ah fuck. Poor guy. I zoom in on the picture, Connor's sleepy eyes, his unusually pale skin. It's the exhausted, stressed look in Rosie's eyes that has me hitting the Call button, slipping out Carter's patio door into his backyard.

"Hey," Rosie answers.

"I'm sorry Connor's sick, Rosie. You okay?"

"Yeah, it's just…" She sighs. "Crap timing. I can't send him to daycare, and obviously Brandon isn't an option anymore." She sniffles, tugging at my heartstrings. "Sorry, I'm frustrated and exhausted because we've been up since two, and it's making me emotional. I'm supposed to be in surgery in two hours, but I'm going to have to miss it."

"I'll watch him. I can take Connor today while you're at school."

"I can't ask you to do that."

"You're not. I'm volunteering. I already did my workout with the guys; I've got the rest of the day free."

"It's not going to be an easy day. He's clingy and emotional when he's sick."

"I like clingy and emotional."

"Adam—"

"Let me help you, Rosie. You can count on me. Plus, I've missed the fuck out of him. Lean on me today."

She hesitates, and I imagine her teeth tugging on her lower lip, the little crease between her brows while she overthinks this. "Are you sure?"

"Sure as hell." I head back through the house. "I'll be there in twenty."

Carter throws his arms in the air, following me to the front door. "You promised to do that TikTok with me!"

"I did not."

"Aw, *man*. But all the girlies love to see you dance."

"No, Carter." I open the door, looking at him in his DILF T-shirt. "They love to see your shirtless daddy content."

"*You could be a shirtless daddy too*!" he shouts out the door as I climb into my truck.

Right now, the only person I'm okay with calling me *Dada* is Connor.

And *shit* is the poor kid ever sick, all red-rimmed eyes and snotty nosed from crying, his skin pale and slick with sweat.

"We'll be fine," I promise Rosie forty minutes later when we're out front of her school. *We might not be fine.* "We've got it under control." *We don't have it under control at all.* I grin at Connor. It's way shakier than I'd like, so I try for plan B, which is two thumbs up. "Right, buddy?"

He heaves, and Rosie manages to get the opened bag into position a split second before he vomits.

"Oh, baby." She wipes his face, worried gaze coming to mine. "I don't know, Adam. Maybe I should stay with him."

"Rosie." I grip her shoulders, squeezing gently. "This is scary because you can't control it. But you aren't going to be able to control him being sick if you're home with him either. I know you just want to be with him, make sure he's taken care of, and I promise you, I'm going to take care of him. He's going to be loved to pieces at home with me and Bear. Right, bud?"

Connor wipes the tears from his face, sniffling. "Dada, Bear?"

Rosie smiles softly, pushing his hair off his damp forehead.

"Trust me?" I ask her quietly.

She watches me for a moment, then nods. "I trust you, Adam."

"Fuck yeah, you do."

"Fuck yeah," Connor repeats quietly, and my smile falls.

"Oh shit. No. Oh fuck. Shit." I look to Rosie. "*Rosie*."

Connor smiles slowly, a devilish sight, little brows quirking. "Oh shit. *Oh* shit! *Shit*!"

I grab Rosie's backpack, sling the straps onto her shoulders, then shove the Starbucks I picked up for her into her hands. "I'll call you if I need anything at all, and I promise I won't swear anymore!" I push her —*gently*—toward the entrance of the building. "Have a great day, we love you!" I stop, popping a fist on my hip, brows furrowed as I replay those last three words in my head. "No, I didn't, um…" My eyes come to Rosie's. She's standing there, clutching her breakfast, grinning at me. "*Okaybye*!" I dash to my side, throw myself in, and tear out of the parking lot without another look in her direction. "Shit. That was a close one, huh, bud?"

Connor grins at me in the reflection of the car seat mirror. "Shit."

Ah fuck.

~

TROUBLE

How's it going?

ME

Great!

Are you lying?

Only a little!

laughing emoji I appreciate you, Adam.

She made it two and a half hours before texting. I'm impressed; I just know her fingers have been itching all morning.

And really, we're doing okay. Tough day, but we're getting through it. He hasn't thrown up in nearly two hours, he's managed to keep down some crackers and water, and he's only fallen to pieces, like, three times, all three times I've tried to put him down. Me? I'm whole. I'm *totally* whole.

"I need help."

"I'll be there in five," Carter says.

I know what you're thinking: *You called* Carter *for advice?* It's the last thing I ever thought I'd do, too, but I have to admit, he's got the dad thing down pat.

I'm waiting on my front porch when he rolls up, a weeping Connor in my arms, his small hand tangled in my hair.

"What is that?" I ask as he strolls toward us.

"What, this?" He touches the hat on his head. "It's my DILF hat."

"I can read, Carter. I know what your hat says. And why do you need a DILF hat when you're already wearing your DILF shirt?"

"To really drive home the point." He holds up the contraption in his hand. It looks like some sort of…backpack? "When Ireland is having a rough day, she just wants to be held. I strap her to my chest, and she's happy as hell." He sizes me up. "We'll probably have to adjust this, because you're smaller than me."

I roll my eyes as he covertly makes the waist larger, because he knows as well as I do who the smaller one of us is.

"I'm gonna put you down for a minute, 'kay, buddy?" I lower Connor down to a chair on my porch, and he screams, grabbing fistfuls of my shirt.

"*No*! No down! Up! *Up*!" He scrambles to his feet, tugging at my pants, wailing. "Up, Dada, *up*!"

"Hey," I soothe, crouching down, rubbing his back. "I know you're upset. My friend Carter is going to help me put this on, and then I'm going to pick you right back up, okay?"

"I'll be superfast, little dude. I promise." Carter straps the contraption around my waist. "Told you you could be a shirtless daddy."

"I don't want to be a shirtless daddy. I want to keep my shirt on." I scoop Connor back up, and Carter shows me how to tuck him against my chest before he clips the shoulder straps together. Connor rubs his eyes with his tiny fists, hiccuping, laying his cheek on my collarbone. "What do you think, bud? You like it?"

"Bus," he whispers softly, pointing down the street.

"You wanna go watch some buses?" I look to Carter. "Can we do that when he's sick?"

"Fresh air might be good for him." He pats Connor's back, smiling. "Nice to meet you, little dude. You'll have to come over for a playdate with Ireland soon, 'kay?"

Connor's wide, glassy eyes move between Carter's. "I-lan?"

"Nailed it!" He claps me on the back. "You got this, Daddy."

"Please don't call me Daddy."

He winks at me, climbing into his car. "You can call *me* Daddy."

My God. Poor Olivia.

I hook Bear to his leash, grab some snacks, and the three of us head out. Connor is quiet at first, watching me as I point out trucks and birds, but Bear wrings a snicker from him when he tangles himself up trying to chase a squirrel up a tree.

"Red car," he whispers, pointing to a car at the stoplight.

"Yes! Red car!" I point at a blue one. "What color is that one?"

He grins, and his little feet start kicking. "Red car!"

"Blue car!"

"*Rrred* car!"

"Close enough! Holy smokes, buddy!" I point at the bus coming down the street. "Look!"

"Woooah-ho-hooo! *Bus*! Big bus!" The bus rolls by us, and Connor waves frantically. "Hi, bus! Hi, big bus!" The bus driver waves back, honking her horn, and Connor loses his ever-loving mind. "Beep-beep, bus! Beep-beep!"

We stop by Wildheart and sign Piglet out for a quick walk. She's confused that Rosie's not with us but elated all the same, tossing her butt in the air like she always does, smacking Bear in the face with it on the way down. By the time we get back to the house, everyone is ready for a nap.

Connor eats half his peanut butter and banana sandwich for lunch, then shoves the other half in my mouth, and I hope to God I don't catch a stomach bug four days before our home opener game.

"Ready for a nap?" I ask, carrying him upstairs.

"No," he replies simply.

"I am. I'm sleepy."

He points a finger in my face. "Dada sweepy?"

"Yeah, buddy. Dada's sleepy. You kept me busy today." I step into my spare room and set Connor on his feet so I can push aside the boxes I set in here the other week, tuck the paint cans away in the closet.

When I straighten, Connor is gone.

"Connor?" I rush into the bathroom, panic gripping my heart when I don't find him. "Connor! Where are you, buddy?"

A giggle sounds down the hall, and I follow the sound to my bedroom. Connor is at the foot of my bed, and Bear has his head under his bum, like he's trying to hoist him up.

"Dada, sweep?" Connor points to the bed, then reaches two hands for me. "Conn'a sweep."

Relief slides through me as I exhale. "You scared me. Thought I lost you for a minute." I lift him into my arms. "You gotta lie down in your playpen."

"No," he cries, grasping my shoulders, trying to pull himself up. "No pen, no pen!" He pats his forehead, the fading mark from Saturday, when he got stuck under his playpen at Brandon's. "Ouch."

I sigh, hugging him to my chest. "You're scared. I know, buddy. I'm sorry." I rock him side to side, and he lays his cheek on my shoulder, sticking his thumb in his mouth. "What should we do?"

He points to my bed again, stifling a yawn. "Dada, Bear, Conn'a, sweep."

"You want me to lie with you?"

His answer is a soft, sleepy smile. I set him in the middle of the bed, and Bear climbs up beside him as I grab extra pillows from the closet, building a makeshift guard around the two of them.

I lie down next to them, and my sigh turns into a full five-second yawn. I rub my burning eyes as Connor curls into my side, Bear at his back, and settle into the warmth. "I'll just lie here until you fall asleep, 'kay, buddy?"

He slides his tiny hand into mine, and I smile at him as his eyes drift closed. His blond waves are scattered across his forehead, teensy freckles lining his nose. He's got that dimple in his chin, the same one as Rosie, and *fuck*, I just can't believe how perfect this little boy is, how damn *lucky* I am. That's all I'm thinking about as I hold his small body against mine and my eyes drift closed, thoughts of him and his mom running rampant in my head.

Rosie sounds the same in my dreams. Soft and sweet as she calls my name, her quiet giggle gliding over me. Fuck, she even feels the same in my dreams, gentle hands that glide up my arm, skimming my jaw, cupping my cheek.

"Adam," she whispers my name again, and when her thumb sweeps over my lower lip, my eyes flip open, finding her amused ones watching me.

"Oh fuck, I fell asleep. *Oh fuck, I fell asleep*!" I shoot up, nearly smacking my face off hers. I grip her arms, steadying her, and look at Connor, still passed out beside me. "Did I forget to pick you up? Fuck, Rosie, I'm so sorry. Connor didn't wanna go down in his playpen, he wouldn't let go of me, so we lied down here 'cause he was tired and I was *so* fucking tired, and he just-he just…" I gesture at my side. "He curled up at my side, this tiny little ball, and he was just clinging to me, and he fell asleep, and I was just *staring* at him, I couldn't believe how sweet he was, how perfect, and I-I-I…I guess I fell asleep too."

Rosie smiles, an incredible, earth-shattering sight that makes me want to drop to my knees at her feet. "My teacher let me leave after surgery. I let myself in when you didn't answer, and found you two right where I expected." She sifts her fingers through my messed curls. "Caring for a little human all day is tiring, especially a sick one." She gestures to Bear, panting happily at her feet. "Me and Bear let you sleep while we made dinner."

"You made dinner? Why?"

"To thank you. I was stressed out this morning because I couldn't be in two places at once, and I hate leaving Connor when he's sick. I thought I was going to be staring at my phone all day, asking for updates, but when you drove out of that parking lot with my son, I felt calm. I knew he would be safe with you, Adam."

She takes my face in her hands, pulling me forward so she can drop her lips to my warm cheek. "Every day, you give me something new to love about you. How lucky am I to find someone who gives me so many things to be thankful for?"

"This is pointless."

I watch Rosie, pacing back and forth alongside the truck on the quiet country road we're parked on. She keeps stopping to think, then throws her arms in the air, saying, *This is pointless,* and starting her strut all over again.

"Why is it pointless?"

"Because I don't even have a car, Adam! And I can't afford one, so it's not like I'm gonna be driving, so why even *learn* to drive, you know?" She props her chin on her fist, staring at me but not really seeing me as her head bobs. "Yeah, it's settled. We'll skip it." She marches to the trunk, gestures over her shoulder, and pats the hood twice. "No driving lessons today! C'mon, everyone! Let's go!"

"Does she do this a lot?" I ask, arms crossed as she struggles to open the door I just locked on her.

"The dramatic stomp-off?" Archie watches her tug at the handle. "Uh-huh."

"Believe it or not," Marco adds, "she has a bigger flair for the dramatics than me."

"Okay," Archie chuckles, rolling his eyes. "I wouldn't go that far. Nobody is as dramatic as you."

"Oh, I've got a friend." I unlock the door for fun, and Rosie's eyes light before she reaches for the handle again. I lock it again. "Sometimes I'm not sure when to push her to try new things and when to let things go. I don't want to force her to do something she really isn't ready for, you know?"

Archie hums, nodding. "Yeah, I know that struggle. The thing is, though, you'll know when she's *really* not ready for something. She'll completely shut down, and your heart will tell you to stop, to hug her instead. You seem to read her well. She's never felt rushed with you. She does need to be talked into quite a few things, though."

"Has anyone ever stopped to think if really *pounding* things into her might work better than *talking* her into something?" Marco wags his brows at me. "Give it a shot, that's all I'm saying."

Connor curls over Marco's head from where he sits on his shoulders, covering his mouth with his hand. It might be for the best. "Mama, tuck?"

"I don't think so, buddy," Rosie says, walking back over to us, hands on her hips as she huffs. "Not today." She thumbs over her shoulder at the truck. "Adam, something's going on with the locks."

"Really?"

"Yeah, they keep unlocking and then locking again."

"You don't say."

"It's weird, 'cause it's almost like when I reach for the handle…" She trails off, frowning at me. It's super frowny, with a side of *I'm gonna castrate you*. "You motherf—"

"Ah-ah. Watch your language around innocent ears."

"Motherforking shirthead." Her eyes narrow, and she pops a hip, pinning her arms across her chest. My gaze falls to her cleavage—*oops*—and she yanks her button-up together, stealing my view. "Don't even think about it."

"Here we go," Archie mumbles.

"And you said she doesn't have a flair for the dramatics?" Marco whispers.

"No, I said her flair for the dramatics wasn't as big as *yours*."

"I'm right here!"

"We certainly know, Rosie."

I laugh, then turn it into a cough when Rosie glares at me. "C'mon, trouble. Let's talk in the truck."

"I know what you're doing," she says as I load her into the driver's seat, the one we've adjusted for her three times. "You're going to give me those eyes—"

"What eyes?" I give her the eyes.

"Those eyes!" She lets me buckle her in. "And then you're gonna ask me what's holding me back from driving in that gentle voice that makes me want to tell you everything, and I'm going to fold!"

I climb into the passenger seat, holding my palm face up between us. Her gaze flicks between it and me three whole times before she finally slides her hand against mine, tangles our fingers together. Fuck, it's a feeling I've missed too much, one that makes everything feel so warm and bright and full.

"What's holding you back from driving?"

She groans, and I chuckle.

"I'm serious. You were excited about our driving lesson today, so I think you *want* to do it."

She saws her lip with her teeth. "I do."

"But you're scared."

She hangs her head. "I'm tired of being scared of simple things."

"It's okay to be scared, Rosie. Just because driving is simple for some people doesn't mean it's simple for everyone. Is it something I can help you work through?"

"I don't think so."

"Wanna give it a shot anyway? You never know."

"I'm afraid of dying," she blurts, then waits, gauging my reaction. When I don't give her one, she goes on. "It's not really death I'm afraid of, but what comes after unexpected death. The thought of never seeing Connor again, not getting to watch him grow up, it wrecks me. And who will take care of him? He has no grandparents. His own father doesn't even—" She stops herself, waving the words off, her nose wrinkling. "I know my parents didn't die in a car accident. But people die in car accidents every single day, and fires are way less likely, and it still happened.

"After they died, I started having a lot of anxiety around the possibility of unexpected death, but once I had Connor, it grew tenfold. Suddenly, I had this little human who depended on me for everything, and all I could think about was what my parents' final moments were like, knowing they weren't going to see me again, that I'd be alone. People always say, 'I can only imagine,' and I always think it's silly, because, like, no, you really can't. But I've been imagining it for so long now, and it's…it's debilitating. There's no other way to describe it. It's like my body quits on me. Fear takes hold of my brain, and I can't do anything but sit there and imagine the worst-case scenario. I get so lost in my thoughts, Adam. Sometimes it feels like they eat me alive."

She sniffles, a swallow so audible it hurts my own throat. When a tear slides down her cheek, I catch it on my thumb. "I know it's only my imagination, but that almost makes it harder, you know? Because if it hurts this much to just imagine it...God, the pain my parents must have experienced in those moments, knowing that was it."

She swipes a hand through the air, dismissing her own pain, forcing a laugh. "So, yeah, that's why I'm scared to drive, even though I'd love to learn. Silly, huh?"

"No."

Her gaze slides to me. "What?"

"Not silly at all. Your fears are real and valid. I can feel your pain, Rosie, and it hurts. I have a thought though. You're feeling what you're feeling, this fear of having to say good-bye to Connor, leave him behind, and that's scary enough on its own...but what if you're holding onto your parents' grief too? What if you're taking on the pain they felt leaving you behind? Their pain that they felt like they were abandoning you?"

Her gaze drops, searching through my words as her chest heaves.

I squeeze her hands in mine. "Can you try something? Close your eyes for me." I smile, brushing her hair off her face as her eyes flutter closed. "I know it's hard, but picture your parents sitting here with you." A tear escapes, tracking its way down her cheek, followed by another, and she clamps down on her lower lip, chin trembling. "Tell them you see their pain."

She shakes her head, tears falling faster.

"Rosie," I whisper, taking her face in my hands. "Please. Tell them."

"I see your pain," she cries softly.

"Good girl," I murmur, swiping at her tears. "Now tell them you can't hold it for them."

She gasps out the words before she falls across the center console, collapsing against my chest. I smooth my palm down her back, holding her close as she cries into my neck.

"What did they say?"

She looks up at me, green eyes dancing in their own rain, crystal clear as it washes away just a little bit of her fears. "'We're not asking you to.'"

"I believe that. They don't want you to hold onto that. Not the pain, not the fears. They want you to remember the love." I wipe away the tears that cling to her lashes as she gives me a heartbreaking smile. "I bet they gave the best kind of love, Rosie. Just like you."

Rosie tosses her arms around my neck, hugging me tight. "Thank you, Adam. Thank you so much."

We spend the next few minutes checking the mirrors, practicing tapping the break and giving the truck just a *little bit* of gas, and when Rosie's ready, she takes a deep breath, gripping the steering wheel.

"Put it into drive," I tell her, watching as she does it. "Good. Now signal left to let people know you're going to be merging into traffic." I glance over my shoulder at the imaginary traffic, Archie and Marco hitting us with two thumbs as they watch from the side of the road, Connor clapping Marco's head. "And when you're ready, take your foot off the brake."

She squeezes her eyes shut and breathes deeply before demanding, "Tell me something good. Tell me about your charity, The Family Project. Why do you do it?"

I smile. "I do it for the kids who are searching for somewhere to belong, searching for safety, for love."

Rosie cracks her lids. Slowly, she releases the brake, and the truck inches forward.

"I do it for the kids who want to give up, because I want to show them what happens when you hold on a little bit longer."

She steps on the gas, just a bit, and the truck moves a little faster.

"I do it so they know there's always someone out there that loves them, that's rooting for them. That it might take some time, but they're going to find their people. I do it for the Rosies."

She beams, bright and so beautiful, and when she comes to a stop at the corner and throws the truck in park, Archie and Marco run toward us with Connor, shouting and cheering. The pride shining in her eyes is unparalleled, a sight I'll remember forever.

"I did it, Adam. I drove down my first street!"

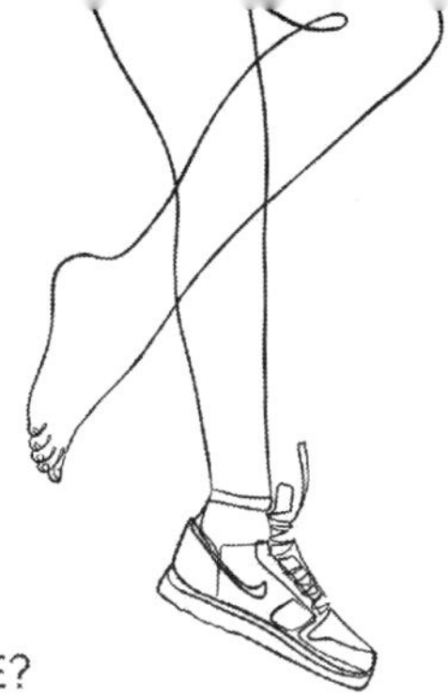

THIRTY-ONE

WHO'S THE REAL MR. INCREDIBLE?

Rosie

"ARE YOU NERVOUS?"

"Me? Nervous? Pfft. Have you *ever* known me to be nervous?"

Adam side-eyes me as we stroll down the sidewalk together, towing Connor along in a brand-new, top-of-the-line, fancy-as-hell wagon he just happened to have in his garage. In the wagon with Connor? Bear. Yes, this wagon is so fancy, it supports this one-hundred-and-forty-pound dog with ease. "Always."

"This would've been an acceptable time to lie, in case you were wondering." I look at Connor, bouncing along in his new favorite ride, clapping his hands and chanting *I-lan,* because Adam told him we were going to go meet his new friend Ireland. Then, I look down at myself, the outfit I changed four times, the jeans Archie swore hugged my ass just right, the oversized sweater I put on after giving up on everything else. "I just want your friends to like me."

"They already love you, Rosie."

"You can't possibly know that, Adam. You're only trying to make me feel better."

"I absolutely do know it. We've been talking about you for three months now. They've been dying to meet the girl who has me smiling at my phone all the time."

Heat touches my cheeks, and I hide my smile. It's been two weeks since Adam and I decided to take things slow, and the man has picked right back up with being a permanent fixture in my life, except it's even better than before, even without the physical stuff.

He finished his preseason games last week, and between all the training and practices and surgeries, we've seen each other every day. Sometimes I wake up to him confirming my Starbucks order, and thirty minutes later he's at my door, helping me get Connor ready for daycare while I savor my coffee. Sometimes he's leaning against his truck when I leave school for the day, a ridiculously handsome smile waiting for me, a goofy grin on Bear's happy face. And sometimes—my favorite of times—he shows up in the evenings with teas and muffins, helps me with Connor's bath, reads him his favorite books and puts him to bed, and then curls up on the couch with Archie, Marco, and me to watch *Jeopardy!*.

He's squeezed himself into every crevice of my life, and everything feels so full I'm nearly ready to burst.

"At least I've already met some of them," I say as we start up a long, winding driveway.

"You mean at the clinic after Bear's surgery when they were all there?"

"No, when they came to Wildheart."

"Hmmm?"

"Garrett and Jaxon? When they came to see me at Wildheart?"

Adam arches a brow. "Pardon me?"

"Yeah, they wore the…the fake mustaches. Did you not know?"

Adam trips over his own feet, somehow kicking a shoe off in the process. "*Fake mustaches*?"

"Back up." I come to a stop, and Adam's still trying to put his shoe back on. "If you didn't know they came to spy on me, where did you think Jaxon got Mittens from?"

He throws his arms overhead. "He told me he heard little meows coming from the dumpster in the parking garage of his condo, and he climbed in and saved Mittens! He sent me a picture of Mittens next to an old sock and a crumpled bag of Doritos and said, 'Look what I found in the garbage!'"

"Wow. That's a really elaborate lie. I'm impressed."

Adam blinks at me, and then, again: "*Fake mustaches*?"

"Garrett's fell off and he ran away after pretending he got a phone call."

Adam scrubs his hands down his face in slow motion. With a sigh, he gestures at the sprawling house before us. "Well, let's go meet the rest of them."

He tucks the wagon onto the front porch and takes Connor's hand in his. When he opens the front door, a lively golden retriever welcomes us by dropping to his back, rolling around on the floor. Bear joins in, and Connor squeals with laughter, dropping to the floor so he can get in on the fun, and I'm busy freaking out over whether I should shake hands, hug, or offer a simple, friendly wave to everyone I meet tonight. I turn to Adam, about to blurt the question, but Garrett Andersen strolls down the staircase, grinning when he sees me.

"Rosie! Welcome to Carter's Palace of Love." He wraps me in a hug as soon as I start shoving my hand out in the space between us. "We're huggers here."

"Well, there was that one time you took a dildo to the face in way of greeting." Jaxon Riley appears behind him, winding an arm around me. "Oh, hey, I can't wait to show you all my pictures of Mitts." His eyes dart to Adam over my shoulder. "Uh, this stray cat, I, uh…found in the dumpster." He winks at me, then frowns at Adam. "What are you grumpy about?"

"*Fake mustaches*?"

Jaxon grimaces. "Oh."

Garrett grits his teeth. "You heard about that, huh?" Suddenly, his eyes widen, and he cups a hand around his ear. "What's that, Jennie? *Coming*!" He takes off down the hallway at the speed of light, leaving Jaxon staring at us.

"So, I guess it's just us. Well, I, uh…" He's nearly as fast as Garrett when he makes a run for it, except he slips at the end of the hall, crashing into the wall. "*Owww*."

"You deserved that," a gorgeous woman says, tossing her long blonde locks over her shoulder. When Jaxon reaches a hand up for her, she nudges it away with her foot. "So cute you think I'm helping you. Cara Brodie gets on her knees for no man." She winks at me, poking the inside of her cheek with her tongue. "Except my husband."

Connor climbs to his feet, pointing at Cara as she hugs me. "Pwetty."

"Oh, bless your soul, sweet boy." She scoops him into her arms. "You have such amazing taste, don't you?"

He runs his hand down her hair, fascinated. "Wooow."

"I did the same thing the night I met her," Emmett Brodie says, nudging my side as he appears at it. He smiles at me before wrapping me in possibly the sweetest, best bear hug I've ever received. "I'm the lucky husband."

Adam's hand slips over my hip, pulling me close, his lips at my ear. "You okay?"

"Oh shit." I clap a hand to my forehead. "I haven't said a word yet, have I? I'm Rosie." I hold my hand out, then pull it back. "Oh right. We already hugged." I wipe my palms on my jeans. "I'm nervous."

"You know what's great for nerves?" Cara asks, transferring Connor to her hip and looping her arm through mine. "Frozen margaritas." She leans close as she leads me down the hallway, the sound of...*singing?* gracing our ears. "You're gonna need at least five."

The sight in the living room is interesting, to say the least. Every bit of anxiety I've been holding onto at the thought of meeting Adam's family melts away as I watch Carter Beckett and his sister, Jennie, putting on a whole-ass show while they sing the karaoke version of "I Just Can't Wait To Be King."

"Wow."

"Yeah," Cara whispers. "You wouldn't believe how often this happens."

Garrett slips up beside us, sipping a can of cherry soda water. "Jennie's ass looks unreal in those jeans, huh?"

"Shut *up*, Garrett!" Carter screams, spinning to us. He stops when he sees me, tossing his microphone over his shoulder. "*Ollie*! Rosie's here!"

Footsteps patter, and a moment later a petite brunette slides into the room, holding her teensy tiny twin. "Oh my God." Are those...tears? "*Finally*."

Jennie dances over, a brilliant, dimple-popping smile on display when she bounces to a stop in front of me, her long chestnut hair tied back with a ribbon. "Hi. I'm the funnier, better looking, and more mature Beckett sibling. Can I give you a hug?"

"I'd love one," I say, swallowing down the emotion crawling up my throat as she gives me a squeeze, so warm, like being wrapped in sunshine. Everyone is so damn *nice*, and I had no less than three anxiety attacks today over the prospect of meeting them.

Carter saunters over, and I swear to God, I'm doing everything in my power to not look at his crotch. It's been shoved in my face seventeen thousand times at the bus stop, I almost feel like we're friends.

"Carter Beckett, NHL captain, Calvin Klein underwear model, GQ's Sexiest Man, and DILF extraordinaire." His chest puffs with pride, and he shrugs. The humble brag rolling off him in waves is astonishing. "Some people also call me Mr. Incredible."

"Oh for God's sake, Carter." Olivia rolls her eyes and sighs. "I'm sorry. He's...well, he's like this all the time. I'm Olivia, and I'm stuck with him for the rest of my life." She passes her daughter off to Carter and squeezes me against her. "It's so good to meet you, Rosie."

Carter shoves his adorable daughter in my face. *"And I'm Ireland, my daddy's biggest fan and his pride and joy."*

"Hi, Ireland," I snicker, shaking her tiny hand. "You are just perfect, aren't you?"

"I-lan!" Connor squeals, tugging at Carter's pants until he plops her down on the floor in front of him. "Woooah-ho-ho," Connor wonders aloud, crouching to look at her, hands on his knees. He waves at her, then pats her fluffy, dark curls. "Hi, I-lan. Hi, baby." He smiles, eyes alight, and points at his chest. "Conn'a hug I-lan?"

"*Olivia*!" Carter shrieks, waving aimlessly. "Get the camera! It's happening!" He tears the video recorder from her hand when she returns with it, and sinks to his belly on the floor, eyes glittering as he records my son hugging this sweet little girl. *"Her first friend."*

He stands, running his hand down his chest as he sighs, and it's then I notice his shirt. It's a picture of him and Ireland, *Daddy* scrawled overtop of it. My gaze goes to Ireland as Connor releases the giggling girl, and I fold my lips into my mouth when I spy her onesie.

Because the picture on it matches Carter's, and scrawled on top of hers? *Daddy's Princess.*

Adam shoves a frozen margarita into my hand. "You've met everyone, seen the Beckett siblings do karaoke, and been subjected to Carter's shirts, which, by the way, he has a whole closet full of. You deserve this. Cara put extra tequila in it."

The extra tequila is wonderful, and so is the strawberry daiquiri Cara makes me next, but if I'm being honest, it's the people that make this night so effortless. To exist here with them, to be at ease with being myself. Watching them welcome Connor into their family, dancing around the living room with him, interacting with him the exact same way they do Ireland. There's no difference here, not with them. Family is family, plain and simple.

And they're treating us exactly like we're theirs.

"He keeps whacking me in the balls every morning. Like, as soon as I step out of bed."

"Maybe sleep with underwear on?" I suggest to Jaxon, who is apparently being abused by Mittens every day.

He flashes me a look of disgust. "No way. I like to free-ball it. My boys love to hang free."

"Okay, well, you could slip a pair on before you get out of bed."

"And take 'em off two seconds later when I go for my morning pee? Nah."

"I might be out of solutions for you then, Jaxon. Wrap your junk, or Mittens will continue to use it for batting practice."

He huffs, sinking back against the couch, but smiles at his screen saver. It's his and Mittens' faces, smooshed together side by side. "He's lucky he's so damn cute."

My gaze coasts the room, finding the same people it's been looking for all afternoon. Adam hasn't been more than three steps away from Connor, and the only time he's taken his eyes off him is to put them on me. Right now, he's sitting on the floor with Connor, Ireland, Garrett, Carter, and Emmett, the kids squealing with laughter as the boys entertain them.

"There's something so innately attractive about men with kids, isn't there?" Olivia asks me on an exhale, her eyes on her husband.

I watch as they aggressively sing the words to "The Wheels on the Bus," actions and all, until Connor and Ireland's shrill giggles fill every inch of this house, and when Adam scoops my son against his chest, hugging him tight and dropping a kiss to his cheek, fireworks explode in my stomach. "*So* attractive."

Olivia turns to look at me, grinning.

"What?"

"He deserves this, you know. You. He deserves you. Someone who sees him for everything he is and doesn't ask for anything more. Someone who loves his gentle heart and matches it with her own. Someone who looks at him the way you look at him."

Adam's eyes come to mine then, a softness that melts me from the inside out, love that shines like the flecks of golden sunshine in his cerulean blue gaze, and when he smiles, my whole world rights itself.

"The same way he looks at you."

I wave a flappy hand through the air to distract from the feelings that are staring me down the nose, demanding me to toss this *slow* notion out the damn window and pick up right where we left off: me, with three little words on the tip of my tongue, meant just for him. "You don't know this yet, but I'm an exceptionally emotional person."

"Oh my God, me too! Even more so after I had Ireland."

"Postpartum hormones are wild. As if I didn't cry over enough things before having a baby. Like those commercials with the puppies, you know the ones I'm talking about? The SPCA ones with—"

"—Sarah McLachlan! Yes! I had to bite my tongue to stop from crying over one the night I met Carter!"

"Is that song necessary? It makes it so much worse."

"Kills me every damn time." Olivia takes my hand, pulling me up with her. "C'mon. Let's make another drink."

She putters around in the kitchen, tossing ingredients into a blender while I examine the tray of snacks on the island. It's BYFS Night—bring your favorite snack—something Adam explained to me as he loaded five boxes of Fruit Roll-Ups into the wagon. You'd think we were at a kid's birthday party by looking at this elaborate setup, mostly made up of several kinds of Oreos, Dunkaroos, Pop-Tarts, and random assortments of fruit snacks and cereals, but apparently, this is just how they like to celebrate the start of their season, and tomorrow is their home opener.

"If you choose an Oreo over a Fruit Roll-Up, Carter will hold that over Adam's head forever," Olivia tells me.

I laugh, peeling open a Fruit Roll-Up, and Adam grins at me from across the room. He winks, mouthing, *Good choice, trouble,* and my insides heat.

"What's this?" I ask, finding a scrapbook among all the food. The front cover shows a picture of Carter in his hockey equipment, holding a smiling Ireland, the words *Daddy Goes to Hockey* scrawled over the cover.

"Carter's been working on that all summer. It's a book for Ireland for when the boys are out of town for hockey. Go ahead and look at it."

I flip through the pages, obviously created with so much love, pictures upon pictures of their family, of Carter on the ice, Olivia and

Ireland in the stands. It goes through their daily routines, morning snuggles and a messy breakfast, walks in the park, doggy kisses, and bubble baths before bed. And then it shows Carter boarding a plane, explains how he's going somewhere far to play hockey but that he'll be thinking of home, and soon, he'll be with his girls again.

On the last page is a photo of Carter with Ireland tucked in the crook of his arm, Olivia held tight against his side. The love reflected in his gaze is staggering, but it's the words beneath the photo that tug at every bit of my heart.

Daddy goes to hockey, but his love stays here.

Carter sidles up next to me, peering over my shoulder, wearing a small smile. "I don't know what I'll do being away from her so much."

"You're really gonna miss her, huh?"

"Uh, yeah. I'm *kinda* obsessed with her."

My gaze flicks to his *Daddy* T-shirt. "You don't say."

"What if she forgets about me, you know? What if she forgets what I look like?"

I look to Ireland, sitting in Garrett's lap, her dad's face on her outfit. "I truly don't think that's possible."

"You're right, Rosie. I should have more shirts made for us. One for every day of the week. Great idea, thanks."

"What? I didn't say—"

"Ollie! Rosie told me to make more shirts for me and Ireland!"

"Carter, you've given that poor girl down the street a full-time job making shirts for you, and she's only fourteen. You need to give her a break."

"Okay." He winks at me. "I'll definitely do that." *Wink, wink.*

"You're a menace," I whisper to him.

"You have no idea how high I can soar, Rosie."

The girls pull me outside, gathering around a fire pit with all the fixings for s'mores while we sip at our drinks.

"I can't believe we're trusting those five alone with the kids," Jennie says as she rotates a stick of marshmallows over the coals.

"Are you kidding me? I found a giant roll of Bubble Wrap in the garage two days ago. When I asked Carter what it was for, he said it was for Ireland when she starts walking. I thought he was joking, but when I laughed, he said, 'Our daughter's safety is not a joke, Olivia.'"

Cara gasps. "He called you by your full name?"

She nods somberly. "Connor and Ireland are possibly *too* safe with those boys in there."

Jennie hands me a gooey s'more, and something thick settles in my throat as I stare down at it.

"You okay?" she asks me softly.

"Oh, yeah. Sorry. This is just really nice. It reminds me of my parents. We used to camp several times a summer, and s'mores were my dad's specialty. I haven't had one in a long time."

Jennie smiles, squeezing my forearm. "My dad passed when I was sixteen. It's weird, isn't it? Doing things now that we used to do then? It's nostalgic in all the right ways, and it makes me feel like he's right here beside me. But it's still hard too. Because sometimes the feeling that he's right next to me is so strong, I look over to say something to him, and…"

"He's not there."

"Yeah. It's almost like I forget how to breathe for a second."

"I know that feeling." I squeeze her hand. "Thank you for sharing that with me."

The four of us settle into easy conversation, and once the boys pop outside to let us know they're going to lay the kids down, Olivia and Cara decide to add *just a little more* tequila to the next pitcher.

"I'm not a violent person—"

Olivia interrupts Cara's monologue with a snort.

"—but if I were given five minutes alone in a room with her—"

I snicker, and Cara points at me.

"You're laughing, but I'm serious. If Courtney was standing on the edge of a cliff, my elbow would absolutely accidentally nudge her ribs *just right*, and we'd never speak her name again."

"Was she really that bad?" I ask. All three of them level me with a look, and I cringe. "I thought maybe the media was embellishing."

"There was no embellishing." Olivia sighs. "She was exactly as awful as they painted her to be, but truthfully, we're just glad she's out of Adam's life. He's always deserved so much more. She never felt like a part of this family."

I look down at my lap at that f-word, the longing that pulls at me when I hear it. But then Cara speaks, coaxing my eyes back up.

"Not like you, Rosie."

"What do you mean?"

"We're a family. We want you and Connor to be part of this family."

Something happens then. The smallest shift but with the biggest impact. Like the final piece was already here, just slightly ajar, and someone tapped it, so gently I'd probably not notice it. Except finally, it slides right into place, this perfect fit that was just waiting to be filled, and suddenly everything is exactly the way it was meant to be.

My heart pounds a relentless beat, and I struggle against the tight grip on my throat, the emotion holding it hostage. Never in my life have I had this, this immediate love, this acceptance without question, without hesitation. It's scary and beautiful and…incredible. It's everything I've ever wanted.

"Thank you," I whisper, and when my voice breaks, these four amazing women throw themselves at me, wrapping me in a hug that fills me all the way up.

And all four of us freeze at Carter's shrill shriek from inside.

"*Ollie*! Come quick! It's an emergency!"

We race inside, sagging with relief when we see the boys standing in the kitchen, piles of Fruit Roll-Up wrappers in front of them, half-eaten snacks clenched in their hands.

Carter holds his rainbow snack up, eyes alight with excitement. "It does tongue tattoos!"

"Jennie!" Garrett shouts excitedly, running over to her. He sticks his tongue out. "Wook at mine!"

Carter rushes over to Olivia, the whole Fruit Roll-Up hanging off his tongue. "Wook! Are you weady? Watch!" He pulls it off, proudly displaying the blue Yoda left behind. "It's woda!"

My gaze slides to Adam, and pink blotches his sharp cheekbones as he smiles shyly at me. Slowly, he sticks his tongue out, showing me the unicorn tattooed there, and it's so fucked up that the only thought in my head right now is how badly I want to take him into a bathroom and mount him.

"I want to ask you if you had fun, but you won't stop smiling and you keep dancing down the street, so I think I know the answer."

I spin around in the cool night air, then dance my way back to Adam, gripping his bicep as he tows a sleeping Connor and Bear along in the wagon. "I had the best time."

"They didn't scare you off?"

"Not even a bit."

"Are you sure it's not the alcohol talking?"

I giggle, inhaling the fresh, crisp air. "Don't you love that smell? God, it makes me so happy, the smell of fresh air. Did you have a clothesline growing up? We did. In the spring and summer, my mom always put my bedsheets outside to dry, and climbing into them at night was the best feeling in the world."

Adam pulls out his phone, tapping away at the screen.

"What are you doing?"

"Making a note to install a clothesline."

"Why?"

"So you'll be this happy every night when you crawl into our bed. Happy wife, happy life, and all that."

I giggle-snort, and I'm so tipsy, I don't even care. "You really think you're gonna marry me one day?"

"Sure as shit do."

"What if I say no?"

"You won't."

"Cocky," I murmur as he opens his garage, picks Connor up out of the wagon, ushers Bear and me inside.

"No. Just sure about you and me."

Beyond all the alcohol running rampant in my system, it's a funny, wonderful thing to hear those words, to know someone is so certain about your place in their future, and the entire walk up the stairs, with him looking at me, I can't stop the heat from rising to my cheeks.

"You'll have to sleep here tonight," he says, showing me to one of his spare rooms. "I took the bed out of Connor's room."

"Connor's room?"

"Yeah." He opens the door to the room where the playpen is always set up, and my heartbeat trips when I step inside.

The once taupe walls are now a misty gray, with white clouds and black birds painted above, snow-capped blue mountains and midnight evergreens below. A dresser sits on one wall, a gorgeous bookshelf filled beside it, and on the other side of the room is a wood-framed bed, shaped like a house, with gauzy white material draped over its roof.

Hundreds of glow-in-the-dark stars dance on the ceiling above us, just like my heart dances in my chest.

"It's a floor bed," Adam says. "The mattress sits on the floor, so Connor won't hurt himself. He was scared of the playpen, so I thought he might like this."

"When did you do this?"

"This week. Do you like it?"

My eyes burn, because believe it or not, alcohol makes me a hundred times more emotional, but goddammit, I'm determined not to cry tonight. "You did this for him?"

"For you both, Rosie. I want you to feel like you have a place when you're here. Like you're…"

"Home."

"Yeah. Like you're home."

Connor stirs in his arms, rubbing his sleepy eyes with his fists. "Dada," he whispers, smiling up at Adam. He looks around the room, eyes widening, wriggling until Adam sets him on his feet. "Whoooa-ho-ho! Birds!"

Adam follows him to the wall. "And trees and mountains too."

"Ma-tins?"

"You got it, bud."

He spies the bed, then makes a run for it, climbing onto the mattress. "Bed! Big bed! Whoooa, big bed!"

"I think he likes it," Adam murmurs, looking back at me. He smiles softly when he sees the tears running silently down my cheeks. "Connor, go give Mama a hug goodnight, and then I'll read you a book in bed, okay?"

He wraps his tiny body around mine, pressing a sloppy kiss to my mouth. "Lub you, Mama," he says, and then dashes to the bookshelf to pick a book while I escape to my temporary room, swatting the tears away.

I listen as Adam reads Connor story after story, as he tells him goodnight and that he loves him, as the bedroom door clicks shut behind him, and his shadow pauses in the light streaming beneath my own door. And when I climb into bed, I listen to the sound of my own breathing, shallow and staggered, the frantic thump of my heart that wants nothing more than to be in the arms of the man I love.

When the house is quiet and dark, and I've given up on sleep, I tiptoe down the stairs, into the kitchen. Moonlight streams through the patio door, and the kettle boils as I root through Adam's pantry for my favorite tea.

I curse Adam's height as I struggle to reach the mugs, the cool air kissing my bare thighs as I press up on my toes, nearly nabbing it.

The cool air disappears, replaced with a sizzling heat that scorches through the thin T-shirt I wear as a body presses up against my back, warm breath kissing my ear. A strong hand grips my hip, pinning me between his body and the counter as he reaches above me, pulls a mug down.

"Imagine your height was above average," Adam's husky voice whispers. "Then you'd only need me for things so much more fun than tea in the middle of the night."

Oh Jesus Christ.

He releases me, midnight eyes casting me an even darker stare as he fills the mug, dips my tea bag inside, and all I can focus on is that he's wearing only a pair of boxer briefs, those flawless abs and those drool-worthy thighs on display beneath the fractured moonlight. "What are you doing up, Rosie?"

"I-I-I…I couldn't sleep."

"Why?"

"I was thinking about…about…why does Carter call himself Mr. Incredible?" *There ya go, Rosie. Much better than telling him you were thinking about sneaking into his room and asking him to fuck the sober back into you.*

"'Cause he thinks he's got the biggest dick."

See, this is where the alcohol gets me in trouble, because instead of nodding, I respond.

"Okay, well, I've seen—*everyone* has seen—the outline of his dick, and is it big? I mean, sure. Yes, of course. But I've had yours in my body—more places than one—and I *know* yours is bigger, so, who's the *real* Mr. Incredible?"

Adam laughs, a deep, rumbly sound that settles low in my stomach, tingling between my legs. "I like you a little drunk."

"You like me all the time."

"This is true." Slowly, he stalks toward me, and my eyes dip down his body, settling without my permission on the bulge in his underwear as he cages me in against the counter. "I like you in your vet scrubs. I like you in the purple leggings you wore that second hike, the ones that clung to your ass." He grips my waist, hoisting me onto the counter, spreading my thighs and stepping between them, hands on my knees, searing my skin. "And I like you in this, my T-shirt and nothing else, with your legs on display and your hips begging me to slip my hand underneath and grab hold."

My brain stops working and my heartbeat drops to my clit, throbbing with need as Adam drags his rough palms over my thighs, taking the hem of his T-shirt as he goes. Dark eyes collide with mine as he pushes that material higher, until it pools around my hips, and my breath gets lost in my throat with no way out. He drops his gaze between my legs as the air kisses the warm, wet spot between my legs, and a heavy breath escapes him.

"I knew it," he tsks, dragging his thumbs over the apex of my thighs, *so close*, and yet not close enough as he smears my arousal, wrings a whimper right from me as I lean back on my hands. "I could smell you the second you walked in here."

"What do I smell like?" I whisper as he brings one thumb to his mouth, sucking me off him, a sight that makes me absolutely feral.

He dips his head, lips finding the hollow spot in my collarbone before trailing up my neck, to my ear. "You smell like trouble, and you taste like it too. Now get back to bed, before I get myself into a whole fucking pile of it."

He steps away, watching as I scramble to my feet.

Heady words stop me at the edge of the kitchen.

"And Rosie? If I find you in my kitchen in the middle of the night again, I'm fucking you right there on that counter."

THIRTY-TWO

IT'S OCTOBER THIRD

Adam

"I'M NOT DOING your TikTok, Carter."

You wouldn't believe how often those words are spoken in this dressing room. You'd think most captains would be hyperfocused before the home opener game, maybe even instilling the fear of God into his teammates, but not Carter. No, our captain is so excited for his daughter to see him play tonight, he's been blaring "My Girl" on repeat, shaking his ass at his cubby, and filming a shitload of content for his TikTok page. He's been trying to get someone to agree to some *Mean Girls*–inspired video for the last ten minutes, but no one's biting.

"Why not?" Carter asks Garrett, frowning.

"'Cause I'm trying to get ready for our game."

"After the game, then?"

"No."

"But it's *Mean Girls* day! This one's so easy! All you have to do is look at the camera and say the date." He crosses his arms over his chest. "I won't give you permission to marry my sister unless you do the video."

"The only permission I need to marry your sister, is your sister's. Plus, you already told me you'd be happy to call me your brother-in-law since I make Jennie so happy."

"*Ssshhh*!" Carter's gaze darts around the room. "I told you that in confidence!"

"You know he got Ireland a jersey that says *Daddy* on the back of it, right?" Jaxon whispers to me. "And Olivia a leather jacket with his number and Mrs. Beckett on it. The man's obsessed."

"You know, Jaxon, Carter was a lot like you before he met Olivia. Maybe worse."

"What's your point?"

I shrug. "Can't wait to see how obsessed you turn out to be for the right woman."

Jaxon stares at me, disgust curling his lips. "Gross. If I ever voluntarily get a woman a jacket that says *Mrs. Riley* on it, just kill me. I've obviously been possessed."

I snort a laugh, doing up the straps on my goalie pads.

"Hey, Adam?" Carter calls.

"What's up?"

"What day is it?"

"It's October third."

A collective groan fills the dressing room, while Carter whoops his fist through the air, his phone pointed at me. "Nailed it!"

I look to Jaxon. "Did I just do the *Mean Girls* thing?"

"You just became Cady Heron, dude."

"Fuck."

Truthfully, I wish I was as relaxed as Carter right now. I'm worked up, and I have been most of the day. With our morning skate and a team meeting earlier, I haven't had the chance to talk to Rosie since I dropped her and Connor off after breakfast. I swallowed the question on my tongue right along with my coffee, and fifteen damn times I typed it out, asking her if she wanted to come to the game tonight, letting her know I'd bought two tickets for them. Instead, I chickened out every damn time, scared she'd say no, that it was too much, too fast. I wouldn't blame her, but I gotta tell you: I'm done with slow.

I'm so damn *starved* for her, the hollow ache inside me begs me to have my fill.

It took everything in me not to sink my fingers inside her soaked pussy last night, not to yank her to the edge of my kitchen counter and remind us both how well she takes my cock. I want to feel her mouth move against mine, feel the way her hips lift and roll, chasing my every movement. I want her fingers in my hair and my name on her lips, and I want it forever.

But more than that, I want her to know how I feel about her.

How utterly devoted I am to her.

How mind-blowingly in love with her I am.

My body has had hers, and fuck, it wants her again and again. But I can do slow. I can stave off the desire, so long as I get her heart.

My phone dings in my cubby, and I pull it out, grinning at the name peeking up at me.

TROUBLE

Have the best time tonight, Adam. You'll be incredible! So big and flexible.

Her message gives me the courage I need to face the two empty seats behind the bench, and as we make our way to the players tunnel, I'm focusing on getting in the zone.

Fog fills the tunnel from the machine up ahead, and the lights in the arena go out, ear-splitting cheers filling the rink as I shake out my nerves, my goalie mask propped on the top of my head. Green and blue spotlights shine on the rink, and Carter goes from goofball to captain in a split second.

"Here we go, boys! Who owns this fucking rink?"

"Vipers!"

"Who works harder than us?"

"No one!"

"And who's taking the win home tonight?"

"We are!"

"Damn right we are, boys! Get your asses out there and show 'em who we are!"

The music starts, and the announcer comes over the speakers, introducing each player as they step onto the ice, until only me and Carter are left.

Carter grabs my head, bringing my forehead to his. "You fucking got this, bud." He claps a hand to my ass as his name is called and skates onto the ice as the arena explodes.

"And finally, ladies and gentlemen, on your feet for our pride and joy, number forty, Vancouver Vipers' Adaaammm Lockwoooood!"

I step onto the ice, raising my stick in the air as my chanted name drowns out the music. It's a surreal feeling, looking into this sea of blue and green, people here just to cheer you on. It's what I love about hockey, the way everyone shows up for each other, stands by your side, believes in you. It's addictive, the support, all the love, but still, as the lights come back on for our warm-up, I keep my eyes off the bench.

Far too many games, I looked right there, the spot just behind it, and I saw my teammates' wives, girlfriends, families. And in the middle of all that love was an empty seat Courtney didn't bother to fill, an excuse she didn't bother to give me. Like a fool, I kept buying that same damn ticket every game.

It's my fault, I know. I didn't even give Rosie the chance to come tonight. And yet I can't look, because I can't bear the thought of associating the painful memories of that empty seat with someone as kind-hearted as Rosie. She deserves more than that.

I cradle my mask in the top of my net, then move to a safe corner of the ice where no one is firing shots at me. Before I can stretch like I planned, the music changes, and I sigh when the "Cha-Cha Slide" comes on.

"Oh shit!" Carter shouts, coming to a stop beside me. "Know what time it is, Woody?"

I sigh again, because I know exactly what time it is. "It's cha-cha time." I point at Jaxon, who's snickering at us as Garrett and Emmett join. "I'm not doing it unless Riley gets in on it this year!"

"Absolutely not. This is your tradition. I wasn't here when it was formed."

"You're part of this family," Carter tells him lowly, catching his jersey and dragging him over. "And this family participates in cha-cha time." He gestures at the crowd, all their phones aimed at us, because since Carter forced this tradition on us during my very first game in an attempt to settle my nerves and stop me from vomiting, they've come to expect it whenever the song comes on. "The people want to see us cha-cha real smooth, Riley, and what the people want, the people get."

"I don't want him standing next to me," Garrett grumbles. "If he messes up, he'll take me down with him. And Jennie likes watching me shake my ass."

Carter yanks Jaxon between us, and he rolls his eyes, standing still as a statue as the rest of us follow the song's instructions, sliding to the left.

"Slide to the goddamn left," I growl at him, shoving him left with my shoulder. "Now right."

"*Criss-cross!*"

I jump in my skates, crossing my feet, and narrow my eyes at Jaxon.

"*Fine*," he snarls, crossing his feet once, then twice. He claps along with the song and at least three-quarters of this crowd, and when it's time to cha-cha real smooth, he does it perfectly, rolling his hips as he spins in a circle, almost like he's been...practicing.

He points one threatening finger in my face the second I open my mouth. "I know what you're about to say, and don't. Just. Fucking. *Don't*."

I grin, focusing on the dance steps as Jaxon nails every single one of them beside me, and when it's finally done, I clap him on the back. "Feels like you're a lot more like Carter than you'd like to believe."

"If you want me to defend your net tonight, fuck off."

Chuckling, I spread my legs wide and sink to the splits on top of the ice, reveling in the pull in my groin and my hamstrings as I get as low as I can.

Garrett sinks down beside me on his knees, spreading his legs. "I'll never understand how you can do the splits."

"Goalie things."

"Jennie says it looks like I'm humping the ice when I do this," he says, bouncing into his stretch. He looks up, wagging his brows, and I know without a doubt he's wagging them at Jennie.

I lean forward, getting my chest as close to the ice as I can. "You think Rosie's gonna watch the game on TV?"

"Nah."

I narrow my eyes. "Thanks, you fucking turtle dick. You could've appeased me and said yes, you know."

Garrett laughs, climbing to his feet with me. "She's not gonna watch on TV." He scoops a puck up with the blade of his stick, flipping it in the air before catching it. Then he points behind the bench. "She's gonna watch from right there."

My gaze snaps to the seats I swore would be empty, and my heart swells when I see it, my two favorite people nestled between people I call family.

I couldn't wipe the grin off my face if I tried, and as I skate toward Rosie and Connor, it only grows. Connor's wearing a tiny version of my jersey, big headphones covering his ears, and when Rosie points to me, a smile ignites his face.

He slaps at the glass as I stop there. "Dada! Hi, Dada!"

I chuckle, placing my gloved hand against the glass, on the other side of his. "Hi, buddy. I'm so happy you're here."

"Hockey!" He points at my stick. "Dada…pay…hockey?"

Rosie's so fucking breathtaking, sitting there in my jersey, I can barely hear Cara losing her shit over the fact that Connor's calling me *Dada*.

"Spin for me." The words are a quiet plea, and my heart slams against my chest when Rosie grins, lifting Connor in her arms and spinning in a slow circle, showing me my last name on her back.

Fucking perfection.

And then she smiles at me, and it's brilliant and detonating and everything I love. "I'm more of a pink girl, but I think I'm rocking the blue and green."

I take my blocker off, pressing my hand against the glass. "Thank you for coming."

Rosie's eyes soften, and she touches her hand to the other side of the glass. "Where else would we be if we weren't here supporting our favorite person?"

The words fill me with pride, and twenty-five minutes later, when the anthems are done and I'm taking my place in net, I'm determined to make them proud too.

I'm not truthfully sure how much of the first period Rosie actually watches. Every time I look at her, she's looking at me. I grin, she flushes, and I grin bigger. By the second period, her eyes are following the play, and when the puck goes from Emmett to Garrett, then up to Carter, and he stuffs it in the net just over Philly's goalie's shoulder, she even jumps out of her seat with the rest of the girls. I'm sure Connor has no idea what's happening, but everyone else is screaming, so he does too.

Carter spins to a stop at center ice, pointing his stick at his wife and daughter. "For my princesses!"

Olivia's stopped burying her face in her hands when he does this, but she sure does still get red as fuck in the face. It all melts away, though, when Carter skates over, touching his hands and forehead to the glass, right against Ireland's on the other side.

I'm playing phenomenally, stopping every shot, but my defensemen are doing their best to keep the puck from making it this far. When there's only a minute and a half left in the game, we've got the only goal, and I'm on track for a shutout, Philly pulls their goalie and throws an extra player on the ice, determined to tie this game.

The play turns over at the blue line during a bad line change, and Jaxon hops off the bench, racing like hell to catch up to the centreman who's barreling down the ice at me. I crouch down, following the puck as I inch out of my net, and when he winds up to shoot, Jaxon pokes the puck free. I nab it with my stick and shoot it off the boards, and just as Garrett grabs it, he's sandwiched against the boards.

The puck springs free, and Philly's right-winger speeds toward me. He pulls his stick back before sending it forward, and I dive to the right, deflecting it with my blocker. Another player snatches up the puck, firing it off before I can climb back to my feet, and I leap to the other side and catch it in my glove at the exact moment Jaxon hammers him into the boards.

The whistle blows, I pull off my mask, grab my water bottle from my net, and squirt a generous helping into my mouth before I drench my sweat-soaked face with it. Rosie's watching me with her mouth open wide, so I wink, watching her face flush scarlet as I pull my mask back down.

With ten seconds left in the game, the puck drops in the circle to my left. When it breaks free right in front of me, clear shot to Philly's empty net, I decide I wanna hammer home my shutout tonight. And maybe, I wanna show off a little.

I cradle the puck back and forth on the blade of my stick as I skate out of my crease, and Carter shoves the only defensemen in my way out of it. Then I pull my stick back and let the puck fly toward the empty net.

The buzzer blares a split second before the clock runs dry, and I find Rosie and Connor, on their feet and cheering.

Right before my teammates tackle me to the ice, I tap my heart twice, then point at the two people who own it.

~

I've never in my life ripped my equipment off as fast as I have tonight, jumped in the shower and scrubbed every inch of me clean before throwing on my suit, not bothering with the wet curls that cling to my skin, leaving water droplets cascading down my face.

My tie makes it back on, but the knot hangs loose and too far to the left, and I'm too buzzed to give a shit.

"Adam, are you—"

"Leaving. Bye."

Laughter explodes behind me as I stride across the dressing room, followed by catcalls and hollers, something about me going to Pound Town and a promise to call me tomorrow so I don't get lost there and forget to get on the plane for Washington in thirty-six hours.

As if I'm gonna spend the next thirty-six hours buried inside Rosie.

Who am I kidding? I'm spending the next thirty-six hours buried inside Rosie.

Cameras and recorders are shoved in my face, when I step out of the dressing room. I push by them, waving over my shoulder, 'cause I'm sure as fuck not hanging around to chat.

Rosie looks up from down the hall, Connor's hand in hers, surrounded by my friends. A beautiful red flush paints her delicate features as I stride toward her, cameras on my heels, waiting to see what I'm going to do.

"Dada!" Connor shouts when he sees me. He dashes over to me on unsteady legs, and I catch him in one arm, hoisting him up to me.

"Hey, little trouble."

He points at Rosie. "Big tubble."

"Adam," she whispers when I stop in front of her. "I—"

I swallow her words, all of them. Whatever the fuck they were, I swallow them with my mouth on hers. Fuck, she's sweet. Like hot chocolate and cinnamon, my first taste of autumn. My mouth remembers all of her, and I devour her savagely, like I've been dreaming of nothing but this all my life.

And I'm gonna take her home and worship her.

I pull back, just an inch, Rosie's trembling fingers on my face, mine buried in her hair.

"Hey, trouble," I murmur, and she grins.

"Hey, you."

THIRTY-THREE

I THINK I'VE TRANSCENDED

Adam

I WASN'T EXPECTING THIS.

Fuck, I was *not* expecting this.

I race around my room, tossing dirty clothes in the hamper, scrubbing at the scuff on the bathroom mirror, washing away the drop of toothpaste that fell to my sink right before I left for my game. I hear Rosie say a final goodnight to Connor down the hall, the click of his bedroom door, and I throw myself on top of my bed, tugging at the covers to make them look neat and tidy.

Fucking figures, the one time I'm running late and don't have time to clean before leaving my house, Rosie comes home with me.

The bedroom door opens when I'm mid–karate chop on a pillow, and when my gaze collides with Rosie's amused one, I stop. Gently, I finish fluffing the pillows, then prop myself up on my side, my cheek on my fist, elbow on the mattress.

"Hey."

"What are you doing?" she asks, and every step she takes closer to me sends my heart into overdrive.

"I was just…I was…cleaning," I finish on a sigh, taking a moment to starfish on the bed before hopping off it, joining her at my nightstand. "I didn't have time to clean before I left for hockey, and I didn't want you to think I'm messy."

"Adam, I'm *so* messy."

"Yeah, but your mess is organized chaos. Mine is just..." I circle a hand around the mess on my nightstand, searching for the word I'm looking for, but all hope is lost when I see what I've left on the table. "Oh shit."

Rosie's gaze follows mine, and when I try to step in front of the table, she elbows me out of the way. "What's this?"

"What's what?"

She holds up the book from my nightstand. "This."

I swallow down the nerves that want to eat me alive. Just when I was feeling so confident thirty minutes ago too. "I've been doing a little light reading."

"Light reading?" She turns the book over in her hands. "*Co-Parent, Not Stepparent: How to throw out the labels and support your partner so you can be the best co-parent you can be.*"

"Okay, well, you didn't have to read the title out loud." *Geez.*

"How long have you had this?"

I rub the back of my neck. "A little while. I wanted to be perfect for you and Connor if you ever gave me a second chance."

She stares at me for a long moment, her throat bobbing. Then, she points at the colored sticky tabs and highlighter on my nightstand. "And those?"

I clear my throat into my first. "I, uh...I've been tabbing the important parts. So I can go back to them later."

"You've been annotating a book about how to be a good partner and stepfather?"

"Yeah, I guess. Well, I mean, the book says one of the most important things is to scrap the stepparent label. You're supposed to love the kid as if they're your own. But that's easy, because, hello, I already do love Connor like he's my own."

Tears well in Rosie's eyes, and they make me frantic. I want to stop them, so I open the drawer and pull out my pen and notebook.

"I have this little notebook. Sometimes I get questions when I'm reading, and I write them down so I can ask you later." Shame creeps up my neck, uncertainty pulling the notebook into my chest, hiding it. "That's weird. I'm saying it out loud and hearing how weird that sounds. You might not have wanted to get back together. And if you did—"

"I do."

I swallow again. "You might not want me to be that involved. You two already have a family. You might not need me, not the same way I need you."

Rosie looks at me, this crease in her eyebrow like she's trying to process the words. She closes her eyes, gives her head this tiny shake, then steps forward, taking the notebook from my hands, lacing her fingers through mine. "We need you."

"You do?"

"Of course. But more than we need you, Adam, we *want* you."

My chest pulls taut, threatening to break open from the strain of my thrashing heart. "Really? Because I've never wanted anything the way I want you and Connor, Rosie. Not a single thing, not even hockey. I want to be your partner, and I want to do all the things together. The adventurous things and the quiet, lazy things. I want to do all the happy things, and all the sad, hard things, too, as long as I'm doing them with you. I want to keep loving Connor exactly the way I do, like he's mine, *ours*, because he fucking feels like it. That kid owns my heart, and there isn't a day that goes by that I don't hope one day *Dada* won't just be a name he calls me because it's a phase, but because I'm the man he can count on to be there for him all the damn time."

"Oh my God," Rosie murmurs. "I love you."

My racing heart skids to a stop. "You what?"

Her eyes widen, and she lets go of my hands. She steps back, and I step forward. "I-I-I…I have to shower!" She spins, racing into the bathroom, slamming the door behind her.

I stare at it for three seconds before I go after her.

Rosie's pacing the room, eyes closed, fingers pressed to her temples. I'm certain she doesn't even hear me enter, not above the roar of the shower and her incessant chanting.

"Think with your brain, not with your tits. Think with your brain, not with your tits. Think with your brain, not with your tits." She throws her arms in the air. "I mean, seriously, Rosie, it's not that damn hard!"

"Why?"

Rosie squeals, spinning to me. "Adam. You heard that."

"Why?" I repeat, backing her against the counter.

Her eyes bounce between mine as she fumbles for something to grab onto, something that isn't me. "Why what?"

"Why do you love me?"

"Oh, *that*?" She waves a flappy hand through the air, gigging anxiously. "Psssh. That was so silly. I love you? Yeah, I say that all the time. Bus driver? 'Hey, thanks for the ride, dude. I love you!' Cashier at the grocery store? 'Thanks for bagging my groceries! Love ya!'" Another shrill giggle, and *fuck me*, I love her hot mess express side.

"Why?" My hand goes to her jeans, and her stomach jumps as I skim the waistband. "Gimme the reasons," I murmur as I pop the button, slowly dragging the denim over her full hips, down her luscious thighs. Christ, she's already wet for me, and we haven't even begun. The dark spot in the center of those dusty rose panties begs me to taste her, to dive my tongue inside her and lick her clean.

And I plan to.

Tonight, I'm taking her back.

Tonight, I'm fucking *done* with slow.

My palms skate up her sides, over her hips and the dip in her waist, dragging her shirt up, guiding her arms above her head as she lets me slip it right off. I reach around her back, flicking the clip on her bra, a guttural groan rumbling in my chest as her perfect, full tits spring free.

Our gazes crash as I scrape my thumbs over her tight nipples, her breath sputtering past her lips.

"Reasons, Rosie. Now."

"I don't feel alone anymore," she blurts, then licks her lip, watching as my fingers creep down her belly. Her eyes flip back to mine. "And it's not about having someone. It's about having *you*. It's about knowing you're my partner, not just a warm body at my side. It's the good morning texts and showing up at the bus stop because it's raining. It's running me a bath and forcing me to unwind while you spend time with Connor. It's double-checking my Starbucks order in case the cooler weather has made me want a warm drink instead of an iced one. It's my favorite tea in your cupboards and a fresh T-shirt waiting for me to slip on for bed. It's loving my son like he's your own, accepting both of us without hesitation." Her lashes flutter, voice lowering. "It's naming the scholarship after the house I grew up in, peonies beneath my parents' tree marking and peonies in your front yard, just so I know my parents are with me. Because I feel you everywhere, Adam, even when you're not here."

Something shutters in her eyes, a hesitancy that tames my hunger for a moment.

I rest my forehead against hers. "What are you afraid of, Rosie?"

"Losing you," she whispers. "Connor's is the only love I've ever got to keep."

"You can keep mine. It belongs to you."

"Promise?"

"Swear it." I hoist her onto the counter, pull off her panties, and spread her legs wide, running two fingers along her drenched slit as she sighs. "Love how fucking wet you get for me," I murmur as I dip my fingers, smearing her wetness over her clit. I sink my hand in her hair and pull her gaze to mine. "Now tell me again, and not the way you tell the bus driver."

She takes my face in her hands, and the love swimming in those sage eyes nearly knocks me to my knees. "I love you, Adam. For everything you are."

I close my eyes as her words seep into my skin, a warmth that spreads through me.

I know this feeling. I felt it when Mom and Dad asked me if I wanted to go home with them, if I wanted to be a part of their family. When they promised to love me forever, and proved it time and time again when I messed up. I didn't have to do anything to earn their love. They just chose me, day in and day out.

And that's what Rosie's doing now. She's choosing me.

All of me.

"Thank you," I choke out.

"For what?"

"Loving me."

"Adam." She sweeps her thumb beneath my eye, coaxing my heavy gaze back to hers. "Loving you came so naturally, like all these years I'd been saving it just for you, and when you walked into my life, all I wanted to do was hand you my heart and tell you to take it. So kiss me, please, because I'm ready to give it all to you."

I've waited too long for this, a partner to walk through life with, a love I haven't had to earn but simply deserved. Because, fuck, we all deserve to be loved without condition.

My mouth takes hers, a gentle nip of my teeth, begging for entry. A soft sweep of my tongue, tasting her slowly. Her back bows as I press two fingers inside her, an unhurried plunge while I savor the beauty below me, every one of her noises, the ones she makes just for me.

"I fell for you that first day, you know. Out there taking care of a dog you didn't have an obligation to. Scared to give up control, to put your trust in anyone else, but willing to do it anyway and for a man you'd just met. Those eyes that smiled first, before anything else. And Jesus, Rosie, I just kept falling. That's all I did, every damn day, fall further, harder, until there was nowhere left for me to go."

I pull my fingers out as she watches me, sink them back in slowly, deeper, over and over, my thumb circling her clit as vines of red heat climb her golden skin and her steady breath turns ragged.

"The second I saw you with that little boy, I knew my heart was yours. You're everything I was looking for. Kind and gentle, with so much love to give. Someone who works for the life they want and won't give up without a fight. You've been through so much, Rosie. So damn much, and not once have you turned around and walked away. Even when I thought you might. When I prayed you wouldn't. When I was fucking terrified you'd give up on me. You stayed, Rosie. And you chose me. Because of you, I know what it's like to be seen, to have every single piece of me loved. I know because you do it every damn day, and fuck, Rosie, it feels so damn good."

I cup her cheek, running my thumb along her lower lip as she struggles to breathe while I bring her closer to the edge.

"That's why I love you, Rosie. I love you, and I've been loving you for a long time."

"Adam," she cries out, clenching around my fingers, grinding her pelvis into the palm of my hand while she comes.

"Love it when you come for me too," I murmur. Dragging her off the counter, I push her toward the steam spilling over the shower door while the water beats down against it. I tug my shirt over my head and yank my pants down, my cock standing proud as I jerk my chin toward the shower. "Now get in there."

When she hesitates, I smile, tsking.

"You feel like being a bad girl tonight, huh? That's okay. I don't feel like being all that nice."

Bending, I grab her behind the knees, hoisting her over my shoulder.

"*Adam,*" she squeals, slapping my ass, making me laugh. "Put me down!"

I whip open the glass door, dropping her to her feet beneath the hot stream, pushing her against the tiled walls. My fingers tangle in her wet waves, melted honey and rose, and I press my mouth against her neck and my cock to her lower back.

"Ready to listen now?"

"No," she breathes.

"Why not?"

"Because I want you to fuck me so hard, I forget all the time we lost where you could've been inside me."

I bury my smile in her neck. "You want me to imprint the shape of my cock in your tight, wet pussy, trouble?"

She grins at me over her freckled shoulder, saucy and charming. "Do whatever you want, Adam. Just as long as I come while you're doing it."

I spin her around, slapping her hands to the tile on either side of her head, gripping her wrists. Trailing the tip of my nose down hers, I find her mouth, stealing a kiss. "Say it again," I whisper.

"I love you."

"Fuck, that sounds good." Jerking her knees up, I wrap her legs around my hips while she slings her arms around my neck. "I don't have any condoms, Rosie. I wasn't expecting this, not tonight."

She brushes her lips against mine. "I'm on the pill. I trust you."

I nod, pressing a kiss to that tiny dimple in her chin. "I love you."

"I know."

"And I'm gonna fuck you like I love you. But first…first I'm gonna fuck you like I should've last night on my kitchen counter."

She opens her mouth, but whatever was about to come out dies a scream when I drop her right on my cock, burying myself to the hilt.

"Jesus *fuck*," I groan, squeezing her ass as she pants, raking her nails down my back.

"You're too big," she cries, and I laugh.

"Oh no, my poor ego."

"Shut up."

"Say it again, baby. It'll only make this better."

Fire sparks in her eyes. "Shut. Up."

"'Atta girl." With one hand braced on the wall and the other on her ass, I drive myself forward. Over and over, harder, faster, deeper, until Rosie's nothing but sharp gasps and whimpered pleas, biting nails and a pair of incredible, bouncing tits I just wanna fucking devour.

I lower my mouth, sucking one rosy nipple between my teeth, and Rosie moans, arching herself into me.

"God. Adam. Oh my…*oooh*. Yes. F-u-u-uuuck."

"You're not speaking English, baby."

"I'm gonna come," she cries, heels digging into my ass, nails raking down my arms. Her eyes roll up, wet hair splayed down her neck, and I grab a fistful of it, dragging her gaze back down to me.

"Look at me while you do it."

"Fuck, Adam." Her pussy squeezes my cock, and I keep thrusting, dragging every last drop from her. When she goes limp in my arms, I pull her off me, toss her over my shoulder, turn off the shower, and stalk across the bedroom.

Dropping her on the bed, I slap her ass and fist my cock. "Hands and knees, Rosie."

She climbs there, slowly, and I grab her hips, yanking her to the edge of the bed, right where I need her. I trail the tip of my finger along her spine, then follow it with my lips.

"You gonna come again for me?"

"Yes, Adam."

"How many times?"

"As many as you want me to."

"And where are you gonna come?"

She sighs, fisting the sheets as I dip my tongue inside her, feasting on her sweet pussy. "On your cock, please."

"Beautiful fucking girl." I run my tongue along her slit, licking up as much of her as I can before I lean over her, fusing my mouth with hers so she can see how good she tastes.

I move back behind her, my gaze trailing every delicious inch of her, the dip in her waist that leads to those wide hips, soft enough for me to dig my fingers into. The curve in her spine that glides down to those dimples on her lower back, right above that immaculate, round ass.

"Fucking *love* these," I rumble, dragging my palms down her back to the dimples, digging my thumbs into her soft flesh. I press my cock against her ass and groan, holding her in place while I fight for control. "You're a fucking goddess, Rosie. This body makes me fucking…*feral*."

"Feral?" she whispers, and when she lifts her ass, rubbing it against my cock, any semblance of control vanishes.

I yank her thighs to me, the soles of her feet hitting the ground, her chest flat on the bed, and I kick her legs wide before I plunge deep inside her. Her back bows off the bed, and she rips the sheets free from the mattress.

"Christ." I grip her hip, holding her there while I pound into her, my other hand gliding up her back, fisting in her wet locks. "Goddammit, I love you. Love fucking you. But mostly…" I bend over her, driving deeper as I angle her face to mine. "Mostly, I love loving you."

She cries out my name as our mouths collide, my hips slapping against her ass as

I climb higher and higher. She clenches around my cock, squeezing me deeper, and when I reach around and rub her clit, she explodes, dropping her face to the sheets to bury her scream.

I pull out of her, flipping her over and tossing her up to the pillows, crawling toward her.

"One more, baby," I plead, spreading her legs, tossing one over my shoulder as I drop my chest to hers. "One more."

She shakes her head, eyes squeezed shut as I sink back inside her, racing toward the finish line. She's already coming, squeezing me again, or maybe she's just never stopped. I don't fucking know, but when her hips lift and she yanks my mouth down to hers, when she tells me she loves me one more time, I let go. I empty everything I have inside her, burying her name in the crook of her neck as we cling to each other, sweaty, breathless, and so fucking happy.

When I roll off her two minutes later, it's only because I'm scared of crushing her.

"That was incredible. Otherworldly. I think I transcended." Her head flops, bleary eyes staring at me. "Seriously, Adam, I don't know how you'll ever beat that."

"I'll spend the rest of my life trying."

"Life goals?"

"My only goal in this life is making sure you spend the rest of your days knowing, without a doubt, how loved you and Connor are." I tuck her into my side, sweeping my thumb over her dimpled chin. "If I succeed, I'll have lived this life right."

She smiles, sifting her fingers through my curls before pressing a kiss to my lips. "You are perfect for us, Adam."

It's not hard to realize how lucky I've gotten in finding Rosie. If it weren't for her, I'm not sure I ever would've found the courage to truly be myself, to give all of me to someone else. I might have lived forever being too scared of rejection, too scared of fake loves and misguided intentions. Now, I get to live my life knowing that somebody has seen it all and still chose me.

That's Rosie.

She unravels every string, and when she puts me back together again, I'm better than I was before. Whole, finally, and I don't think I've ever been whole.

THIRTY-FOUR

NO-NUT NOVEMBER

Adam

"Pink's my favorite color."

"It's one of mine too." It wasn't up until four months ago, but now when I think of pink, I think of everything bright, fresh, and captivating. I think of Rosie.

But instead of telling this preteen girl that, of all the options I was presented with earlier today, I chose to dress as the pink crayon because the color reminds me of the fistful of hair I had in my hands this morning while Rosie took my cock as far down her throat as she could, I settle on: "It makes me happy."

The girl in front of me grins as I take my picture from her hands and uncap my marker. "My name is Skylar."

"Skylar," I repeat, scrawling her name across the picture before signing mine, finishing it with my jersey number. "Here you go, Skylar." I dump a whack of candy in her plastic pumpkin bucket. "Happy Halloween."

"Thanks!" She looks at Jaxon, her eyes moving over him with disgust. "I *don't* like green. It reminds me of puke."

Jaxon crosses his arms over his green chest, and his green crayon-tip hat dips down over one of his eyebrows. "Yeah, well, I *don't* like butterfly queens. They *also* remind me of puke."

Skylar gasps, the tip of her tall butterfly wings smacking Jaxon in the chin when she twists and storms off.

"You fucking suck with kids," I say under my breath as she tosses him one last glare over her shoulder, one he gives right back.

"I'm good with Ireland. She only cries, like, thirty percent of the time I hold her, and she laughs when I blow raspberries on her cheeks. And Connor's, like, my best bud."

This is true, but it might have something to do with the fluffy cat Jaxon brings over to my house every time he comes to visit. Jaxon loves showing off all the tricks he's taught Mittens, and Connor loves to roll around on the floor with Mittens and Bear. He even calls his stuffed kitty Mittens now.

"Why the fuck am I dressed as a crayon?" Jaxon grumbles, tearing open a mini–Kit Kat. "And why the fuck am I the only one who wasn't allowed to wear pants with my costume?"

I don't know, but he looks hilarious in his green crayon dress, with his green crayon-tip hat, and his hairy legs on display. "It's Carter's world; we're all just living in it."

"Did he tell you what costumes he's making us wear tonight for trick-or-treating?"

"He says it's a surprise."

"He said the same to me, but then he did this high-pitched giggle, promised it would be 'spicy,' and then ran away."

I'm as scared as everyone else. We haven't been home and game-less on Halloween in five years. That Halloween, Carter made us all dress up as Britney Spears. I still have nightmares of seeing him in his schoolgirl outfit. I was stuck in red latex, Garrett was dressed as a sexy stewardess, and Emmett was nearly naked with a stuffed snake around his neck.

We did win Best Group Costume that night, though, so…

"I heard about the Britney Spears debacle," Jaxon whispers. Frightened eyes bounce between mine. "This year will be better, though, right? Because he has a kid now? So he won't be so…Carter-y?"

Before I can answer, a microphone screeches. Jaxon and I look up, watching as Carter—dressed as a purple crayon and with his purple-crayon daughter strapped to his chest—steps onto the stage set up out front of the arena doors.

"No," Jaxon murmurs as a screen is lowered behind Carter.

"He's really doing it," I whisper.

"I thought he was joking," Garrett mutters, appearing on my left.

"Someone call Olivia," Emmett mumbles, on Jaxon's right. "He needs to be stopped."

"Is everyone ready for Vipers Karaoke?" Carter calls out at the gathering crowd. To our horror, they explode with cheer. "Twenty dollars gets you the song of your choice here on stage with a Viper of your choosing—"

"What?" Jaxon gasps.

"I did *not* agree to this," Garrett growls.

"No," Emmett groans.

"Holy fuck," I sigh.

"—and all the proceeds go back into the community to help fund sport programs for underprivileged youth. So multiple songs are not only welcome but *encouraged.*"

Jaxon pins his arms across his chest. "Nobody better pick me, 'cause I ain't singing."

A small girl wearing a sparkly pink dress with a fluffy skirt and a tiara approaches Jaxon, tugging on his crayon gown with her gloved hands, batting her blue eyes. "Excuse me, Mr. Riley. My name is Mia and I'm a princess. I wanna sing a princess song with you."

His eyes melt as he stares down at her, and when she clasps her hands and hangs her head in defeat, Jaxon groans. He takes her hand in his, pulling her toward the stage where Carter waits with a shit-eating grin.

"C'mon, Princess Mia. Let's go pick a princess song."

~

Thirteen. That's the number of songs Jaxon's sung this afternoon.

"He acts like he's not one of us," Carter muses, watching as Jaxon wraps up his performance of *Moana*'s "How Far I'll Go" with a girl dressed exactly like her. "But I knew he was a Puck Slut from the moment he stepped off that plane from Nashville a year ago."

Garrett pulls off his blue crayon hat and messes up his hair. "When can we go home? I wanna take Jennie to Pound Town once quick in Carter's bathroom before we go trick-or-treating."

Carter shoves his elbow into Garrett's rib cage.

"*Ow*! I'm telling!"

"I'll chop off your dick if you touch my sister in my bathroom."

"You can't." Garrett gets this slow, smug smirk on his face, and his chest shakes, already laughing at his own joke. "It's her favorite ride, right along with my face."

Jaxon thumbs at Garrett as he rejoins us. "Where did the balls on this one come from in the last year?"

"Jennie," Emmett and I answer simultaneously.

"I just know she's gonna look sexy in her costume. I won't be able to resist her."

I arch a brow, peeking down at the photo on my phone, the one Rosie sent me a half hour ago, after they left here and went back to Carter and Olivia's. It's a group shot of the girls and Connor, and they're all dressed as different animals and bugs.

I flash my phone at Garrett. "She's a butterfly."

"A *sexy* butterfly."

"You'd fuck Jennie in a garbage bag."

"As if you wouldn't fuck Rosie in one."

Touché. "Jennie's not gonna wanna touch you in your crayon dress."

He gestures aggressively at himself, runs his hands over his crayon-covered hips. "Jennie's gonna be *all over* this."

"Uh-huh."

He jabs his finger into my chest. "Just you wait. She's gonna be begging for me. I'll have to tell her no."

Jaxon snorts a laugh. "As if you'd ever be able to tell her no."

Carter's chest puffs. "Yeah, I gotta tell Ollie no all the time."

Everyone laughs, except for Carter.

"What? I do!" He frowns, hands on his hips. "Well, I could if I wanted to. I just never want to."

"You absolutely could *not*," Emmett argues. "Not even if someone paid you."

"Wanna bet?" Carter pulls a wad of cash from his wallet. "Five hundred bucks says I can."

"Oh, I'm *so* in." Garrett holds up his own money.

Emmett crosses his arms. "What are the terms?"

Carter thinks for a minute. "No-Nut November."

"No-Nut—" I bury my face in my hand. "What?"

"The terms are simple. Five hundred bucks each, and we're all betting on ourselves. No sex, no jerking off, no nutting—period. We start tomorrow, November first. Whoever lasts the longest gets the pot. Twenty-five hundred dollars."

My face is still in my hands, so I drag them down it in slow motion. "I can't believe we're having this conversation dressed as crayons."

"I can't believe I'm not wearing any pants," Jaxon says, and then, "I'm in."

"*You*?"

"What? I'm not in a relationship."

"You still fuck nearly as much as the rest of us," Garrett argues.

Jaxon runs a palm down his proud chest. "Yeah, I'm hard to resist."

"I'm absolutely not in," I tell them.

"Aw, come on," Carter whines.

"I just started having regular sex a month ago. I'm not about to give it up." Also, I'm kinda scared of Rosie. She likes to be fucked to sleep the night before a big surgery, or an important test. It helps her unwind and take her mind off it, otherwise she's up all night hyperfocusing. She also likes morning sex, and shower sex, and the other afternoon I fucked her on my kitchen counter while Connor was napping upstairs. I'm not gonna be the one to take that from her.

"Then bet on me," Carter says so simply, like it's...logical. It fucking isn't. That's why I snort the loudest, most incredulous laugh. "I won't let you down, Adam, I promise. Plus, we're on the road fourteen days in November. Which means I only have to resist Olivia for sixteen days. I can do it. I can."

He sounds so confident, it's both comical and sad. After all these years, Carter thinks I don't know him. After all these years, Carter doesn't know himself.

"No."

"Don't bet on me," Emmett says. "I know exactly how this is gonna go when I drop this on Cara. Hint: not fucking well." He shakes his head. "And goddammit, I love my wife, but I am *terrified* of her."

"You can bet on me," Garrett assures me. "Don't worry. Jennie's not the boss of me."

I blink at him. "My money's on Jaxon."

"*Fuck yeah*!"

Carter stretches his arms overhead. "Yeah, just wait 'til the girls see us in the costumes I picked out for us tonight. They're gonna be on their knees, begging for a piece."

~

"Are you—"

"Yes."

"Adam." Rosie folds her lips into her mouth, but it doesn't stop her laughter. It shakes her entire body instead as her eyes roam down my body, then back up. Down again, then up. Down once more, and finally that laughter breaks free. "I can't handle this," she cries, hands on her face, and I'll tell you this: she's definitely not on her knees, begging for a piece.

She's so fucking adorable in her ladybug costume, and I'm…I'm fucking…God, I can't even say the words.

Somehow, Carter's found a way to top the Britney debacle.

There's a manly shriek from the downstairs bathroom, and I know Jaxon's just discovered his fate.

"I'm *not* wearing this!"

"You have to!"

"I'm not dying my hair!"

"It's just colored hair gel! It'll wash right out!"

Rosie and I exchange a look. "Ginger."

She peeks over her shoulder, then steps toward me, pushing me back into the bathroom I just stepped out of. "You know," she murmurs, trailing her hand down my cropped orange tank top, over my bared abs. "I think this suits you. Orange might be your color."

"I'm gonna be fucking freezing."

She smiles, pressing herself against me, sweeping her mouth over mine. "I'll warm you up after."

"That reminds me, Carter wants to do No-Nut November. No sex for the whole month."

"But I start a new rotation on Monday. I'll be up all night overthinking everything if you don't put me to sleep. And also, just no."

I chuckle, kissing her pouty red lips. "I may have let him talk me into this ridiculous fucking outfit, but I will not let him talk me out of you." My eyes go to my reflection in the mirror, and I sigh at all the orange. I'd rather be in my crayon costume. "Do I look okay?"

Rosie presses her lips together and nods. "Mhmm."

"That's not convincing."

"Well, I love you anyway." Slender fingers lace through mine, and she tugs me out of the bathroom.

All eyes lift to mine, and Carter, who's wearing a purple dress with a black lace overlay, spreads his arms wide. "Ehhh! There he is!"

The girls explode with laughter, and Rosie finally lets hers go beside me.

"Aw, c'mon!" Garrett throws his arms in the air. His blond hair is pulled into high pigtails, and he's wearing a skintight pink dress and knee-high socks with his runners. The finishing touch is the gold choker around his neck that says *BABY.* "Adam got to be Sporty Spice and I'm stuck as fucking Baby Spice?"

Emmett gestures at his gold spandex jumpsuit. "Fuck off. I'm fucking Scary Spice. I'm wearing fucking *spandex*." He aims a pointed look at his crotch and drops his voice to a whisper. "You can see *everything*."

Cara rubs his chest. "And we love it, baby."

Connor peeks up from the mat he's playing on with Ireland, his eyes lighting. "Woooah-ho-ho! Dada! Orange Dada!" He leaps up, toddling over to me, strokes a hand over my orange cargo pants, and grins up at me. "I lub you, orange Dada."

"I love you, too, Mittens." Mittens because he's dressed as a kitten, and he's been walking around calling himself Mittens.

The basement door slides open, but nobody comes out. Then, after a minute, one running shoe appears, followed by a Union Jack sock, attached to a long, hairy leg. Slow as molasses, Jaxon steps into the hallway, clothed in red booty shorts and a matching tank top, showing off a sliver of his torso, and his brown hair now shines a vibrant red.

"Nobody say a word," he mutters, walking into the silent kitchen with his head down. "Not a fucking *word*."

The slow clomp of his shoes sounds against the kitchen floor as all eyes follow him. When he pulls a beer from the fridge and starts to down it, the snicker-snorts start, choked and muffled.

Jaxon closes his eyes and drops his head back with a groan as laughter explodes around him. "Fuck it, I don't care. I look fine as fuck, and everyone knows Ginger Spice was the hottest Spice Girl."

"Okay, well—" I gesture at myself "—it was clearly Sporty Spice."

"No way," Garrett argues. He twines a tiny pigtail and pops a hip, pink lollipop in his hand. "Baby Spice, all the way."

Emmett gestures aggressively at his outfit. "I'm in. Fucking. *Spandex*."

"You're all wrong," Carter says. "It was Posh Spice. She was the hottest one. That's why I'm dressed as her." He points his foot in his runners, and my eyes go to the black string he has laced up his calves like some sort of decoration. When he flexes one calf, the string breaks. "Aw, damnit. *Ollie*! My muscular calves broke my string again!"

"Well, stop flexing them!"

"I can't simply stop flexing my muscles." He shakes his head and scoops up Ireland, who's dressed as the world's cutest puppy. "C'mon, puppy girl. Let's get you into your Posh Spice costume."

Olivia plants her fists on her hips. "She's happy in her puppy costume."

"She wants to twin with Daddy, though. Yes, you do, little princess, don't you? Daddy even got you a leather jacket to keep you warm." Despite Olivia's protests, he heads down the hall with Ireland in his arms, singing "Spice Up Your Life" as he goes, and ten minutes later, he returns with his Posh Spice twin, except she's still wearing her puppy ears.

He holds her out to Olivia. "Compromise." Leaning into me, he hides his whisper behind his hand. "If I only have one night left, gotta make it count."

He doesn't only have one night left; he knows it as well as the rest of us do, including Olivia, who rolls her eyes and whispers something in his ear, something that has his eyes bulging as we all head toward the front door.

We stop on the front porch for a photo op—several, actually, until Carter's satisfied—then head down the street, one terrifying group that definitely shouldn't ever be seen in public.

But as I look around at my friends, the way everyone simply accepts their place in this unit, how permanent it is, I know this is everything I've ever wanted out of life. Family who chooses to stand next to you every day, even when you're a six-foot-five man dressed as a Spice Girl and embarrassing the fuck out of yourself.

I look down at the tiny hand in mine, his other hand tucked into his mama's as we walk down the street, and *fuck*, everything just feels so damn *right* in this world.

Rosie's gaze slides to mine, cheeks flushing when she catches the goofy smile stuck on my face. "What?"

"I love our family."

Her eyes move over our people, and she smiles the most beautiful smile. "Connor and I are so lucky to be a part of it."

Cara pops her head over her shoulder. "And *we're* so lucky you two are a part of it."

ME

Where is everyone?

I've been at the rink for fifteen minutes now, getting ready for our morning skate, and the other four still aren't here. I'd like to hear their excuses, since *fucking my wife/girlfriend/random girl I met at the gym all morning* can't be any of their reasons. No-Nut November commenced nine hours ago. I'm the only one with a license to be buried nine-and-a-half inches deep inside my woman.

And I was, in case anyone was wondering. Rosie and I got up with the sun, and coffee on the balcony turned into…well, fucking on the balcony. Sue me for not wanting to take advantage of a gorgeous sunrise over the mountains.

The door to the dressing room opens, and Jaxon walks in, hair a mess and sunglasses on, Starbucks in his hands.

He sinks down beside me with a sigh, stretching his legs out and crossing one ankle over the other. "Sorry I'm late. I slept in. It was amazing. Maybe a break from sex is what I needed."

"It's been nine hours. I don't think you can deduce that yet."

"Feel like I can." He sips his coffee and eyes me. "You got laid six ways to Sunday. You lucky fuck."

Before I can answer, the door swings open with so much force, it bounces off the wall. Carter strides in, his fly halfway undone and his shirt on inside out. He pulls a wad of cash out of his pocket and slaps it down on the bench beside me.

"I'm out."

"You're out?" I throw my arms out wide. "It's been nine hours!"

"Ollie put her bumblebee costume back on this morning, except without a top and no panties on under her tutu." He laughs, running a hand over his mouth. "We played this game where she—"

The door bangs open, and Garrett waltzes in, whistling. He tosses a stack of bills down, and Jaxon gasps. "You too?"

"Jennie got a new toy. Said she didn't need me anymore." He shrugs. "Had to show her that she does, in fact, need me."

This time when the door opens, it's a slow creak. Emmett sticks his head in, peeking in before he ambles on in, running a hand through his mussed blond hair. "So, uh…how about that No-Nut November, huh?"

"Carter and Garrett are both already out."

"Oh, thank *fuck*." He counts out his money, adding it to the pile. "Well, it started with Cara refusing to dismount me at midnight. Then I argued that it didn't count because we started *before* midnight, so *technically*, it was Halloween sex. Then she said, '*Technically*, Emmett, I don't *need you* to make myself come.'" His eyes glaze over. "She popped on that fucking audiobook they're listening to, and started… she started…she spread her legs and I…I…I tried. I really tried."

Garrett squeezes his shoulder. "I know, buddy. I know."

Jaxon leaps to his feet, tossing his arms overhead. "Are you fucking kidding me? Was I the only one taking this seriously?" He scoops up the money, aggressively tucking it in his pocket before he points a finger at them, one after the other. "Fuck you. Fuck you. And fuck you." He points at me. "Thank you for believing in me, but fuck you, too, because you had sex and I had none."

"Okay, so. Hear me out." Carter braces his hands out in front of him and grins expectantly. "Destroy-Her-With-Your-Dick December."

Silence hangs in the air for only the briefest of moments. Then, suddenly, the empty spot on the bench where Jaxon's winnings just were is overflowing with a fuckton of cash all over again.

"I'm in."

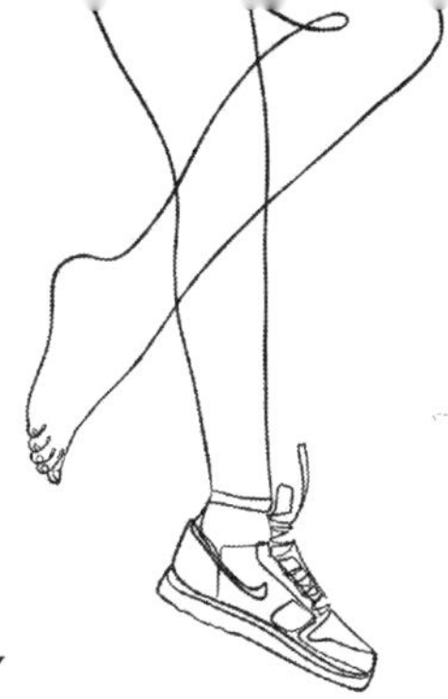

THIRTY-FIVE

TWENTY-FIVE AND CAN FINALLY DRIVE

Rosie

"No."

"Rosie, you can do this."

I look up at the building on the other side of this windshield. *Vancouver Drive Test*. Absolutely forking *not*. I pin my arms across my chest and shake my head. "Adam, no. I can't do this. I-I-I…I'm not ready. I'll fail."

"When have you ever failed at anything?" Adam twists in his seat, taking my hands in his. "Rosie, you've been practicing so much. You're doing incredible, and beyond that, you're an extraordinarily safe driver."

Translation: anal. I'm an anal driver, and we both know it. Adam has lovingly reminded me that I can go a teensy bit over the speed limit and still be safe, but I'd rather continue driving my way: taking my foot off the gas pedal and letting us coast every time I get one or two miles over.

"I already know the examiner is going to be so impressed with how well you maintain the exact speed limit at all times."

I narrow my eyes at the amusement dancing in his. "I know you're laughing at me in your head, *Adam*."

He chuckles, pulling my hand to his mouth, sweeping a kiss over my knuckles. "I would never laugh at you. I only laugh *with* you."

"I'm not laughing," I argue, lifting my shoulder to nudge Piglet's tongue out of my ear when she sticks it there from the backseat. She settles on licking my temple. "Is this why we picked up Pig? Brought Bear? So everyone can watch me fail? And on my birthday, no less."

"Connor, tell Mama she's not gonna fail."

"Mama no fail!" he shouts from the backseat.

I can't tell you how often I've wished I had the same faith in myself that Adam and Connor have in me. They make it seem so easy, so natural, the way they believe in me. What I wouldn't give to live one day inside the head of a person who never second-guesses themselves.

Adam runs his thumb over the dimple in my chin. "Stop that."

"Stop what?"

"Overthinking. Forgetting how amazing you are, how many strides you take day after day to be better than you were. You get behind the wheel every single day, whether it's with me, Archie, or Marco. Whether we're practicing for two hours or just running to Starbucks. You constantly put one foot in front of the other and work on your goals and your fears. You inspire me every day, Rosie. Even on your hard days."

"Do you wake up every day and think to yourself, 'What can I say to Rosie today that'll make her fall even more in love with me?'"

"Pretty much. I need you head over heels if I have any hope of getting you to change your last name one day. Every morning I wake up and ask myself how I can get us one step closer."

"Shut up," I say, all giggle-snort as that familiar heat climbs up my neck. Scuffing at the floor of the truck, I mumble, "I can't believe you didn't tell me."

"Rosie, what would you have done if you knew three weeks ago that you had your driving test today?"

"I would've lost at least three nights of sleep catastrophizing everything that could possibly go wrong, had a handful of anxiety attacks, and I definitely would've thrown up this morning."

He smiles gently, brushing my bangs back. "I wanted it to be a surprise so you weren't stressing and in your head about this for weeks. It was too much time for you to second-guess how much you've learned in these last two months." With my chin in his hand, he brings my lips to his. "If you're not ready, or you simply don't want to—it doesn't matter the reason; you don't need an excuse—just say the word. I'll turn this truck back on and we'll go get birthday cupcakes. There isn't a rulebook saying you have to do this. But you *can* do this, Rosie. And if we leave here today without trying, that's okay. As long as you walk away knowing you're capable." Another kiss, this one everything so inherently Adam. Sweet, soft, that bit of force that coaxes me wide open. "I believe in you."

I glance at my son in the backseat, chattering on to the dogs who look at him like he's their whole world. His sweater says *Mama is a superhero,* and when Adam dropped him on the bed this morning wearing that, I thought it was simply a sweet gesture for my twenty-fifth birthday.

"Do you really think I'm a superhero?" I whisper to Adam.

"I know you are. I've seen it with my own eyes. You take the impossible and make it possible."

Truth is, I feel like most things in this world are possible with his hand in mine.

Maybe that's why I take a deep breath and step out of the truck.

And maybe that's why, fifteen minutes later, when I drive off with the examiner in the passenger seat and Adam, Connor, and the dogs on the walkway, holding a poster board that says *Go, Mama, Go!* I feel like I might *actually* be a superhero.

And maybe, just maybe, when I pull up to the curb forty-five minutes later, that's why I get to jump down from the truck, hold up my final grade with shaky hands, and shout out a sentence I never thought I'd get to say.

"I'm a licensed driver!"

"I have five cars. You can use one of mine."

I open my mouth to politely decline, but Carter holds up a hand.

"Wait, it's six. I have six cars. 'Cause Ollie won't let me get rid of Red Rhonda."

Olivia's face lights. "You can borrow Red Rhonda! She's such a great little starter car. I got her used when I was seventeen. She—"

Carter covers her mouth with his hand, pulling her back against his chest. "Once she starts on Rhonda, she doesn't stop. And trust me, Ro, ol' Rhonda isn't gonna get you anywhere, except stuck in a ditch."

Olivia frowns, ripping his hand away. "That was one time. She just needs new snow tires and she'll be good as new."

Carter's gaze locks with mine, and he shakes his head, discreetly cutting a hand across his throat.

"I'll probably keep up with the bus while I save. Maybe that'll be my first big purchase after I graduate in the spring, when Connor and I get our own place."

"You mean when you move in with Adam?" Carter asks, then grips his shoulder when Olivia gives him a little whack there. "Ow! Don't make me tie those hands up, Ollie girl."

She rolls her eyes. "The move-in discussion is one for them to have, not them plus you."

"But—"

Olivia silences him with nothing but the fierce look in her eyes.

"Fine," he grumbles. "But it's not like Adam's gonna let her go somewhere else. He's *pretty* obsessed with her."

My gaze flicks to Adam beside me, only to find him already watching me. He winks, and the simple action, paired with him pushing that giant wagon with both Connor and Ireland inside, *and* Bear and Dublin, Carter and Olivia's golden retriever, sends a heady rush of blood to my head. He's so innately at home in this role as a family man, like he was made to fill these shoes, and damnit, he does it so well.

It's been two months since we've seen Brandon, and I haven't heard from him once. I knew that was it, the moment we walked out his door. I knew there would be no going back, that he would take the easy way out, the one he'd probably been searching for since the beginning. But if I'd had a shred of doubt, it would have dissolved in flames the night Archie came home from work, said he saw a pile of Connor's things set next to the trash on the curb out front of Brandon's condo.

The picture in my head was gutting, and once Connor was in bed for the night, I curled up on the couch and cried in Archie's arms. The knowledge that it was so easy for Brandon to let go of Connor, to liken it to taking out the trash, it hurt like hell.

And yet, Connor hasn't asked for him once. His days are filled with more love now than they ever were, people who put themselves in his life because they want to be a part of it, and my boy is thriving, absolutely glowing. I have so many incredible people to thank for that, but the one who's made the biggest difference recently is the man standing next to me. The one who picks him up early from daycare while I'm still in clinic, keeps him home for the day because he missed him so much while he was traveling. Sings and dances with him in the living room. Walks him to the local school at dismissal time just so he can see all the buses coming and going. Lets him make a mess at the kitchen counter while they make breakfast together. Wears bubble beards and bubble hats with him. Reads to him while they're lying in bed at night. Loves him, unconditionally, the way a child is meant to be loved.

Nostalgia stokes a warm fire in my chest on this chilly November evening, reminding me of the childhood I had, all the ways my parents loved me and showed me every day. All I want to do is give Connor a childhood like the one I had, and I hope somewhere, my parents are looking down at me, proud of the life we're living.

Proud of me.

"Sorry, fellas. We'd love to give you two special permission, but you have to leave the wagon here. The bridge isn't fully accessible, unfortunately."

"The bridge?" I swing my head around, realizing for the first time that we've veered off Capilano Road, that we're now in the entryway to some sort of park, talking to a smiling attendant. I watch Adam and Carter take the kids out of the wagon, securing them to their chests in carriers. The sight is so fucking attractive, but I can't fully appreciate it in this moment. "What bridge, Adam?"

"Right on time too," the attendant continues. "The lights go on in five minutes."

"Lights? What lights? Adam, what lights?"

He just smiles, taking my hand, pulling me forward. My heart threatens to pound right out of my chest, because the only bridge and lights I can think of are the ones my parents were supposed to take me to see exactly thirteen years ago, on my twelfth birthday.

"I thought we were just going for a walk," I rush out, stumbling down the path, my hand suddenly clammy in his.

"You didn't think I'd let your birthday pass without giving you something you've always wanted, did you?"

"You already did," I argue. "You taught me to drive. I'm a licensed driver today because of you. You fed me breakfast in bed, and no one, not ever, has done that for me." And because I'm nervous, and freaking out *just a little,* I lean closer and whisper, "And you did that thing with your tongue, remember?"

"Ah," he hums. "Yes, I did. And with my fingers too. And then you did that thing you do, what was it, three times over?"

"Four," I murmur, the memory of his name on my lips while I came this morning still such a vibrant, beautiful, incredible memory.

"Right, well, let me give you one last thing." He stops and pulls me back to him, pausing to look at his watch. 4:28 p.m., it says, right on track for this late-fall Vancouver sunset, and Adam smiles. "I need you to close your eyes for me."

My chest pulls taut, and I shake my head. "I'm scared."

Connor touches my nose. "Mama no scare."

"I should be brave?" I ask him quietly.

He nods. "Mama bwave."

"Okay. I'll be brave, but only because it's easy to be brave with you two beside me."

Adam's fingers lace through mine, a tender squeeze that urges my eyes closed. Gently, he leads me forward, and when we stop again, I grip his hand so hard I'm afraid I might cut off fingers he may or may not need in order to catch pucks; I'm still not totally sure of the logistics of hockey.

While I wait, my heart thuds a quick, unsteady beat, a buzz of electricity that pulses through me, to the tips of my fingers and all the way down to my toes. I breathe in the fresh air, listen to the sound of birds singing overhead, twigs snapping and rustling leaves, and hundreds of memories flood my brain. Memories of times so long ago, spent in places just like this, where the two people who loved me more than anything showed me how to appreciate nature, how to fall in love with the way it grounds you, makes every worry seem so small.

Sometimes life has a funny way of reminding you that the permanence of death isn't quite as all-encompassing as we believe it to be. That despite the lack of physical evidence, the people we part ways with are never all that far. That they linger with us, show up sometimes at the strangest, most inconsequential moments.

Because as I finish smiling at the thought of my parents, at the moment Adam's lips touch my ear, whispering for me to open my eyes, I'm graced with the most magnificent view, one I've waited over half my life to see.

In a plush forest of deep green, vibrant colors dance with the swaying trees, glitter down below in the running river, twinkle against the purple and coral sunset, and wind like glowing vines around a bridge I'd given up walking along.

For my twenty-fifth birthday, Adam is giving me the gift my parents couldn't deliver on my twelfth birthday. But more than that, he's giving me them. There's nothing I feel more right now than the certainty that my parents are right here at my side, that they've never left.

Speechless, I stare out at the Capilano Suspension Bridge, the river and the trees, the millions of twinkly lights that make this day glow. And when I look into Adam's eyes, it's not just the lights that dance in them, but the same love my parents showered me with, day in and day out. A silent tear runs down my cheek at the powerful feeling, so palpable I lean into it, close my eyes, and drink it in.

Adam catches my tear with his thumb. "I know this was supposed to be something special you and your parents did together, and I can't replace that, but I thought..." He gestures behind me, and I turn to see all our friends join us next to Olivia and Carter. Archie and Marco, Garrett and Jennie, Cara and Emmett, and Jaxon. "I thought this family might be a decent runner-up."

"Please say yes," Carter whispers over my shoulder. "My ego can't take the hit."

"Your ego is big enough to take at least a hundred hits before it's in danger," I whisper back, sniffling.

"Damn it, she knows me too well already."

I wipe the tears from my eyes. "You guys are here for me?"

"Where else would we be?" Archie asks.

Cara smiles. "We're family, Rosie. We show up for each other."

Jennie slaps at her cheeks. "I'm not crying, FYI. It's just, you're crying, and the lights are super pretty, and I love birthdays, and-and..." She chokes on a quiet sob as Garrett rubs her back. "I have really bad allergies."

Adam grips my hand. "I mentioned we love super hard in this family, right? Any more and it'd be downright suffocating."

Suffocating? But it's the opposite. These people, the way they love so openly and without limits, it's so goddamn refreshing. I've been searching my entire life for these people, for this kind of love, and I didn't just find it in one person; I found it in a whole group of them. Surrounding myself with their love is like coming up for air at the last moment, having life breathed back into you.

I think about it all night, as we wander the lit trails, have hot chocolate above the river, as we talk and laugh and enjoy every moment together. And when Adam and I are lying in bed later that night, all I want to do is say thank you.

I run my fingers through the dark smattering of curls on his chest, stuff my leg between his, desperate to be as close as possible to my person as his fingertips trail down my back.

"Can I tell you something?" I murmur into the silence of the night.

Midnight eyes fall to mine, a handsome, lazy smile hooking the corner of his mouth. "Anything, gorgeous girl."

"Earlier tonight, you said you wanted to give me something I've always wanted. But I already have that, Adam, because I have you. You gave me you. And I've always wanted you, even before I knew you. My heart knew you were out there, that we'd find you one day." I skim his jaw, fingers sliding into his hair as I guide his mouth to mine. "How lucky am I to have my dreams come true?"

"Am I really your dream?" he whispers against my lips. "Promise?"

"Swear it."

THIRTY-SIX

NOBODY'S GONNA KNOW

Adam

"You're fucking embarrassing."

"Oh, what? So you and Carter can bring your kids to family skate, but I can't bring mine?" Jaxon flings his arms into the air before propping his fists on his hips. His cat, Mittens, meows from where he's strapped to his chest, in a—*fuck, this pains me to say*—cat carrier. "Double fucking standards."

Garrett looks up from his knees, where he's lacing up Jennie's skates. "I'm scared you might be losing it, bud."

Jennie cringes. "I hate to say this, Jaxon, but I think you might need a—"

"Don't say it. Don't fucking say it, Jennie."

"—girlfriend."

There go his arms, up above his head again. "I told you not to say it! Mittens has a touch of separation anxiety, that's all. And we were just on the road for eight days." He takes Mittens' paw, jiggling it. "You hate when I leave you, don't you, chunk? Yes, you do. Daddy hates leaving you too."

Rosie snorts a laugh, and Jaxon narrows his eyes at her. She folds her lips into her mouth, pretending to button them, then leans into me as I tie Connor's brand-new hockey skates. "I think we all know who's the one with separation anxiety."

I chuckle, watching as she looks down at her skates, swings them gently, her fingers gripping the bench as she breathes deeply. She sure isn't experiencing separation anxiety from a cat right now, but I know my girl is feeling a little anxious. "How are you doing, trouble?"

"Me?" Her brows jump, and she lays her hand on her chest. "Fine. I'm fine, Adam."

"Wanna try that again?"

She sighs, long and loud, back to staring at her skates. "I'm nervous. I've never skated before. I think I'm going to make a fool out of myself, but I'm so happy to be here and doing something that means so much to you."

Her hesitant gaze flicks to the crowd of children who've just exploded through the doors, rushing to find spots on the benches in our locker room to get skates on too. Kids from Second Chance Home, joining us today for a family skate, because they're part of our Viper family.

I cover Rosie's wringing hands with one of mine, tipping her chin up until she's looking at me. Over the past two months, I've told Rosie all about my charity, the Family Project, the work we do with the foster community. She loves my stories, and she's so damn proud of me, and as much as I would've loved to drag her along to meet everyone, I've never asked her. I've never wanted to put her in a position where she's forced to relive parts of her childhood she wishes never happened.

But this, inviting the kids to be a part of our family skate, to help decorate the tree at the arena, it was her idea.

"I don't want to remember what it feels like to go unnoticed," she admits quietly. "To feel unwanted. But then I don't think the memory has ever really been far, and I guess I'm just…dreading seeing myself in someone else, someone small and perfect and innocent who deserves to be the center of somebody's world. Someone who shouldn't have to be wondering how they can change themselves, make themselves more lovable so somebody will choose them."

She's got the biggest heart, my Rosie, and it shows in every one of her decisions, every thought that wanders through her head. I know she's passed that quality onto her son, too, because Connor reaches up, laying his hand on her cheek, and tells her, "Conn'a choose Mama."

She kisses the inside of his palm. "I choose you, too, Connor."

"I think spending some time with these kids when you've had such heavy emotions surrounding the foster system is brave of you, Rosie.

But you don't always have to be brave. If it ever becomes too much, you can step away, okay? Just let me know whether you want to step away by yourself, or with me. I'll support you however you need to be supported."

Grateful eyes look up at me. "Thank you."

Chestnut pigtails catch my eye, and I find Lily hovering by herself in the corner, watching Connor, Rosie, and me. When I wave at her, her ears burn bright red, and she looks away.

"That must be Lily," Rosie murmurs. "Why don't you go say hi? Connor and I will make our way out to the ice with the others and wait for you on the bench." She drops a kiss to my lips and stands on shaky legs, looping one arm through Jaxon's as Garrett scoops Connor up, and I watch them disappear.

Lily twines a pigtail around her finger, scuffing at the floor as I approach her.

"Hey, Lily-bug. I'm happy to see you."

Brown eyes dart to mine. "Was that your family?"

"Yeah, that was Rosie and Connor. Do you want to meet them?"

She lifts a shoulder. "I don't want to bother them."

"You wouldn't be bothering them."

"It's okay. I'll just stay here."

I frown. "You're not gonna skate?"

"I don't know how."

"Well, I'll teach you." I hold my hand out to her. "C'mon. Let's go find a pair of skates that fit those teensy feet of yours."

"Will you promise not to let go of my hand? I'm afraid of falling."

I hold up two fingers in a promise. "I will not let go of your hand unless you ask me to. You can trust me, Lily."

Her nose wrinkles, and slowly, she slides her tiny hand into mine. "I trust you, Adam."

I'm not sure what I've done in this life to deserve her trust, but I know I'm never going to do anything to break it.

With a pair of skates on her feet, a helmet on her head, and her hand in mine, we walk through the tunnel and out to the rink.

"*Adam*!" Rosie screams, the biggest smile I've ever seen splitting her cheeks as she clings to Olivia and Garrett, gliding along with them. "Look! I'm doing it! I'm skating!"

"*Dada*!" Connor waves from the ice, where he holds onto the little red skating aid, Emmett holding onto it from the other side as Connor takes tiny, quick steps. "Dada, hi! Conn'a pay hockey!"

"Look at you, little trouble! You're doing it! And Mama too!"

"They're just learning too?" Lily asks, tugging on my hand. "Like me?"

"Just like you, sweetheart."

Her chest puffs. "Okay. Let's do this."

"That's my girl," I whoop, stepping onto the ice.

Lily freezes at the last second, dropping my hand and hugging the boards. "No. Wait. I'm scared."

I crouch down in front of her. "That's okay. Sometimes the best things in life are a little scary. We can do them at our own pace. There's no rush."

She peeks around me, watching all the kids zipping around the ice, having fun, and then those ginormous brown eyes come to mine. "I think maybe if you held me, that might be okay. Can you do that?"

As if I'd ever be able to say no to her.

I scoop her into my arms, sitting her on my hip, and she clings to my neck as I glide onto the ice.

"Don't go too fast," she whispers, and when I do a little spin, she giggles. "This is kinda fun."

Carter skates up beside us, Ireland in his arms, her outfit complete with her tiny helmet, *Daddy* jersey, and the teensiest skates I've ever seen while she chomps on a silicone hockey skate teether. "Hey, Lil. Wanna go for a spin with me? I'm way faster than Adam."

She shakes her head, hugging me tighter. "I want to stay with him. You talk too much."

"Wow," Carter mutters as I bark a laugh. "A dagger right through the heart. I don't talk too much, Ireland, baby, do I?"

"You absolutely do," Olivia answers as she joins us, holding Rosie's hand.

"Look at you," I murmur, pulling Rosie into my free side. "Managed to ditch Garrett, huh?"

"*And* Olivia said it didn't feel like I was crushing the bones in her hand anymore!"

Olivia laughs. "You're a much better student than Cara. It took me weeks to teach her."

"I wasn't motivated enough," Cara says, skating in a wobbly circle around us. "Emmett was already obsessed with me. I showed him how I won the award for most tacos eaten in five minutes in university, and he dropped to his knees and begged me to marry him."

Cara, Olivia, and Carter skate away, and Rosie smiles at Lily.

"Hi, Lily. Adam's told me so much about you. I'm Rosie."

Her cheeks flame, and her legs grip my waist tighter as she mumbles, "I like your pink hair."

"Thank you. It was my mom's favorite color."

"Is your mama in heaven?"

Rosie's eyes flicker. "She is."

"Mine too."

She hesitates, then tentatively reaches forward, squeezing her arm. "You must miss her very much."

"I miss her butterfly kisses the most," Lily whispers. She taps her nose. "She gave me them right here whenever I was sad or scared."

A small smile hooks the corner of Rosie's mouth. "My mom used to give me those too."

Lily's face lights. "Really? So you know how to give 'em?"

"I do."

"Maybe if you give me one, then I won't be scared to skate." She looks between us, excitement bubbling, then dying just as fast as she shrinks into herself. "Unless you don't want to. You don't have to. Maybe I should sit on the bench."

Rosie steps forward on two wobbly feet, taking Lily's face in her hands. My heart thumps a heavy, unsteady beat as I watch her press featherlight kisses along the bridge of Lily's crinkling nose, watch that little girl's smile burst like sunshine.

"I think I could try skating now. I feel kinda brave right now."

When I set her on her feet, she slips a hand each into mine and Rosie's, and Rosie's eyes come to mine. The way they dance says it all: she's in love, which is pretty much exactly what I figured would happen when these two met. After all, it's been the same for me since that first time Lily slid over on the couch, asked me to read to her.

"I tried taking steps at first too," Rosie says as Lily clomps between us. "But Olivia told me to try to keep my feet on the ice and wiggle my bum and hips a little bit."

"Like this?" Lily shimmies her hips, looking up at Rosie as we slowly glide forward.

"Just like that."

"I'm doing it," she whispers. "I'm really doing it! Look at me!"

"You're doing so great, Lily-bug." I smile at Rosie. "You both are."

"*Dada*!" Connor races toward me with his skate aid, Emmett's hands on either side of him. "Dada!

"Buddy! Look at you!"

"He's fast as fuck," Emmett says, stopping Connor before he crashes into us. "I mean, fast as…fuck." He cringes. "I'll try better next time, I swear." Crouching down, he holds his hand up, grinning when Connor slaps it. "Thanks for skating with me, dude!"

"Bye, dude!"

"Oh my gosh." Lily wriggles free from our grasp, putting her hands on her knees as she crouches down to Connor's level. "Hi, Connor. You're so cute. I'm Lily. Can you say Lily?"

"Woooah-ho-ho. Lily! Hug? Conn'a hug Lily?" He spreads his arms wide and steps into her, and the two of them go tumbling to the ice, a giggling mess.

"I think he likes me! I can be your best friend, okay, Connor?"

I pick the two of them up, setting them on their feet, and Lily takes his hand in hers.

"C'mon, Connor. I'll keep you safe, okay? Your mom gave me butterfly kisses, so I'm super brave right now."

"Yeah! Bwave!"

"Be careful, you two," Rosie says, sliding her hand into mine as we glide slowly behind them, watching their quick, teensy steps in their skates. "Not too fast, okay?"

Warm, mossy eyes come to mine, and she grins that goofy, magnificent grin. "Uh-oh."

"Uh-oh? Uh-oh what?"

"Uh-oh, I think I just fell in love."

~

One of the things I love about Rosie is that she doesn't just fall. She's a head-over-heels, all-in, whole-world type of lover. If I hadn't already been sure of it, I certainly would be now. Because in the week following the family skate, Rosie hasn't stopped talking about a certain brown-haired girl who stole her heart.

"Are the kids allowed to go out with families?" she asks as we stroll through the mall, on the hunt for a gown for her to wear to my Christmas gala next week. It's the first of its kind, an extension of sorts to the tree lighting ceremony my charity, The Family Project, holds every year. Except this one is a fancy dinner and dance, involves alcohol, and costs a fuckton more money. But it's a night out for us, and I can't wait to see Rosie in her dress, and then peel it off her later.

"You're thinking of Lily again."

"Maybe she'd like to go for a hike with us and the dogs. Something casual, a change of scenery."

That's the first suggestion. The next five hundred roll in, in quick succession, and I don't think she even pauses to breathe.

"Oh! I know! We can go to the suspension bridge again and see all the Christmas lights! She'll love that!"

"We could take her out for a pancake breakfast and hot chocolate."

"Or dessert. Everyone loves dessert!"

"Oh, hey, there's that new Disney movie coming out. Maybe we can take her in the new year."

"What about the train at Stanley Park?"

"Do you think she likes buses as much as Connor?"

"I know she loves doing her loom bracelets. What else does she like? Does she like to paint or color?"

I follow her through a store, watching as she gushes over gorgeous dresses and then talks herself out of them, telling herself it won't work on her body. Each one she puts back, I hang over my arm, and she just keeps keeping on with ideas for Lily.

"Can I ask you something?" She spins around, frowning when she sees my armful of gowns. "Adam, what are you doing with all those?"

"Is that what you wanted to ask me?"

"No, I—Those won't suit me. I'm too…I have too much…"

"There's nothing about you that's too much, Rosie. Everything about you is just right. You love these dresses, so you're going to try them on, and if you hate them, that's that. But give them a chance."

"Bossy," she mumbles, sorting through another rack. She pulls out a satin crimson dress with thin straps and a thigh-high slit, her eyes lighting. "Excuse me, could I bother you to check if you have this in a twelve?" she asks one of the sales attendants.

"Absolutely." She takes the dresses from me. "And I'll get a fitting room started for you."

Rosie brushes her bangs aside. I helped her touch up her hair yesterday, and the normal coppery pink is more vibrant, a stunning shade against the golden freckles on her nose and cheekbones. "What would you think about having Lily join us for Christmas? She could come over in the morning and we could put some presents under the tree for her. I know they do that stuff at the home, but…I don't know." She drops her gaze, mindlessly runs her fingers along a shimmery dress. "I want her to feel special. I hated Christmas without a family. It felt so lonely, even though I was surrounded by so many people."

"Yes."

"Yes? Yes, you'll think about it, or—"

"Yes, let's have her over for Christmas. I'll check with her social worker to make sure it's allowed and if it's something she'd be up for."

Her gaze rises to mine, thoughtful, curious. Slowly, she slides her arms around my waist, pressing up on her toes to touch her lips to mine. "Thank you."

I'm about to coax her mouth wide open, see if she'll let me slide my tongue in there for just a quick taste, but a throat clears beside us.

"I'm sorry," the sales associate apologizes. "We don't have any twelves left, but I do have some tens. Would you like to try one?"

"Oh shoot. That was my favorite. Um…" Rosie drums her fingertips against her chin, then waves a hand through the air. "That's okay. It probably won't fit."

The sales attendant holds the dress up next to Rosie and glances at me. We both nod.

Rosie looks up at us with hopeful eyes. "Yeah? You think?" She waves off my reply before I can give it. "No." She frowns. "Okay, maybe. What the hell, right?"

The sales attendant leads us back to the fitting rooms, and I collapse into a plush, oversized chair as Rosie disappears into her little room. There are at least twenty women roaming this store, and the only other man is sitting on the opposite side of the changeroom, buried under a pile of dresses, watching sports updates on his phone from what I can hear. He looks at me, and I give him a half wave that he returns with a nod and the bump of his fist twice against his chest.

Solidarity, brother, he mouths.

I scroll aimlessly through my phone while I wait for Rosie, checking in with Carter to see how Connor's doing over at their place. When five minutes turn to ten, and Rosie's silence turns to grunts, I make my way to her door and knock gently.

"Everything okay in there?"

"Um…yeah. No. I think…I think this dress is…not for me."

"Let's see."

"Um…no. No thanks. I think I need to go up a size."

"Whatever makes you feel comfortable."

"Or something less revealing, maybe."

Less revealing? I'm totally not proud of the way my dick rises to attention, like his presence has just been requested. I press a little closer to the door, mostly because I want in but also because I don't want my buddy over there to see the hard-on I'm suddenly sporting.

I knock again, lowering my voice to a whisper. "Lemme see, baby. I bet you look perfect."

The door cracks open, and Rosie steps aside, eyes trained on the floor as she lets me in. I close the door behind me, my gaze falling down her body in that tight little dress.

She tucks her hair behind her ear and gestures at the body I can't take my eyes off, the one filling every inch of satin so flawlessly, sending a rush of blood to my throbbing cock. "Curse of the mom bod, am I right?" She forces a chuckle, and when I don't say anything, her eyes come to mine, delicate voice cracking. "Adam? Why aren't you saying anything?" She reaches for the zipper on her back. "This was silly. I can't pull something like this off. I don't have the body—"

She gasps as I push her against the wall, jaw grasped between my fingers. Wide green eyes stare up at me, her cheeks flushed with the same heat that pulses through me.

"I mean this in the politest way possible, Rosie, I swear, but for the love of God, shut up. And if you don't, if you say one more thing about this body that isn't praising how fucking *exquisite* it is, I'm going to do us both a favor and shut you up with my cock in your mouth."

My hand slips to her throat, squeezing it gently, holding her in place as I dip my head and drink her in once more. Crimson satin squeezes her waist, stretching across her full hips. The slit up her thigh is sky-high, begging my hand to slip below and find out how warm she is, how wet. My eyes climb up, zeroing in on the deep plunge in her cleavage, the heave of her full, plush tits. The tip of my finger skims her side, runs up the center of her chest, traces the swell of her breasts, along her collarbone and to that dainty strap that hangs off her shoulder. I slip my finger below it, toying with it, before I grip it and haul her forward.

"Feel like making some noise for me, trouble?"

Her eyes dart to the door. "Here? But—*oooh*."

"Good start, angel," I hum, stroking her pussy through her panties. "I'm gonna take these off, okay?"

She nods frantically and lifts her foot, like she thinks I'm gonna slip them off. Instead, I ball the flimsy lace in my fist and rip.

"Oops."

"Asshole," she breathes, hiking her leg around my hip as I drag my hands up her thighs, gripping two fistfuls of her ass.

"Aw, see, I was gonna be nice and fuck you slow and gentle so you could keep quiet." I shove the dress up over her hips, and a shiver races down my spine at the sound it makes when it rips. "Now I think I'll make sure everyone in here knows my name."

"Adam—"

"Louder, baby." I plunge two fingers inside her wet pussy. "Let them know who your pussy is soaked for."

"Oh *God*." She tears at my coat, yanking it off my body, pulling at the buttons of my shirt, and rolling her pelvis against my hand when I return it between her legs.

"Adam, baby. Not God. How many times do I have to tell you?" I steal her mouth, drowning her moans with my tongue, nipping along the edge of her jaw until I find her ear. "Or do you need me to fuck it into you?"

"Yes," she whimpers, pulling at my belt buckle, yanking down my zipper. "Please."

"Tell me how perfect this body is," I demand, teasing her clit with the head of my cock. "Tell me and you can have my cock."

"Fuck," she rasps, watching my cock slip through her slit.

"Tell me."

"Perfect," she cries. "My body is perfect."

"And who does it belong to?"

"You," she whimpers, breathless as I push inside her.

"And this pussy? Who's fucking it? Who owns it?"

"You, Adam. God, *you*."

"That's my good fucking girl, Rosie."

My fingers slide up the back of her neck, grabbing the hair at her nape as I hold her against the wall and fuck her. Her nails rake down my shoulders as she lifts her hips, urging me deeper, harder. My hand glides along her shoulder, grabbing hold of that delicate strap. I pull, ripping it, and her incredible tits spring free, bouncing in my face as she rides me.

"You're a fucking masterpiece, sweetheart. Made just for me, I swear to God." I pull her head taut, bringing those eyes to mine. "I'm gonna worship this body for the rest of my life."

"Please," she begs. "I don't want you to stop."

"Couldn't if I tried." I drop my forehead to hers as I drive myself forward, over and over, the door shaking on its hinges. "Christ, Rosie. You're so tight, so fucking wet, squeezing me so good."

Palming her breast, I suck her nipple into my mouth, teasing it with my tongue, pulling it gently between my teeth as she writhes and cries, pleading for more.

"I'm gonna come. Adam, I'm gonna…*oooh fuck*. Please, Adam."

"You're asking so nicely." I drag my mouth up her throat as pressure settles in the base of my spine, my balls tightening. Grabbing the backs of her knees, I hike her legs up against her sides, pushing them wider, plunging as deep as I can, until my name leaves her mouth on a loud gasp. "Fucking *Christ*, I never thought I'd love hearing my name so much."

Her head lolls over her shoulder, hooded and dazed eyes hooked on mine as I pummel into her, savoring the way she squeezes around me as she fights for air.

"Hold on," I demand, as my orgasm barrels down my spine.

She shakes her head, squeezing me tighter.

"Hold the fuck on, Rosie."

"I-I…I can't. Oh *fuck*, Adam. Oh *God. Please*." She lifts her hips, and when I pound into her, she explodes around me, crying out my name, dragging hers from my throat as I empty myself inside her, my palm slamming against the wall.

"*Fuck*, Rosie."

Her heaving body goes limp in my arms, and I struggle for air as I grin down at her damp face, kissing her swollen lips.

Five minutes later, when we're dressed and the changeroom is…well, it's as clean as one would reasonably expect, we exit the changeroom.

All five sales associates, a handful of women, and my buddy, who's still sitting in the chair under a mountain of clothes, stare at us, speechless and slack jawed.

I hold up the hanger with the shredded dress. "We'll take two, please."

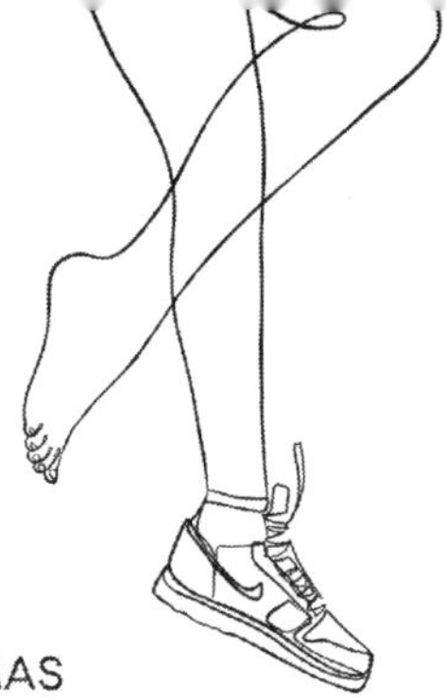

THIRTY-SEVEN

HOW THE GRINCH STOLE CHRISTMAS

Rosie

"I'M scared to leave you with them."

Cara rolls her eyes, sipping her shimmery red cocktail. "Say that one more time, Adam, and I'll give you something to be scared about."

"You keep saying that like Rosie's not already one of us," Jennie adds.

"She joined the book club. She's officially infiltrated the group. There's no turning back now." Olivia slaps Carter's hand under the table and holds up her butter knife. "Carter, I swear to God, if you try to slip your hand under my dress one more time, I'm going to saw it off. We're at a fundraiser for kids, for fuck's sake."

Carter pouts. I've learned no one does it quite like him, except maybe his sister. Something about those Beckett dimples, maybe. "Yeah, but there are no kids here, and your legs keep peeking out of that slit."

Garrett tosses back his water. "Yeah, Carter. Take her to the bathroom instead. Jennie and I have already been."

"You motherfucker," Carter seethes, launching himself across Olivia, a battle of slapsies ensuing between the two adult men, or overgrown children, whichever you prefer.

"*Sister*fucker," Jaxon corrects, and Emmett high-fives him.

Adam stands, folding his napkin and placing it on the table. "Yeah, see, this is exactly what I mean."

"Rosie can hold her own," Carter says.

Emmett tosses his arm over my shoulder. "We're gonna tell Rosie how you got your nickname Woody."

Adam's eyes widen. "No."

"I thought it was because his last name is Lockwood?"

"They caught Adam jerking off on his first road trip in his hotel room," Jaxon tells me.

Adam shoves a finger in Jaxon's face. "You weren't even there, twat-waffle!"

The table goes silent, and then promptly explodes with laughter.

Carter makes a claw with his hand. "Rawr."

"I love getting him riled up," Garrett says.

I chuckle, grabbing a fistful of Adam's crisp white button-up, tugging him down to me. "I'll be fine. I know exactly who these people are, and I choose to love them, and you, anyway."

"Was that an insult?" Carter whispers. "It felt like an insult."

I press my lips to Adam's as the emcee introduces him. "You look so handsome. I won't be able to take my eyes off you up there." He grins, and I pull him closer, my lips at his ear. "Then maybe you can take *me* in the bathroom."

I swear I hear it, the way his heart speeds up, his slow swallow.

Am I normally this bold? Of course not.

Do I have a penchant for sex in semi-public places where someone could potentially catch us ever since Adam fucked me so hard my soul left my body in that changeroom last week?

...

Yes.

Listen, it's out of my hands tonight. This party goes until eleven so that the boys can board their plane to Tampa forty minutes later. If I want him one more time—and I do—I have no choice.

I peck his lips and smile up at him as he struggles with the buttons of his suit jacket, wide eyes bouncing between me, the hallway that leads to the bathrooms, and the stage where everyone is waiting for him.

He walks away, and Cara's lips touch my ear. "I knew you had a freaky side."

I arch a brow, because I know for a fact that Adam received a call for help in his group chat last week that involved some sort of mix-up with handcuffs and lost keys. If that wasn't enough, Cara slid into our girls' chat forty minutes later to ask Olivia if she *liked what she saw* when she and Carter came to save the day.

Cara just smiles a devious smile, wagging her brows, and I roll my eyes, turning my full attention to Adam as he takes the stage.

He's always a dream, whether covered head to toe in hockey gear, in a hoodie and a pair of sweats, naked and sleep-rumpled in bed, or in nothing but a thin pair of pajama pants hanging low off his hips and my favorite five o'clock shadow while he makes us French toast and bacon over the stove. But tonight, with his normally unruly curls tamed, a fresh shave, and a midnight blue suit that looks like it was made just for him, a crimson tie that matches my dress, he's immaculate. A picture of confidence and control, someone who knows what his purpose in life is and is proud of every step he's taken.

I'm proud of him too.

"Good evening, everyone, and thank you for joining us tonight at the first annual Tinsel and Ties Charity Gala. My name is Adam Lockwood, and I—"

"Fuck yeah, Woody!"

"Take it off, baby!"

"—have the most supportive and inappropriate friends in the world, apparently." The crowd laughs, and he smiles. "Most of you know me as the goalie for the Vancouver Vipers, but I'm also the proud founder of The Family Project, a charity that supports local foster agencies here in British Columbia. All proceeds go directly back into our community, and tonight in particular, we're raising money to open our first ever sports summer camp." His grin is so boyish, so adorable as he rubs the back of his neck, a sweet flush painting his cheekbones at the hoots and cheers. "I'm really proud, but mostly, I'm proud of this community. None of this would be possible without the amazing people who come out and support us every time, who donate their time—and their money, thank you so much—just to put a smile on a kid's face. And while I know how much it means to these kids, I can't tell you how much it means to me. Because I was that kid."

Adam drops his eyes for a moment, and when he looks up, they come to me. There's something in them, something sad and yet so damn grateful, and it sparks a hope in me I didn't know I needed, not right now. "The truth is, I was so damn lucky to find my forever family. And if I hadn't found them, I wouldn't be where I am now, with a whole crew of people I call family." He gestures at our table. "My teammates, and their incredible wives. My spectacular girlfriend, and our beautiful son."

My heart leaps to my throat at that three-letter adjective he's tossed in there so casually, like he doesn't even have to think about it. His mouth quirks as he watches me start fidgeting, tugging at my dress, shifting in my seat.

"If I can help even one child find the love I've found, I know I'll have made a difference. Thank *you,* folks, for coming out here and making a difference too."

Adam heads through his standing ovation, his hand on the button of his suit jacket as he approaches me. Music starts, drowning out the applause, and he takes my hand, pulling me out to the dance floor.

"Why're you crying, gorgeous?" he asks, spinning me out before hauling me into his chest.

"I'm so proud of you." I sniffle, wiping away the tears. "And also, you said *our*. You called Connor *our* son. And all I've ever wanted is for someone to love him as endlessly as you do."

"I was thinking, maybe one day in the future…" He clears his throat, and I'm thrown by the sudden shyness, the uncertainty.

"Spit it out, Woody."

He grins, and right here on the dance floor, in front of everyone, pinches my ass. "It's Adam to you, and when I'm inside you, God is also acceptable." Blowing out a low breath, he spins us in a slow circle. "I was thinking, in the future, when we get married—"

"You have to ask me first, you know."

He narrows his eyes. "If we manage to make it to the bathroom, everyone's definitely going to hear my name coming out of that mouth, trouble." He arches a brow, and when I fold my lips into my mouth, continues. "Would me adopting Connor be something you might want? Obviously, we would talk to him about it, too, and see if he wants that, but—"

I throw my arms around his neck, hugging him so tight, and he chuckles.

"Is that a yes?"

"He'd be the luckiest boy in the world to be able to officially call you his dada." My hand slips into his hair, and I press my lips to his. "But you've been his dada from the moment he laid his eyes on you, Adam."

His soft exhale rolls down my neck, and as we move from one song right into the next where he refuses to let go, I can't get my mind off a little brown-eyed girl who stole my heart on a pair of skates.

"Have you ever thought of fostering any of the kids from the home? Or...adopting?"

His hand glides slowly up my back. "It's something that's always been on my mind, to be honest with you."

"Really? How come you've never asked me if it's something I want?" Because truthfully, until recently, the thought of ever stepping foot into a foster home again made me sick to my stomach. I've wanted to leave all those years in my past, but now all I can think about is giving someone the childhood I wished I had. The family I lost, and the one I've found now.

Adam brushes his thumb over the dimple in my chin. "Because none of those things are deal breakers to me, Rosie. There are so many ways for us to give back to this community. It doesn't have to be by foster or adoption if it isn't something that fits our family. I also recognize how different our experiences were within foster care, and you're still sorting through those emotions. The last thing I'll ever do is put pressure on you."

His hand goes to my hair, drifting across the jeweled barrette, twirling a wayward lock around his fingers before he tucks it behind my ear. "How we make a family doesn't matter to me. Whether we open our home to kids who were born to someone else, whether we make five babies or Connor is our one and only, and he and Bear convince us to buy a farm filled with animals to play with. What matters to me, at the end of the day, is that I'm with my family. And my family is you and Connor."

With my cheek on his chest, I breathe in the comfort, the security, the way he loves me so completely, without conditions. "Thank you."

"For what?"

"For being you. For not making me feel pressured either way. For everything you do that makes this world a better place for kids like Connor and Lily. For kids like twelve-year-old me, who hoped one day they'd find someone who cared as much as you do." I take his face in my hands. "You're a good man, Adam Lockwood. I love you."

"You do, huh? How much?"

I arch a brow. "What do you want?"

He grins, shrugging. "Been thinking about what Carter said a few weeks ago, at your birthday."

"He says a lot of things. In fact, he almost never stops talking."

Adam chuckles. "About you and Connor moving in after you graduate."

My pulse spikes. "Oh. Don't worry about that."

"I'm not."

"Cool." My head bobs. "Yeah, me neither." I try to back up, put the teensiest amount of space between us so he can't hear the way my heart rattles against my rib cage, but his palms press against my back, pulling me right back in until I bounce off his chest.

"Connor's room is already made up, and you don't have much stuff at your place with Archie. Should be a quick, painless move."

My jaw drops, and Adam smirks, two fingers on my chin to close my mouth.

"You're not surprised, are you? You heard Carter say I was obsessed with you, right?"

"I mean, it's not as if I haven't thought, you know, 'How cool would that be, if everything was still perfect in the spring, and Adam maybe wanted us to stay forever, and—'"

"I want you to stay forever, Rosie. I was thinking we could start the year off in our house, together."

"The year? Like-like-like…the new year? In two weeks, that new year?"

"The very one."

"But-but-but—" *Jesus, Rosie.* "That's so soon."

"Respectfully, I don't give a fuck how soon it is. Why should I wait on something that brings me so much happiness?" He cups my cheek, guiding my gaze to his. "If it's not something you're ready for, and you feel like it's too fast, that's okay. Communicate that with me, and I'll back off." He dips his head, nuzzling my neck. "But if you're on the fence and open to persuasion, I can take you to the bathroom and show you what we could do every single morning on our bathroom counter."

"Mmm…" I sway into him as he kisses his way up my neck. "What if I want to paint our bedroom pink?"

"Done."

I think about his SUV, the one I've been driving to and from school since I got my license. "And if I hit a curb with your car? Oh, *or* what if I backed into your truck *with* your car? Huh? What then?"

He drops his head, pressing his quiet, rumbly laugh against my shoulder. "Do you want to hear how the first thing I'll ask is whether you're okay? And then tell you that it's okay, they're just cars? Or do you want me to tell you how I'll bend you over the hood of it later that night, when the house is quiet, and pretend I'm furious? Because I'll do both, Rosie."

Sounds great. Okay, Rosie, let's level this bad boy up.

"What if I have a creepy ceramic doll collection I haven't told you about and I want to display them for everyone to see?"

"Then I'll build you a fucking shelf for your creepy dolls so their eyes can follow me everywhere I go in our house, so long as it's *our* house. Just move in with me, *please*."

"Geez," I mumble, hiding my smile against his shoulder. "No need to beg. I was gonna say yes."

"Fucking troublemaker," he murmurs against my lips, then glances at his watch. "We've still got over an hour before I need to be on that plane. How many times do you think I can make you come in that bathroom before then?"

"Gross," Carter whispers, killing the moment as he appears beside us. "Your bathroom orgasms need to wait. The DJ's about to put our song on."

"Our song? What—" Adam's brows pull down, his mouth set in a grim line as the "Cha-Cha Slide" starts spilling from the speakers. The boys gather around him, clapping their hands to the beat, and Adam tries to hang onto me like Jack tried to hang onto that door. There's not enough room for him on my door, though, and this Titanic is sinking, so I smile at him as I let him go.

"My brain genuinely can't comprehend why I find this both utterly mortifying and yet such a fucking turn-on," Olivia whispers as she pulls me to safety.

"Oh, I love it." Cara traces the shape of her lips with her pointer finger as she watches her husband dance. "Emmett sometimes puts it on while he's cleaning. There's nothing like watching your man cha-cha real smooth with a Dyson in his hand."

"I love when Garrett shakes his ass," Jennie tells us on a sigh. "He's such a bad dancer, and it makes him a hundred times more lovable."

"Adam's been teaching Connor how to do the Macarena. Connor calls it the Macaroni, so now every time Adam puts his hands on his ass and jumps, he sings, '*Heeey, Macaroni*!' It's the most attractive thing *ever*, and I jumped on him as soon as Connor went down for his nap this afternoon."

"That man was made to be a dad," Cara says, nodding.

The song comes to an end, and the boys bow to their cheering crowd before they start ambling over.

"Who's got first dibs on the private bathroom?" Cara asks. "Because I—" Her eyes widen, and her face goes a volcanic shade of red as her gaze narrows on something over my shoulder. "I must have died and gone to hell, because I know Satan's whore didn't really just rise from the ashes and walk the fuck in here."

Adam's easy grin slips, and the blood drains from his face. He grips my hand, pulling me behind him, and I grip his suit jacket as I peek around him, at whatever is causing the commotion.

A stunning redhead strides toward us in sky-high stilettos and a fur jacket. It's not until she stops before us and slips it off, showing us the glittery royal blue dress below, do I notice that she is really fucking pregnant.

A low gasp fills the room, and Cara mutters something about the spawn of Satan.

The redhead smirks at her, crossing her arms over her chest. "Charming as always, Cara." Devastatingly beautiful and equally evil blue eyes move over me with disdain, and my stomach somersaults as Adam tucks me tighter against him.

"What do you want, Courtney?"

"Oh, that's simple." She tosses her fiery red locks over her shoulder. "I want you to step up and be a father to the baby you put inside me."

Adam

"What the fuck did you just say?"

I slam the door behind us, the cold, fresh air doing nothing to soothe

the fire torching my insides. Rosie's tucked into Olivia's side, her gaze so lost as it moves between Courtney's belly and me.

I feel like my goddamn head is going to explode.

"I'm pregnant," Courtney says.

I snort. "Clearly."

"The baby is yours, Adam. And if you'd had picked up the phone any of the hundred times I tried calling you, or showed up to the meeting you set up with me, you'd know that."

"Absolutely fucking not. We haven't slept together in a year and a half."

She scoffs, rolling her eyes. "So you're just going to pretend that night at your place didn't happen? In July, when you had that party?"

"*What*? I didn't touch you! I don't even remember you being there!" My gaze flicks to Rosie, and I see the way she's backtracking, adding up dates in her head, and I fucking *panic.* "Rosie, I haven't so much as *looked* at another woman since you came into my life, I swear it."

"This is disgusting," Courtney spits. "I figured you regretted it when you woke up the next morning and tried to play it off like nothing happened, when you kicked me out of what used to be *our* house. But I can't believe you, Adam Lockwood, golden boy, would really act like you had nothing to do with this. You found me in nothing but your T-shirt, for fuck's sake."

"That doesn't mean shit." It's not me who says it, but Carter. "Everyone knows you're nothing but a conniving, vindictive old shrew. All you ever do is try to break everything good because you lost the best thing you'll ever have. You're lying."

"Then what the fuck is this?" Courtney shoves her phone in his face, in Rosie's before I yank it from her hand. "Pretty damning evidence whose bed I slept in that night."

The photo is me, passed out in my bed. Next to me? Courtney, in nothing but my T-shirt.

I shake my head, searching my brain. Like it was that morning, it's foggy as hell. "I had too much to drink. I did…I did those keg stands." I look to Jaxon, pleading for answers, but he just shakes his head, his eyes sad for me, like he wishes he could help.

"I told you that morning, dude. You ran out of the pool when you saw her come in, and I never saw you again."

I tug at my hair. "I don't remember."

Courtney steps forward, one hand on her belly, the other on my arm. "We can be a family again, Adam."

I jerk away from her touch. "I have a family."

"A *real* family. You've been playing house with that girl for long enough, don't you think?"

"Don't fucking talk about her," I growl lowly, looming over Courtney.

"This is our son. *Ours*, Adam. The one you always wanted. The one we dreamed about having together."

My stomach roils, and I place a hand over it. "A baby won't change anything between us. And I have the son I always dreamed of having."

"This rich, martyr stepdaddy act is getting old, Adam." She spins to Rosie, a huff of laughter escaping her nose. "Wow, talk about getting lucky, huh? You must be thrilled that your *woe is me* sweet little single mama act worked. You think you're set for life now, huh?"

"Enough," I roar, blood thundering in my ears, my heart hammering. "Don't fucking speak to her. Don't even *look* at her. You're so goddamn beneath her, she can't even fucking see you."

Rosie rushes to my side, tucking her shaking hand in mine, placing her other hand over my heaving chest. "This conversation is over," she tells Courtney. "You shouldn't have come here tonight."

"Don't you dare talk to me like that, you bitch."

"No," Cara growls, stepping between Rosie and Courtney. "Don't *you* dare talk to *her* like that. In fact, life would be immensely better for everyone if you just. *Shut. Up.*" She swings her hip out, pinning her arms over her chest. "You should be ashamed of yourself for ruining such a special night for five minutes of fame. Like the woman told you, this conversation is over. Now get. The fuck. *Out.*"

"You're a bitch," Courtney spits out.

"Proud of it, babe." Cara wiggles her fingers at her as she storms down the street. "Enjoy your trip back to the fiery depths of hell."

As luck would have it, our team bus pulls up out front at this moment, and the doors open as the rest of the team filters outside.

Coach raises his brows at me. "Everything good here?"

No.

"All good, Coach," Carter replies, his grip on my shoulder shaky.

"All right. Everyone on the bus. Wheels up in forty."

"Rosie, I swear—"

She silences my frantic words with her mouth on mine, her trembling fingers pressing into my jaw as her soft lips move with purpose. When she pulls back, it's the quiver in her chin that breaks me, the way her gaze wobbles as she stares up at me. "We'll…we'll figure this out, Adam. Okay?"

I climb on the bus and watch my pink-haired world slowly fade from view, and I can't help the thoughts that claw their way in, setting up shop inside my brain.

Will we figure this out?

THIRTY-EIGHT

TOO PRETTY TO FIGHT

Adam

I'M AN EMOTIONAL HOCKEY PLAYER.

I think it comes with the territory of being a goalie. Losses are hard, and I've always found it hard not to lay blame on my shoulders. Even worse, when something's going on in my personal life—like, say, finding my long-term girlfriend riding her side piece in our bed—it distracts me. My thoughts are elsewhere, and sometimes that leads to careless mistakes.

Not tonight, though. Because tonight I'm not broken.

I'm fucking furious.

Tampa's left-winger races down the boards, around our exhausted defenseman. Jaxon took a careless penalty a minute ago—the result of someone chirping in his ear—so we're down one man, and I've been throwing myself all over this net to stop the countless shots.

Tampa's captain soars across the blue line, into our defensive zone, calling for the puck. The winger sends it across, right through the legs of my defenseman, and the captain winds up, firing the puck at me at lightning speed. I dive to the right, my glove coming up right on time to catch the puck before it can hit the back of my net. The whistle blows, I drop the puck in the ref's hand, and grab a drink of water as our lines change.

"Jesus fuck," Carter mutters, clapping a hand to my head as he circles my crease.

"You're not letting a single thing by you tonight."

"Nope."

He gives me an assessing once-over. "You okay?"

"Nope."

I haven't seen Rosie in forty-eight hours, and aside from a couple texts, we haven't had the chance to talk. She worked all day yesterday, had twelve hours of clinical today, and she's been driving herself up the wall studying for the NAVLE, her veterinarian licensing exam in January.

As I look around this arena, all I see are ways I've added to her stress.

Where do I send my application for baby mama #3?

I'll let you shoot 'n' score & I won't ask for more!

I'll take 2 minutes for hooking if it's with Woody!

Jesus fuck, who lets these girls in here with those signs? For the first time this season, I hope Rosie isn't watching.

Carter follows my gaze. "She knows better than to put any stock in those signs."

"Doesn't mean they won't make this harder on her."

I toss my water bottle back in my net, getting into position at the edge of my crease as everyone lines up for face-off. The whistle blows and the puck drops, and I slide left and right as the play moves around our end of the ice. The shit-disturber centerman trying to block my view of the puck is pissing me the fuck off, so I slip forward and shove him out of my way.

"Get the fuck out of my net, Marchanbo."

"Feeling testy tonight, Lockwood?" Dark eyes flick to the women slapping the glass, shoving their signs against it. "I thought you let just anyone score these days."

I track the puck as it passes between players, around the back of my net, as Garrett pins someone against the boards, trying to dig it free.

"That's why you've got two baby mamas, right?" He glides in front of me, and I shove him out of the way as Jaxon's penalty ends and he jumps out of the box. "How many more do you think are out there? I bet women have been poking holes in condoms for years, trying to get a piece of the golden boy."

"Fuck off."

"I like the one with pink hair. Seems spunky. And that ass? *Oof.* Love me something to grab on to."

I chuck my stick and gloves to the ground as I get in his face. The play around us skids to a halt when I grab him by the collar. "You shut your goddamn mouth."

"Think her kid will call me Daddy?"

My fist rears back before I hurl it forward, a lot like I did the last time we saw Brandon, when he made sure Rosie knew how disposable she and Connor were to him. Because here's the thing: everyone thinks I'm some sort of golden boy, that I'm docile and sweet all the time. But the second you open your mouth and insult the two people I love more than anything in this world, you're gonna see a whole new side to me, one that's anything but docile.

Marchanbo wipes the blood from his cracked lip, chuckling under his breath, a sound I barely hear over the roar of a crowd who loves to see fists fly. "Guess you're not all that golden," he murmurs, right before he launches himself at me, tearing off my helmet.

I catch his fist in my hand before it can connect with my jaw. Right before I let mine fly again, another body collides with Marchanbo at full speed, crushing him into the boards.

Jaxon's chest heaves as Marchanbo slumps to the ice at his feet. "Don't touch my fucking goalie." He tosses my mask at my chest. "Here. Your face is too pretty for black eyes."

~

It feels like I have them anyway, two black eyes. Everything hurts, a throbbing ache behind my eyes and in my temples that hints at the exhaustion running rampant through me, dragging me toward the ground as I head back to my hotel room. All I want to do is bury my sorrows in a bucket of beer and a platter of deep-fried pickles, then collapse in my hotel room with Rosie's face smiling back at me from the other side of my phone. But I don't have any of those things.

I stare down at the last two messages from Rosie as I kick my shoes off inside my room. One is pregame, Connor in his Vipers pajamas. The other is halfway through the third period, right around the time I clocked Marchanbo in the face, and she repeats Jaxon's words back to me.

TROUBLE

Have I ever told you your face is too pretty for black eyes? Your face is too pretty for black eyes, Adam.

I've read it at least twenty times now. It's about the only thing that's put a smile on my face today.

The truth is, I don't know how to face Rosie, and it's killing me. I'm afraid of what I might see reflected back in those pools of sage. I know the same old kindness will be there, and all that love. But it's the hesitation, the disappointment that might overshadow everything so intrinsically Rosie…those are the things that will gut me.

I don't give a fuck about my reputation. Not that the media is twisting my words from my speech at the gala, where I called Connor *our* son, and guessing that he's biologically mine. Not that Courtney's giving them her best sob story, that it wasn't her that did the cheating in our relationship, but *me*. That she found out about my *mistress* when she caught me visiting Rosie and Connor in the hospital, just hours after he was born. All of it, a load of fucking shit that paints me in the worst light, and I don't give a flying fuck.

I don't give a fuck about my reputation, but I give a lot of fucks about Rosie's.

Homewrecker. That's what they're calling her. It's on every Vipers' fan page, her picture and Connor's as she loads him into the back of my SUV at the damn grocery store. And I did this to her.

It's because of me.

She stuck with me through one mess; how can I ask her to stick with me through a second, this one way messier than the first?

My head whips up as the door opens behind me, my friends strolling in mid-conversation, arms filled with bags.

"What are you doing here? I thought you were going to the bar?"

Carter unloads piles of take-out containers. "You said you weren't in the mood, so we're staying in with you." He hands me a mountain of deep-fried pickles. "You have to stop looking like that."

"Like what?"

Garrett drops a box of Fruit Roll-Ups on top of my pickles. "Like this entire shitstorm is your fault."

"It is," I say simply.

Carter shakes his head. "You know, this feels entirely too reminiscent of that night you came home to Courtney cheating. Back then, you wondered if it was your fault. If you could've loved her better, given her more of what she needed. But it's the same story now as it was then. You couldn't have prevented this. Whether you answered her phone calls or went to that meeting. She wants something from you, whether it's a dad for her son or money to support herself."

Jaxon cracks the top off a beer and hands it to me. "She wants both, and she thinks you're nice enough to accept your fate without questioning it."

Emmett takes my treats and sets them on the small table in the corner. I shake my head, squeezing it between my hands as I sink to the chair there.

"That's not my baby. No fucking way. I know I was drunk. I know I don't have the best memory of some pieces of the night, but…there's no way I would sleep with her. There's nothing she could ever say that would make me second-guess our relationship status, no matter how many drinks I had."

Honestly, it makes me sick to my stomach to think that she was in my bed at some point that night, even if it was only to take a picture.

My phone rings, my publicist, Angie, on the other line. I accept the call and put it on speaker as I tear open the box of Fruit Roll-Ups and peel one apart. "Any news?" I close my eyes, press my fingers against the headache pounding there as I wad the Fruit Roll-Up into a ball and toss it in my mouth. "Sorry. Hi. How are you?"

She chuckles. "There's no room for pleasantries right now; I get it. I made a fake Instagram account and followed Courtney. Looks like she's been seeing the same guy off and on since you two split. But there are no pictures of them together after June."

It takes a moment for the words to sink in, but when they do, hope sparks in my chest.

"I think she was already pregnant at your party, Adam. My best guess is this guy bailed on her when she told him, so she came to your party hoping you'd sleep with her."

"So she could pretend it was mine."

"Bingo."

Carter shakes his head and drops an entire slice of pizza in his mouth. "I saw this on Maury once."

"That's *literally* what Maury's about," Emmett tells him.

"Yeah," Garrett whispers. "Keep up, you donkey."

"Shut *up*," Carter whispers back, and I slap his hand away when he reaches for one of my Fruit Roll-Ups.

"What should I do?"

"Guess you just gotta wait and do a paternity test when the baby is born," Emmett suggests.

"No way." Jaxon jabs at the table. "Demand that shit now. There are tests they can do before."

"I don't even want to know *why* you know that, Jaxon," Angie says with a sigh. "The boys are right, though, Adam. You have two options. You can see how much money she wants to go away, or—"

"Fuck that." Sure, I can afford to pay her off, but I have a thousand better ways to spend that money. The summer camp I'm opening next year, Connor's education, a garden full of peonies in the backyard, and an engagement ring that Rosie never wants to take off her finger, to name a few. "She's not getting a cent."

"*Or*," Angie continues, "you request a paternity test. This all goes away one or another. I know it feels so much more complicated than this, but really, it's that simple."

She's right about one thing: nothing about this feels simple. It's a game of waiting, and I've done enough waiting in my life.

Life started the moment Rosie and Connor walked into it, and all I want to do is dive headfirst into the rest of it. I should've never been put in a position where I had to forget how to love myself, how to be proud of everything that makes me who I am, but it took finding them, letting them love me, to remember how.

And I won't let Courtney steal that from me all over again.

"What's he doing?" Garrett whispers.

"I don't know," Jaxon murmurs. "That's, like, his fifth Fruit Roll-Up."

"I don't think he even realizes he's been eating them this entire time," Emmett adds.

"I'm worried about him," Carter says quietly. "He's not even doing the tongue tattoos. He's just...eating them whole."

I stick my hand in the box, frowning when I come up empty. "Did you get me more than one box?"

Without breaking eye contact, Garrett slowly slides another box across the table. "So, hey, big guy, we were thinking—"

"Emmett, get Cara on the phone. I need her advice."

He leaps from his seat, dashing across the room to grab his phone. "She's been preparing for this her entire life."

It's nearly one a.m. when I'm walking up my driveway two days later, desperate to crawl into bed after our road trip. It's been too many days of missed calls, pictures sent from different time zones, and overanalyzing toneless text messages.

I miss Rosie so goddamn much, my alarm is already set for six a.m. so I can drive myself to Starbucks, fill up on everything that makes her warm and smiley, and show up at her door before she takes herself to school. If it wasn't the middle of the night, I'd be at her door right now, begging to come in.

I fiddle with my keys at the front door, pausing when the porch light flicks on. The door opens, and Rosie stands there in nothing but my T-shirt and my thickest socks, and Jesus fuck, I've never been so happy to see pink.

"You're here."

"Where else would I be?"

My stomach dips, the weight on my shoulders easing. "You're not going anywhere?"

"Why would we do that? Connor and I were a family before we found you, sure, but now…" She shakes her head, eyes shuttering at the thought of a future she doesn't want, the same one I don't want: one without each other. "Something would always be missing without you, Adam."

She takes my hands, pulling me into the warmth of the house, the warmth radiating off her. Gentle fingers brush my curls off my forehead, and a tender smile touches her lips.

"We don't only choose you when it's convenient and easy and happy. We choose you through all the hard, challenging moments in between. That's how families love each other, Adam. And Connor and me? We'll always be by your side."

She swipes at the lone tear running down my cheek before pressing her lips to mine.

"There's no better view than right here beside you."

THIRTY-NINE

ATE AND LEFT NO CRUMBS

Rosie

FOUR DAYS IS FAR TOO long to be apart when what we need more than anything is each other. It's far too much time for overthinking, for catastrophizing, the things I normally do best. It's time I didn't need to figure out how to handle this situation, because I've known from the moment those words left Courtney's mouth.

All I can do, all I *would* do, is stand by Adam's side.

But the surprise he wore when he found me waiting for him, something about it broke me. I've spent so much of my life believing I wasn't enough. That if I was better, somebody would choose me, give me the love I so desperately wanted. Adam's spent months building me up, helping me realize it was never about me. That I'd always be enough for the right people. But at one a.m., the terrified look in his eyes told me he wasn't so sure *he* was enough.

And now, I'm dedicating the rest of my life to making sure this man next to me never questions his worth again.

I look up at the boutique coffee and pastry shop and swallow my annoyance. Of course Courtney requested Adam meet her at their old favorite date spot. Adam looks just as annoyed beside me, with a side of nauseous as he grips the manila envelope in his hand.

He hates that it's come to this. After everything this woman has put him through, this kind man I get to call mine would rather she just see herself out of his life silently.

"We don't have to do this," I remind him gently. "If it's not what you want, Adam, we can wait until the baby is born and request a paternity test. We can wait this out quietly."

He shakes his head, and the envelope scrunches beneath his tightening grip. "She lost the right to quiet when she brought you and Connor into this. I've tolerated a lot of her bullshit, but I refuse to tolerate that." He takes my hand in his, squeezing as his eyes come to mine. "I love you, Rosie. Thank you for standing by me."

I hope one day he'll understand that there is no other place for me and Connor than at his side.

All I've ever done with love is lose it.

But I won't lose this. Not Adam, not this life we're building together.

I refuse.

The bell over the door jingles as we walk in, and heads rise, eyes bulging when they see their very own Adam Lockwood.

"Adam." Courtney stands, a wide grin stretching across her cheeks. Even after all the ugly things she's done, she's still painfully beautiful. So much so, that for the briefest moment, a seed of insecurity blooms.

And then Adam squeezes my hand, and I bury that seed so deep, refusing to give it roots to grow.

Courtney's bright blue eyes dim when they spot me, her jaw setting in a harsh line as we approach the intimate booth she picked in the back corner. Its location does nothing to stop all the wandering gazes from following us. "I thought it would be just the two of us."

"It's fitting that, if I'm talking about the prospect of expanding my family, my current family is present, no?"

She crosses her arms over her chest. "I'm not sitting with her."

"You're right; she's not sitting." He drops the envelope on the table in front of her. "We aren't staying."

"What is this?"

"A letter from my lawyer. He's sending you one via email too. It should be in your mailbox in…" He checks his watch. "Two minutes ago." Then he smiles at her, sadistic and devastatingly handsome. "Selfishly, I had to see your reaction in person."

There's a slight tremor in her hands that she tries to hide as she opens the envelope, pulls out the letter. Her eyes move over the words, and any hint of confidence she was managing to hold onto slips from her face, droops in her shoulders.

"You're suing me?"

"For two-point-five million," he confirms, pointing out a spot on the document.

"But you-you…you can't do that."

"I can, actually. Your bullshit sob stories have accomplished nothing but harm my reputation. I might've let it go, but then you dragged people I love into it. You know, I really can't comprehend how you thought dragging my name through the mud was the best way to get to me, but then again, you haven't always made the best decisions."

"I can't afford that," she splutters. "I don't have that kind of money. I'm having a baby!" Her gaze flicks to me, lighting with fire, jealousy for something she gave up. "What kind of toxic bullshit is she planting in your head? You would turn away your own flesh and blood and the mother of your child for some bitch and her offspring? The kid's dad didn't want him, and he didn't want her either."

One moment, Adam is solid and steady beside me, my hand tucked warmly inside his. The next, he's looming over Courtney, an energy so feral it makes the hair on the back of my neck rise.

"Keep her name out of your fucking mouth," he whispers, the words so lethal, tinged with venom, Courtney fumbles backward, her hand at her throat. "This isn't a goddamn game anymore, Courtney. You can't play with people's lives like they're yours to manipulate. I'm tired of being your fucking chess piece."

I step forward, laying my hand gently on his back, watching his shoulders drop, his heaving chest deflating as his breath slows to steady.

Courtney watches the exchange, and I see it in her eyes, the desperation for this to work, the knowledge that it's not, that she's watching her so poorly thought-out plan slip between her fingers, fall to pieces at her feet. And in all her despair, she gives it one last go, throwing herself at Adam, gripping his coat in her tight fists. "Please, Adam. *Please.* You can't do this to me. You can't. This is our chance. We can be a family. A *real* family."

"I have a family, Courtney, and she's standing right here! I have a family who's chosen me day in and day out, who loves me for who I am, and you have no one. You. Have. *No one.* So what the fuck are you still doing here? Why are you still in Vancouver? In Canada? For fuck's sake, Courtney, *go home.*"

She shakes her head frantically, tears building in her eyes. To her

, they look genuine, but I'm almost certain they're there because th right here was her last-ditch effort. She doesn't care about Adam, and she most certainly doesn't deserve him.

"You'll never get rid of me," she whispers. "I'm not leaving. You can't just brush me under the rug because you've got a new girlfriend."

"I'm not brushing you under the rug. I'm telling you right here, right now, that you have no place in my life. None of it belongs to you, and it never will again. That baby isn't mine, and we both know it."

Her glazed eyes bounce around the coffee shop, a volcanic heat climbing her neck, erupting in her cheeks.

"Here are your choices, Courtney," Adam starts quietly. "You can prove it right now, take a test and prove that baby is mine. But when the results show I'm not the father, I'll sue you for defamation, and all the money will go directly to the young mother's shelter downtown. Or you can admit this baby isn't mine. You can make a public announcement that you were lying, that Rosie had nothing to do with our relationship ending. I don't give a fuck whether you tell them the truth about who cheated, as long as you tell the truth about Rosie. We're gonna resolve this one way or another, but none of these involve you and me and a future together."

He threads his fingers through mine, and together, we turn toward the door. We only make it three steps before he turns back around.

"And no offense, Courtney, but fuck you. Fuck you for using me to make you happy until you decided you didn't need me anymore. For taking what you wanted and leaving me with nothing. For staying for everything I gave you and giving me nothing in return. You gave me *nothing*. Not love, not happiness, and sure as hell not your respect. You took my confidence and all my self-worth, and I hurt someone I love because you made me feel like she wouldn't be able to love me for me. *You* did that. And I fucking let you."

He rubs his jaw, a low chuckle rumbling in his chest. "You know, oddly enough, I wouldn't change a thing. Otherwise, I would've stayed in a miserable relationship, and I wouldn't have found Rosie and Connor. I wouldn't know real love, what it's like to feel it, what it's like to be loved that way, if it wasn't for them. And I will *always* choose them." He points a shaking finger in her face. "Fuck you. Full offense."

She blinks those baby blue eyes and sniffles, her mouth opening, almost as if she might actually try her luck at responding.

But I'm so proud of my man, the way he's stuck up for himself, because it's never easy to do. And now I want to show him exactly how it feels to have someone always on your side. So when she spits out her first word, I hold up my finger, silencing her.

"You gave up the right to your happy ending with him the moment you chose to hurt him instead of love him. Now I'm going to give him the happy ending he deserves. Every day, I'm going to choose to respect him. Every day, I'm going to choose to lift him up instead of tear him down. Every day, I'm going to choose to stand by his side. Every day, I'm going to choose to love him. Every *damn* day, Courtney, I'm going to *choose* him, and he's going to choose me back. And that's *our* happy ending."

He hasn't stopped looking at me since we left the coffee shop.

He was looking at me as he held the door for me, and he was looking at me when he tripped over the curb and fell against the hood of his truck. He was looking at me as he tucked me into the passenger seat, smacked his forehead off the door frame. And he was looking at me the entire drive home when he nearly ran a red.

He's still looking at me now, even as I kick off my shoes in his front hallway, hang my coat in the closet. I feel his gaze touch my back as I stroll down the hall and into the kitchen, gabbing on about anything and everything to distract me from the fact that, between all the staring, he hasn't spoken a single damn word to me since we walked out on Courtney.

"Are you still up for dinner and drinks for Christmas Eve at Carter and Ollie's tomorrow? I found gingerbread Oreos at that little grocery store on the other side of town. I picked them up for Carter." I open the fridge, bulging my eyes at nothing as the cool air brushes my cheeks, a welcome reprieve from the sear of Adam's gaze. I grab a water bottle and close the door, guzzling half of it while I lean against the counter. "Jaxon said he's bringing Mittens, so Connor will be psyched. Hey, did you see the weather forecast? It's supposed to snow. Imagine that, huh? Snow."

I drain the rest of the water, letting it sit in my cheeks for a moment as I bob my head. Then, I do what I do best, make a fool out of myself when I forget to swallow before opening my mouth. "Marco—" I sputter the water into my hands, waving my hand around like I'm not choking, my eyes watering. "Marco was measuring my room yesterday. Says it'll make a nice yoga studio. Then Archie reminded him he hasn't done yoga in two years, so Marco looked him dead in the eye while he ordered a new mat and five outfits from Lululemon." I force a chuckle as I head for the garage to recycle my bottle. "Yeah, I'm really gonna miss—*ah*!"

Adam stops me with his hand wrapped around the back of my neck. Slowly, his fingers creep up into my hair, and he pulls my back against his chest. Soft lips touch the shell of my ear, hot, shuddered breaths rolling down my neck, pebbling my nipples beneath my top.

"Lose the fucking clothes, trouble."

"Clothes? But—"

"Lose. The fucking. *Clothes*."

I tear at my hoodie, yanking it over my head. The jeans go next, and when one pant leg gets caught around my ankle, Adam pushes me against the wall, holding me there with his hand between my shoulder blades while he ditches my pants. His palm slides slowly down my spine, and he flicks the clasp on my bra, guiding the straps down my arms. Thumbs hook in my panties, and the torturous speed he drags them over my hips, down my legs, has me trembling.

His chest presses against my back as he palms one breast, his other hand pushing between my legs. I sigh as he strokes me, and he hums as I soak his fingers.

"What did you say back there? At the coffee shop?"

I close my eyes, trying to remember the words that left that stunned look on Courtney's face while he plunges two fingers inside me. "That I choose you. Every day."

"Mmm. And that last piece? About the happy ending?"

"It's you. You're my happy ending."

He shudders, his hand coasting up to grip my throat as he opens his mouth on my neck, slow, wet kisses and grazing teeth. His bulge presses into my lower back, and I smile as the realization hits. He's turned on. I stuck up for him, to someone who's done nothing but hurt and disrespect him, and he's turned on.

"I love you, Adam. I'm always going to love you."

There's a brief pause where his movements still and he rests his forehead on my shoulder, like he's savoring the moment. And then he spins me around, tosses me over his shoulder, and carries me back into the kitchen.

He drops me on the island, a starved look in his eyes as he holds my gaze and discards his clothes behind him. Jesus, I've never seen him so hard, standing so tall, so proud, his cock bobs against his belly button.

"Spread your legs," he demands, fisting his cock. "Show me that perfect, wet pussy."

I set my feet flat on the counter, baring myself to him. His deep-belly groan sends a shiver down my spine, and heat settles in my clit, throbbing with need as he wraps his fingers around my ankles, settling himself between my legs.

"That's a good girl, angel. Want me to show you how good?"

"Yes, please."

I'm hot all over, a wild, unrestrained need for this man to bury himself inside me until he's all I can feel, until I can't remember my own name.

He guides me down to my back, spreading me out on the countertop, pressing tender kisses along the inside of my thigh. Electric blue eyes flip to mine, and my teeth press into my trembling lower lip as I watch his tongue flick out, licking me slowly from bottom to top.

"I'll never get over the way you taste," is all he says, barely a murmur, and then he dives in.

God, it's everything I've ever wanted, the way he eats me. Feral and starved, like he needs me to survive. Reverent and all-consuming, like he worships every inch of this body. He laps at my pussy, sucks my swollen clit into his mouth, sinks two fingers inside me, and fucks me until I see stars, bucking my hips and tearing at his soft curls. And when he's done, he pulls me up, yanks me to the edge of the counter, and wraps my legs around his hips.

Fingers sift through my waves, tightening around them as he forces my gaze to his, drops his sweet mouth against mine for a long, slow kiss. And when he drives himself inside me, pulling a cry from my throat as his fingertips dig into my hip, I swear to God I see the light.

"If I'm your happy ending, you're my heaven. There's nothing else I need from this world. I could live here forever, in this place where I'm yours and you're mine. There's never been anything more beautiful than this version of paradise. I'm certain of it."

FORTY

CHRISTMAS DICKSICLES

Adam

"Welcome to Santa's Village. Have you been naughty or nice this year?"

I karate chop Carter's wrist, making him drop the teensy Santa hat he just tried to put on my head in his front doorway.

"Ohhh-ho-ho," he muses, scooping up the hat with an irritating smirk. "Ollie girl, change Adam's mark on my naughty or nice list! He's been a bad boy this year!" He leans into me and Rosie, a hand at his mouth. "It's okay. Ollie's been *very* naughty."

"*Carter*! I can hear you!"

"It's like she's got supersonic hearing. I'm sick of it. I never get away with anything." He scoops Connor into his arms, plopping a loud kiss on his cheeks before he sits him on his shoulders. "C'mon, little dude. Your bestie is waiting for you. I got you matching reindeer outfits. We're having a photoshoot."

"Jesus," I mutter, grabbing Rosie's hand as we follow Carter into the living room. There's tinsel draped across the ceiling, mistletoe hanging in the doorway, giant candy canes, twinkly lights, and a small pink Christmas tree, bedazzled to the nines. "It looks like Santa's elves threw up in here."

"Carter wanted Ireland's first Christmas to be special," Olivia says, wrapping Rosie and me in a hug. "Merry Christmas, you two." Rosie's package crinkles against Olivia, whose eyes widen. "Are those—"

"*Gingerbread Oreos*!" Carter shrieks, tearing the package out of her hands. "I've been looking for these everywhere!" He hauls Rosie into his arms, twirling her around. "I love you, I love you, *I love you*!"

The front door opens behind us, and Jennie steps through the door, a dazzling, dimple-popping smile on her face as she holds out her hand. "We're—"

Garrett pushes by her, doing a twirl in the entryway. "—engaged!"

"Garrett, you donkey." Jennie glares at him, fists on her hips. "You stole my entrance!"

"Oops. Sorry, sunshine." He scoops her into his arms, twirling her as she squeals with laughter. "We're engaged!"

The girls dash forward, embracing the both of them, and when Jennie frees herself, she dashes over to her brother. Carter hauls her into his chest, hugging her so tight as he whispers in her ear, and when she pulls away, I swear he wipes a tear from his eye.

Then he holds his hand out to Garrett and tells him, "I'm lucky to call you my brother-in-law," and when they embrace each other, every woman in the room bursts into tears.

Rosie flaps at her face. "I'm not stable enough for this."

I grip her chin, tilting her face up, and press my lips to her tears. "I love your unstable heart."

"That's good, because it's yours."

Jaxon steps inside, Mittens tucked under his arm, the two of them in matching Christmas sweaters. He looks at the scene unfolding around him, crying girls and Jennie and Garrett kissing under the mistletoe. "They get engaged?"

I nod.

"Cool. I'm the only single one left. That's okay. Mitts and I don't need no one but each other, right, chunk?" He nuzzles Mittens' face. "No, we don't. We don't need no mean, scary girl putting our balls in a vice."

"You're not gonna have any balls left to put in a vice if your cat keeps using them as batting practice," Rosie murmurs, and Jaxon guffaws.

"I'll have you know I started sleeping with underwear on, so the problem is solved."

Rosie arches one brow.

"Fine. Whatever. The problem isn't solved. I refuse to wear underwear to bed." He points a finger in her face. "Shut up."

Mittens leaps from Jaxon's chest to Rosie's, nuzzling her chin, and Jaxon glares as the two of them walk away, finding a spot to snuggle on the couch where the rest of us join while Jennie and Garrett give us the details on how their engagement went down. *Explicit* details, right down to what color Jennie's underwear was. Apparently, it's a very necessary detail, Jennie argues when Carter says it not, because they matched perfectly with the sapphire on her ring, a pleasant surprise for Garrett when he got to take them off after she said yes.

"You can't tell me that's not some soul-mate shit," Garrett says. "Panties matching her ring?"

It sounds like a coincidence, but he's so psyched about it, I just nod and tell him, "Oh, for sure. Definitely soul-mate panties."

I sigh, watching as Carter sticks antlers with bells on them onto Connor and Ireland's heads. Then he plops matching ones on Bear and Dublin, and when Connor snatches up Mittens, holding him to his chest and kissing his forehead, Carter attaches a tiny pair to the cat too.

Carter flattens himself on the floor, aiming his camera at the most chaotic group of reindeer I've ever seen. "Okay, guys, look over here. Ireland, baby, look at Daddy! Connor! Connor, look at your favorite Uncle Carter! Dublin!"

"Mittens," Jaxon calls, jingling his keys above Carter's head. "Mittens, look at Daddy! *Pss-pss-pss*!"

Fuck it. If I can't beat 'em, might as well join 'em.

"Bear!" I clap my hands. "Up here, buddy! Connor, look at Dada! Say cheese!"

Connor holds up the candy cane, grinning at me. "*Cheese*, Dada!"

"*No*, Dublin, don't eat that!"

"Ireland, baby, Connor's nose isn't a chew toy."

"*Mittens*! Not the tree! No, not the—*Not the tree*!"

The pink tree goes toppling to its side, the dogs trample over it, the cat takes off like lightning, scattering pink ornaments in every direction, and Connor's just sitting there shrieking with laughter as Ireland stands on her wobbly legs, her arms wrapped around his head while she gnaws on his nose.

I sigh, turning to Rosie, and my heart stops at the two silent tears streaming down her face as she takes in the utter commotion around her.

Olivia lays her hand over Rosie's. "You okay?"

She sniffles, wiping at her face, head bobbing. "I forgot what Christmas is supposed to feel like. Thank you for reminding me."

I watch the two of them embrace, and I'm struck by how easy it is for me to forget. To forget that Rosie has missed out on so much, silly traditions, ridiculous antics, embarrassing family you wouldn't trade for the world. I've never known what it's like to be lonely on a holiday, to crave something so deeply, something that so many people take for granted.

Even over this last week, in all my anger, confusion, in all my fucking *hurt,* I've never had a need to want for anything more than I have. Everyone I need to get through this shitstorm has stood firmly by my side, reminding me that, whatever the outcome, I don't have to do it alone.

Rosie hasn't had that, not until now, and I know this family is going to give her everything she's been missing.

"Hey." Carter nudges my side, offering me a beer, inclining with his head toward his patio door. "Let's head outside for a bit."

I leave Rosie with a kiss and follow the rest of the boys outside, taking a seat around the small fire Carter's tending to.

He holds up a bag of marshmallows and a package each of candy cane and gingerbread Oreos. "Christmas s'mores?"

"Oooh." Garrett rubs his belly. "I could fuck with those."

"How you feeling?" Emmett asks me as we roast marshmallows.

"Better than I was two days ago. Cara's advice was right, I think. Threatening to sue, to serve Courtney in public like that." There were so many eyes on us, watching. Normally, I do everything in my power to avoid the media. They're bloodthirsty and ruthless, which is the only reason anybody with a brain would spread that bullshit story about Rosie being my mistress and Connor being our secret baby.

I'm not sure Courtney even realizes the mistake she made yesterday. She thought she had me pegged as the same nice guy who let her walk all over him all those years. The lawsuit shocked her, and in her haste to grasp at any straw, she tripped over her own lie and admitted that I wasn't Connor's biological father.

Now I can only hope that, somehow, word spreads.

"I won't tell Cara you said she was right. She's almost never wrong. In fact, she keeps track of every day that goes by where she's *not* wrong. Her current streak is one hundred and forty-seven." Emmett runs an exhausted palm over his face. "I should know. It's written on my bathroom mirror in pink lipstick."

I chuckle, sipping at my beer as the fire toasts my marshmallow. "I need to see her walk out of this city and never, ever come back. This chapter of my life needs to end, and I don't feel like I can truly put it behind me until she's gone for good."

Carter raises his beer. "To killing off Courtney." He looks around at our blank faces, our beers still in our laps. "What? Is that not what we're…yeah, no, obviously what I meant was…to gently…*guiding*… Courtney…out of this city. Obviously. Obviously, that's what I meant."

His eyes slide to Garrett, and then roll. "And I guess to Garrett and Jennie, so lucky to have you as a brother, can't wait for you to marry my sister, I know you'll make her happy, blah blah blah, I love you."

"You just said you love me," Garrett whispers.

"No, I didn't."

"Carter just said he loves Garreeett," I sing.

"Carter loves Garrett, Carter loves Garrett," Jaxon adds.

Carter smooshes a roasted marshmallow between an Oreo. "Whatever. Real men love their friends. I read somewhere that there's a direct correlation between how much love a man shows other men and the size of his cock."

"Ah," Emmett hums. "That explains your pocket rocket."

Carter stills, his gaze slowly rising to meet Emmett's. "Excuse me?"

"Your tiny dick. That explains it."

Carter rises from his chair. "Excuse. The fuck. Out. Of me."

"Everyone knows Adam is the biggest," Garrett adds, and I shrug but also nod, because, yeah.

"You son of a bitch. I just welcomed you to my family." He leans closer, trying and failing to whisper. "I told you I love you, and this is how you repay me?"

"There's only one way to know for sure." Jaxon stands, reaching for his belt buckle.

"There are children here," I rush out. "We're not whipping our dicks out."

"Of course not." He walks to the snow-covered grass and turns his back on us, the sound of his zipper echoing through the frigid Christmas Eve air. He smiles at us over his shoulder, and then spreads his arms wide, face-planting in the snow.

"*Ooou, fuck*!" He scrambles to his feet, jumping back and forth as he tucks himself away. Then, with a grin, he points at the snow, some sort of distorted snow angel, and, uh…a perfectly shaped imprint of his cock. "Beat that, fuckers."

"No. No way."

I shake my head, backing away.

"I'm twenty-six. I'm not dipping my dick in the snow to compare sizes."

~

I dipped my dick in the snow to compare sizes.

Honestly, I don't want to talk about it.

"That's clear shrinkage!" Carter shrieks. "From the snow! 'Cause it's cold!"

"If you have shrinkage, we all have shrinkage!" Garrett screams back, arms flailing. "That doesn't change the fact that Adam's a half inch bigger than you!"

"Three-eighths! Three-eighths of an inch, not a half!"

The patio door slides open, four beautiful, concerned women staring back at us with mugs of boozy hot chocolate in their hands.

"What's going on out here?" Olivia asks, shifty eyes moving between us as we shiver, wet with snow.

"Nothing," Carter lies quickly. "Nothing, Ollie."

Cara looks at Emmett, raising a brow, and that motherfucker folds like a lawn chair. "We were comparing dicks by dipping them in the snow," he blurts, then breathes out a deep sigh of relief. "Adam's got Carter beat by a half inch."

"*Three-eighths*!"

Rosie's amused gaze comes to mine. "Adam, you didn't participate in this, did you?"

Heat rises to my cheeks, even though my junk is fucking frozen solid. With an anxious chuckle, and a sheepish grin I hope is equally charming, I sidestep to the right, showing her my slutty snow angel.

"Sweet holy mother of Jesus," Cara murmurs. "Look at that dicksicle. Rosie, how are you upright?"

She opens her mouth to tell everyone how sweet and respectfully I fuck her, but the trill of my phone slices through the night air. My heartbeat thumps in my chest at the name on my screen.

"It's my lawyer."

Rosie rushes to my side, and my friends crowd around me as I answer the phone.

"I know it's Christmas Eve, Adam, but I figured you'd want answers as soon as I had them," my lawyer tells me. "Courtney refused the paternity test."

"Of course she did," I growl, and Rosie slides her hand into mine, squeezing gently.

"She refused the paternity test because the baby isn't yours, Adam."

"What?"

"You didn't sleep with her that night. You were asleep in your bedroom, and she snapped that picture to make it look like you two had been together. She was five weeks pregnant already."

I didn't sleep with her.

"I also issued her a no-contact order for you and Rosie, and was explicitly clear what types of ramifications there might be on her Canadian visa should she choose to break it. This is over, Adam, for good. And if you need a little proof to help you feel confident in that, I suggest hopping on Twitter. A minute of scrolling will give you all the satisfac-tion you need."

I pull up the app as soon as we disconnect, my heart racing at the content littering my feed. Links to gossip articles detailing Courtney's scheming, all her lies. Posts in support of Rosie and me, people sending their best wishes to our family. I click on a video that has tens of thousands of shares, watching a repeat of yesterday from a different view: me and Rosie, a united front, and Courtney, desperate and caught in her lies.

"How did they get this footage?" Rosie asks.

I look up at her, at my friends surrounding me, and my hands tremble. "I don't know. But they're incredible."

"Wow," Cara murmurs, doing a piss-poor job of hiding her sneaky smile behind her boozy hot chocolate. "It's almost as if someone knew you'd be there, at that exact coffee shop, at that exact time, and made sure they were situated within earshot of that exact devil, so they could record that exact conversation, only to turn around and leak it. Hmmm."

She sips her drink, licking the whipped cream from her top lip. "I wonder who that possibly could've been."

"That was you?" I ask quietly. "You did this?"

"Rather easily, my man. And quite frankly, I'm insulted you two didn't notice me. Yes, I had my big sunglasses on, and yes, I was wearing Emmett's hideous scarf his nana knit him that I'd usually never be caught dead in. But there's no one alive with hair this gorgeous, and you should be able to spot it from a mile away."

"You did this for Adam?" Rosie whispers, green eyes glassy.

"I did it for my family. For Adam, and Connor, and you. Because nobody gets away with hurting the people I love."

Rosie throws herself at Cara, wrapping her arms around her neck, burying her face in Cara's long blonde hair, while I stand here, too shocked to move.

"There's one more thing," Cara says. "Search the hashtag *deportcourt*."

My feed floods with pictures of my ex. The same picture, over and over again, of her with a baseball cap pulled down low, a baggy sweater, and a scarf wrapped around her neck, covering half her face, like she's trying to go unnoticed.

There's no mistaking that red hair, though.

Just like there's no mistaking the luggage at her feet.

Or the runway behind her.

My feed updates, a new tweet appearing with the same hashtag. A simple picture of a plane taking off, and two words I was beginning to think I'd never see.

She's gone.

I toss my phone at Carter's chest, wrap Cara in the tightest, best hug, and take Rosie's face in my hands.

"She's gone?" she whispers. "Really?"

"She's fucking gone."

A sprig of mistletoe appears above us, held up by Carter. "I really wanna have a group hug, so we all need you to hurry up and kiss."

Rosie giggles, that adorable scrunch of her nose making me smile. I kiss that first, then the dimple in her chin, before finally—*fucking finally*—taking her mouth. It's soft and sweet, unhurried and tender, and it tastes like freedom. Freedom to love with everything I have. Freedom in letting go. Freedom to be who I am and to know with certainty that all of me is loved.

Then, our friends come around us, winding arms and tender squeezes.

And this? This feels like family.

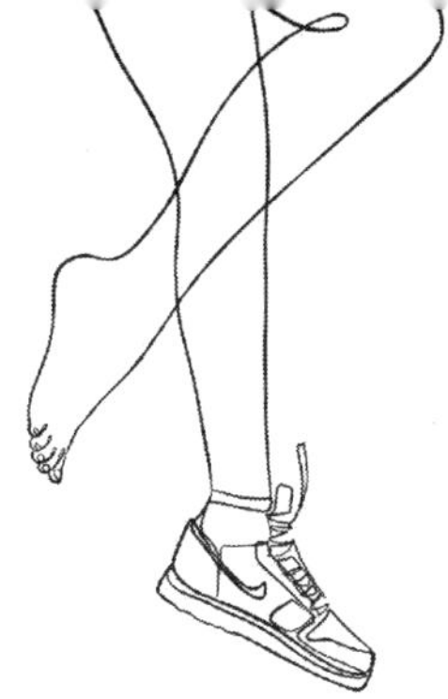

FORTY-ONE

PUZZLE PIECES

Rosie

"AND HERE'S Adam at eight years old, passed out in the pantry."

"Is he wearing underwear with dog Santas on them?" He definitely is, and it's the *only* thing he's wearing. He's also halfway toppled out of the pantry, folded onto the bottom shelf, his cheek on the floor, dark curls scattered around him.

"Those were his Santa Paws underwear," his mom, Bev, tells me. "They were his favorite. He wore them every day. I had to fight with him to let me wash them. Such a strong-willed boy."

"And he's in the pantry because…?"

"He wanted to catch Santa in the act. And he's wearing only underwear because he wanted to show them to Santa.

"*Mom*." Adam levels her with a *what the fuck* look from across the room. "Who actually travels with photo albums to show off?"

"I do." She flips the page. "Oh, oh my God! Look at him here! He was thirteen and started growing this precious little mustache."

"Oh my God." I look at my gangly boyfriend, his shaggy hair in desperate need of a cut, wide grin finished with braces, and about eight strands of facial hair he looks *so* proud of. When I find Adam's scowl, he narrows his eyes.

"Don't," he whispers. "Don't you dare."

"You look…" I fold my lips into my mouth, my shoulders shaking with the laugh I keep trying to swallow down. "So cute."

"I wanna see!" Lily sets down the bracelet she's working on for Connor and kisses his forehead. "I'll be right back, okay, Connor? You stay right here." Then she kisses Bear's head, and Piglet's next, and when she gets to Adam's dad, she just blushes. "You stay, too, okay?"

"I wouldn't dream of going anywhere," Deacon tells her sincerely, holding up his Rainbow Loom, his wrist already decorated with several colorful elastic bracelets. He's much better than Adam, who's still struggling with his first bracelet. "I'm learning so much about making bracelets."

Lily's been with us all day, showing up at nine this morning in a beautiful red dress that was waiting for her beneath the Christmas tree at the children's home this morning. She was crying when she got here, and I was worried she didn't want to be here with us until she wrapped herself around my legs and thanked me for wanting to spend time with her. She took to Bev immediately, the same as Connor did when we picked her and Deacon up at the airport on our way home from Carter and Olivia's last night.

She's been more hesitant with Deacon, but Adam said she's a little nervous with men, just like Piglet. But both girls have been inching closer to him all morning, and now Piglet's draped over his lap, paws in the air, and I know she's enjoying a break from the shelter this Christmas.

"How big was Adam when you adopted him?" Lily asks Bev.

"Adam was five years old when we adopted him."

Lily's face lights. "Hey, I'm five! Maybe someone will adopt me, too, like Adam."

Bev smiles, raking her fingers through Lily's hair. "The family who finds you is going to be such a lucky family, Lily."

My throat tightens, and my gaze collides with Adam's. I haven't stopped thinking about Lily since I met her, and lately, I've been thinking what it might look like to one day open our home up to someone who needs one. Someone who needs some extra love, because we have so much to go around. It's as scary as it is empowering. When I was in foster care, I tried everything in my power to make myself more *adoptable*, as if that were ever a real quality. It's taken me years to come to terms with the fact that there was nothing I could do. It was never up to me. And now, I'm in this incredible position, one where I have the power to change someone's life for the better.

And yet there's something inside me that's scared. Something that keeps me from taking that final step. Something that worries I won't be the right choice.

I've found all these people who are perfect for me, but I'm nervous I won't be perfect for *her*.

"Goddammit," Adam grumbles from the living room. "*Lily*! I need help with my bracelet, please!"

"Again?"

"It's not—I can't—my fingers are too big!"

"Well then how come your dad can do it?" she yells back, then wraps herself around my middle, hugging me tightly before she skips back to the living room. "You just gotta believe in yourself, Adam. If you say you can't do it, you never will." She sits down beside him, and he looks down at her like she's one of the few reasons he breathes. "Don't worry. I won't give up on you."

"Puzzle pieces," Bev murmurs beside me.

"Hmm?"

"I've always thought people were like puzzle pieces. That we spend our lives searching for someone who's shaped almost as if they're just for us. You find each other, and you get this funny, excited feeling in your stomach the closer you get, the more you learn about them. And then, suddenly, something slides into place, this perfect fit, like you had this space saved just for them. And when they squeeze themselves in, it feels like your puzzle is finally complete."

She smiles, watching her husband and son as they pull out all the toys Connor and Lily opened this morning, pulling out the mini–hockey net, showing the kids how to hold the little sticks.

"I thought Deac and I found all our pieces when we met in college. And then we found Adam, and it's like a new space opened up just for him. And then I *really* thought we were done." She covers my hand with hers, squeezing tenderly. "Looks like we found a few more pieces."

All I've done the past six months is find more pieces, filled my life with so many incredible people. But do I have more space? Do I have room for one more? How will I know? I start with the most logical question.

"Did you always want to adopt?"

"Nope. Never even wanted kids."

"So how did you wind up with Adam?"

Her soft brown eyes follow Deacon as he covers Connor's hands on his hockey stick, helping him shoot and score on Adam. "Because Deacon's heart is every bit as big as Adam's is. He had too much money and nothing to spend it on. After a few fundraisers with his team, he started volunteering with a few homeless youth programs. Then he started organizing his own fundraisers, trying to find these kids families to love them. Adam came along one day, those big blue eyes and curls for days, shy as could be. Deacon started popping into the home whenever he could. He'd find any excuse to go see that little boy. He said as sad as Adam was, his eyes always lit with so much hope whenever someone sat down with him, paid him any amount of attention."

I press my hand to my chest, over the heart that aches for a little boy who just wanted someone to love him. As different as our experiences were, we've had a lot more in common than I realized. The connection isn't as settling as I thought it would be; it breaks me knowing he ever felt the same way I did.

Bev chuckles quietly, watching as Lily squeals with laughter as Adam misses her shot, collapsing to his back in defeat. "That boy stole my whole heart, and he did it without even trying. Deacon hosted a low-key event at the park one day, trying to get kids interacting with potential families. Adam didn't want to talk to anyone but us. He brought a little foam football, told us he'd saved up all his chore money so he could learn to throw it like Deacon did on TV. That was the first time that boy made me cry. The second time was twenty minutes later, after he fell and scraped his knee. I cleaned it up, patched it, and kissed it better. He looked up at me with so much love in those tear-filled eyes, covered my hand with his, and said I'd make the best mama to the luckiest kid in the world. We started the adoption process the next day." She wipes away her tears as mine roll silently down my cheeks.

"Sometimes you're not born to your family, not your forever one. Sometimes you are, and tragedy strikes and separates you until you can be together again. And sometimes, despite it all, you find your family. You choose each other every single day, over and over. When you find the people who come into your life and make it whole, you don't hesitate, Rosie. You grab it before it's gone, because life without them is no longer living. It's simply existing."

"Sorry I'm crying," I cry, slapping at the tears streaming down my face.

She laughs, pulling me into her embrace. It's everything Lockwood, warm and bright and so fucking steady, the safest place to be. "I thank your parents every day for setting you on our son's path that day. For letting us hold onto you. And I thank you, Rosie, for making our family whole."

It's wild, isn't it? How you can spend years searching for love, for acceptance, and right before you accept that it's not for you, someone sweeps in and showers you in it. It's like Adam took one look at my heart and said, "This is what you want? Let me give you more." He didn't just give me him; he gave me the family I'd been searching for all these years.

A small hand tugs on mine, and troubled brown eyes peer up at me. "Are you okay, Rosie?" Lily asks me. "I saw you crying."

I crouch down before her, brushing her bangs off her forehead. "I'm okay, sweetheart."

"Were you thinking about your mommy and daddy in heaven?"

"Yeah, I was."

"Can I give you something to help you feel better?"

"I'd like that."

Two tiny, gentle hands cup my cheeks, and I close my eyes as Lily presses featherlight kisses across my nose. "There," she whispers. "Butterfly kisses." She turns to leave but pauses, smiling back at me over her shoulder. "I think Connor's the luckiest kid in the world. He's got the best mama."

My heart catches in my throat, a few special kisses and two little sentences from a five-year-old girl that sound identical to the ones a five-year-old Adam said some twenty-one years ago.

Adam joins me at the counter, tucking me into his side as we look out at our Christmas.

"Did you get everything you wanted?"

My gaze slides to Lily, and my heart patters against my chest as she helps Connor onto the couch, snuggles up with him and Deacon and Bev and the dogs.

The perfect fit.

Adam's palm touches my lower back, gliding up my spine, his thumb moving over the nape of my neck. "You know what I was thinking?"

"What?"

"We have five bedrooms, and only two of them are being used."

My chest rises and falls quickly. "Yeah?"

He looks at Lily, and when she grins at us, he grins too. "Yeah."

"For fuck's sake, Marco, I haven't even left yet!"

I prop my fists on my hips in the doorway of my bedroom. Oh sorry—Marco's Zen Den. That's what he's calling it now. I guess that's why he's changing my soft-glow white pot lights out for warm amber bulbs, why there are bamboo branches in a large ceramic vase in the corner, and why he's currently plugging in a diffuser.

He fans the mist at his face and inhales deeply, then winks at me over his shoulder. "Gotta get rid of all the bad juju."

"There's no bad juju! Connor and I don't have bad juju!"

Okay, so as it turns out, I'm more attached to this little apartment and this tiny bedroom than I realized. It should be simple to pack up and leave today, to officially begin the new year at my new home. And it is. But I underestimated the hold this place has on me.

This was our home. This is where I found out I was pregnant, and the couch in the living room is where Archie held me and assured me I'd be such an amazing mother. This bedroom is where Connor slept when he came home from the hospital, and where I spent that entire night just staring at him, refusing to believe I'd created something so damn *perfect*. This home is where he smiled for the first time, and these walls heard his laugh before I had to share it with anyone. He learned to crawl, learned to walk, and learned to love right here in this home.

"Oh God. Fuck. *Archie*! Help! I made her cry!" Marco rushes to my side, pulling me into his chest. "I was joking about the juju, Ro. You have the best juju. No one does juju like Rosie Wells-slash-soon-to-be-Lockwood. *No one*."

"What did you do now?" Archie asks with a heavy sigh, entering the room.

"He didn't do anything," I choke out, flapping at my face. "I'm just—" *hiccup* "—really gonna miss you guys!"

"Aw, Rosie." Archie embraces me tightly, and Marco piles on top. "You know we're not going anywhere."

"You two are the only family I've known for so long. I don't want to lose that."

Archie swipes at the tears falling from my eyes. "We'll always be family, Ro. And we are so proud of you, and so happy to see you growing your family. You are deserving of everything good you've found in this world."

"You're two of the best things I've found," I murmur.

"We get that a lot," Marco whispers, and I snort through my tears.

Twenty minutes later, I've got the last of my things loaded into my backpack. One bag is all I have left, because Adam and Archie already took everything over to Adam's place—*our place*—yesterday.

"Oh hey." Archie stops me in the doorway after my fifth good-bye, handing me a folder from the bank. "Take this."

"What is it?"

"A savings account for Connor. I opened it when you found out you were pregnant." He rubs his neck, lifting a shoulder. "Been putting your half of the rent in there every month for his education."

My chest cracks wide open, and my heart falls at my feet. I don't have the words to tell him how much this means to me, so in true fashion of a girl who has too many feelings and has never learned how to properly express all of them, I hurl myself at his chest and weep.

He rubs my back, his breath catching in his throat. "If you don't get out of here in the next ten seconds, I'm gonna cry, too, and I don't wanna cry."

"I love you, Arch. Thank you for being my best friend."

"I love you, too, Rosie. Now get your ass on home."

I can't wait to, but it's the new year, and I can't let one of my favorite girls celebrate all on her own, so I stop at Wildheart on the way. The vet tech who got saddled with holiday duty waves at me from the cat den when I walk in.

"Hey, Rosie." She follows me through to the kennels with one of the ten-week-old kittens from a litter someone found on the side of the highway. "What are you doing here today?"

"Just wanna see Piglet." I haven't seen her since we dropped her back off on Christmas Day, and I don't think I've ever gone so long without seeing her. "I'm gonna take her for a quick walk."

"Piglet? Did nobody tell you?"

"Tell me what?" I grab her leash off the hook, already reaching for her favorite treat in my pocket as I approach her kennel. My feet skid to a stop, and my knees wobble, like they don't know how to keep me upright anymore. Then I read the sign hanging from Piglet's kennel, and when my coworker whispers the same words, my heart shatters.

"Piglet's been adopted."

It takes me an hour to pull myself together enough to get behind the wheel.

An hour of convincing myself this was everything I wanted for my Piglet. A home. A family who will love her beyond a shadow of a doubt and treat her right. A family that chooses her for the rest of her life.

She deserves this, a forever family. The same as I found mine.

I guess I was just holding out hope that my forever family…well, that it could be hers too.

Ugly sobbing and snorting all kinds of snotty fluids isn't quite how I pictured driving up to this house for the first time since it's officially become my home. When Adam watches me from the front porch as I step out of the car, I can tell it's not how he imagined it either.

It's a mild day, the dusting of snow we got yesterday melting beneath the bright sun as Connor rides his new bike along the walkway. Adam's gaze comes my way, and all the worry in his blue eyes steals his excitement as he stands from the front steps.

Connor stops the bike with his feet, climbing off and racing over to me. "Mama!" He hugs my legs tight, his big green helmet smooshed against my thighs. "I lub you, Mama."

"I love you, too, baby." The words come out super croaky, and when Adam takes my hand and pulls me into him, a fresh wave of tears falls.

"What's wrong?" he whispers, rocking me side to side. "Did you change your mind? 'Cause you're not allowed. I'll lock the doors and won't let you leave."

I laugh a snorty, strangled laugh, then cry some more. "I'm fine. I'm totally and completely one hundred percent fine."

"Uh-huh. You wanna try that again?"

"I-I-I-I went to visit Piglet on my way over and take her for a walk, but she wasn't there. She-she-she—" I swipe the heel of my palm against my nose. "She got adopted! It's so good, right? That's so good. It's excellent. It's *amazing.* She found a-a-a—" A choking sob hurls me forward, and I bury my face in Adam's chest. "She found a family!"

Adam slips his hand beneath my sweater, his cool palm a heavy weight on my back as it glides up and down, over and over. He doesn't say anything, just holds me close while I cling to him. Then, he takes my hand and my bag, pulling me toward the front steps.

"C'mon, Connor. Let's show Mama how we filled our home today."

I scrub at my raw eyes as Connor dashes to the front door. "What do you mean, filled our home?"

Adam smiles, and even in my borderline hysterical state, I recognize what a beautiful sight it is.

If home is a feeling, I feel it when I see that smile.

When he opens the door, a chorus of barks greets us as Bear leaps forward, showering us in kisses, soothing my sore heart. And then a flash of brown and black fur catches my eye, and I look up as the most beautiful German Shepherd steps forward, happy pink tongue hanging out of her mouth as her gorgeous brown eyes blink up at me. She takes three steps before leaping into the air, whacking Bear right in the face with her butt when she spins, and I drop to my knees as I wrap my arms around her neck and bury my cries in her fur.

"Piglet."

A crocheted pink peony is fixed to her collar, and I take the heart-shaped tag with her name on it between my fingers. On the back is my phone number and a simple message: *If I'm lost, please call my mom.*

"You did this for her?" I whisper, staring up at Adam through blurry eyes.

He shakes his head. "I didn't do a damn thing but fall in love with a girl and her dog one day in the forest. And then they brought me that little boy, and together, all of us, we made a family."

"Meow!"

My head whips up at the tiny mewl, just in time to catch a tiny blob of grey fluff that launches itself off Bear's head and scurries up my shoulder. The kitten nudges my jaw with its little head and then digs its piercing claws into my sweater, hanging down my chest and dropping into my lap.

Adam rubs the nape of his neck. "Oh, and, uh, that's Dinosaur. We went to visit the cats while we were waiting for Piglet, and I, uh…well, Connor looked up at me with these hopeful eyes, and I…" He sighs, a sheepish smile as he shrugs. "He wanted to name him Dinosaur. I couldn't say no."

And then he grins, scooping Connor into his arms, helping me up, and tucking me into his side. He takes my chin in his hand, tipping my face, dropping the sweetest lips to mine as another puzzle piece slowly clicks into place.

"Welcome home, Rosie."

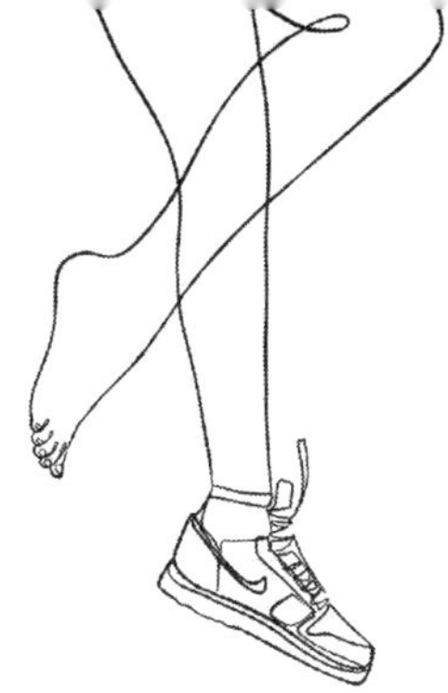

EPILOGUE

OOPS

Rosie

May

"Do you think she'll like it?"

I step back, my bare feet warm on the hardwood planks, the early morning west coast sun streaming through the windows in our living room, bathing the scene before me in light. Pink foiled balloons, spelling out her name and what this day means to us. Her favorite breakfast laid out on a blanket on the floor, because picnics are our favorite way to eat as a family. *Up* ready to go on the TV, because there isn't a movie she loves more.

Warm hands land on my arms, coasting up to my shoulders where his fingers slip beneath the straps of my tank top. Adam guides me back against his chest, broad arms coming around me as he drops kisses along my shoulder, up my neck.

"She's going to love it. She'd love it without all this, Rosie, because she loves you."

I smile, swaying against Adam as he kisses my cheek. "I love her so much. It feels like we were made for each other." I turn into him, draping my arms over his shoulder as he grips my hips. "That's how I knew she was it for us, the same way I knew you were it for me. Your mom told me people are like puzzle pieces, and when you find the pieces that fit with yours, you don't let go."

"She's our puzzle piece."

"The perfect fit."

He threads his fingers through mine, tugging me toward the staircase. "C'mon. Let's go get the kids up."

Adam pauses outside of Connor's room, his ear at the door. Small voices drift through to us, and he smiles as our gazes collide. When we open the door, everyone is exactly where we expect them to be.

Connor is tucked beneath his blankets still, huddled up by the pillows, his thumb in his mouth. Bear and Piglet are curled up together at the foot of the bed, and Dinosaur—who is a bit of an asshole, by the way—is draped over the edge of the mattress, belly up, his head on the floor, paws stretched out overtop.

And Lily sits cross-legged atop the pillows, a book in her hands as she reads to Connor and the animals, the same as she does every morning before breakfast.

Lily's been living with us for six weeks now. The day after Christmas, Adam contacted her social worker and asked about becoming foster parents. On January second, we began our twelve-week PRIDE pre-service training, and as soon as we were qualified, Lily moved in with us.

It hasn't always been easy. There have been tears and so many fears, long nights and even longer days. Exhaustion ran rampant as I finished up my rotations before graduating, and everything feels harder when Adam isn't here, but he checks in on us every night. And despite all the tough days, every single one has been worth it. Because beyond it all, there's been the bravest leaps and bounds, breathtaking smiles, so damn much laughter, and more love than I ever thought possible.

And now, after nearly six months, Adam and I are officially adopt ready.

"Good morning, sweethearts," I greet the kids, taking a seat on the floor beside the bed. Connor and Lily rush over, climbing into my lap for a squeeze before they run to Adam. "Did you sleep in here with Connor last night?" I ask Lily as Adam scoops them into his strong arms, setting a kid on each hip.

Lily lays her head on Adam's shoulder, nodding. "I don't like sleeping alone. Me and Connor, we make each other feel safe."

My heart warms at the love she has for Connor, so deep and endless, and I'm happy she's found another way to help herself feel more at home here, safer. We've heard her bedroom door creak open every night this week, stuck our heads out, and watched her pad across the hall with at least one animal on her heels, creep quietly into Connor's room. And five minutes later, we've cracked his door, found the two of them fast asleep beneath the glow of the moons and the stars stuck all over his ceiling.

Lily wiggles down Adam's body, rushing over to me and taking my hand. "Can you help me get ready, Rosie?"

Adam tosses Connor onto his shoulders. "I've got this one."

Like clockwork, my throat grows tight at the sight of Lily's room, neat and tidy, barely lived in, her bag in the corner of the room like she's only visiting. She unzips it, pulls out the clean laundry I washed yesterday, the clothes she put right back in there. And I ask her the same question I do every morning.

"Would you like to unpack your bag today?"

She shakes her head, spreading out a few options on the bed. "It's better this way. In case you want me to go, I can leave fast."

Her pain wraps around my heart like an angry fist, squeezing. The same old feelings resurface, the reminder of years spent feeling unwanted, unworthy of love, slapping me in the face. It's not better this way, and I would do anything for her to believe that.

For now, I crouch beside her, laying my hand over hers, staring into those innocent, wide eyes. "We love you very much, Lily. Whenever you're ready to unpack your bag, you let me know, and we'll put everything away together. Our house wouldn't be a home without you."

That little nose crinkles when she sniffles. She twirls the dusty pink ends of her chestnut hair around her fingers, the temporary dye we put in last weekend when she said she wanted hair like mine. "Could you put braids in my hair this morning? I want to match you."

Fifteen minutes later, with matching French braids and in her favorite dress—the one she was wearing when we asked her if she wanted to come live with us—we head downstairs. My heart gallops, growing more anxious the closer we get. When we see the boys in the living room, waiting beneath the balloons and among our mini-zoo, Lily stops.

"Lily Day?" she whispers, curious chocolate eyes moving between us and the pink foil balloons. She cocks her head. "I thought my birthday wasn't until June."

"It is. But today we want to show you how grateful we are to have you in our family. We have loved watching you grow, Lily. You are fierce and brave and gentle, and you are such a caring and spectacular sister to Connor."

Her eyes flash at that s-word, and when Connor runs over, wrapping himself around her, she closes her eyes, sinking into his love.

"I lub you, sista," my sweet two-year-old tells her.

Adam kneels in front of her, taking her tiny hands in his big ones. "We love you, Lily. We love dance recitals on Saturday mornings, picnics on the living room floor, playing Dr. Lily, veterinarian, with the dogs and cat. We love snuggling up and reading your favorite books over and over, rainy days spent watching movies, and your art on the fridge."

As Lily's chin trembles and tears flood her eyes, Adam reaches into his pocket and pulls out the pink and purple bracelet he made last night, after she was fast asleep. He slips it on her wrist, running the tip of his fingers over the small addition, the dangling silver letters. *A, R, L, C.*

"One for each of us," he tells her, and when that first tear slips free, he catches it on his thumb. "You're our puzzle piece, Lily. Our family isn't complete without you."

I run my hand down her braid, smiling through my own tears. "We want you to stay, sweetheart. Forever."

"You-you-you…" She sniffles, chin quivering. "You want to adopt me?"

I nod. "You've been part of our family for a while now. But if it's okay with you, we'd like to make it official."

She takes the skirt of her dress in her fists, looking to Adam. "Does that mean I get a jersey like Connor's to wear to your games? One that says *Daddy* on the back?"

Adam grins, walking over to the coffee table, returning with a small blue and green jersey. He unfolds it, showing the back to Lily, his number set below that very word, the one Adam feels so lucky to be called by Connor, the one he's been hoping Lily would someday feel comfortable calling him too.

Tears cascade down Lily's cheeks as she rubs her eyes with her shaking fists. "Does that mean I can call you Mommy?"

My heart shatters, and I pull her into my chest. "If you want to, sweetheart. I would be so honored to be your mommy, and I'm going to love you forever, just like your mommy in heaven."

A sob cracks from her throat, and she clings to me as we cry. Connor wraps his little arms around us, and Adam takes all three of us in his. Somewhere, there's a cat meowing his disapproval that he's not in the middle of this hug, and two dogs dance around us, sticking their tongues in our ears, licking away our tears.

When we break away, Lily looks at me, scrubs the tears from her eyes. Red-rimmed and tired, it's the renewed hope in them that paints over the fissures in my heart like glue, mending pieces of me I didn't think could ever be fixed again.

And then she takes my hand and says, "I think I'm ready to unpack my bag today."

~

She wears her jersey to Adam's play-off game that night. Proudly displays that five-letter name on the back, a devastating smile and so much color in her cheeks as she points at him stretching on the ice and tells everyone, "That's my daddy."

"Holy fuck," Cara mutters under her breath.

"Yeah," Olivia says on a sigh.

"We all knew it," Jennie hums.

"What?" I ask, my eyes on Adam as he sinks farther into his stretch, his legs straight out at his sides as he does the splits and somehow manages to wink at me and wave at the kids at the same time.

"Adam," Olivia says simply. "He's a bigger DILF than Carter."

Carter tosses his leg up on the bench, stretching and glaring. "How dare you! I'm standing right here. No one out-DILFs me, *Olivia.*"

Cara points at Adam, fixing his brand-new goalie mask over his face as he skates over. "Adam just did, babe."

"Dada!"

"Daddy!"

Connor and Lily jump at the glass, smacking their hands against it as Adam stops in front of them.

Connor's eyes light, and he points at the artwork on Adam's mask. "Pic-ta! Dada, Mama, Conn'a, sista! *Oooh-ho-ho*! Bear, Pig-it, Dino-saw! *Chomp-chomp*!"

Being a dad has never suited a single person alive more than it suits this man, I swear to God. I've lost track of how many times I've jumped on him the moment he leaves their rooms after reading them a bedtime story, tucking them in for the night. And I did the same damn thing when Adam came home four nights ago, showed me the new mask he'd made with Lily's artwork on it, a drawing of our family.

Lily's chin quivers. "I drew that picture. You put it on your helmet?"

Adam nods. "Gotta keep my family with me when I'm on the ice." He lays his palm against the glass, and Lily smiles, stepping forward to lay hers on the other side.

"Here, Connor," she says softly. "You put yours here, right next to mine."

There's a sniffle beside me, and the distinct click of a camera. Lennon, the team's new photographer and social media content manager, and newest addition to our girl crew, sniffles. "Got it." She flaps at her eyes. "That's it. That's the sweetest picture I've ever taken. The girlies are gonna go feral over this."

Jaxon knocks on the glass. "What about me? Did you get my picture?"

She ignores him, snapping a picture of Carter and Ireland next. "Perfection. Utter perfection."

"Lennon? Did you get my picture? Look at this." Jaxon shimmies backward, dropping to his knees, spreading his legs wide. "Look how low I can get."

"Not as low as Adam," she murmurs, flipping through her pictures.

"Len? Did you see me? Want me to do it again?"

"Yes, Jaxon," she finally calls, rolling her eyes for only us to see, her chestnut coils bouncing from where they're piled on top of her head as she finally swings around to give him her attention. "I saw you. We're all *so* impressed."

He grins, so boyish and proud, and I snicker. Between the two of them, I'm not sure which one annoys the other more, but I'm certain they both enjoy it.

A gentle tap on the glass in front of me draws my gaze there, finding Adam watching me, his mask propped on top of his head.

"We're pretty lucky, huh, trouble?"

"The luckiest."

He smiles then, devilish and so sure of himself. "I'm gonna marry you someday, you know."

I grin, that same giddy feeling in my stomach every time we have this conversation. "What if I say no?"

He pulls his mask down, fixing it over his face. As he backs away, he winks at me. "You won't."

And at the end of the game, when they win in overtime, Adam looks at us, and he taps his heart three times.

~

We're up at the crack of dawn the next morning, the kids and all the animals packed up in the truck for our hike. Yes, even Dinosaur.

The sun had only just broken through the horizon when Adam dropped the kids on me in bed, hand-drawn cards and a bright bouquet of pink peonies for me on Mother's Day, requesting a sunrise hike. The Starbucks warm in my hands helps chase away the sleepies from a night spent celebrating with our family and friends, but I'd get up early every day for the rest of my life, so long as it's this family I'm getting up early with.

Fractured rays of amber filter through the branches as we walk, the slowly rising sun warming this wooded trail. Connor and Lily dance ahead of us hand in hand, the dogs close behind, the cat trying to claw his way to the front of the pack.

"What are you thinking about?" Adam's deep timbre crackles in the quiet forest as birds wake one by one, their morning songs becoming louder as we walk deeper.

"How I never imagined myself walking a cat on a leash."

He barks a laugh, his hand squeezing mine. "Dinosaur doesn't like when we all go out without him."

Uh, yeah. The cat has the biggest case of fear of missing out I've ever encountered. All eight pounds of him also thinks he's as big and ferocious as his canine siblings—who are, by the way, *terrified* of him—so he pretty much runs our household now.

Lily and Connor stop to inspect a bug crawling up the trunk of a tree, and the animals dash over, the five of them huddling together as the fuzzy orange and black caterpillar slowly ascends.

"I can't believe how my world has changed in the last year. I have everything I always wanted but never dared dream I'd actually have. Everything I'd grown to believe I wasn't deserving of. I thought I needed to be better. Do something to stand out. Dye my hair to get people to notice me. So badly, I just wanted to be chosen. I wanted someone to look at me and say, 'That's her.' I just wanted someone to love me for who I was without having to change a single thing about myself, Adam, and then I found you. And not only did I get your love, but I learned how to love myself better because of the way you loved me, so wholly."

Adam's fingers tighten around mine, pulling me to a stop. The emotion shining in his eyes reflects exactly what I feel in my heart—so damn much gratitude for the love of a lifetime. I take his face in my hands, guiding his mouth down to mine.

"The only choice I ever had was choosing to step foot on this very trail that morning. Fate took care of the rest. That's what I'm thinking about."

"Marry me," he blurts, then blinks rapidly, like he can't believe those words just left his mouth. "Ah shit. That wasn't how that was supposed to happen."

"I thought you was gonna do it at the tree," Lily scolds, hands on her hips. "Where her parents are." She taps her foot. "And you have to give her the ring, Daddy. That's what's gonna make her say yes."

"I'm so sorry," he rushes out, and I'm not sure if he's apologizing to me or Lily. He grabs my hand, dragging me along as he dashes up ahead to that old tree, the one with my initials and my parents', surrounded by a rainbow of peonies that have just begun to bloom. My heart tries to crawl its way up my throat as he turns back to me, pulling a small velvet box from his bag with trembling hands. "Hey, uh, forget what I said back there a minute ago, 'kay?"

"Forgotten," I whisper as he drops to one knee.

The dogs sit at his sides, and Dinosaur drops to his back, rolling around in the dirt as he meows. Connor tugs the box from Adam's hands, opening it, and the rising sun catches on the most gorgeous diamond.

"*Oooh,*" he coos, shoving it in my face. "Pwetty, Mama."

"I thought you was gonna wait for the sun to come all the way up," Lily reminds Adam. "'Cause you said she's like a sunrise."

Adam drops his head, a tired laugh shaking his chest. When he looks back at me, it's with the softest smile, so inherently Adam, tender and calm, so patient. "I should've expected this to go exactly opposite of how I planned it, huh?"

I nod, tears already gathering in my eyes. "That's parenthood for you."

"But maybe it's exactly how I planned it, because all I need is you right here, surrounded by all the love that makes this family exactly as perfect as it is. That's the only thing I've ever dreamed of." He turns to Connor, taking his tiny hands in his. "Connor, buddy, I fell in love with you the moment I met you, when you threw your shoes at my chest and demanded I put them on your feet. You are so clever and curious, and you love with your whole heart, just like your mama." He pulls Lily in to join them. "Lily, you are everything kind and patient in this world, and the day you asked me to read with you, I knew I loved you." He squeezes their hands. "I love you both, and I'm so proud and grateful to be your dad. Now what do you say I make Mama my wife?"

"*Yeah*!" they scream, and Connor trips over his feet, face-planting against Adam's chest as he grabs hold of his neck.

"I lub you, Dada." He points at me, holding the ring out. "Gib Mama wing?"

Adam takes the ring from the box with shaky hands. His gaze touches the heart carved into the tree, and when he closes his eyes, presses his hand against the very spot my parents once touched, my tears spring free.

He opens his mouth, hesitates, then closes it, shaking his head. "I practiced this a thousand times. Every single word I wanted to say, I said it in front of the mirror, in the shower, Christ, Rosie, I even recited it in front of the guys last week. And now we're here, and I'm looking up at you, and the only words I can think of are *thank you*. Thank you for trusting me with all of you, your fears, your insecurities, your past, and your future. Thank you for letting me into your life, for making me feel like I belonged there." He hangs his head, breathing out, and I reach forward, running my fingers through his soft curls until he gives me his eyes again, electric blue and shining with tears. "Thank you for giving me a second chance. Thank you for taking the time to see all of me, to know all of me, and thank you for loving it all. Thank you for showing me what it means to be loved without reservation. Thank you, Rosie, for being you."

Glittering golden rays dance through the forest as the sun finally breaks through the trees, bathing my family in a dazzling, breathtaking warmth I can feel all the way to the tips of my toes.

Adam smiles, a stunning, magnificent sight, the tremor in his touch disappearing as he slips my hand into his. "You've been my best friend and my partner through all of this." He slips the exquisite ring on my finger, the teardrop diamond the same rosy shade as my hair. "Now I want you to be my wife."

He catches me against him as I fall to his lap, a soft laugh that skates down my neck as I toss my arms around him and cry for a love I spent my life dreaming of.

"You didn't phrase it as a question," I cry.

"Because you're not allowed to say no; I already told you." He shifts me back, brushing my waves off my damp cheeks. "Do you know how I knew? How I knew it was you?"

"How?"

"Sometimes people say they know they've found the one because they turned their world upside down, took everything they thought they knew and shook it up. But you? Not you, Rosie. You didn't throw my whole world off balance. You centered it. It was like you were my gravity, and every moment I was with you, everything settled into place. My fears, my insecurities, my hopes, and my dreams. I was at peace with everything, as long as you were by my side." He tucks my hair behind my ear, his thumb sweeping over the dimple in my chin as he smiles. "With you, I found my gravity. That's worth so much more than my chaos."

We stay there all morning, me and my family, have breakfast on the bridge, splash in the cool creek down below. And when it's time to leave, Adam takes a pocketknife from his bag and adds *C*, *L*, and *A* to that heart forever marked in the tree.

I take Lily's hand in mine as Adam perches Connor on top of his shoulders, Bear, Piglet, and Dinosaur leading us home.

"We'll have to come back in January to carve in one more initial."

Adam's gaze slides to mine. "One more?"

"Mhmm. When we're a family of five." I shrug. "Or eight, I guess, including the animals."

"Family of…" He trails off, ticking off each of us on his fingers as he counts beneath his breath.

Lily gasps, and Adam's eyes snap to my stomach when she places her hand there.

"I know it's a little earlier than we planned, and you had high hopes for a spring or summer baby so you could be off with us, but it looks like we made a—"

"A winter baby." His words escape him on a breath. His chest rises sharply, and that tremor in his hands from earlier returns as he brings one to his mouth, rubbing it, before hesitantly reaching out, laying his palm over my stomach. Blue eyes flip to mine just in time for me to track the single tear that escapes, running down his cheek. "We made a winter baby?"

I grin, covering his hand with mine, and shrug.

"Oops."

The End.

ACKNOWLEDGMENTS

First and foremost, to Megan, because this book would be nothing but eleven chapters of my tears, and I'd be rocking alone in my closet right now. I truly don't know how to thank you for everything you've done to help me bring Adam and Rosie's story to life, but I hope you enjoyed the podcast you got to tune into every day with my thousands of voice notes. I can't wait to plot seventy-five books with you, and laugh at all the relevant, genius videos you create about them. I'm so grateful for you, and wildly lucky to call you a friend.

To my girls, Erin, Hannah, and Ki, I don't know what I'd do without you, other than get more sleep. Of all the amazing things writing has brought me, the best by far is you three.

To Michelle, thank you for taking the time to let me pick your veterinarian brain. I know it's not perfect (no fourth year vet student has as much free time as Rosie), but I hope you enjoyed it.

To Paisley, for your undying patience with me, and for making me feel safe handing my stories over to you. I'm sorry your search engine is all kinds of funny because of my books.

To Nicole, for being with me since day one, and for taking one look at Adam's name on paper and saying, "Mine." You know how to pick 'em.

To Ellie and Autumn, for everything you've done for not only my books, but for me. I'm so thankful to have you on my team.

To Alana, for bringing my boys to life via stickers. You are an incredible artist.

To Miss Bizzarro, always, because once upon a time I was twelve years old, and you made the impossible feel possible.

To my incredible alpha team, Megan, Autumn, Nikki, Allie, and Kristen. You guys have angel-level patience with me, whether it's me taking two weeks to update, or me scrapping the first twenty-eight chapters and starting over.

To my readers. This would probably be a good time to thank you for your patience, huh? THANK YOU. Not only for that, but for your support, your love, lifting me up every time I need it. I adore you, and I appreciate you so darn much. Thank you for loving my Vipers.

To my son, for being the cutest inspiration for Connor, and to my daughter, because you are well worth every delay.

And to my older brother. I'd never let you read my books, but I know somewhere, you're proud of me. I miss you, so damn much.

From the bottom of my heart, thank you.

ABOUT THE AUTHOR

Becka is a steamy romance author, self-proclaimed sarcasm queen, professional procrastinator, and a superfan of dragging her readers through hell and back on the way to a happy ending.

When she's not staring blankly at her computer screen or deleting close to two hundred occurrences of the word *just* from her manuscript, she can be found teaching kindergarten (*gasp!*) in Ontario, Canada, and mom-ing with her two children and her animals.

Though she's always been an avid reader and forever dreamt of becoming an author, Becka didn't begin writing books until after the loss of her brother. While she loves to include all the fun stuff like heat, humor, and alpha men who are secret teddy bears, her writing comes from a place of heavy emotions, and she often can't resist letting those emotions seep into her pages.

More in the *Playing For Keeps* series:
Consider Me - Carter & Olivia's story
Play With Me - Garrett & Jennie's story

Still to come in the *Playing For Keeps* series:
Fall With Me - Jaxon & Lennon's story
Breathe With Me - Emmett & Cara's story

Printed in Great Britain
by Amazon

29170912R00245